ALSO BY OLIVIA WILDENSTEIN

THE KINGDOM OF CROWS

House of Beating Wings
House of Pounding Hearts
House of Striking Oaths

HOUSE
OF
POUNDING
HEARTS

House of Pounding Hearts

OLIVIA WILDENSTEIN

sourcebooks
casablanca

Copyright © 2023, 2024 by Olivia Wildenstein
Cover and internal design © 2024 by Sourcebooks
Cover design © Olivia Wildenstein and Miriam Schwardt
Cover type by Antoaneta Georgieva/Sourcebooks
Cover images © ead72/Depositphotos.com, fivespots/Depositphotos.com,
scis65/Depositphotos.com, Givaga/Depositphotos.com
Map © Olivia Wildenstein
Map art by Chaim Holtjer/Chaims Cartography
Internal art © Grace Zhu

Published by Sourcebooks Casablanca, an imprint of Sourcebooks
P.O. Box 4410, Naperville, Illinois 60567-4410
(630) 961-3900
sourcebooks.com

Originally self-published in 2023 by Olivia Wildenstein.

Cataloging-in-Publication Data is on file with the Library of Congress.

Printed and bound in the United States of America.
LSC 10 9 8 7 6 5 4 3 2 1

Getting lost is part of the journey.

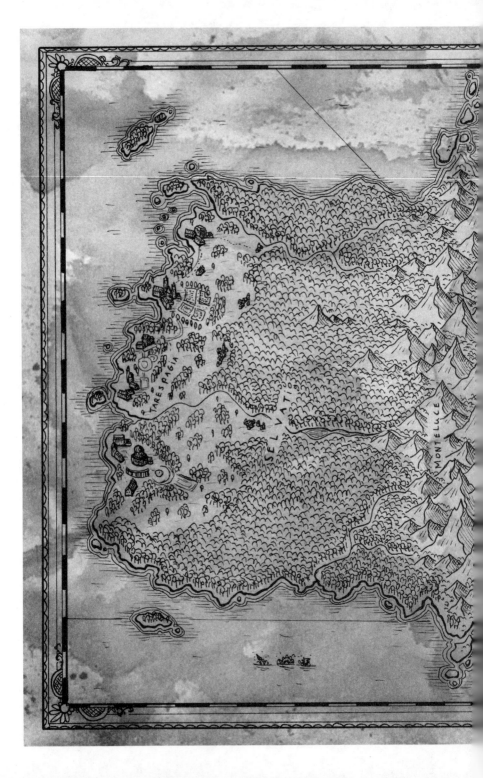

LUCIN GLOSSARY

Altezza—Your Highness
bibbino/a—baby
buondia—good day/good
   morning
buonotte—good night
buonsera—good evening
Caldrone—Cauldron
carina—sweetie
castagnole—fried dough rolled
   in sugar
corvo—crow
cuggo—cousin
cuori—heart
dolcca—honey
dolto/a—fool
furia—fury
generali—general
Goccolina—Raindrop
grazi—thank you
-ina/o—affectionate ending to
   first names
Maezza—Your Majesty

mamma—mom
mare—sea
mareserpens—sea serpent
merda—shit
micaro/a—my dear
mi cuori—my heart
nonna—grandma
nonno—grandpa
pappa—dad
pefavare—please
piccolino/a—little one
piccolo—little
princci/isa—prince/princess
santo/a—holy
scazzo/a—street urchin
scusa—sorry
serpens—serpent
soldato/i—soldier/s
tare—land
tiuamo—I love you
tiudevo—I owe you
zia—aunt

CROW GLOSSARY

adh (aw)—sky

ag—and

ah'khar (uhkawr)—beloved

álo—hello

bahdéach (bahdock)—
beautiful

behach (beyock)—little

beinnfrhal (benfrol)—
mountain berry

bìdh (bye)—food

bilbh (beehlb)—dumb

bròg—shoes

chréach (kreyock)—crow

cúoco (coowocko)—coconut

Dádhi (daji)—Dad

dalich (daleh)—sorry

dréasich (dreesseh)—dress

éan (een)—bird

fás—not yet

fihladh (feelaw)—leave

fin (fion)—wine

fios—know

focá—fuck

guhlaèr (guhlair)—okay

ha—I

*ha'rovh béhya an ha théach'thu;
ha'raì béih (haroff beya
an ha thock thoo; haray
beh)*—I wasn't living until I
met you, merely alive

ínon (eenon)—daughter

Ionnh (yon)—Miss

khrá (kraw)—love

leath'cinn (lehken)—half-Crow

Mádhi (maji)—Mom

mars'adh (marsaw)—please

mo—my

moannan (meanan)—mate

moath (mof)—north

*mo bahdéach moannan
(mo badock meanan)*—
my beautiful mate

Mórrgaht (mawr-got)—
Your Majesty

murgadh (murrgaw)—market

né (neh)—no

o ach thati—oh but you do

rahnach (rawnock)—kingdom

rí (ree)—king

rih bi'adh (reebyaw)—king of the sky

ríkhda gos m'hádr og matáeich lé—much longer and I may kill him

sé'bhédha (shehveha)—you're welcome

sí (see)—she

siér (siuhr)—sister

siorkahd (shuhrkaw)—circle

tà (taw)—yes

tach (tock)—the

Tach ahd a'feithahm thu, mo Chréach (tok add a faytham thoo, mo kreyock)—The sky awaits you, my Crows

tàin (tawhhn)—ass

tapath (tapoff)—thank you

thábhain (hawben)—tavern

thu (too)—you

thu leámsa (too lehawmsa)—you are mine

tuiladh (twilaw)—more

uhlbheist (ulbeeheist)—monster

HISTORICAL TIMELINE

MAGNABELLUM
Great War waged 522 years ago between the Kingdom of Luce and the Queendom of Shabbe. Costa Regio won the war and became the first Fae king of Luce.

BATTLE OF PRIMANIVI
Battle waged 22 years ago between a Lucin mountain tribe and the Fae. Costa's son, Andrea, who had ruled over Luce for the last century, was killed. His son Marco Regio took over, won the battle, and was crowned king of Luce.

1

T he captor became the captive. The gatherer, the gathered. The—"

"Aren't you being a tad dramatic, Piccolina?" Phoebus flops down beside me in my sky kingdom cell. "Gods, this mattress."

"It's too soft."

"No such thing as too soft. Unless we're discussing penises."

"Which we're not. We're discussing the man-faced harpy who's imprisoned me in his stone nest."

Phoebus flexes his lips into a smile. "Man-faced harpy. Cute."

"It's not meant to be cute. It's meant to be slanderous." I glower at the ceiling that I've glowered at for the last three days. I'm surprised my incendiary gaze hasn't transformed the wooden rafters to sawdust or pulverized the stone roof beyond.

My friend's smile only increases. "Although I'd love to discuss your sexy jailer, I've come on a mission."

"Horrible people aren't sexy. As for your mission, if it's to get me to come out of this room, my answer is a resounding *no*."

Phoebus stretches his ridiculously long limbs and yawns. "He takes all his meals in his private chambers, so you won't cross paths with him in any of the taverns."

Of course, Lorcan Reebyaw doesn't dine with his people.

Kings never do. I still cannot believe I brought him back to life.

Although I'm the maker of my own misfortune, I will never forgive Bronwen for misleading me with her stupid prophecy. Yes, I should probably have questioned it instead of jumping feetfirst into the mission like I jumped feetfirst into the canal the night Ptolemy Timeus threatened my serpent, Minimus.

Any jumping I do from now on will be thoroughly thought out.

"Tell Syb and Gia to come over with a barrel of wine. Oh, and tell them to bring Antoni, Mattia, and Riccio."

"Not going to happen, sweets. I'm the only man allowed inside your bedchamber."

I fling my glower on Phoebus. "Says who?"

"The big bad crow."

"Serpent ass," I mutter.

"I've always wondered...*do* serpents have asses or just tails? Or are their asses inside their tails?" His green eyes glitter, and although I've no doubt these musings have crossed Phoebus's mind many a time during his twenty-two years of life, at the moment, I sense he's using these inane questions to soften my mood.

Except my mood will not be softened.

"Actually, that's a lie. One other man is allowed to come see you."

I sense he'll speak my Crow genitor's name—Kahol Bannock. Sure enough, those are the four syllables that roll out of Phoebus's mouth.

My father is another male I've been refusing to see. I'm not ready to meet the giant with the twisted nose, square jaw, and stony mouth.

I still cannot believe he had a part in making me. And not with the woman I've called Mamma my entire life but with a Shabbin witch.

A Shabbin witch!

Although I've yet to confront Lore to learn my full history,

I've fathomed that Bronwen must've been the one to switch Mamma's—I mean, Agrippina's—baby with me, and that is what disintegrated the mind of the sweet Fae I love with all my heart.

Unless Bronwen broke her mind so she'd keep me—the Crow-Shabbin changeling—a secret?

It's the first time this theory forms, and it makes so much terrible sense that I want to storm the mountain to find both Lore and the scarred soothsayer.

I sit up and ball my fists so hard that my phalanges whiten. "Fine. Let's go to the tavern."

Phoebus blinks up at me. "Really?"

"Yes, really."

He rolls himself into a sitting position and rubs his palms. "Oh, the favor Syb will owe me."

"Favor?"

"She bet me you'd never come out of hiding."

"I'm not hiding."

"Right, you're sulking."

"I'm not sulking."

Phoebus grins.

"Shall I remind you that friends don't take pleasure in their friend's melancholy?"

He scoots off the bed and plods over to my side, extending his hand. "You do realize that your man-faced harpy is not evil incarnate."

"Don't you dare take his side! He locked me up. He lied to me. He *used* me." I leave out the part of me using the Crow king first. I've yet to explain the prophecy I gobbled up to my friends.

If it doesn't come up, why share it?

Thinking about the Fae prince I made king simmers my insides. I may presently loathe the sky king more than the earth king, but I'm no fan of Dante Regio, who, after everything I did for him, abandoned me.

3

Dante doesn't deserve a gram of my respect. As for my love, he lost that the day he called me a traitor and looked upon me as though I were some demon spawn hungering for Fae blood.

I clap Phoebus's hand with a little more vigor than necessary. "I hate men." At his dramatic gasp, I add, "Except you."

He pretends to wipe his brow on his apple-green shirtsleeve. "You had me worried there for a minute."

"As long as you don't lock me in a stone palace or leave me behind, I will love you forever."

His throat dips. "You know that if I could, I'd take you with me."

I steal my hand from his. "Please, Pheebs. I beg you, don't leave me here. *Please.*" My voice breaks even though my eyes stay dry.

He sighs before gathering me into a hug. "Fine. I won't. I'll stay as long as you stay."

"That's not—"

"—what you want. I know. But it's the best I can do if I care to keep my limbs attached to my body, which I do."

"They'd regenerate."

"Not if an iron beak or talon pries them off."

I pull away, spine arching to peer up into his face. "Did Lore or some other Crow threaten you?"

"Not me specifically."

I grit my teeth.

"Look, I think you'd be doing yourself a great disservice by leaving. I hear there's much unrest in the capital. Most Fae are unhappy that Marco's dead and that the Crows have returned."

I flick my gaze toward the windows that give onto the ocean and the island of Shabbe beyond. I've no doubt making me face the pink rock is part of Lore's punishment, the same way keeping me in the room contiguous to his is.

Thankfully, there's no door between our rooms, and the stone wall blocks out all sound, but I swear I can feel him on the other side. Several times, I've woken up in the middle of the night with

4

the distinct impression of his yellow eyes beaming from a pocket of darkness. If he did pay me unwanted visits, though, I've yet to catch him—the same way I've yet to hear him speak through our stupid mind link.

Although I'd like to believe he isn't plucking the thoughts from my head because I've figured out how to shield my mind, I'm not delusional. I doubt there's any way for me to keep an all-powerful shape-shifter with the ability to create storms and send visions from penetrating my skull.

Lore's either bored of viewing all my unpleasant thoughts or too busy ruling his charcoal-eyed, feathery folk. After all, he has so many more minds to trespass into now that his people have been resuscitated.

My head is yanked brutally back. "What the underworld are you doing, Pheebs?"

"Brushing out that snarled mess atop your head before a Crow mistakes it for a nest. Now hold still."

My head is wrenched back anew. "With what are you brushing it? A garden rake?"

"No, although I should ask Lore if we can get one. Your hair may be short, but it's preposterously bushy."

I twist my head, abandoning many hair follicles to whatever instrument of torture Phoebus wields. "You're to ask Lorcan for nothing. Don't owe that man a thing."

Phoebus is smart enough not to attempt to appease me. Once he's done torturing my scalp, he ambles toward the adjoining grotto, which someone transformed into a closet. "So what are we wearing?"

"I'm not changing."

"Piccolina, you've donned Gia's clothes for the past three days. We need to get you—"

"I'm not wearing any of those clothes. I don't know who they belong to."

"They belong to you. Lorcan had them made—"

My glare stops Phoebus's explanation, or so I assume.

"The *man-faced harpy* had them sewn solely for you."

I hike up my chin. "One more reason not to wear them."

He sighs. "Well, at least splash yourself liberally in perfume, because you smell like the inside of a conch shell." My tapered gaze makes him add, "Which I'm sure smells lovely to Crows. I hear they're fond of mollusks."

I watch his lips for a twitch that would hint at humor. Phoebus remains alarmingly solemn, so I visit my private bathing chamber, which I refuse to show appreciation for. Anytime even a modicum of wonder creeps up, I squash it down.

I riffle through the many glass vials of scented oils arranged in an earthen pot, nudging aside the bars of soap flecked with dried herbs and flowers that remind me of the ones Nonna would cook and sell for coin.

As I uncap one of the vials, my heart swells with emotion for this woman who raised me like her own even though I wasn't hers at all. I hate the way I left and want nothing more than to run into her arms. Would those arms close around me, or would they push me away?

I dab the oil on my pulse points, then furtively sniff my shirt to see if I really smell like a beached shell. I don't.

Ass.

Phoebus was probably trying to trick me into changing. Except wearing any gifted outfit would be construed as a peace offering, and I will only offer that man-bird peace if he offers me my freedom.

I thumb the cork back into the vial and return to the bedroom to find Phoebus examining a painted mural that I refuse to find pretty. "I'm ready."

"For…*war?*"

I smile for the first time in days. "No, I'm ready to drink my weight in wine. Whyever would you think I look ready to kill?"

"It's your eyes. They glitter."

I snort as Phoebus crooks his arm and I loop my arm through. "I promise not to inflict harm on anyone who doesn't deserve it."

"Perhaps leaving this room is an unsound idea."

Like the vines Phoebus can grow from his palms, my smile matures, its roots sliding through my rib cage and capturing my heart. Just as they begin to buoy the deadened organ, a Crow plummets through the same hatch opening Lore carried me through days ago.

I hold perfectly still, hoping the shape-shifter will be a stranger. Odds should be in my favor since I know all of two Crows—well, one, really. I tighten my grip on Phoebus's biceps when the black feathers melt into smoke that congeals into a man with citrine eyes. Out of all the Crows in the sky kingdom, why must *he* be the first I see?

Lore's gaze sidles up my body. "Feeling rested, Behach Éan?"

I cast my attention on one of the torches hooked into the stone wall, pretending the royal monster isn't standing there, mere breaths away.

"Don't mind her." Phoebus pats my hand. "Her mood's always rotten before she eats."

I ferry my widened gaze over to my friend.

Former friend.

Phoebus pins my arm under his to keep me from shooting back into my cell. "We were about to remedy that."

If he invites him to join us, I will—

Another Crow lands beside Lore and shifts into skin. My heart holds still again, and I pray to the Fae gods—even though they probably won't listen to me since I'm not one of their children— that it isn't my father.

Lo and behold, it isn't.

A woman with long black hair that gleams sapphire like Lore's and features as sharp as her alter ego rises from a crouch, and although her shoulders don't graze her king's, she stands close.

A little too close for a subject, if you ask me.

Which, I'm aware, no one *is* asking me.

She doesn't smile at me or thank me for being instrumental in her return. Maybe she hasn't regained the use of her voice. She pivots toward Lore and says something in their tongue, proving that her vocal folds are, in fact, in tip-top shape.

He nods, eyes not leaving mine. "Imogen, meet Fallon. Cathal's child."

Her eyes taper on me, so I narrow mine right back. Childish, I'm aware. Finally, she nods. I don't.

He steps toward the archway under which Phoebus and I stand. "I hope you'll find our food to your liking, Fallon."

I smile up at him, making sure it's all teeth. "You know my love for carrion."

A slow smile spreads over his mouth, and although he shows no teeth, I can feel them pressing into the curve of his lips. "We stock plenty of birdseed. Phoebus, make sure she gets a generous ration?"

My friend, who isn't my friend anymore, grins.

"Imogen, my chambers. Now. We've work to do."

I don't watch him leave, but I do watch her follow.

She sticks so close that if he were in his other form, her head would be up his tail, lodged somewhere in that indent I once mistook for a detonating switch. I shove the visual aside and yank Phoebus forward. "Let's leave them to their *work*."

"Someone sounds—"

I elbow him in the ribs, cutting off both his speech and breath. Even though a door claps shut, these shape-shifters have exceptional hearing.

Besides, I'm *not* jealous.

I'd have to care about the winged male, and I absolutely don't.

2

The Sky Tavern, or Awhawben as Phoebus tells me it's called, is excavated in the gray rock of Monteluce. Wooden beams support thick ropes strung with rows of glass lanterns. Every wick burns with a flame, providing light in the otherwise dusky cavern. Yes, there are windows, but they're as minute as the ones in my cell.

Like the mural behind my bed, the walls are decorated with landscapes of chalk and ink. I study them thoroughly, and not because I find them pretty; I don't. Just like I don't find the wooden mezzanine with its driftwood furniture lovely in the least.

This prison may sit in the sky, but it's still a prison. No amount of starlight will ever make it sparkle. To think I begged Lore for a glimpse of it the day we crested the mountain.

"Oh my gods, you got her to come out of her room!" Sybille's voice bangs against my eardrums.

I find her waving from a table in the corner—if an egg-shaped room can be considered to have corners. I'm glad to see the table sits under the mezzanine and not smack-dab in the middle for all to peer at, because *all* are peering. The room grows so quiet I can hear the sweeps of eyelashes amidst the charcoal-streaked faces twisted toward me.

Overwhelmed by the attention, I burrow into Phoebus's side and tug him toward where Syb sits with Antoni, Giana, Mattia, and Riccio. "You didn't warn me there'd be people," I hiss.

"Not only is it mealtime but it's a tavern. Since you used to work in one, I assumed you'd figure that out on your own."

For some reason, it didn't strike me that we'd run into anyone but my friends and a couple casks of wine. Said friends are watching me just as quietly as the rest of the patrons. Although it's only been three days, I feel like Giana, Antoni, Riccio, and Mattia have aged years. The stress of the last few weeks has clearly taken its toll on the lot of them.

Sybille shoves Riccio aside so I can slip onto the bench between them.

Giana smiles at me from across the table where she sits beside Antoni. "So what do you think?"

"Of?"

She gestures to the tavern. "The sky kingdom."

"I like our earthly one better. It's more colorful."

Phoebus, who lowers himself beside Riccio, flips his shoulder-length locks back, exposing his peaked ears. Although proud of my friend for not hiding what he is, I worry a Crow will morph into a bird and peck off the points. "She's only traveled from her bedroom—"

"Cell," I correct.

Phoebus rolls his eyes. "From her *cell* to here, so she hasn't seen much of it."

"I've seen more than enough." I pile my hands in my lap, atop the scratchy pants Giana lent me after she arrived with Bronwen. They balloon around my thighs, which have grown as reedy as they were before my first blood cycle.

Even though Nonna is not a curvy woman, my thinness would horrify her. All things considered, though, my gaunt body would probably give her little pause in comparison to the news of my lineage. My heart gives a painful squeeze at the idea of her finding out.

"How have you been?" Antoni's voice springs me out of my glum contemplations.

"Deeply annoyed. And you?"

"Impatient to receive my boat."

"I wouldn't hold my breath if I were you. Lore doesn't need you anymore, so he has no reason to get you a boat."

The few conversations buzzing around us stop after I utter the sky king's name.

Mattia's bushy blond eyebrows bend. "He promised us one, and he's kept his other promises. Why so negative?"

"I don't know." I shrug. "Could have to do with the fact that he's holding me hostage."

"Because you're the only person who can handle both obsidian and iron, Fallon." Riccio raises a tankard of something to his lips.

Thanks to Sybille nudging her drink in front of me, I find out it's wine, but it's not bubbly like the one we drink in Luce; it's flat and earthy, like sun-warmed berries crushed against loamy soil. *Delicious.*

Obviously, if asked, I'll pretend to thoroughly dislike it. I drain the contents of the metal goblet before smacking it down on a tabletop that's so black I assume it's obsidian, but the surface is grainy and full of knots like wood. Not to mention that obsidian is poisonous to Crows.

"Hey, Connor," Phoebus calls out to the brown-skinned male with blackened eyes who's carrying a platter of drinks to a nearby table. "Tuiladh fin ag bidh mars'adh."

As Connor replies with a nod, my fingers tighten on the stein, the foreign syllables running on a loop inside my mind—*twilaw fine ag bye marsaw.* Not one is familiar, but then again, my knowledge of my father tongue consists of ten words or less. "Since when do you speak Crow?"

"Since yesterday. Connor is giving me lessons." Phoebus trails the barkeep—tavern owner?—with his eyes. Does anyone own anything in this realm, or does everything belong to Lore?

"Why?" I ask.

"Because I thought it was the congenial thing to do while we live amongst them."

Sybille presses her mouth to my ear. "Also, Pheebs is trying to get into that male's pants."

I blink at Phoebus. "What about Mercutio?"

He stabs his fingers through his golden hair. "What about him?"

"You liked him."

"Well, you liked Dante." Phoebus turns back toward me. "And look how that turned out."

I sandwich my lips. "Except Mercutio didn't discard you in the enemy realm."

"Crows aren't the enemy, sweetie." Sybille wraps one hand around mine and squeezes my fingers gently.

I steal my hand from hers and return it to my lap. How can she say this when they're keeping me locked up here?

"I'm glad you finally saw Dante's true colors," Giana says while Antoni watches my face for a reaction.

Since I neither want to think about Dante nor dissect our obsolete relationship, I change the subject. "So what else have the lot of you been doing besides converting to Crowism?"

Riccio snorts. "Crowism."

"Resting, exploring, meeting new people." Giana steals a crumb of cheese off a wooden platter littered with fruit rinds and blackened vegetable stems. "Communicating is challenging as most Crows don't speak Lucin, but the few who do help us translate."

A girl with braided, inky hair and inkier eyes glides through the tavern as though she were more serpent than bird. She stops beside our table and smiles. It's not that I was expecting her to growl or caw…

All right, I was.

"Gia, álo."

Giana snaps her gray eyes onto the newcomer. I don't miss the fierce glitter that turns them silver. "Hello, Aoife."

"You room for one more?"

"Of course." Giana shuffles to make room for Eefah.

"You must be Fallon. Such a pleasure to make meeting."

"To meet you," Phoebus corrects her.

"Ah, tà. *To meet you.*" The words unspool with accents on all the wrong syllables. Where Lucin sounds like harp music, Crow sounds like rocks jouncing down a riverbed—raw, wet, and guttural.

The woman's smile exposes teeth that are slightly crooked yet don't take away from her overall attractiveness—a beauty that both Giana and Riccio have clearly noticed.

"Aoife is Imogen's sister," Phoebus explains.

Beneath her black mask of makeup rests the same small feather that adorns every Crow's cheekbone. "You met Immy?"

The memory of Lore's *colleague* abrades my already tetchy mood.

"We ran into her and Ríhbiadh on our way over." Everyone at our table—and not at our table—grows quiet when Phoebus drops Lore's last name.

"Well, I'm nice one." Eefah leans over the table, her long braid swishing past shoulders that are wider than Giana's but not quite as wide as Riccio's. Probably from all the flying.

I try to remember if Imogen's were as wide, but the hallway in which we met was dark, and I was rather busy glowering at my jailer.

"You and I have so much in common, Aoife." Sybille grins tauntingly at her older sister, who rolls her eyes.

"I personally prefer Gian—" Before Phoebus can pop the last

a out, Sybille pinches an orange rind off an otherwise bare platter and launches it at our friend's pretty face. It hits his tall forehead and slithers down his nose before plopping onto the table. "Just proving my point, Syb." He knuckles the slimy juice off his skin. "Oh, and you'll pay for that later."

She smiles as though daring him to get her back. Which he will. Phoebus always strikes back, but unlike Sybille, who's of the *act first, ask questions later* tribe, Phoebus is imbued with an inordinate amount of patience.

"So Imogen works with your king?" I ask.

"*Your* king?"

"Morrgot. Or whatever it is your people call him." The Crow word leaves a bad taste in my mouth, because for the longest time, I thought it was Lore's name. Well, his birds' name—name*s*. It was Dante who corrected my awry assumption by offering me the translation: *Your Majesty.*

"*Your* people?" Eefah's brow puckers. "Cathal is father, no?"

"Yup." Sybille bumps her shoulder into mine.

Eefah's forehead smooths. "You are Crow too, Fallon. Lorcan Ríhbiadh is *your* king too."

"Lorcan Reebyaw will *never* be my king." My avowal is met with vicious hisses.

Hmm... There are few things I enjoy more than being challenged, Behach Éan.

My gaze snaps to the tavern entrance where I expect to find Lore. When I don't see him, I scan every shadow for golden pinpricks. **That wasn't me challenging you.**

Yet I feel challenged.

Although I think the words, my lips also shape them. "It's not a challenge."

"What's not a challenge?" Sybille asks.

"Nothing," I grumble.

"I'm guessing Fallon took after her birth mother." Riccio rubs the stubbled edge of his jaw. "I hear the princess of Shabbe was quite the looker."

The blood drains from my face. "You know?" I stare around the table, seeking scrunched brows but finding none. "You *all* know?"

"Lazarus told us," Sybille says softly, as though she senses that speaking any louder would make me snap.

I hunt the dim tavern for the giant Fae healer with the silver hair but don't find him amongst the patrons.

"He assumed we already knew since Antoni knew," Giana adds.

I whip my gaze toward the boat captain. Although his irises are the same blue as Dante's, they somehow seem darker tonight, like the ocean that stretches between Luce and Shabbe instead of the midday sky. "Since when?"

He inhales deeply, his jaw as stiff as my spine. "Since that night in the woods with Bronwen."

The night he trailed me to where Bronwen was waiting for me with Furia. How I miss the stallion Dante rode away on. One more reason I have to loathe the new Fae king.

"Zendaya was great beauty." Eefah sighs as Connor returns with a jug, which I hope contains more Crow wine, and a platter piled high with grilled vegetables and fruits.

No dead animal in sight. No seeds either.

"*Was?*" I look away from the colorful mound striped black like everything else in this kingdom. "Is she dead?"

"No." The answer comes from behind me.

I twist around on the bench, my gaze climbing up…and up… and up.

"Your mother is alive." The gruff timbre accenting the male's Lucin raises the fine hairs on my arms.

Eefah gasps and rambles something in Crow I don't catch, because every gram of my attention is concentrated on the male swathed in smoke.

"Àlo, daughter."

3

Time stops as I take in the man who made me, this elusive father I've only just learned about.

Although I've seen him in visions, the glimpses I've had of him don't compare to the actual person. He's taller, larger, and completely more terrifying in real life.

His nose looks to have been bashed in by an entire mountain, his whiskered jaw is jagged enough to saw through tree trunks, his hair is a chin-length storm cloud, and his eyes…they're the darkest shade of black, darker than the murder of Crows that cloaked the sun the day Lorcan roused his people. They are eyes that have soaked up all the rage in the world and stored it.

This rage and the blood it enflames are the only things this man and I have in common. In no other way do we resemble each other.

The air beside Kahol darkens and heaves with more smoke as another Crow appears. I know before the person has even firmed up that it will be Lore. I'm not sure why or how, for his misty shape isn't darker or denser than other shifters'. Perhaps I merely expected him to come since he so loves to hover.

I do not hover; I watch over you, Lore has the audacity to murmur into my mind.

I'm not a child, Reebyaw, and I'm no longer in danger, so feel free to let me fucking be.

Lore's expression blackens at my use of the foul word. I decide to use it frequently from now on.

"Shall we take this reunion to a more private place?" His voice is low yet resonates everywhere.

"I'm fine right here." I only say this to pester him. In truth, I'd prefer not to be ogled by a bunch of strangers.

"Very well." His eyes flash with something both molten and chilling. "Fihladh!" Lore's command echoes over every glass lantern and windowpane, springing people from their seats. To my tablemates, he says, "Until further notice, Adh'Thábhain is closed. Please exit the premises."

I take it that the word he bellowed—*feelaw*—means leave or something along those lines. Bench legs scrape the stone floor as Mattia presses away from the table to ease himself up.

Only Sybille remains seated. I don't realize she's snatched up one of my hands until I feel her long, calloused fingers fold over mine. "If you want me to stay, I can."

"Me too." Phoebus hovers, half standing, half sitting.

I'm uncertain what I want.

"Leave. Please." Kahol's voice is so thick and raspy it sounds edged in sorrow, but I must misconstrue the emotion, because this man looks as capable of weeping as I look capable of fitting through those tiny openings in the rock.

I may have tried.

Good to know.

I narrow my gaze on Lore's as I squeeze Sybille's hand. "Go. I'll be fine."

Although hesitant, both she and Phoebus head toward the large doors that Connor pulls shut behind him once the room has emptied.

Lore lays a palm on Kahol's shoulder, making the massive male jerk, then nods toward the bench across from me. Without glancing away from my face, Kahol circles the table and drops so heavily onto the wood that it groans.

As Lore lowers himself into the seat that Phoebus vacated, my stomach gurgles, and although the scent of food is alluring, I don't think I could swallow anything. Except wine. That would probably go down nicely.

I reach out for the pitcher, but Lore beats me to it and pours some dark, fermented juice into the goblet in front of me before filling one up for my father.

I drink while my father stares and stares at me as though I were the oddest creature he's ever laid eyes on.

"I thought you died the night Regio and his army ambushed us in the Isolacuorin temple. I heard his general say—" He closes his eyes. "I heard him tell Marco that Daya bled the child out. That it was done."

Although I sit here, proof that it wasn't *done*, my father's features remain crinkled as he relives his nightmarish memory.

"But of course, she'd find a way to save you." When his lids reel up, his eyes are wet. "Thank Mórrígan that Agrippina was there. Thank Mórrígan she kept you a secret."

"Why *was* she there?"

"She was there," Lore says, "to warn Cathal and Daya that it was an ambush."

"She arrived too late to save us." The saddest smile contorts my father's mouth. "But in time to save you."

"How *did* she save me? Did she fish me out of the puddle of blood?"

"Daya placed you inside Agrippina." Lore says this slowly, as though believing that the pacing of his delivery may help my mind make sense of his ludicrous explanation.

"What do you mean, *she placed me*?"

"Your mother sent you inside Agrippina's womb." At my rumpled brow, Lore adds, "With magic."

Wait…*what?* I look between my father and Lore a great many times. I was magicked from one body into another? Although I sensed I was a changeling, the news of how I swapped wombs is stupefying. It does explain how my grandfather *saw* me come out of Agrippina, though.

I've lived my entire life surrounded by people with elemental power, yet the concept of being transferred like a virus is utterly mind-blowing. "How did she do it? Did she click her fingers and *poof?*"

Lore smiles. "Shabbin magic comes from your blood, so there's no clicking of fingers. There is much pricking of fingers, though, for sigils are drawn with blood."

I study my fingertips, expecting them to shimmer, but all that shines is the coarse skin atop my calluses. Although I doubt my father or Lore will wrinkle their noses at my decidedly unfeminine hands, I slot them beneath my thighs. "How do you know I'm truly Daya's daughter?"

Lore drums his fingers. "Besides the fact that you share most of her traits?"

"I used to think I shared many traits with the woman who birthed me."

Lore shifts forward in his seat, making his leathers creak. "Daya sent Bronwen a vision before Meriam bound her magic so that your aunt could look after you and send you to wake me when it was time."

The emotion glazing my father's eyes is so potent that it rips tears from the giant man. As they carve through his makeup, he murmurs words in his tongue that sound soft in spite of their guttural pronunciation.

Is he swearing a lethal retribution upon all those involved in the ambush, or is he crying because I was saved?

"What happened to Agrippina's child?"

"Agrippina was with child?" The bear of a Crow across from

19

me scrubs at his wet, bristly cheek, smearing the black.

"I'm a changeling, which means I was changed. Is…" My tongue slips out and wets my lips. I cannot bring myself to utter the word *mother*, much less think of the Shabbin who gave me life as such. I have a mother whose name is Agrippina. Though she may not love me—may never *have* loved me—I cannot find it in my heart to replace her just because we do not share the same genes. "Is Daya raising Agrippina's baby?"

"Agrippina was never pregnant," Lore replies calmly.

My eyebrows all but collide. "I don't—I thought for there to be a changeling, babies had to be exchanged?"

A mild smile plays on Lore's mouth. "Shabbin magic is rather extraordinary."

Rather? It's wholly bewildering. "Where is Daya? In Shabbe?"

"That's the one place we know she is not." Lore pinches a spear of asparagus from atop the stack Connor deposited on our table and raises it to his lips.

"How?"

"Because we've been flying around the Shabbin wards for days and have seen neither hide nor hair of your mother." Kahol must grind his teeth, because his jaw is all harsh angles.

I frown. "How is that possible?"

"Bronwen believes Meriam may have bound Daya's magic." Lore snaps off the crisped spear with teeth that flash white against his dusky lips.

"Meriam?" Why does the name sound familiar?

"Meriam was Costa's Shabbin lover. The woman who doomed us and whose blood fuels the wards." Lore's explanation makes the memory of our conversation whizz around my mind. "Meriam is also Zendaya's mother. Your grandmother."

My back straightens as though my articulated spine had transformed into a serpent tusk. "I'm related to the sorceress who damned your people?"

"*Our* people. You may reject your heritage, but you're no less a Shabbin or a Crow, Fallon."

I roll my lips, not feeling like I belong anywhere or to anyone.

You belong. Lore growls. **You belong—**

Before he adds *to the sky*—which he's appropriated—or to the pink dot on the horizon, I ask, "If my mother isn't in Shabbe, where is she?"

"I do not know." My father wraps his giant fingers around the tankard of wine. Metal scrapes against metal like chalk against slate. It takes me a second to realize the sound came from him, from his nails that have elongated and hooked into iron talons, even though the rest of his body has remained humanoid. "I do not know. I cannot feel her." Kahol crushes his goblet, and wine sloshes out.

Feel her?

They are mates.

I blink. **Mates can feel each other?**

Yes.

If he cannot feel her, then how does he know she lives?

Hope.

Is Lore telling me to hope, or is he saying that my father does not actually know?

"We will find her, Cathal." Lore curls his fingers around one of my father's leather vambraces, which I doubt he has much need for, considering the breadth of his bones and muscles. "We will find her and bring her home. But first we must bring down the wards so the rest of our people can return. We need the manpower."

"You mean *birdpower?*" The correction slips out before I can stifle it. *Neither the time nor the place, Fallon.*

My impertinence wins me two sets of pointed stares. On the upside, it's heaved my father out of his chasm of despair.

"Not everyone's returned?" I ask.

Lore drums his fingers. "The Crows who sought refuge in

21

Shabbe are confined there."

Unlike my father, whose nails are spiky and pewter-colored, Lore's are blunt and nude. They never glided over my skin, yet I distinctly remember the feel of his ghostly fingers slithering over my body. He stops drumming them and flattens both his palm and lips.

What? Did he think I enjoyed being touched without my consent? I refocus on my father. "So how do we bring down the wards?"

"We wait until Priya has tortured Meriam's location out of one of the Fae the serpents dragged to her shores."

Good serpents.

"Or until Dante figures out where his brother hid her," my father interjects.

"My grand—" *You're not related to him,* I remind myself. It may very well be the first time I'm glad I'm not a Rossi. "The general was closest to Marco. He'd know."

"Your grandfather was not retrieved."

"He's alive?"

"If he is, he has not shown his face around Luce yet."

"What about Commander Dargento?" I ask hopefully. "Has he washed up on Shabbe?"

Smoke begins to waft off Lore's iron pauldrons as though the man were about to shift into his bird. "No."

My pulse quickens as I recall the odious Fae with black hair and amber eyes who threatened to murder everyone I loved. "Is he dead?"

Not yet. Not. Yet. Out loud, Lore says, "Imogen overheard Dante's soldiers chatter about the commander's miraculous return. Although we've yet to set eyes on him, we're to believe he's made it back to Isolacuori alive."

4

Both my stomach and my heart harden at the news of Silvius's survival. "Good," I end up saying.

"Good?" Lore pops out the word as though it tastes vile.

"Yes. *Good.*" I squeeze my mug to test if it's malleable; it's not. "Because I wish to be the one to pierce his heart with an iron blade."

My father draws in a ragged breath. "What has the man done to you, ínon?"

Eenon?

It means daughter in Crow.

Lore's translation doesn't make the title any less jarring. Jarring but also...nice. I have a father. He's real. He isn't exactly what I expected, but he cares. Or at least he seems to care.

Cathal cares deeply about his family.

I side-eye Lore, my anger dwindling a fraction. "Silvius Dargento is a detestable man who's threatened to kill everyone I love."

My father still clasps his misshapen tankard, which buckles some more beneath his talon-tipped fingers. "Has the man ever... harmed *you*?"

"No. He never dared because he feared there'd be consequences.

Up until a few days ago, I was the general's granddaughter and the prince's friend."

A dark look stains Lore's expression, and although I don't catch any of his thoughts, I sense they have to do with one or both of the aforementioned Fae.

My father speaks some words in Crow, and Lore answers, golden eyes flashing behind intermittent wisps of black smoke. How I wish I understood their tongue.

Lore slides his still-tapered gaze toward me. *I'll send a tutor in the morning.*

I said I wished. I didn't say I wanted.

Lore rolls his shoulders forward and drops his forearms onto the table. *Am I to understand that you do not want to kill Silvius?*

How did you arrive at that conclusion?

You said you wished to be the one to score his heart.

I gnash my molars, because there's little I hate more than people using my own words against me.

My father misses our quiet exchange because his eyes are pinned to the spilled wine surrounding his warped tankard.

How do you say Pappa in Crow? I ask.

Dádhi.

"Daji?" The title feels odd on my tongue, but not altogether unsavory.

Kahol's blackened eyes jolt off the tinted puddle and perch on my face.

"What were you and Lore discussing?" I ask.

For a full minute, he stays quiet, either still perplexed about the title I tossed at him or busy dissecting what to share with me. He releases the mug and seizes a balled napkin.

As he wipes his hands dry, he says, "I suggested bringing the commander up here to grant you your wish, but Lorcan has opposed himself to my idea."

I stare around me at the stone and lanterns. I may consider

these grottos my prison walls, but to everyone else, this place is a safe haven. "Silvius shouldn't be allowed inside the sky kingdom. However, I should be allowed out."

Lore's nails spring out and gouge the ebony wood. "Well, you are not."

"Why? Why are you keeping me locked up here? I've set you free. I've brought you back."

"Until the wards fall, you are the only Shabbin capable of removing obsidian from my skin if Dante fails to control his subjects. Or himself." Lore's dark cuirass creaks from his deep inhales and deeper exhales. "I will not risk cursing my people thrice."

I may still detest my situation, but at least now I understand the reason I'm caged. "So once the wards fall, I'll be free?"

The two males exchange a loaded look that makes my vertebrae click into a straight line.

Don't keep me in the dark. Not after all I've done. Not only is it unfair but it's also unkind.

"Once you've undone my curse for good, you'll be...free."

His hesitation makes me wonder what type of freedom he's alluding to. *FYI, I don't consider death a form of freedom.*

There'll be no dying. Lore's sullen mood gentles the slightest bit. *I promise, Behach Éan.*

I nod, somewhat appeased. There's still the subject of curses and breakers of curses—a.k.a. me. "What did you mean by *for good*?"

My father is still toweling his fingers even though I suspect no wine lingers. "Before you were born—before you were even conceived—Bronwen foresaw Daya and I having a daughter who'd possess the power to break the Crows' obsidian curse forever."

I gape. "That's why you called me the curse breaker? Not because I *unstaked* you."

Correct.

Wow. So much for believing myself powerless and useless. "And do tell, how will I swing this curse breaking?"

Lore sighs. "Bronwen hasn't yet seen how you'll do it."

"Let me get this straight. You plan on keeping me in the sky kingdom until Bronwen gets a vision?"

Yes.

"What if she only *sees* how I break your curse in, like, six decades from now?"

"We were trapped for five hundred years, Fallon. And then again for twenty—"

"I'm not spending the best years of my life trapped in a cavern in the clouds, away from civilization."

Lore releases a muted snort. "Are we not civilized enough for your taste?"

I joggle my head.

My father doesn't seem to mind my comment as much as Lore, because what he plucks out from all I said is "The best years?"

"Unlike you, I'm not immortal." My origin smacks me upside the head. "Or am I?"

"As long as your magic is bound"—the Crow king gazes toward the glassed-in openings that overlook the dense spill of the Racoccin woods—"you are not immortal."

My father swallows, probably because my unfortunate state reminds him of my mother and her bound magic. "Another reason you must stay here, ínon. No harm can come to you up here."

"No harm, perhaps, but also no good," I mutter, calculating how many slippers I'll go through pacing these stone hallways. "I will grow dottier than a Fae high on sprite urine." At Kahol's rumpled brow, I add, "I've not tried it; I was merely told about its effect. Besides, I'm not Fae, so pee probably wouldn't affect me. What will affect me, though, is being trapped up here. I'll develop highland fever. You do not want that. Trust me. Ask my friends. They'll tell you how impossible and maddening I can become."

Come to think of it, losing my mind may incite them to toss me from their nest...

My predicament draws a smirk to Lore's lips. "It is not your predicament that amuses me, Fallon, but your thought process."

Kahol makes a choking sound, and his face reddens...purples. Oh, Cauldron, what did he ingest?

"Lorcan!" I yell, because Lore's ass is still in his seat.

Kahol lurches to his feet so suddenly that it topples his bench. The bang thuds as loudly as the frenzied beats of my heart as I also leap to my feet, ready to vault over the table and pump his chest. I've only just found the man. I cannot lose him to—to—

I scan the food platter to figure out what he could've eaten...a spear of asparagus? A carrot? I cannot lose my father to a vegetable.

He's immortal, Fallon. Lore's words douse a little of my anguish. "You will not lose him to produce."

"No." My father's brow glistens with fury. "No!"

I don't—I don't understand... "What's going on?"

Lore tips his head, golden eyes steady on his friend's. "I meant to tell you."

My eyebrows bend in confusion.

"You meant...?" My father spits, barking out a laugh that freezes the torrent of adrenaline inside my veins. Sober again, he sweeps both his palms down his face, smearing his black makeup some more, and growls like a Selvatin leopard.

"What the underworld is happening? Is this some side effect from being a crow-shaped block of obsidian?" Although my voice is high-pitched, neither man pays me any mind.

No. Is that a smile in Lore's mind voice?

I'm probably imagining his internal delight, because he sports the look of a bad tidings' carrier.

"You know how it works, my friend." The king is calm, whereas

27

my heart has morphed into a thieving halfling being chased by an entire battalion of Fae *and* a couple serpents. "You know one does not choose."

"Sí mo ínon!"

I sense my father's roaring something about me being his daughter.

"I'm aware, Cathal, but it could've been worse. She could've ended up mated to Aodhan."

Color leaches from Kahol's streaked face.

"Who's Aydawn, and why are we discussing me being mated to him?"

"For all my desire to bring my Crows back from Shabbe, I wouldn't mind leaving that one behind."

Okay, so Aydawn is a Crow, and apparently not a favorite of Lore's. It doesn't ferry me any closer to understanding what has gotten my father's armor in a twist.

Kahol squeezes his lids shut and drops his head back. He seems to be imploring the sky for strength. "If you hurt her, Lore, you better pray for Mórrígan to lend me mercy."

"Have you met your daughter? Odds are rather high that I'll be in need of your pity more than your mercy." Lore utters this with a kinked smile that my father does not return.

"Can one of you please explain what the underworld's going on?" When Lore pins me with his citrine stare, my hands find purchase on my hips. "What?"

"I need—" Kahol's throat dips. "I need to fly." He looks at me, then at Lore, and then he says something that includes my biological mother's name, Mórrígan's, and a whole lot of headshaking before he streaks across the tavern, liquefying to smoke long enough to squeeze under the closed doors.

I grab every piece of information that's been tossed my way over the course of this strange get-together and stir, trying to smooth the lumps, but many remain.

"Do you remember when you mind walked into that memory of Bronwen and me on that hill?"

"Yes. She explained she could not marry you, which disappointed her father."

"Why couldn't she marry me?" Lore stands and circles the table toward me, gait unhurried.

I pivot as he stops on the other side of my bench. "Because you didn't do it for her."

The male-faced harpy grins now. "I see you memorized her speech word for word."

"Just get to the point."

His eyes glow, and suddenly, I'm back on that hill, this time standing so close that I catch the striking green of Bronwen's irises as well as the tapered points of her ears.

Oh my Gods, Bronwen is Fae!

While my mouth opens around a gasp, hers opens around the words *"Cian is my mate."*

So flummoxed by the shape of Bronwen's ears, I don't turn toward Lore when he answers, *"I've heard. He hasn't stopped speaking about it since you penetrated his mind."*

All the air exits my lungs as Lore releases me from this memory and sends me into another, the one where I stood before him naked and asked what he wanted to talk about, and he said… he said…

I yank myself out of that memory before his lips shape the words, yet they chase me back to the here and now: *"You're the one who penetrated my mind, Behach Éan. Again."*

The weight of my shock makes my ass knock into the table and tip over a wine goblet. Dampness courses down my leg, soaking into Giana's woolen slacks. "How do you—" My throat is so dry I have to gulp down my wadded saliva several times before I can form my question in full. "How do you cancel it?"

Lore arches a single black eyebrow. "Cancel it?" He sounds

entertained, which is ludicrous, because there is *nothing* entertaining about this situation. "Mating bonds are not supper bookings."

I grip the edge of the table with quaking fingers. "But this can't—we can't—I object."

The male has the audacity to laugh at my crumbling hopes and dreams. It's not that I was still holding out hope to marry Dante, because that ship sank along with his brother's galleon, but I *was* eager to choose my own destiny.

A realization stills my inner chaos, and I shrug. "So what if we have a mystical connection."

Lore's laughter wanes, and his eyebrows level out. "What do you mean, *so what?*"

"You can penetrate all your people's minds, so penetrating mine isn't all that special. As for my ability to enter yours, I'll just—I don't know—stifle it."

His pupils dilate, taking over the gold. "Crows have one mate, Fallon. *One.* I've waited for mine—for *you*—for centuries, and your reaction is *so what?*" Although smoke doesn't leak from his nostrils, it does bleed off his black fighting leathers.

"How exactly were you expecting me to react? I don't love you, Reebyaw. I barely like you. Frankly, until a few minutes ago, I flat out loathed you."

Silence grows between us, heavy and cold like Tarecuorin satin. I eye the door I long to run toward, then the man I long to run from.

The man who's accepted what the Cauldron has thrown his way.

Who the Cauldron has thrown his way.

This situation is utterly absurd. Marriages of convenience are one thing—one thing I believe should be abolished immediately—but mating bonds? Gods, I can't decide if I want to cackle at the ludicrousness of it all or pour my thoughts out *extremely* loudly.

Lore must realize that my will is stronger than any argument he may throw my way, because his contours fade. When cool air licks up the side of my neck and drifts across the edge of my jaw, I assume he's tossed open the tavern door. But then the gust hinges my neck backward, forcing my face to tilt and align with his hazy one, and I realize the air isn't coming from the hallway but from his shadows.

You know how I feel about challenges, Behach Éan.

Frustration steals across my cheeks. "For Cauldron's sake, that was not a challenge!" I unscrew my face from his ghostly grasp. "Go slither over someone else, Morrgot. Someone who cares for your attention."

Someone like Imogen, I think to myself, but since my thoughts always find their way into his mind, he must catch my suggestion.

His vaporous eyes scour mine for a heartbeat longer before flashing into oblivion like polished coins tossed into the murkiest canal. Although I try to kick the male from my thoughts after he leaves and my friends return, he lingers like a musty smell, dampening my mood.

Which only dampens further when Imogen walks into the tavern an hour or so later, hair mussed, makeup smudged, and mouth scraped raw like the doxies at Bottom of the Jug. "Lorcan has asked me to convey the message that your boat is slated to arrive in the morning, Antoni." Unlike her sister, her grasp of Lucin is flawless.

Antoni raises the gaze that's sat heavily on my face since he regained his seat. Like the others, he's curious about all that was said. Unlike the others, he hasn't pried. "I thought it wouldn't be ready for another week."

"As the Fae say, he pulled strings." Imogen casts a cursory glance my way before whirling on her black boots and returning to wherever it is she came from—probably Lore's bedchamber.

The male evidently wasted not a minute.

5

S plinters of sunlight wedge themselves through my lids, and
I groan. I'm not ready for this day to commence.

Not after last night.

Not after I learned the Cauldron decided I was incapable of
choosing my own mate. Sure, my track record is far from spectacular, but I'm certain I'd have eventually picked the perfect man.

I try to flip over onto my stomach, but I encounter a body—a
tall, broad, warm body. I spring upright like a jack-in-the-box.
When I catch a curtain of shoulder-length blond hair, a wave of
relief crashes over me, followed by a tidal wave of nausea.

I race to the bathing chamber and throw up in the toilet bowl.
Just when I think my stomach is empty, more fluid shoots up and
singes my throat. I hover over the metal bowl, watching the vis-
cous liquid drain down a fist-size hole that leads to what Eefah
explained was called a septic tank.

Sadly, the septic tank doesn't lead into the sea. Not that I'd fit
through the hole, but holes can be broadened if necessary. Seeing
as how the sky kingdom's waste flows into a grotto lined with
some precious stone that purifies it before sending it back into
pipes that gush water over one's head, drilling would be pointless.

The Crows' system is strange but brilliant. Especially since I used the shower on my second day of captivity, and the water does not smell foul. I stare at it now, contemplating slinking underneath it. I probably should.

In slow motion, I peel my desiccated body off the floor and crawl to the wall. Hand over hand, I hoist myself upright and spin a metal dial. As cool water splashes over me, I close my eyes, lift my head, and flatten my palms against the smooth stone.

Cauldron, I am never drinking alcohol again.

The water thins, then stops dribbling. Have I used up the entire sky kingdom's supply? It seems unlikely, but many unlikely things have happened to me, so I won't put it past my luck.

I find a sparkly eyed Sybille standing in front of me, armed with fluffy gray cloth and a blinding smile.

"Syb?" I pluck wet locks of hair off my forehead and scrub my eyes to ascertain I'm not confusing my friend with a towel rack. "Someone's awfully cheery this morning."

"You realize you showered with your shirt and drawers still on?"

I dip my chin, which sends my brain listing into my forehead and my body hurtling into the wall at my back.

Her smile grows and grows. "Someone's still drunk."

I have to close my eyes, because her teeth are too bright.

She sighs, and then her fingers latch onto the hem of my shirt and roll it off me. "Need help with the underwear, or can you manage?"

"I can manage." It's a feat that almost sends me sprawling into the floor, but thanks to Sybille, I avoid adding a bruise to my already-thudding head.

Once naked, she wraps me in what feels like a hunk of clouds. I wish she could use her air power to dry my hair, but the sky kingdom stifles Fae magic. A shame, for Phoebus's vines would've proved mighty helpful in my grand escape.

"Seriously...what's put you in such a stellar mood? And *where* did you come from?"

"From Mattia's room." Sybille waggles her brows. "The good mood is also courtesy of the strapping blond sailor."

My eyes jolt open, but the movement feels as though Nonna were scrubbing them with her bristly broom, so I drop my lids and squint instead.

"Gods, I should've confiscated the pitcher of wine when you decided that matching Riccio glass for glass was a sound idea."

"I was feeling competitive."

"Is that what drove you to drink your weight in sky wine?"

"Absolutely."

"So it wasn't Imogen's mussed hair and makeup?"

"Her hair and makeup were mussed? Didn't notice."

Sybille sighs. "You may be able to pull off lying with most people, but I know you too well. You took one look at that female Crow's face, and you dunked yours inside your tankard."

I toe a small puddle that has yet to vanish down the slender grooves in the stone floor. "I do not care about that female Crow or her sex-tossed hair."

"*Wind-tossed.* I have it on good authority she was scouting the Fae lands and *not* Lore's private chambers last night. Speaking of whom…you've yet to relate your conversation with the fearsome monarch. Spill. I'm *dying* to know."

Still processing the notion that Imogen may not be the sex fiend I thought her to be, I say, "He just reminded me that I'm the only one who can remove obsidian from his body, and that is why he couldn't let me leave, yaddy yadda."

"Yaddy yadda? New expression?"

"You're all abandoning me." I add a little pout, because one, I hate that she's leaving, and two, I want to steer the conversation off Lore before I reveal the mating bond I've zero intention of upholding.

Her smile melts away. "You asked me to go check on your grandmother and mother and to pack your clothes. If you want me to stay, I'll stay."

I sigh. "No, no."

"Fal…"

"No. Go. Just come back quickly. Maybe with them? You think they could be convinced to move here?"

She smooshes her lips together and side-eyes the lump of wet fabric on the floor. "Don't get your hopes up, all right?"

I nibble on my lip as we reemerge inside my bedroom where Phoebus is still dead to the world. At least *he's* staying. I try to take comfort that I'll have one friend and ally in Reebyaw's realm.

After I sink onto the bed, Sybille vanishes into the adjoining closet. "Dress or pants?" Her voice sounds muffled, as though she's wedged herself in between the preposterously dense row of outfits.

"Neither."

She pops out of the stone chamber, balancing a slew of hangers that clink like bones.

I shake my head, which angers the throbbing between my temples. "I'm not wearing any of those clothes."

"Then I guess you'll be wearing that towel for the remainder of the day."

It barely covers my intimate bits. I glance around the room for Giana's pants but cannot locate them.

"There was a wine stain down one leg, so I tossed them."

"What do you mean, *you tossed them*? Where?"

"Into your laundry chute."

"I have a laundry chute?"

She nods toward the closet. "There's a trapdoor in the wall that leads to a washroom. It's mystifying that you haven't explored your new bedroom."

"This isn't my new bedroom. It's my provisional dungeon."

Sybille rolls her eyes. "It's the nicest dungeon I've ever seen."

"Still a prison."

"Must you argue so loudly? I'm sleeping," comes a deep grumble.

"Clearly." Sybille grins. "We're about to leave, Pheebs. I thought you may want to wish us a safe passage."

"No. I just want to go back to that dream I was having of Connor."

"Rude." Sybille blows a lock of wavy black hair out of her eyes. Although she hates the natural curl, I think it softens her. "So"— she holds up two different outfits—"dress or pants."

"Towel."

She tosses the hangers onto the foot of my bed. "You are *such* a Crow."

I tuck my sodden hair behind my ears. "What is that supposed to mean?"

"That you're stubborn," Phoebus mutters.

Out of the corner of my eye, I spy apple green. I toddle over to Phoebus's discarded shirt. "You don't mind if I borrow your shirt, do you?"

"The only thing I mind is your yammering right now."

I smile.

Sybille wrinkles her nose as I replace the towel with my friend's silken shirt. "You do realize you're going to smell like male sweat all day?"

Phoebus burrows under the rumpled sheets. "I sweat rose water."

Sybille snorts. "No one sweats rose water, Pheebs, not even purelings."

I sniff the material, and although the fabric doesn't exactly scream rose bushel, it doesn't smell overly musky either.

Sybille walks over to the bed, and then she jumps. Right on top of Phoebus, who yelps. "I just wanted a hug," she says. "You know, in case we don't make it back."

I release the fabric I'm still sniffing. "Why wouldn't you make it back?" The shirt's hem brushes against the goose bumps that have risen on my thighs.

"Well, we did help the Crows return."

Although my head thumps, I'm fully sober now. "You also helped Dante snag the throne."

Phoebus encircles Sybille's body in a hug and slides his chin into the crook of her neck. He must shift his jaw around like he used to do when he realized that spot was ticklish, because she squeals and attempts to lever herself off him. "If Dante so much as touches a hair on your body, Fallon will sic her favorite Crow on him."

"I don't have a favorite Crow."

He snorts. "Lies. So many lies."

"If only she wasn't immune to salt..." Sybille's eyes sparkle as she presses her cheek into Phoebus's chest and gazes up at me.

Phoebus too is staring, but he seems elsewhere. "If Dante attacks any of you, Syb, I guarantee Lore will retaliate with a beheading or some limb culling. Can you imagine if he went for Regio's cock?"

"Cocks aren't limbs, Pheebs." Sybille's voice dims as though it were emanating from inside the sewage conduit.

I blanch as I relive the memory of Marco's severed head, and then I must swoon, because when my lashes sweep up, Sybille and Phoebus are crouched over me, palms smoothing down my hair, my cheeks, my arms.

"Oh my Gods, Piccolina. Are you all right?"

"Obviously not. She just fainted, Pheebs. Why did you have to mention severing essential body parts?"

"Because I'm only partly awake." Phoebus helps me sit and holds me as Sybille inspects whether my skull incurred any damage. "No one's getting beheaded or delimbed."

"*We* might if we break Lore's curse breaker." Sybille snags her lip as though she actually believes this is a possibility.

"I'm all right. I promise."

"You just went down like a sack of parsnips," Sybille says as someone knocks. "Come in!"

"No," I hiss because what if it's Lore? Or my father? Phoebus is wearing underwear, but I'm not. I probably should put some on. I tug on the hem of the shirt to cover as much of my legs as I can.

"Actually, don't—"

The door swings open.

"—come in," Sybille finishes softly as my visitor springs the door open with his fingertips.

6

Y our curse breaker is fine." Phoebus swallows, angling his large body behind mine.

Since my friend is not a prude, I imagine he fears retaliation from the male who stands in my doorjamb, wearing a scowl beneath his freshly applied war paint.

"Super fine." Sybille squeezes my shoulder, digging her nails into my skin. "Right, Fal? Right?"

My best friends' squeamishness may have brought a grin to my lips were it not for the presence of Imogen at Lore's side. I do not let myself wonder whether they spent any time apart. As far as I'm concerned, they can spend every bloody second of every bloody minute of every bloody hour together.

Lore's fingertips glide off the studded door, and although he doesn't smile, his eyes seem incandescent. Probably a trick of the light since the sun beaming through the narrow windowpanes drapes right over his face.

"Your friends are insisting on saying their goodbyes before they are carried down to their new vessel." As he lowers his arm, his vambraces scrape smoothly over his leather cuirass.

"How nice of you to personally deliver the message. One would think a king would have better occupations."

Slowly, the corner of his mouth curls up. "Hardly. Besides, the day's beheadings have already been seen to."

Sybille's intake of breath echoes through my sleeping quarters.

"He's kidding, Syb." Phoebus mustn't be too certain, though, because his hot breath smacks my earlobe a second later, "Right?"

"Lorcan was known as the Crimson Crow. Since his plumage isn't vermilion, I imagine he earned his nickname for some other reason." I shoot Lore a frigid smile as I press my palms into the smooth stone and swivel onto my side before levering myself up as gracefully as one can manage when one is wearing no underwear and a man's shirt.

Lore's smile vanishes when I start toward the door. "Your clothes, Fallon."

I glance down at my bare legs. "What about my clothes?"

"You seem to be missing many."

"And yet...I'm not. Do you mind moving aside, Morrgot? I have friends to hug."

The skin beneath his tattoo twitches, spasming some more when he peers down the loose V-neck, which must reveal more cleavage than I'd normally be comfortable with.

I filled your closet with clothes.

"Not my closet and not my clothes."

Fallon. My name comes out as a growl. *Those clothes were sewn for you. They've never graced another body.*

"I don't want to keep my friends waiting."

His fingers ball into fists that leak dark smoke. I expect him to shift at any moment, but he surprisingly stays two-legged. And even more surprisingly, he backs up, allowing me to step around him.

"Good morning, Ionnh Báeinach." Imogen inclines her head ever so slightly. Although her hair is neatly plaited and her makeup freshly applied, my mind conjures her up like she looked last night on her way out of... I'd have called it work, but Imogen is no doxy.

"Imogen," I say as I walk past her. "Had a pleasant night?"

"Yes. Most pleasant." Her gaze streaks through the shadowy darkness, surely toward her beloved king.

An arm weaves through mine, its familiar weight untethering me from the bitter girl I've become within these walls. To think that arm will be out of my reach soon. I'm two seconds away from begging Sybille not to leave, but I think of her parents and how worried they must be. Yes, Giana will be home soon, but one daughter doesn't replace the other.

Fetching me clothes and checking on my grandmother and mother are excuses to give Sybille her freedom. I may be trapped, but she shouldn't be.

"I'm going to try and land an audience with Dante once I get home," she murmurs. "To see if he can work something out with Lorcan."

"Work what out?"

"Ensure your protection so that you can roam Luce freely."

I don't want to flatten Sybille's optimism, but Lore will never let me out of these walls. Not until the wards are removed. "Syb, if you do manage to speak with Dante, make sure to tell him not to trust Dargento."

She nods just as we reach the air hub, or whatever the Crows call this three-storied stone room topped with a narrow glass cupola that I've only ever seen opened. I crane my neck and gaze at the bright blueness, letting it trickle into me and wash away the drabness of these unscalable walls. Sure enough, Mattia, Riccio, Antoni, and Giana stand there, waiting amongst a few Crows.

The only one I recognize is Eefah, who is chortling at a story Riccio tells. Her laughter peters out at the sight of my damp hair and unconventional attire.

Giana steps up to me, her gray gaze traveling between me and a spot over my head, which I assume must be Lore, because it's too high to be Imogen. Unless it's Phoebus? I chance a glance over my shoulder and my eyes land on the Crow king's. Although his body is limned in smoke, the taut lines of his neck and the strain in his jaw are in sharp focus.

He's wound awfully tight for someone who spent his night fornicating. I don't mean to hurl this remark into his mind, but that's where it goes.

Fornicating? You must have me confused with the male whose eye sockets I'm about to hollow.

My neck cracks from how fast I whirl my attention back around to find Antoni staring fixedly at my legs.

"The tides are turning, Greco, so speak your goodbyes quickly." Lore's voice slithers off the gray stone, as dark as the cloud he's slowly turning into. "I wouldn't want your new vessel to end up docked in Shabbe instead of the Tarecuorin wharf."

I suck in too much air. *Are you threatening them?*

I may be possessive of what's mine, Behach Éan, but you'll learn I'm not petty.

Says the man ready to spoon out eyeballs. And—once more—*I'm not yours.*

A beat of silence vibrates between us, rife with many unsaid things.

Your friends would be safer in Shabbe, so it's hardly a threat.

Giana grips one of my hands and lifts it, clutching it tight. "Promise you'll behave?"

I'm taken aback by her parting words.

My expression must display my frustration, because she sighs. "I know how much you want to leave this place, but please don't." Although she speaks quietly, I've no doubt the Crows surrounding us can hear her. After all, their hearing is unparalleled. "There's still so much left to do, and I don't want to have to worry about you on top of everything."

Whose side is she on? Clearly, not mine. "Then don't worry about me." I tug my hand free.

Her gray eyes flash silver from the sting of my retort.

"Pheebs is staying. He'll ensure she doesn't get up to too much trouble." Sybille tightens her arm around mine before letting go.

"I'm not some rambunctious child," I mutter.

"Yes, Fallon, you are exactly that," Giana replies.

My ego splatters at my feet. I may be young in age, but that's no fault of mine. As for rambunctious—

"What Gia means to say is that you're spirited and a tad stubborn." Sybille glares at her sister, who merely shrugs a shoulder.

"Take good care of yourself, Fal." Antoni shifts on the mirror-smooth stone as though debating whether to approach the *rambunctious child.*

I shove away Giana's hurtful comment. "I'm going to miss you, Antoni." Although I don't say it to anger Lore, I can sense the Crow king's discontent through our mental bond.

Gods, to be free of it… Will it fade, I wonder, or must I actively work on shielding my thoughts from him?

Two more people arrive. Although the man is a stranger, the woman isn't.

"Thank you for all your help, Bronwen." Giana touches the older woman's shoulder. "I wish you much bliss and happiness with Cian."

My sour mood momentarily lifts as I follow her gaze to the male at Bronwen's side—her mate, my uncle.

Granted, Keeann seems as warm as the stone beneath my bare toes, but still… I have an uncle. Who's married to the woman who led me astray.

She did not lead you astray.

She said I'd rule Luce beside Dante.

She said you'd be queen. She never once mentioned Dante.

Two bulky men with black stripes on their faces and a small feather tattooed on their cheekbones morph into monstrous birds.

"Fal." Mattia and Riccio raise two fingers to their foreheads in salute as they climb aboard their feathered steeds. Where Mattia grins at being airborne, Riccio's ruddiness leaks right out his cheeks.

Sybille and Giana climb atop the shifter sisters' backs.

Sybille alternates between eyeing the hatch and eyeing me. "I should stay."

I shake my head. "I promise to behave."

"And wear actual clothes?" She bobs her head toward my outfit.

"Once they reappear from the laundry."

"I meant—"

Crow Imogen—or is it Eefah?—flaps her wings, cutting off my friend's speech and breath, but only momentarily.

"I meant the ones in your closet! Love you, Fal!" Sybille yells, right before vanishing through the hatch.

Antoni dares approach me. I think he's about to hug me, but a glance behind me—at Lore, I presume—stills his advance. Is this to be my future? No male daring to hug me? Well, besides Phoebus?

Antoni holds out his hand. Because we've never shaken hands, I stare at it a beat too long.

Finally, I reach out and take his palm, which feels very dry, like…

Oh…

My eyes grow wide as I realize it isn't his skin I'm feeling.

"See you soon, Fal." Although he doesn't blink, I read the warning to stay quiet about the note he's just given me.

As I slip my hand from Antoni's and tuck my fist at my side, tendrils of Lore's smoke curl around my neck and collarbone.

Don't touch me. With my unencumbered hand, I whisk away the spiderweb texture of his magic, yet I swear I can still feel it cling to my skin.

My hands are at my sides, Behach Éan.

I turn to scowl at him. *With any part of your body.*

Then do not touch other men.

Although I want to smother this mental bond as soon as possible, my molars and lips are wedged too tightly to allow words through. *Who I touch is none of your concern. Besides, it was a handshake. Hardly worth getting your feathers in a bunch.*

While Lore's golden eyes rove over Antoni, his attention presses into my spine, prompting me to square my shoulders. "Your gold and your mansion await, Greco."

I startle. "A mansion?"

"In Tarecuori." Antoni casts a long look at the king he helped resurrect.

I wonder if he regrets it.

Perhaps, but I doubt he regrets his newfound prosperity. As Antoni climbs atop another giant bird, Lore says, "Imogen will be at your house tomorrow evening to discuss your visits to Rax. I've also tasked her to be our go-between with Vance from this point forward."

"Who's Vance?"

"The unofficial leader of the Racoccins," Lore explains just as the Crow carrying Antoni takes off.

"Safe travels, Antoni!" I call out as one more friend is swept away.

Once the air stops churning and I find myself alone with Lore, Keeann, and Bronwen, I scan each one of their faces. "What exactly are you planning?"

"An alliance," Lore offers.

"You're allying yourselves with the humans?" I ask.

"They could do with a friend in this Fae world, don't you think?" Keeann's voice isn't quite as deep as my father's, but it rumbles and rises just the same.

Before I can answer his question, which, granted, was surely rhetorical, Bronwen inhales a sharp breath.

"What is it, ah'khar?" Keeann whirls to face her.

"Pierre Roy is coming."

7

P ierre Roy, the king of Nebba?" I ask Bronwen, whose eye-
lids are still pried wide.

"Or the Butcher of Nebba. The man has many names."
Lore has sidled in so close that the heat of his skin and the chill of
his mood lick up one side of my body.

I stare at the harsh cut of his face, made even harsher by the
charcoal stripes he wears. "It seems to be a trend amongst kings."

Lore smiles even though there really isn't anything funny
about our little aside. To Bronwen, he asks, "Is he coming to collect his daughter?"

"No." Sweat dots Bronwen's patchwork of creamy-brown and
pinkish skin. "He comes for his daughter's nuptials."

Lore's mouth flattens. "Correct me if I'm wrong, Bronwen,
but I rather clearly recollect separating her betrothed's head from
the rest of his body."

Bile lurches up my throat, because I too recollect this.

"Eponine will marry Dante."

My fingers go slack, and the little note Antoni slipped me flutters to the floor. "Dante?"

Bronwen's white eyes shine like twin moons. "Yes."

My pulse lurches…teeters…stumbles.

Dante will marry Eponine?

Although my love for the Fae ruler has wilted, the idea of him marrying the woman who was supposed to be his sister-in-law is farcical.

"I expect King Vladimir of Glace won't be too pleased with this turn of events." Lore's comment draws me back into the deep stone well where sunlight penetrates but does not warm.

"Considering the track record of Bronwen's predictions," I mutter, "it may not come to pass."

Although Bronwen is blind, her face veers toward me. "All my predictions have come to pass, child."

"Yet here I stand, crownless and stateless."

Bronwen opens her misshapen mouth—I assume to tell me off—but instead, a sharp inhale stabs the weighted air.

"Ah'khar?" Keeann cups her cheeks between paw-like hands.

"They were looking." She sweeps her fingertips across her forehead, grazing the new hair growths darkening her shaved scalp.

Her words dredge up the memory of something Lore had let slip during our travels. He'd told me Bronwen had struck a deal with the Shabbins: use of her eyes in exchange for the power to see the future.

The idea that a resident of the pink isle is currently spying on us causes goose bumps to bloom everywhere on my body.

"Can you tell who was looking?" I ask.

Her eyes cling to Keeann's, and although I may be wrong, I think they're carrying out a silent conversation. After almost a full minute, she replies, "No."

Is it me, or was her pause a couple beats too long?

Keeann glides his hands down his mate's face before turning toward Lore, who suffuses the air between us with the black coils of his smoke.

"Cian, gather the Siorkahd." The Crow king pivots but doesn't pound straight off into the darkened hallway. His gaze strokes over my upturned face before falling to the stone beneath my feet.

He crouches, and my heart screeches to a halt. Using his middle and index fingers, he clinches Antoni's folded note and carries it upward.

I assume he'll read it or confiscate it or…I don't know, *swallow* it.

He holds it aloft.

When I don't take it, he circles my wrist with fingers that are as cool and soft as his smoke and presses the parchment into my palm.

You're not even going to look at it?

He closes my fingers over the paper with the gentleness of a man handling breakable things. *I trust you.*

Except the king of Crows trusts no one.

As he swirls down his torchlit hallway, becoming one with the shadows, I call out, "Since when?"

Without so much as a backward glance, he says, *Since you walked into my bedroom unclothed. You said it was symbolic, that it showed you meant me no harm. I choose to believe this, Behach Éan.*

Heat crawls up my collarbone, floods my neck, and submerges my cheeks. *It wasn't real!*

I wait for him to retaliate with a quip dripping with his usual velvety barbs, but all I get is booming silence. When I turn back around, Bronwen and Keeann are gone, and I am alone.

Alone with Antoni's note.

What did Lore mean about trusting me?

He trusts me *not* to read it, or he trusts me not to keep what's written from him?

Crumpling the paper in my fist, I return to my ~~bedroom~~ cell on feet gone numb from the icy stone.

One would think summer would warm the sky kingdom, but

between the altitude and the narrowness of the windows, the Lucin heat doesn't permeate the pale gray rock.

As I near my door, it unbolts as though by magic—except it's not magic. It's a bare-chested Phoebus. "I'm off to find some food."

And here I expected to find him burrowed beneath a mound of pillows. "Some food or some Connor?"

"If I'm lucky, both." He sends me a saucy wink that makes me shake my head but that also makes me grin, something I haven't done in too long.

"Hey, Pheebs?"

"Yes, Piccolina?"

"Thank you for sticking around, even if you're only staying for...*the food*."

He chuckles. "I'm staying for you. *Food* can be had anywhere."

"Bring me back some?"

"This may come as a surprise, but I don't care to become a eunuch."

"Um, what?"

"Losing the family jewels. Which, come to think of it, should be called *my* jewels since—"

"I know what a eunuch is, but why would you be castrated for bringing me back food?"

"Oh, I thought you meant for me to return with Connor."

His comment startles a laugh from me. "This may come as a surprise," I recycle his words, "but I was not alluding to a three-some, you fiend."

The man grins, which sharpens the edges of his beautiful face. "So just food?"

"Yes. Just food."

"And wine?"

"No wine." I palm my churning stomach. "Anything I ingest is bound to be pickled considering the amount I drank last night."

Barking out a laugh, Phoebus strides away. Once he's out of

sight, I close the door and cross to the sliver of glass that overlooks Mareluce. Atop the liquid carpet of blue bobs a wooden vessel varnished entirely black. I try to make out my friends, since I imagine this is their ship, but I'm too far above and they too far below.

Antoni's note crinkles in my fist. I finally unfold it and read his scrawled words.

I blink, because it's a poem.

It's not that I thought a sea captain incapable of penning verses, but here I was expecting a hand-drawn map of the sky kingdom's weaker points.

Wishful thinking.

Lore's realm probably has no weak points.

> *You've scored yourself into my heart,*
> *Like a knife through the darkest of wood.*
> *But apparently, Fallon, you aren't meant for me.*
> *However, you are meant to be free.*
> *Tonight, sit at my table and drink in my honor.*
> *I may be gone, but my affection*
> *and attention, they linger.*

My heart hastens, flooding my veins with so much blood that I must lean against the wall to stay upright.

What would Lore have done had he read this? I may not consider myself his, but the Crow king is possessive as fuck. Would he have punished Antoni for his sentimental parting?

I press my palm to the unbreachable glass. "You crazy, crazy man. Why would you risk your life to proclaim feelings neither of us could ever act upon?"

Not that I acted upon them when I had the chance. I was so obsessed with Dante that I convinced myself getting him on the throne was my sole purpose in life. I even gave that ungrateful Fae my virginity. Granted, hymens aren't prizes, but still, I gave Dante everything. But my tongue was too sharp and my ears not sharp enough.

I picture him standing on his metal wharf, watching the Nebban vessel glide closer to his shores, long braids embellished with jewels snapping against his white uniform. Unless he now sports gold like Marco wore.

I swap out the white for gold, close my eyes, and picture him again. My imagination is so vivid that it even adds smells—lemon, brine, eucalyptus—and sounds—Dante's smooth voice, Gabriele's breezy one. When my brain tosses in Tavo's and Silvius's voices, I fling my lids up. For all my desire not to be here, I wouldn't want to be there either.

I head to the unmade bed and straighten the sheets with the military precision Nonna taught me. After rereading Antoni's note, I slip it beneath the mattress. I should probably toss it in the piss pot, but it's my first love letter, and even though I don't pine for the captain, I find owning a love letter terribly romantic.

How I would love to share it with Mamma. She so loves romance.

I cut my daydream short.

Agrippina, not Mamma.

Curling my fingers into fists, I raise my gaze back to the island that seems to float atop the ocean like a swirl of strawberry gelato.

The birthplace of my ancestors.

Sorceresses…

I want to both shiver and shudder that I descend from women who use blood to cast spells.

To think that one day, a drop of what runs through the web beneath my skin will make me just as feared as they are. I take comfort in the fact that Phoebus, Sybille, and the others know what I am, and they haven't shunned me.

The desire to understand more about my heritage and learn how my powers will be unbound tempts me to plow through the wall behind which Lore resides—or use my door and then his. I've no doubt he'll skirt the truth, for the day my magic is liberated, I become vulnerable to obsidian *and* get sucked out of Luce.

A lose-lose for the Crow king.

I suppose it's not much of a win-win for me, unless…

Since I'm only half-Crow, perhaps I'd only become half stone. Still not ideal.

If my lower half becomes a block of obsidian, I can kiss walking around goodbye. If my upper half becomes stone—well, definitely not ideal.

Lore would probably know what happens to half-breeds.

The floor tips. The stone wall blurs.

I'm suddenly standing in a room lined with books and more books. Thick leather spines embedded with gilt lettering. Some titles make sense, while others are clearly not in Lucin, what with their oblique dashes and apostrophes smack in the middle of words.

I whirl on myself, because where the underworld am I? I almost lose my balance when my nose grazes black leather and a hard arm bands around my back. I crane my neck and gulp when I meet a familiar golden stare.

8

Y ou cannot stay away, can you, Behach Éan?" His scent whispers over the tip of my nose, wind-spun sunshine and summer storms.

Giving Lore my best eye roll, I dig my palms into the hard leather covering an even harder chest. "Let go."

His arm falls away so suddenly that I stumble backward and whack my tailbone into a bookcase.

"Why am I here?"

"Inside my mind? Because you're my mate."

"Your mind is a library?" I choose to skip over the second part of his answer.

A slow smile snares one corner of his mouth. "When I'm awake, my mind is anywhere my body is. When I'm asleep, my mind is any place my dreams take me."

Huh. "What's the scope on this mind link thingy?"

"Mating bond."

I shoot him a withering look, which I hope translates what I think of him insisting on calling it a mating bond.

His smile grows. "Did a lash fall into your eye?"

I frown.

"Your left eye is twitching a tad manically."

I snap my eyes wide and jack up my chin. The new look I hurtle his way does nothing to scare off his smile. "The scope, Morrgot? Focus. What's the scope on this mind link?"

"Mating bond."

"Mind link." My stubbornness only amuses him further.

"There's no scope. As long as both our hearts beat, we can penetrate each other's minds."

Well, merda. "Then how come Kahol cannot penetrate Zendaya's mind?"

My enquiry does away with his smile. He turns so somber that black smoke begins to thicken around him. Tendrils dart through the air between us and ribbon around my bare calves and ankles.

For once, I don't tell him off, because his intent isn't to infuriate me. I doubt he's even aware of how deeply his emotions are causing him to smolder. "You think she's dead, don't you?"

"In all honesty, I do not know, but I pray the reason he cannot enter her mind is because Meriam drew a bloody sigil on her daughter that interferes with their bond."

"By bloody, you mean…"

"With blood."

The concept of painting people with what runs through our veins unsettles my stomach further. "So for us to be unlinked, a Shabbin witch would need to swirl a little blood on my skin? Or preferably, on your skin?" I wrinkle my nose. "The sight of blood makes me queasy, except during my monthlies, which…is completely off-topic and of no interest."

His smoke rushes back inside his flesh, or wherever it is his smoke goes.

"Anyway." I rub the skin over my collarbone that's undoubtedly become splotchy with a blush and focus on the books instead of the renewed upward curl of his lips. "I should…um…go." I close my eyes and focus on my ~~bedroom~~ cell. After about three and a half seconds of intense concentration, I crack my lids open.

Lore sears me with a smirk.

"How do I get out of here?" I grumble.

He leans a slim hip against a high desk covered in yellowed maps. "You must *want* to leave."

I gawk at him. "I want nothing more."

"If you wanted nothing more, then you'd be back inside your body, Behach Éan."

I blow out an annoyed breath that lifts a piece of my now-dried hair and focus on Phoebus returning with food. My stomach looses a deep growl, and that growl projects me back into my body, which is, surprisingly, still in the exact spot I left it.

Oh my gods, I left my body.

I can leave my body.

This is *wild*.

And completely undesirable—but really, *really* wild.

And the worst part, I can't even tell my best friend, because he'll wonder why I can mind walk, and I'd prefer not to get into details as to why.

Come to think of it, no one can know about this.

Absolutely no one.

Your father is not much of a gossip.

I jump at the sound of Lore's voice inside my mind and squint around to see if he's projected more than his voice, but no smirking, smoldering male darkens my sleeping quarters. **What about you?**

Do I strike you as someone who enjoys pouring their heart out to people?

No. Yes. I don't know. You're not a total tomb.

Your secrets are safe, Behach Éan. Now, I must get back to plotting my next war.

I snort until—**Wait. You're plotting a war?**

How are empires grown and thrones seized?

Which throne are you plotting to steal?

A beat passes, then: **Your princeling is safe. For now.**

My bedroom door opens so vigorously that the studded wood smacks the wall.

Phoebus teeters beneath the weight of the platter he holds. "I brought you everything you could possibly desire."

What I desire is my freedom, and no one but the Crow king can hand that to me.

9

I stand on the threshold of my closet, stomach so full it juts through the green fabric of my borrowed shirt. I contemplate the row of hangers and the line of shoes. Lore has seemingly planned for any and all occasions. There are as many gowns as there are pants and blouses, all of them running the monochromatic gamut.

After opening and shutting every drawer, Phoebus trails his fingers along the skirt of a dress made entirely of black feathers. "Stunning."

"Ghastly. Birds must've been plucked to make it!" I add with a hiss. "Lore may consider his Crows superior to Fae, but Fae don't weave clothing from their own people's skin."

Phoebus's nose wrinkles as he releases the gown. "You have an unprecedented manner of ruining a good thing."

"Why are we in here anyway?"

"Because you have a sauce stain over your right boob." He pokes the spot as though I may have forgotten about it. Considering how hard I scrubbed it, it hasn't slipped my mind. "It'll draw attention during our excursion."

"Attention to what? How clumsy I am at eating?"

He smirks. "That too."

I shrug. "Don't much care what people think about me anymore."

"How blasé you've become, Piccolina."

"Disillusioned, not blasé."

On a sigh, he turns back toward the racks, grabs a black shirt, then pinches a drawer open and hooks something peach and shiny.

"Pheebs, I'm not—"

"The shirt's for me. Wouldn't want to give complexes to your kinfolk." He gestures to his lean torso that's packed with tight muscles—not quite as large as he'd like, but that he's still proud of. Especially since he was the kid with the concave chest and toothpick legs.

However often Sybille and I told him he was handsome, until he stopped growing like a reed and started packing on weight, he just wouldn't believe it.

"This, though, is for you." He tosses the scrap of satin at my face. "It can get quite drafty around the castle. Wouldn't want you to catch a cold."

"I wasn't aware one caught colds through their nether regions."

He snickers, but I indulge him. In case there are stairs or drafts that blow up the hem of his shirt.

"Maybe wear slippers?" he suggests as he adjusts the drapey black blouse that's a tad short, hitting the waistband of his slacks. Somehow, he makes it work.

I eye the row of shoes. That would be one more concession. I'm not ready to wave a white flag in Lore's face, even if it's just to thwack him with it. What I am ready for, though, is to make the most of my confinement.

"New shoes mean new blisters. My feet are still recovering." After poking my legs through underwear that feels woven from warmed oil, I head out into Lore's realm.

Phoebus cranes his neck. "That's as far as I've come to date."

I turn on myself to take in the cavernous stone room covered with trellises of vertically growing—"Is that squash?" I stride closer to one of the leafy wall panels and slide my fingertips over the heart-shaped frond poking from a green bulb.

"Tà." A woman with black hair shot through with silver, blackened eyes, and the same feather tattoo that graces every Crow cheek loops twine around the stem of another swelling bulb, securing it to the crisscrossed wood. "Squash." After clipping the twine with an elongated, iron talon, she sets her attention on me and speaks a string of Crow words, none of which I pick up until the very last one. "Beinnfrhal."

"I know *benfrol*," I proclaim with childish excitement. I whirl toward Phoebus, who gazes down at me with a soft smile. "It means mountain berries. I tasted them during my journey across Monteluce. They're the most delicious fruit ever."

The woman's black eyebrows gather over a slender nose that's so straight and symmetrical it reminds me of Lore's.

Which is a rather odd thought to have.

One surely brought on by exertion. Phoebus and I have been trekking for hours, and I do mean *hours*. The sky shining through the large hatch in this three-storied cavern of a room has turned a gorgeous bronzed lavender.

Soon night will drape across the sky kingdom. A night I may have to spend curled in some hallway because I don't think I'll make it back. My feet are *killing* me. Of course, I refuse to admit this to Phoebus, who keeps eyeing them and pointing out all the comfortable shoes I could've been wearing.

By kilometer fourteen, I threatened that if he didn't stop spotlighting my silliness, I'd tell Lore that my friend was lining up suitors for me. For all his ensuing eye rolls, Phoebus has palmed his *jewels* more than once since I dropped my menace.

"Fallon?" The woman pronounces my name like all the other

Crows, twisting it into a foreign word that sounds like a brook tripping over smooth rock. She nods to another section of the oddly shaped cavern and gestures for me to follow.

And I do. I may have felt many emotions when I was brought up here against my will, but chariness toward these people has never been one of them.

At the foot of one of the trellises, her outline blurs into a cloud of black. I take a tiny step back as she transforms into her other self. Although large, I've noted the females aren't quite as big as males, and no male is as imposing as Lore.

She swoops upward, her black feathers glimmering sapphire as she nears the opened hatch.

"What do you think she's trying to show you?" Phoebus's breath catches in my hair.

"I'm not sure."

She flies to the very top of a wall, her wings beating like a hummingbird's as she levels off and snatches something with her iron beak. My heart misses a beat when I spot the slender branch dotted with pink berries—benfrol.

Did she fetch them because of how excited I became when she mentioned them?

The woman doesn't land. Instead, she puffs into smoke that coalesces into her two-legged shape. With a smile that presses slender wrinkles around her mouth, she removes the branch from between her human teeth and tenders it.

I return her smile. "Thank you…" As I take her offering, I point to her. She frowns, so I point to myself and say, "Fallon," then point to her again.

She touches the base of her neck and says, "Arin."

"Thank you, Arin."

She smiles, dark gaze flitting over my features, studying them.

I twist a berry off the stem and pop it into my mouth, and Great Cauldron, it's just as I remember—syrupy with the slightest tang.

Phoebus grabs a pink pod, sniffs it, then tosses it inside his mouth. When he moans and reaches for more, I skip away from him and hurry to fill my mouth with as many as I can pack. It's silly and childish, and if my cheeks weren't so full, I'd melt into a puddle of laughter.

He grabs me around the waist and tickles me until I concede the almost-bare branch. "Dear gods, how old are you, Fallon?"

In between bursts of laughter, I lick the sweet berry juice off my lips. "It's all the walking," I say, barely able to keep a straight face. I swipe what feels like pink drool off my chin, then plop my finger into my mouth.

"That's bringing out your animal nature?"

The mention of my Crow nature smothers my delight.

Phoebus heaves a sigh and presents me with the last berry as a peace offering. "Here. Take this magical fruit and giggle again."

I cross my arms. "It's just fruit. Plus, I'm all out of giggles."

"A shame. It was such a lovely sound." The deep voice spurs my heart, hastening its beats.

"Àlo, Mórrgaht." My sycophantic friend sketches a bow.

"So you've uncovered my favorite spot in the kingdom." Lore glides out from someplace behind me.

"How funny." Phoebus sweeps the branch he holds like a magic wand toward the trellises dripping with fruits and vegetables. "It appears to be Fallon's favorite too."

I sear him with a glare that makes him wink. "My favorite place is my home in Luce."

Lore looses an exaggerated sigh. "Because my kingdom is such a drab penitentiary."

Phoebus swings the branch in my direction. "The stubborn streak is quite strong in this one."

Where Lore affords him a pleasant smile, I grumble, "Should've shipped you back and kept Syb."

Phoebus mimics his heart being broken, or whatever

smooshing both palms over his chest and moaning like a sow in heat is supposed to mean. "I'm going to see if I can get your wonderful gardener to pick us some more delicious fruit."

He plods across the airy space toward Arin, who smiles before shifting and flying back up to fetch him another branch.

Lore links his hands behind his back, making his broad chest jut out. "So how was your adventure?"

"I doubt you're here to gather my opinion on your home, so get to the point."

"You're right." One of his eyes narrows a little. "I'm actually here to visit my mother."

I was, quite possibly, less shocked the day I learned Lore could transform into a man. "You have a mother?"

"Did you think I hatched from a cabbage?"

"No—I—" When a smile threatens the edges of his mouth, I mutter, "I know how babies are made, Lore. I know they don't sprout in produce."

"How fortunate for your future mate."

A blush steals across my cheeks. "We call them husbands where I come from. And yes, I suppose he'll be extraordinarily pleased when I spread my legs instead of hand him a trowel and a packet of seeds."

Lore chokes on air or perhaps on one of the bees cartwheeling about this magical greenhouse. When his face tips backward and laughter spills from him in deep, gravelly ripples, I realize he swallowed no bug.

I hate how much I enjoy his laugh.

A beautiful laugh does not a beautiful person make, I remind myself before I can forget that the man standing before me has stripped me of one of my fundamental rights.

He sobers, yet his eyes keep dancing. "What am I going to do with you, Little Bird?"

It's a rhetorical question, yet I say, "You could start by setting me free, Morrgot."

That snuffs out the light in his eyes and turns the gold matte. We keep staring at each other, and although tension billows, there is no awkwardness. After all, how can one feel awkwardness before a man who's seen one naked? Who's heard all about one's nipple burns and silly crushes on Fae princes?

I deemed the Crow king a friend. Someone who merited my trust and my respect. Someone I could count on. But then he had to go and ruin it all by being greedy and selfish.

He must hear my thoughts, because his lips flatten and his irises, which I considered matte, blunt like tarnished metal. His hands break away from their knot as he strides past me toward where Phoebus and Arin are attempting to carry on a conversation.

Lore's soundless footfalls peter out when he reaches Arin. The older Crow tilts her head to look up at him. Slowly she cups his jaw, drags his face down, and presses her cheek to his. I've come across many Crows in my hike across this rocky kingdom, and the only ones who pressed cheeks were mothers with their children.

Which means…

Which means that the woman Phoebus called a gardener is no horticulturist at all.

10

My mouth must gape, because Phoebus traipses over to knuckle it shut.

"Did you know?" I hiss, watching mother and son interact.

"Do you really think I would've called her a gardener if I had?" He gnaws the life out of his bottom lip. "Thank the Cauldron she doesn't understand Lucin."

Arin runs her thumb across the hollow of Lore's cheek, smoothing the edges of a black stripe.

He has a mother.

Lore has a mother he never mentioned—not once—during our voyage through Luce.

Lorcan Reebyaw has a mother.

A mother?!

"Should I be worried?"

"About?" I finally tear my gaze away from Arin and Lore.

Phoebus's head is tipped and his eyes tapered. "About these berries melting my brain and robbing me of my sanity, since clearly, they've done away with yours?"

My crossed arms jolt. "The man has a mother, Pheebs."

"Many men have mothers. Actually, *all* men have mothers. You do know how babies—"

"Not you too," I mutter.

"Why is this upsetting you so?"

"Because I spent *days* with him. Just him and me. And not once did he mention his mother was alive."

"And he was supposed to tell you *why*?"

"Because—because—" I toss my hands in the air. "You're right. He had no need to share anything private with me. He still doesn't." I add that last part, because I can feel Lore's gaze on my face.

I pluck Phoebus's hand and drag him toward the hallway opposite where we came from, energy restored. Since most of my blood is concentrated between my face and heart, I can barely feel my feet, which is quite fortunate considering I plan on putting as much distance as possible between me and the shifter.

If he'd trusted me, he would've told me about his mother.

"This isn't the way back," Phoebus says as we slip beneath a stone arch and the ceiling slopes violently downward, probably because of the topography of the summit over our heads.

The sky is a deep purple flecked with stars by the time we pass beneath an archway that opens onto a grotto as voluminous as the vertical orchard, except this one boasts communal tables girdled by market stands. Each stand is equipped with firepits atop which are roasted produce, fish, and meats that put the harbor market's wares to shame.

The crisscrossing strings of lanterns trickle as little light as the moon through the cupola carved into the jagged rock ceiling, but torches have been welded, not only into the uneven walls but also around each stand.

"Antoni told me about this place. It's called Murgadh'Thábhain, which means the Market Tavern. It's at the epicenter of the kingdom. It's both a marketplace—the only one for that matter—and a tavern."

I roll the foreign words over my tongue: *Murrgaw Hawben.*

Phoebus's gaze narrows on the openings peppering the rock and the black wisps streaking in and out. "Huh. This must be proletariat housing."

"Why do you say that?" I ask.

"No doors. Stacked rooms."

"Or it's their version of a brothel."

"Or that."

"We do not have brothels in the sky kingdom, because we deem the act of coupling sacred." Lore materializes out of a shadowy pocket.

I wonder how long he's been there and *why.*

I make sure to wipe all traces of wonder from my expression and turn, pretending he isn't present. Perhaps if I pretend long enough, he'll vanish.

"Who lives here then?" Phoebus asks.

I glare at him for engaging Lore.

"The younglings."

One of Phoebus's blond eyebrows quirks up. "You separate children from their parents?"

I'm about to traipse away but linger to hear the answer.

"No. Chicks, as we call our very young children, reside with their parents until they decide they're ready to leave the nest. Then they're given a lodging here or in the north, where they live for free until they pick up a craft and become contributing members of society."

Phoebus's other eyebrow pops up. "Any caste member gets access to free housing?"

Lore gazes around at his people, eyes gleaming like faceted stones in the darkness. "Crows do not have castes."

"You have a king," I toss in, incapable of keeping my mouth shut. My self-control is pitiful, which is probably why Lore has such easy access to my brain.

The edge of Lore's jaw ticks. "So very observant, Behach Éan." His sarcasm makes my lips pinch.

Our discussion—or shall I call it what it is?—altercation doesn't go unnoticed. The noise level has greatly decreased as most Crows stare openly in our direction.

A young boy approaches and extends a stein toward Lore, arms shaking a little. Liquid sloshes out and plops onto the smooth, shiny stone beneath his feet. He inclines his head in a diminutive bow and says something that ends with Morrgot.

"Tapath," Lore says before taking the metal goblet from the boy and drinking.

Unlike our kings, he doesn't have someone else taste it for poison or salt or the Cauldron only knows what people have tried to slip our rulers.

Believe it or not, Fallon—his golden eyes find mine over the lip of his cup—*you are the only Crow who desires me dead.*

I don't respond, neither out loud nor through the mind link. Instead, I steel my spine and walk away.

You never asked about my mother. His words slow my retreat.

Without turning, I say, *And you never asked about my chafed nipples, yet I told you all about them. Tell me, will I be meeting your father next?*

My father passed before the Shabbins gave our clan magic. His timbre has turned so grave that I regret having asked. I hear him swallow. *Mother would like to sup with you.*

I'm supping with Phoebus.

The invitation was for the two of you.

We're not hungry. I mutter at the same time as I hear Phoebus say, "Starving. We'd love to join you and your mother for dinner."

I glance over my shoulder, hoping my friend was agreeing to dine with someone else's son, but sure enough, he's nodding at Lore, who must've tossed the question out loud at the same time as he tossed it into my head. Never mind. Phoebus can have dinner with every Crow in the kingdom for all I care.

I keep going, exhaustion be damned. Unfortunately, when I swivel my head back around, my escape is cut short. I collide into a woman toting drinks, all of which spill over me before clattering onto the stone, creating a din that echoes against my eardrums long after the last metal goblet has finished rolling about.

Even though the lighting is dim, I don't miss how the woman blanches.

Since the pileup was my fault, I mumble an apology she may very well not understand and pluck at my shirtdress to unglue it from my drenched skin before attempting to wring some of the reddish juice out.

A heavy bolt of fabric drops over my shoulders, startling me out of my rigorous squeezing. I start to say thank you, but my gratitude withers on my lips, because of course, who should come to my rescue but the king himself.

I grip the edges of my newfangled cloak.

Please keep it on. It may be dark, but Crows have unparalleled sight. I'd prefer to be the only man familiar with the shape of your body.

Too late for that.

His pupils constrict.

Dante is well acquainted with every millimeter of my body.

Lore's outline flickers as he heaves fumes that thicken to the point where I hold my breath to avoid suffocating on him.

As briskly as it rushed out of him, his smoke retreats and reshapes his too-near and too-large body. *I was going to go after your princeling's throne last, but you've convinced me to start with his.*

I wheeze out the dwindling air in my lungs, then suck in a fresh lungful. *You may gain a throne, but you'd also gain an enemy.*

When you have as many enemies as I, one more matters not. Now please, come to the table. Mother is waiting.

I don't want to dine with you, Lore. I don't want—

Before I can finish my sentence, Lore shifts into his Crow, snatches me, and carries me into one of the dwellings, startling a half-naked male off his mattress.

11

L ore must tell him to scram, because the boy nods, shifts, and soars right out of the small grotto-like room that contains one bed, one desk, one chair, and one closet.

I stumble away the second he untalons me. "What is wrong with you?" I screech at the monstrous bird just as a loud bang echoes through the air, followed by flashes of light and a rumble that vibrates the very stone.

Has Lore created the storm? It is one of his many powers after all.

He fractures into smoke before knitting back into flesh. "You want your freedom, fine. When the sun rises over Mareluce, I'll fly you out of my dreadful home and let you get back to your beloved Dante and your beloved profession. Perhaps you'll even get lucky and receive a visit from your princeling. That is if he isn't too busy fucking every female with a pulse. After all, he *is* king now. Everyone wants to bed a male in a position of such power. I should know," he adds with a curl of lip that chills my blood. "All I ask in return is for you to put aside your rancor and dine with my mother. Do you think yourself capable of that?"

Thunder claps Monteluce anew, quickening my pulse and my breaths. I try to space out my inhales, but it's of no use. "Will you be attending this meal?"

His nostrils flare with breaths as shallow as my own. "My mother would worry if I left after I promised I had time to sup with her, so yes, Fallon, you'll have to endure my presence."

"And you truly will fly me out of the sky kingdom in the morning?" The wine-soaked fabric flutters against my prickling skin.

"I may assign the job to another Crow, but yes…you'll be escorted out of these walls."

"Phoebus too." My voice is thin, but unlike the rest of me, it doesn't tremble.

"If he wants to leave, he'll get an escort."

If he wants to leave… What if he prefers to stay? The thought hadn't even crossed my mind.

Do we have a deal, Fallon?

One dinner against a lifetime of freedom… "What's the catch?"

"The catch?"

"Your bargain sounds too good to be true."

"I'm no Fae. I do not bargain."

"You've just bartered my obedience against my freedom. That's called a bargain."

He doesn't tell me I'm wrong because he knows I'm not, even though bargains do not register on Crow skin like they do on Fae flesh. "There's no catch."

"So I won't be guarded by your Crows everywhere I go, what with being your curse breaker?"

"We've found Meriam, so we no longer have need of you."

His answer feels like a slap.

Two slaps.

"You've found Meriam?" When he stays quiet, clearly uninterested in sharing any more information with someone outside his inner circle, I say, "She stabbed you with obsidian once before. You expect she won't do it again?"

"I expect she'll want nothing more than to turn me into a

71

block of iron, but I'll have rid her body of blood, which will end her and her malefic magic. The wards will come down, and the Shabbins will be free. I'll be sure to keep plenty in my employ to combat our curse."

"You've got everything figured out, haven't you?"

"I've had time to strategize."

We study each other in silence for a long moment. I may know his Crow form well, but I haven't let myself study his human form at length.

And now…now it'll forever stay unfamiliar, because we've reached a fork in the road we've been traveling together since Bronwen sent me on my fool's errand, and I—fool that I am—accepted, few questions asked, none answered.

The fight drains out of me. "If Bronwen ever figures out how I can break your curse, come and find me, and I'll help."

Although he knows the shape of every one of my features, his gaze lingers on them all. "Tapath."

I fathom *tapoff* means thank you. "How do you say 'you're welcome' in Crow?"

"Sé'bhédha."

"*Shehveha*," I repeat as the storm begins to ease, outside and inside.

12

Lore transforms into a Crow. Instead of snatching me, he drops low and extends his wing, and although I cannot imagine it feels nice to be stepped on, he doesn't flinch when I use his wing as a ladder. Gripping the hand-knit coverlet draped over my shoulders with one hand, I curl the other around his neck, my skin sinking into his black feathers.

I try not to squeeze too hard but end up strangling him when he lurches from the cubbyhole in the rock to carry me back down to the flickering torches and effervescent crowd. We land beside the communal table at which Arin and Phoebus have taken residence.

Where she smiles, he gapes at me with the same amount of horror and distress he regarded me with that day in his family vault when we unhooked Lore's first crow from the wall.

I sink onto the seat beside his and squeeze his thigh under the table to reassure him that I'm all right, but he must not be reassured, because his knees keep bouncing.

Crows from every market stand come forth with earthenware bowls filled with creamy dips and thinly sliced fish, wooden chopping boards topped with roasted meat and plump vegetables flecked with herbs, and baskets of flatbread browned and streaked with oil.

Arin speaks to us, but since she speaks in Crow, Lore has to translate. "I hope you have a large appetite, because every vendor plans on bringing you their specialty."

I return her smile. "Trekking across your home has cleaved a pit in our stomachs."

Phoebus, always so quick with niceties, remains too perplexed to pitch one in.

A jug and metal goblets are set before us and filled with Crow wine. Although I said I'd never drink again, I drink, mostly to take the edge off my raw nerves.

The nectar is just as delicious as I remember it to be. "You should sell this wine in Luce."

Although most of the Crows farther down the table from us use their talons to spear and cut food, Lore picks up a fork and a knife, as does Arin. "Why would we do that?"

"For profit."

"We've no need for coin."

I lean back in my chair. "All right. Then trade it for things you do need."

"Perhaps once we're more settled."

I'm tempted to snort at his euphemism. Clearly, he means once he's taken over all three kingdoms and, perhaps, even a queendom. Since I swore to be congenial, I steer the conversation away from his politicking. "Is it made from purple grapes or green ones like faerie wine?"

"It's actually made from beinnfrhal."

That must be why I prefer it to Fae wine.

Arin touches her son's arm and says something. I pick up one word: *Zendaya.*

"Mother says you take after Daya."

I pat my lips on a napkin. "So I've heard." I try to recall the one and only vision I had of her, but I was so focused on what was being said that I cannot recall her face. Only the shade of her eyes.

Would you like another glimpse of her?

I blink at Lore. *I believe this may be the first time you've asked for permission to penetrate my mind.*

He sets his cutlery down and waits for my answer, which I give him in the form of a nod.

The Market Tavern fades. Actually, it merely lights up. Sunlight filters through the windowed hatch in thick beams that illuminate the pale gray stone and catch on the dust motes, making them glitter like tinsel.

A woman laughs, and it raises goose bumps over my skin, because somehow, the sound is familiar. She sits with her back to me, auburn waves flowing all the way down to her tailbone.

I pad closer, a ghost in Lore's memory, stopping only when I stand in front of the table where she sits with a slew of other women and men. Like theirs, her face is smeared with black stripes and bears the black feather I've spied on every Crow cheek—every Crow except Bronwen.

Does ink not adhere to her damaged skin? I don't give this thought room to grow, knowing I have little time and so much to absorb.

Zendaya's stare arrests me yet again with her arched brown eyebrows that shade long-lashed pink irises, a hue that doesn't exist in Luce or in Nebba or even in Glace. I didn't inherit the color, but it's seeped over the blue, turning my irises a shade of violet that has perpetually given Fae pause. Her skin tone is also different from mine, a burnished shade of olive that resembles baked earth.

Mine is peach, like my father's.

The one feature I seem to have inherited from no one is the shape of my face. Zendaya's is a perfect oval and my father's a perfect square. Mine? Nonna calls it heart-shaped because of my pointed chin and high cheekbones. I used to think I took after my mother, Agrippina, because she too has a pointy chin and prominent cheeks.

Obviously, I do not.

I press away the sadness that always encroaches on my heart when I think of the secrets surrounding my origins and concentrate on this window Lore is allowing me to peer through.

Zendaya's lips, full and pink, slice open around a smile that is so bright it seems otherworldly. My heart twists at the sight of her mirth, then twists some more at the melody of it. I wonder if she's laughed in the past two decades.

I wonder if she is alive.

My eyes latch on to the pearlescent shell pendant nestled in the hollow of her neck. Although the shell is white, the tip is a rusted red.

My mother stands, one palm flush with the table, the other flush with her abdomen—a tightly rounded abdomen. Her fingers stroke the lump, and although I'm no longer lodged inside her and I've never felt her caress, my skin pebbles from the phantom touch.

She looks up at the sound of wingbeats. Giant Crows descend like cannonballs through the hatch, feathers dissolving into smoke before conjoining into flesh. One of these monstrous creatures lands right beside her. Once Kahol morphs into skin, Zendaya's arms rope his neck and tug his face down to hers.

My heart tips, pouring heady beats into my bloodstream at the sight and feel of so much love.

How different my life would've been had Meriam not come between them...between all of us. The thought leaves me feeling like a traitor, like an ungrateful child. Nonna and Mamma gave me everything, and how do I repay them? By imagining my life elsewhere, surrounded by other people. People who aren't Fae.

Heat veils my vision. I close my eyes when a wet trickle curves down my cheek.

When I open them again, the Market Tavern is dark and Lore's hooded stare is bright. Phoebus and Arin watch me too. Where

Arin's mouth is squeezed into a grim line, Phoebus's is wedged so tightly that he can barely fit the flattened bread he's smeared with a yellowish dip.

I palm away the tear and shoot him a smile that does nothing to soften his worry.

When Lore's gaze slips to his mother's and their heads bend close, Phoebus props his mouth beside my ear and hisses, "Are you crying? Why are you crying? Did Ríhbiadh make you cry? I don't even care that he's outfitted with iron appendages. If he's hurt you—"

I turn my head, our noses almost colliding. "He showed me a memory of my mother."

Phoebus's pupils shrink against the green. "Oh. Good. I do prefer to engage in fights I have a chance of winning."

I smile.

"Which mother did he show you?"

"Zendaya." A current races down my spine as I picture her hand resting on…me. "I think I take more after my father. Speaking of whom…" I turn toward Lore and wait until Arin finishes whatever she's telling him before asking, "Will I get to see him before I depart?"

"Depart?" Phoebus's voice hits a note he hasn't reached since puberty.

"Lorcan's allowed me to return home. Isn't that wonderful?"

My friend's lips part and his fingers too. His open-faced sandwich topples onto the plate he's piled high with a little of everything. "You don't sound as though you find it wonderful."

"Yet I do. I find it very wonderful."

He rubs his fingers on his napkin, eyebrows bending like windblown fronds.

"Will you be coming home with me or staying?"

He hesitates, frowning at Lore. "I'll go back with you, Piccolina, but in my opinion, it's a shit decision."

I swallow at his reproof but remind myself that it comes from the heart. Phoebus is worried, and for good reason. Before departing from Monteluce, Dante told me I'd be safer away from Luce because the Fae would see me as the traitor who murdered their king.

Those words had pounded the last nail in the coffin of my feelings for him. After all, he was the one who'd demanded his brother's head, not I, yet he blamed me. I wonder if that's the story he told upon taking the throne in Isolacuori and anointing himself king with a crown soaked in blood.

I hunt the depths of Lore's eyes for the answer, but he reveals nothing, so I attempt to penetrate his mind but bang into an obsidian wall with no beginning and no end and not a single fissure. I almost ask him to let me see what he's seen and heard, but deep down, I don't want to know, for it may influence my decision.

I turn back toward Phoebus. "Good thing I didn't ask for your opinion, Pheebs."

He launches the smeared bread into his mouth and chews on it like a rabid animal, then seizes his berry wine and slugs it down, the apple in his pale throat moving like a razor blade. "When are we to leave?"

"In the morning," I say.

He nods. "Good. That gives me some hours to yell at you."

"Phoebus," I sigh.

He holds out a palm. "Save it for the conversation we'll have behind closed doors."

Another sigh balloons through my aching chest. "It doesn't sound like it'll be much of a conversation."

He pivots his body so that it's angled away from me and gives Arin his undiluted attention. Although Lore doesn't pat Phoebus's back, I can tell my friend's irritation pleases the shifter.

"Nothing and no one can change my mind."

"Oh, I've no illusion you'll be staying, Fallon," Lore says. "As for your father, you asked if you'd see him. He's scouring the three kingdoms for Daya, so I fear he may not return in time to see you off."

I'm so shocked by this news that my fingers loosen around my makeshift cloak. The heavy fabric glides down my arms and settles like a shawl in the crooks of my elbows. "Isn't that dangerous?"

"He isn't alone."

I'm glad to hear my father didn't charge into this reconnaissance mission all by himself, but still…

The gold in Lore's irises shivers before it hardens, along with every line in his body. "Crows do not do well without their mates."

I don't think his intent is to guilt me, yet that is the emotion that wells behind my thumping breastbone. *I wish I could've been the mate you deserve, Lore.*

He doesn't respond to that. I suppose there isn't much of a response to give.

Nevertheless, his silence irks me, and however much I try to concentrate fully on Arin and the questions she asks about my childhood and passions, questions that Lore translates, my mind wanders to other places.

To my little blue house in Tarelexo with its frescoed walls and fragrant wisteria.

To my loyal pink serpent with his rings of scarred flesh.

To the gloomy Racoccin woods steeped in mist.

To the white barracks where I spent one afternoon with Dante, convinced it'd be the first of many.

To the mountain pass I scaled on the back of my beautiful stallion.

To my first awed glimpse of the sky kingdom.

To the pureling tribe that attacked me for sacks of gold.

To Selvati and the man who sacrificed his life to help Lore and me.

To Tarespagia and the horrible Rossi women.

And to that final horseback ride the day my world tipped and changed forever.

Over and over, I shepherd my straying mind back to the here and now. To this woman intent on getting to know me even though I've chosen to abandon her son and his people. Soon, like the Fae, the Crows will consider me a defector. The girl who reneged on her heritage for one that doesn't even belong to her.

Maybe I should sail to Shabbe.

Don't.

I jump at the sharpness of Lore's voice. At the fervency limning that one word.

Not until I've destroyed the wards.

I study the harsh angles of his face made even harsher by his dismal mood. *I swear not to cross the wards until you've killed Meriam, Lorcan Reebyaw.*

He doesn't look at me again for the duration of the meal, nor does he look at me after he flies me back through the hallways of his kingdom toward my ~~cell~~ bedchamber and departs with his mother, who carried Phoebus.

Phoebus, who shuts the door so hard it all but splinters the wood and shatters the stone frame. Phoebus, who yells until his voice goes hoarse and we both have tears running down our faces, because leaving is a risk. But I cannot hide inside a mountain while the world crumbles. Only cowards hide, and I may be many things, but I'm not a coward.

"Leave the fighting to people who enjoy it, Piccolina. Please. You're not immortal."

"But I could be." I gaze up at the ceiling from where I lie sprawled on the bed, my head cocooned in the crook of Phoebus's arm, my left hand intertwined with his right one over his gurgling stomach. "If I found Meriam and made her unbind my magic, I could be."

"You could also be dead."

My intent when bartering for my freedom wasn't to partake in this fight between Shabbins, Crows, and Fae, but the more Phoebus and I talked—after he was done with his heated monologue—the more I realized that I could make a difference.

If she dies, so does her evil magic.

My mother will be free.

Shabbins will be free.

Perhaps Meriam wants me dead, but to kill me, she needs to find me, which makes me the perfect bait.

13

I jolt awake to the sound of thunder.

I groan and turn into the warmth of Phoebus's body, attempting to fall back asleep. My neck creaks from having spent the better part of the night being propped on a hard bicep.

I reach for my pillow and stuff my face against it, but I know there's no going back to sleep. My heart is up and racing even though my body has yet to pare itself from the sheets that smell a lot like a distillery. I realize, with abject horror, that the smell is coming from me.

With another groan, I walk my carcass over to the bathroom, each step sending needles of pain inside my heels and bone-deep aches inside my calves and thighs. The temptation to spend the day holed up in bed is strong, but my desire to accomplish something useful is stronger.

Not to mention I fought hard for my freedom, so it would be nonsensical to delay it. What if Lore reneged on his deal? Unlike the Fae, Crows aren't held to their bargains with rings around their arms and marks over their hearts.

If he went back on his decision because I failed to jump on the opportunity to leave, it would ruin more than my mood. It would ruin my fledgling plan that grows and grows as I scrub every corner of my body with scented oil.

When I smell like a rose dipped in cream and honey, I turn off the shower and walk to the closet. Giana's pants have not reappeared, and neither has her blouse, but I wouldn't have worn them anyway.

Today I feel like wearing something that fits, something that was made—apparently—for me. I select gray suede leggings that I pair with a blouse that could almost double as a dress. I cinch the breezy white material with a belt studded with silver coins. On closer inspection, they look like Lucin coin, what with the emblem of the sun stamped onto the surface.

I wouldn't put it past Lore to have clothes woven from actual Fae money.

The outfit is different from what is fashionable in Luce, but I'm different, and as hard as I once tried to fit in, I've no desire to anymore. The girl who left Luce isn't the one who's returning to it. I comb my hair, then plait it and secure it with a black ribbon I steal off one of the dresses.

Ready for the next chapter in my life to begin, I wake Phoebus, who mutters for me to go away.

So I do. I give him one extra hour of slumber while I go off to find us some breakfast.

The tavern is mostly deserted at this time. Either Crows sleep in, or they're off, flying around, gathering small prey to warm their bellies.

I wrinkle my nose at the memory of the rabbit Lore tried to feed me when we were ascending Monteluce, before I explained I couldn't stomach meat or fish of any kind. I didn't ask if it was a Shabbin trait. I haven't asked many questions.

Someday, I will, because *someday*, Luce will be at peace, and Shabbe will be free of Meriam's yoke.

As I take a seat at the table where I ate with my friends, my mind strays to the news that Lore delivered last night—the part about Meriam. Did the queen of Shabbe torture her location from one of the Fae castaways, or did Lore's people find her using their own methods? And if they found Meriam, then why is my father looking for Daya? Why isn't he interrogating the Shabbin sorceress who started this whole mess? I thought Meriam was holding her prisoner.

Connor comes over, and although he doesn't smile, he mumbles good morning with such a strong accent that it takes me a moment to realize he isn't speaking Crow.

"Buondia indeed," I say with a smile. "Can I please have a platter of cheese, fruit, and brown bread? Oh, and a jug of coffee?"

Connor nods and retreats toward the bar set against one of the curved walls. I see him exchange a couple words with a fellow Crow server whose light-brown hair strikes me as odd. Not everyone has black hair, but as far as I know, none possess hair so pale. The same way none have eyes any other color than deep brown. Well, besides Lore.

The brown-haired Crow lifts his eyes, which are black, and stares at me, and although I may be misreading his expression, his features seem stamped with disgust.

Sure, I've not been as sweet as gelato since my arrival, but I doubt I deserve such loathing.

Peeved, I draw my attention away from him and his condemnatory mien.

Sybille would roll her eyes and tell me not to give his mood a lick of thought. I concentrate on the fact that I'll see her soon. And Nonna and Mamma, wherever Giana has hidden them. They're probably out of hiding by now. After all, Marco is dead. Perhaps I'll even visit Antoni's new lodgings. A house on Tarecuori must be so grand.

In spite of the storm raging outside, rainbows begin to tinge my mood anew. By the time Connor brings out the food, I am buoyant.

I grip the edge of the table to drag the bench closer. As the wood creaks against the stone, my fingertips sink into shallow grooves. I think they may have been carved by iron talons, but the furrows are rounded and vary in size. I don't bend to look under the table, but I press my fingers deeper into the wood before carrying them to my face.

My tongue palpitates with heartbeats when I make out three letters on the tip of my middle finger.

Someone's whittled words onto the underside of the table!

I suck in a breath as I realize I sit where Antoni sat during the one and only meal we shared. The poem still tucked beneath my mattress pricks the backs of my lids. Although I don't remember it word for word, I recall him saying something about a *knife scoring words into his heart* and his injunction to *sit at his table.*

It was no love poem!

It was a missive to lead me here!

The wood is so dark and the light so dim that unless I slide underneath the table with a candle, I won't be able to read his clandestine message. But crawling under the table would attract attention, and I don't need anyone reporting my odd behavior to Lore. Not only would he keep me locked up, but he'd also surely go after Antoni.

If what my friend wrote is insurrectionary. Perhaps it's just another farewell note, a sort of little treasure hunt to keep me from growing bored.

Even I realize what utter serpent shit that is.

Sensing the paler-haired Crow's attention, I snatch a cheese stick and nibble on it while I brush the underside of the table to feel where the message begins. Once I've located the first word, I press my fingers into it.

By the time I've collected all the words from the first line, I've wiped the plate clean of cheese. The food sits like damp sand inside my stomach, which clenches when the next letters begin to imprint on my fingertips—STA. I know how the word ends before I've pressed it into my flesh.

My stomach has become one giant knot by the time I finish deciphering Antoni's missive. He may not have signed it, but a Crow would know it was written by a Fae, because Crows have no need for stairs, what with being endowed with wings.

A secret staircase inside the esplanade column...

Does Lore know of its existence? Did he have it built? Isn't it a safety risk for his people?

I try to recall the one and only time I wandered on horseback across the esplanade. The columns had all seemed so smooth. How did I miss the seam of a door? Because Lore rushed me away from the top of the mountain, or because I was too busy gaping wondrously at the castle?

"I was hoping to catch you before you took leave of us, Fallon."

I jump at Bronwen's voice, smacking my knee into the dark wood. The metal cutlery jangles against the black ceramic plates and knocks into the tumbler of coffee that's long gone cold.

"May I?" My aunt gestures to the bench beside mine as though she can see it.

"Of course. Do you need help?" I start to lean over to slide the bench out but stop when she shakes her head.

"I know the sky kingdom like the back of my hand, every nook and cranny, every knot in the wood and furrow in the stone."

My pulse prickles. Is she hinting at the hidden staircase? Is she aware that I'm aware of it? Can she *see* what lurks inside my mind? "Have you come to sway me from leaving?"

"No. I've seen your destiny, and for it to unfold the way it needs to unfold, you must leave."

My skin prickles for a whole other reason now. "Do tell what my future holds, Bronwen? Perhaps the Glacin crown this time, or is it the Nebban one?" My tone is salty, but how could it not be when she led me astray with a prophecy that only served *her* people?

86

"It has not changed, Fallon. You will still be queen of Luce."

"Dante is marrying his brother's betrothed. You said so yourself."

"Luce has only one true king, and that king isn't Dante," she all but yells.

Sheesh. Could she speak any louder? "Old me may have been interested in crowns, but new me longs for a small life."

"You are the curse breaker, Fallon."

"I'm aware." The Cauldron only knows how I'm succeeding at keeping my cool. "And I will curse-break, but I'll do so calmly and quietly, without exchanging oaths of eternal love."

"After you kill Dante, you will get your calm and quiet life."

Fire. My blood becomes fire. "*Kill* Dante? You must have me confused with some other curse breaker, because I could never kill him!"

But Bronwen, unlike Connor and the six other Crows present, isn't listening. "You will plot and plan his death."

Like a kettle heated past its boiling point, rage gushes through me. I palm the table and jerk to my feet, the legs of the bench screeching as I shove it backward. My fingers dig inside the grooves Lore's talons left behind the night he confessed to our mating link. "I may not love that man anymore, but I certainly will not plot his death."

Her purple-tinted lips remain shut, and her glazed white eyes are fixed on the stone wall behind me.

Although tempted to storm out, I'm suddenly struck with a thought—clobbered, more like—and a snort escapes me. *Of fucking course.* "Lorcan put you up to this. It's a ploy to get me to stay put, isn't it?"

"No." Her face turns toward me like a sunflower seeking the warmth of the sun, but all she'll get from me is bitter frost. "Lorcan still believes he will slay Dante and lose his humanity doing so, for that is what will happen if he's the one to remove your former lover from this world before the obsidian curse is lifted."

A blush steals across my cheeks that Bronwen's aware of my afternoon with Dante on the barrack island. "You mean he'll be turned into an iron statue. Let me guess. I'll be the one to stab him?"

Her eyes mist over with tears that begin to fall, tripping over the runnels of her scars. Is she weeping for the friend she may lose, or is there something more she's seeing that she's yet to share?

"No, Fallon, because you'll already be dead."

14

I pad back to my sleeping quarters on feet that have gone as numb as the rest of my body. All the anticipation I felt upon waking has been washed away by Bronwen's prophecies.

A murderess or a dead girl.

My two options.

Both rotten.

However disappointed I am in Dante's behavior, I do not want him dead and cannot imagine anything swaying me to remove him from this world.

Nevertheless, the idea of dooming Lore and his people doesn't sit well either. Especially considering that in that scenario, I'm the dead one. I've no desire to visit the next world. I've so much left to do and see in this one. So many adventures left to go on, so many men left to kiss and kin left to find.

Even though I'm not fond of my origins, I am curious to meet these sorceresses I descend from. Perhaps I should sail to Shabbe until this battle for thrones ceases. Why didn't I have the prescience to ask Bronwen what would happen to Dante and Lore if I left Luce for good?

Yes, I'd be breaking my vow to the Crow king, but he's found Meriam. It's only a matter of time before the wards fall. And then…

And then I'd come back into play whether I wanted to or not.

I clutch my stone windowsill, the pink isle fading and reappearing beyond the slashing rain.

What if *Lore* penetrated the wards? Sure, he'd never head there willingly, but what if I could trick him across?

Everyone has a weakness. All I'd have to do is uncover his.

Or I could simply turn him into a block of iron and ship him through the wards on Minimus's back.

Oh, how angry the Crow king would be, but at least he'd be safe. Dante would be safe. And perhaps I would be as well. Or I'd still be dead, but at least the two of them would get to hate each other for another few centuries.

"Connor…" Phoebus mumbles from where he lies flopped, fully clothed, on the bed. I think he's mid-dream when he adds, "You promised to bring me back breakfast, Piccolina, but I see neither food nor dark and handsome Crow."

Worried my expression will display my moroseness, I keep my gaze riveted to Shabbe. "A pale-haired Crow was serving the food today. I seem to remember you find brown-haired men boring."

He yawns. "Seeing as the brown-haired male is Connor's son, bringing him back here would've been awkward."

"His son?" I whirl away from the window this time, Bronwen's prophecies slipping to the back of my mind.

"Yes. According to Aoife, he had him with a mortal woman a few decades before the Crows' first slumber."

I suddenly worry that Phoebus has taken a fancy to a male who may never return his affection.

It's happened before, and it cracked my friend's heart.

"He swings both ways. I've checked. Not that it matters, since we're leaving." Phoebus expels an exaggerated sigh. "My prospects are dwindling to Racoccins or Selvatins."

"Why would you say that?"

"Because of my allegiance to a certain someone." He cocks me a half smile. "It's fine, though. I'm starting to prefer extra-rugged men."

"Stay."

The emerald color of his irises hardens as he props himself up to sitting. "Quiet, Piccolina."

"I'm not jesting, Pheebs. It'd be safer for you to stay."

"Where you go, I go, even if it's into the human swamp lands."

A knock forces me to drop the matter. *For now.*

"Come in." My pulse, which beat with dread and then with guilt, now beats with an oxymoron of an emotion—glum antici-pation. I want to leave, and yet I don't.

I'm expecting our escorts to have arrived, but the male who stands in the doorjamb is not equipped with wings.

"I heard you were leaving." Lazarus, the fire-Fae who worked as a healer beneath two Fae kings, looks between Phoebus and me. The Crows' passion for face paint has rubbed off on the mammoth male, who's adorned his amber gaze with black stripes that make him look like a seasoned warrior.

"We are. Shortly. Will you be coming home with us?"

He steps over the threshold without closing the door behind him. "My home was killed two decades ago, Fallon. I've nothing left in Luce."

His *home* was Dante's father, Andrea Regio, who was murdered by his own son, even though Marco blamed the Crow king to sway public opinion against the shifters. Andrea, like Dante, was willing to broker a peace treaty to end the age-old feud; Marco wasn't.

"I'll be staying here until the wards fall, in case Lorcan has need of me." Lazarus plays with a sapphire brooch pinned to the stand-up collar of his midnight-blue tunic. It's only when he lowers his fingers that I notice the two entwined letters—L and A. Is the A for Andrea, or does Lazarus's family name begin with an A? "Then I'll head to Shabbe."

His destination makes my gaze spring off the shimmering sapphires.

"Shabbe, huh?" Phoebus crosses one outstretched leg over the other and stretches his arms, which makes the black blouse he borrowed from my closet yesterday rip at the seams.

I briefly wonder what Lore will do with all these clothes once I'm gone. Gift them to all those girls who throw themselves at him because he runs a kingdom? Girls like Imogen?

Instead of dragging the shirt off his head, Phoebus tears off what remains of the sleeves until he's left with a chemise that displays the rounded knobs of his shoulders. "I've heard your healing crystals come from there. Is that hearsay?"

"No. It's accurate." Lazarus raises his hand to the thirty hoops that line the shell of his right ear as though to ascertain that the little colored beads, which contain magic, are still speared through. He doesn't check the other ear, which is fringed with just as much hardware. "That's the reason for my visit, actually. Phoebus, I brought you an earring that will counter the effect of iron on your blood and help you heal, as long as the injury isn't to your heart."

As Lazarus approaches, Phoebus sits up straighter, swinging his legs off the side of the bed. "I've been meaning to ask you for one." My friend presses his hair aside to give Lazarus access to one of the many holes he's kept free of the baubles worn by the moneyed Fae.

Back in school, his ears dripped with expensive gewgaws, but ever since he rebelled against the Lucin caste system by cutting off his ties with his family, along with his waist-long hair, he's barely ever worn anything other than the occasional gold stud.

"How does the gem work, Lazarus?"

"You rub it between your fingertips, then smear the salve on your injury."

I wonder why he's equipping Phoebus with one only now.

Why not when we were transported into the sky kingdom, where more iron exists in a square meter than in the whole of Luce?

Lazarus flicks his gaze my way. "I have a crystal for you as well, Fallon."

I cross my arms. "I'm immune to iron."

"Not to counteract iron. Merely to heal your injuries in case anyone hurts you." The silver-haired Fae strides toward me, his silken blue pants and fluid shirt snapping around his limbs like seawater.

"You make it sound as though our return to Luce will be met with violence."

"I don't know how you'll be received, Fallon. I'd hope Dante will prove fair, like his father"—his throat dips with a jagged swallow—"and protect you and your friends, but he's young and eager to be popular, and most rise by stepping atop others."

I want to defend Dante, but I'm no longer the naive girl who thought him incapable of wrongdoing. All I can do is take care not to stand in his way, for I'd prefer not to be used as a stepping stone—*again*.

The healer inspects my ears, which are on full display since I've bound my hair back. It strikes me that I've stopped being pre-occupied with their shape, what with being surrounded by people with similar ears.

"My lobes aren't pierced, Lazarus."

"By choice?" he asks.

"Yes." Why adorn something you prefer not to attract attention to?

"The crystal cannot rest on your skin, or its magic will wear off."

I tip my head to give him access to my right ear. "I'm no longer opposed to piercing them."

Phoebus gawps at me, because he's one of the only souls aware of my former reticence. "Are you certain?"

I nod, and his surprise turns to an emotion akin to misty-eyed pride. I don't think it deserves pride, but my decision *is* rather momentous. Today marks the first day Fallon Rossi Bannock ceases to be ashamed of what she is not.

Lazarus unhooks the sapphire pin adorned to his collar, then rubs one of his many crystals—a purple bead—and slathers whatever magic he's extracted from it onto the brooch's stem before aiming it at my lobe.

I shake my head and tap the cartilage up top, right where a point would stand had I been born a pure-blooded Fae. "Here."

Phoebus's mouth goes soft at my request, because he understands that will draw attention to my curved shells.

"Very well." Lazarus pinches the top of my ear between his large fingers. "It'll sting, but only for a moment."

Before my next swallow, he stabs the bar pin through the cartilage, and although the pain is shallow, I hold my breath as he slowly slides the needle-sharp accessory back out and produces the definitive hoop. He rubs the translucent amber crystal hooked onto it between his thumb and index finger and applies the magical salve to my new hole.

My skin burns before cooling almost immediately. I release the air trapped in my lungs as he spears the hoop through and secures it. Although it weighs next to nothing, its presence fills me with renewed bravado.

"Knock, knock." The chirpy voice emanates from Eefah, who stands in the doorway, black hair plaited into two long braids that start at the crown of her head. "I come to fly you to Luce. Are you all pack?"

"Yes." I crane my neck and shoot Lazarus a smile. "I hope I'll one day be able to repay your kindness."

The tall healer inclines his head, his heavy silver locks draping over his shoulder, swallowing one shapely ear whole. "Stay alive. That'll be payment enough."

"I've no intention of dying." My lips remain curved in spite of the dread gaining traction inside me.

"Andrea had no intention of passing to the next world either." His grief-stricken tawny gaze scrolls over my features one last time before he turns and ambles out of my borrowed room, vanishing into the abounding darkness.

"Nice earring." Eefah's smile is all crooked teeth and genuine sweetness. "When you getting Crow tattoo?"

I blink at her. "Um." I sense that saying *never* would collapse her delight, so I swap the word out with a vague declaration. "I haven't decided yet."

"Here I assumed you were all born with it." Phoebus stands, his new green crystal glittering as brightly as his eyes, in spite of the purple circles rimming them.

I've no doubt that the second he gets home, he will slip under his bed sheets and hibernate for a month.

"No. We receive when we fly the nest."

As he slips his huge feet into the green suede moccasins that somehow survived his swim in Mareluce, he asks, "How come Bronwen doesn't have one?"

The corners of Eefah's mouth turn down. "Because Costa Regio sent Fae-fire on Bronwen when she choose marry Cian."

I startle. "Wh-what?"

"So that's why she's disfigured..." Phoebus murmurs. "How crazy that she knew Costa Regio personally."

Eefah's eyebrows join. "Costa *is* father to Bronwen."

My jaw drops in time with Phoebus's.

"You did not know?" The female Crow swings her inky eyes between our two startled faces.

My ears buzz, and although I don't feel duped, I do feel foolish for not knowing of their kinship. "Is Dante aware of it?"

"I do not know."

"Her ears aren't pointed," Phoebus remarks.

"Because Costa cut tips off with steel blade. He was cruel man. An uhlbheist."

"*Ulbeeheist?*" Phoebus repeats.

"A monster."

I'm still reeling over the fact that my aunt is also Dante's. Which means she's a Regio. Which means—"Bronwen is the rightful queen!" I whisper gasp.

Eefah wrinkles her button nose. "Cian is mate. Not Lorcan."

It takes me a moment to make sense of her comment. "There's more than one throne in Luce, Eefah."

"Only for moment." She makes her index fingers kiss. "One day, one throne."

Has Bronwen broadcast her newest prophecy? I hope not, because I stand by what I told Bronwen—I will *never* murder her nephew.

The air churns with wingbeats, then heaves with smoke as a second Crow materializes beside Eefah—Connor.

As he exchanges a few quiet words with Imogen's younger sister, Phoebus's slack jaw snaps closed, and he rushes to put order in his pillow-mussed hair. Under other circumstances, I would've grinned at his preening, but my staggered brain is incapable of bending my lips, much less shutting them.

Eefah turns back toward us. "Imogen not free, so Connor come with us. I hope okay?"

While Phoebus proclaims that we'll *make do*, my lips tighten, and I stare at the wall that separates this room from Lore's, imagining Imogen's unavailability is due to being caged by a certain someone's bedsheets.

15

My teeth have been welded shut since Eefah and Connor flew us out of the sky kingdom.

However hard I try to find joy that I'm headed home—and by sky to boot—I get assaulted by another image reel of Imogen and Lore tangled together that dampens my mood like the storm dampens my clothes and the vibrancy of the Racoccin woods.

The only reason I can come up with for why their coupling infuriates me is because it proves that Lorcan Reebyaw is no better than Dante or any of the other monarchs—all of them philanderers with loose morals and looser slacks.

I'm starting to believe that loyal men are an endangered species. Perhaps Sybille is right and I should lay to rest my romantic aspirations of finding *the one*. I'm done reading romance novels.

I'll visit the Great Library in Tarecuori, the one Nonna forbade me from entering because blood is needed to gain access. Though she hadn't known the true nature of mine, she'd known there was something curious about it.

There, I'll borrow medical, religious, and political journals. Essentially, any story that contains plenty of gore and a healthy dose of horror instead of heartwarming banter. I might as well harden myself to the world and prepare my mind for the battle I plan on participating in.

The prospect of stepping into the five-storied temple of knowledge smooths over my prickly mood, which smooths over some more when laughter rolls out of Phoebus as the wind whips his hair into a blond storm cloud.

"We're flying, Fal! *Flying!* Look how small that marsh looks!" He jabs at the air with his chin, arms bound tightly around his winged steed's neck. "And those people! They're sprite-size!"

Through the jumble of raindrops, I catch the upturned faces of Racoccins wading about, up to their knees in mud, harvesting their drowned crops. I'm uncertain if Lore is behind the storm, but if he is, he needs to let up, or he'll end up ruining the humans' source of income and food.

Phoebus hollers a "Hello!"

While no adult shouts back a greeting, a gaggle of children wave, running as fast as their little legs can carry them, splashing through the mucky field, soiling both their skin and ratty clothes. Though their faces are grimy, I don't miss their cheeks lifting into smiles at the sight of our giant mounts.

Like a cloth against fogged glass, their wide-eyed delight clears away the rest of my irritation.

To think that one day, I'll be able to soar without the aid of another Crow.

To shift into smoke and feathers and cast spells using droplets of blood.

My heart skips from rib to rib, and I thrum with absolute exhilaration that wanes when a fleet of white-garbed sprites swoops through the air and forms a roadblock in our trajectory. "Corvi, you're trespassing on Lucin soil. You are requested to stop immediately!"

"They're carrying us to our homes. In *Luce!*" Phoebus's golden hair is plastered to either side of his face now that we've stopped.

"Because we"—he points between me and him—"are Lucin citizens."

"By decree of the king—" The sprite barking this gets walloped in the face by a massive raindrop, which causes his head to twist sideways and his slight body to sink.

"No Crow is permitted beyond the Racoccin forest!" another sprite, one wearing a jacket with garish gold buttons, finishes. I take it he's the battalion leader.

"Cauldron, calm your wings, sprities. These kind birds are merely dropping us off—"

Phoebus's quip is cut short with a shrieked "*Kind*? They chop our people in half!"

My stomach lurches because I remember Lore slicing them in half. At the time, I'd believed he'd killed them to protect me, but really, it was to protect himself. To ensure I could go on collecting those scattered pieces of him.

"Land immediately, corvi, or we'll use obsidian darts to *make you* land."

Ten sprites have already produced black sticks as slim as needles from the quivers strapped to their waist.

To avoid breaking the tenuous amity between the Crows and the Fae, I nod. "We'll land. Eefah?"

As she begins to swoop down, I swipe my waterlogged lashes against my shoulder. Beyond the white cloud of buzzing faeries unspools the islands of Tarelexo—home. We're so near, I can almost smell the wisteria vine that hugs my little blue house. In no more than thirty minutes, we'll reach the ferry that'll sail us across to the wharf in front of Bottom of the Jug.

One of the sprites tapers his eyes on my winged escort. "And the birds go back to where they came from."

Eefah's head swivels toward Connor, and she releases a caw that the rumbling sky seems to amplify. She tucks her wings in time with Connor, and we drop so fast that my stomach jounces into what feels like my throat, even though I'm fully aware that is anatomically impossible. I cringe, dreading the idea that her landing will cost me a few bones, but her wings deploy, and her talons kiss the muddy ground.

She fans out a wing to help me down. As soon as I'm steady on my feet, I brush back the hair that's escaped my braid.

Two sprites hiss in unison, "It's a girl!"

It takes me a moment to realize why they assumed I was male—the pants. I really need to make these fashionable amongst Fae, for women deserve to discover the comfort and convenience of trousers.

"The Serpent-charmer. It's the Serpent-charmer! Warn the king!"

Before my next breath, every winged soldier positions a dart stick in front of his mouth.

Eefah morphs into skin. "We go back, Fallon! Connor—"

"No." I shake my head, because I fought too hard to come home to fall back at the first sign of tension. "We come in peace," I tell the battalion.

The sprite with the gold buttons sniggers. "The king killer comes in peace?"

Phoebus breaks away from Crow Connor and springs in front of me and Eefah.

I try to press out from behind my friend to glare at the sprite, but Phoebus takes his role as my shield exceedingly seriously. "I did *not* kill Marco Regio."

"Fallon, please. Lorcan turn me into forever Crow if anything happen to you." Eefah's voice squirms with nerves.

Although the sprites keep their distance, they fly higher to get a line of sight on me behind Phoebus, but Connor spreads his wings, screening Phoebus and me.

Eefah mutters, "Don't like this."

"You've got your information wrong. I did not murder your former monarch."

"We know what happened. *All* that happened." Gold Buttons's taunt exacerbates my anger.

"You've obviously been misinformed, you stunted canker blossom," I mutter.

Phoebus snorts. "Canker blossom?"

"I heard the doxies discussing them," I murmur.

"You do know what they are?" A smile sounds in Phoebus's voice.

"I'm imagining it's no flower."

"No indeed."

Although silly, our discussion helps quiet my nerves. It does nothing for Connor, whose feathers heave with black smoke, or for Eefah, whose skin keeps losing its solid edges as she attempts to shield the parts of me that Connor and Phoebus don't shelter.

"Do you know who I am?" Phoebus yells at them.

"A traitor," a sprite hisses.

Phoebus shoves his blond hair aside to show his ears. "I'm Phoebus Acolti. So let us through before I bat you out of our way with a cypress branch and have you expelled from the army."

"You've got no authority here, pureling."

"King Dante says"—a sprite pants, flushed cheeks puffing out from his rapid flight—"that Fallon Rossi is not"—another rough breath—"to be harmed. And we are…to give her…safe passage… to wherever she desires to go."

My pulse hastens with gratitude but also with relief that a few days in power have not turned my former flame into an unpredictable despot.

"Come home, Fallon. Please." Eefah sounds on the brink of a meltdown.

I clasp her arm. "I've got to find my mother and grandmother first." I don't mention which ones. If I'm lucky, I'll find both sets.

Her dark eyes flash before glazing over like slick marble. "Guhlaèr."

"*Guhlair?*" Although Phoebus's body is still tense, he turns to face us.

"It means *okay*." Eefah's lids swoop down, whisking off the veneer of her daze. "Lorcan says okay to let you go into Fae land."

I raise my gaze to the sky, surprised the Crow king is listening, since I pictured him otherwise engaged. "It's not his choice." I wait for a retort, but no words drum between my temples. "Is he near?"

Without meeting my stare, Eefah says, "No."

Lies have no taste, yet her breath smacks of deceit.

Without gazing upward, I murmur through the bond: **You promised not to follow.**

Silence.

If you can hear me, Lore—which I imagine you can—please stay away from Luce. You heard the sprites say they've been granted permission to use obsidian. Every Lucin has probably been armed with it.

The air churns as Eefah shifts into her beast.

Before she takes off, I say, "*Shehveha* for the ride, and for your kindness."

She nods her round head before snapping her wings and vanishing skyward, iron talons glinting in the veiled sunlight. Connor follows suit, vanishing after Eefah past the leafy canopy.

Wings beating as briskly as their pulse, the sprites watch them ascend but don't follow.

"Crafty demons," one mutters.

I aim a glower his way. "Crows are more civilized than most of the Fae I know."

Phoebus spears his fingers through mine and tugs me against his side. "Although I'm not opposed to heading back to the sky kingdom immediately, I advise you not to engage if you care to see Syb and find Ceres and Agrippina."

"You won't be finding the Rossi women," Gold Buttons proclaims, his words holding my lungs in a vise.

"Why not?" The words come out strangled.

The buttons on his white jacket gleam like Lore's eyes. "Because they're gone, Serpent-girl."

"Gone where?" Phoebus asks, because I'm breathing too chaotically to fashion words.

"Rumor has it they sailed to Shabbe to escape the shame you brought upon your family."

My heart thumps at the memory of Lore telling me Bronwen and Giana had gotten Nonna and Mamma away to safety. Did he mean Shabbe?

I wrench my head back and glower at the pewter air. *They were brought to Shabbe?*

Silence.

Answer me, godsdammit. Tears sit heavy on my lashes. *Answer me!*

I told you they were safe.

The tears escape and mingle with the raindrops. *In Shabbe, Lore.* My voice cracks like my heart.

It was the safest place for them.

Perhaps, but all my hopes and dreams of reuniting with them, of hugging them, of explaining why I left and brought back the Crow king...all of them pop like soap bubbles. *Did they at least* know *where they were being taken?*

"Why's the girl looking at the sky?" one of the sprites exclaims.

"The Crows must've stayed. Go check the trees!" Gold Buttons commands. "Now!"

His entire squadron jolts like a spooked shoal of fish.

"Fucking now, soldati!"

Four sprites crawl higher, complexions as milky gray as Montelucin stone.

Phoebus squeezes my hand. "Fal, what do you want to do?"

I scrub away the tears. "Right now, I want to yell at Gia, and then I want to set sail toward Shabbe."

Thunder growls, then peals through the sky in time with forks of lightning.

You set sail for Shabbe, and I will personally see that you're returned to my home where you'll stay until the wards collapse.

I gnash my molars at Lore's threat. *I will never go back to your home.* Never. *I hate your nest, and I hate you.*

A laugh that raises the waterlogged fine hairs on my arms echoes through the bond. *Go see what's become of your home before you decree my nest so terrible.*

16

Phoebus keeps my hand tucked in his as we trudge across the soggy marshlands, the haze of white sprites pressing around us, thinning the already stifling air. Although he tries to get me to make conversation, my anger and disappointment take up too much space to allow my mind to latch on to any topic.

With a sigh, he drapes his arm around my tight shoulders and hugs me to him, finally growing as quiet as me.

When we reach the dock, I'm soaked to the bone. To the marrow. And although it's still summer, my body is racked by shivers.

Phoebus holds me tighter, water running over the slight dusting of gold hair plastered to his tanned skin. "I don't think I've been this wet since Dargento tossed me into Mareluce to swim with the serpents."

My blood heats at the memory of what my friend endured at the hands of the evil commander.

My vengeance will be so fucking sweet.

"I hope he's rotting in Filiaserpens." The corners of his eyes are crinkled as though he's remembering the pain and the fear. "Or better yet, in Shabbe."

Fearing it may panic my friend, I don't confess that the hateful man's alive and in Luce.

Unfortunately, the sprite nearest us publicizes both.

Phoebus's grip turns crushing. "What?"

"The brave commander made it home."

"Brave?" Phoebus chokes out. "The man is a smarmy and scheming brute!"

Although I still tremble from cold and grief, I squeeze my friend's rigid fingers and murmur, "He'll be dealt with, Pheebs." I stare over my shoulder in the direction of the sky kingdom buried beneath gray billows of rain. When I look back at Phoebus, his green eyes are wide with shock and trepidation.

"We'll have a war on our hands if the Crows get involved," he whispers back.

War is already on our doorstep, because Lorcan Reebyaw isn't satisfied with the lot he was given. I bite the depressing confession from my tongue before it springs off it and scores Phoebus's face with more worry. "Not the Crows. Dante owes me."

We stop to let a horde of grimy-faced, bald Racoccins pass. Although the sprites yell at them to keep walking and keep their stares turned downward, many pause to catch a glimpse of who could warrant such a dense escort. When one of the humans sucks in a breath and elbows his friend, I assume they've figured out who the auburn-haired girl with the round ears and violet eyes is.

"You struck a bargain with Dante?" Phoebus's clammy fingers dent my skin as we start up again.

"Not exactly. I'm not a Fae, remember?"

He swallows, the rumples of worry and fatigue deepening in spite of the miniature smile tugging at his mouth. "How could I forget, piccolo serpens? Or should I say piccolo corvo?"

His ribbing blows away some of my tension. "You should say neither."

He smiles down at me as we pad out of the cypress forest

toward the waterfront. Our boots squelch against the coarse hodgepodge of sharp rocks and broken glass that make up the Racoccin beach. When a strip of gauze bearing a maroon stain catches around my ankle, I wrinkle my nose and hinge at the waist to pluck it off. A malodorous gust snatches it from my fingers and carries it back into Rax, where waste makes up a good deal of the scenery.

I focus on breathing solely through my mouth as I attempt not to step into anything dubious. I hope that one of Dante's first orders of business will be to clean up this part of the kingdom. I hope he'll prove himself worthy of the sunray crown I helped place upon his brow.

After being flogged by more noxious gusts and washed-up debris, we finally reach the splintered pier that sags into the dark waters of the Racoccin canal. The ferry is fast approaching, bobbing toward us like a tavern patron after one too many jugs of wine.

A soft cry lifts out of the boat as a woman springs up, attempting to catch the unraveling bands of her turban, but the wind snatches it out of her grasp.

"Take your damn seat before you end up in the drink along with your headpiece, human!" the Fae captain barks at her.

How I wish I had magic to help her, but I… "Phoebus! Help her."

He wrinkles his nose. "I'll buy her ten new turbans, but there's no way I'm diving in there."

"I mean grow a vine or something."

"Oh, that I can—"

"There'll be no frivolous use of magic," a sprite spits out, lurching in front of us to make sure he has our attention.

I gesture to the bobbing red fabric that resembles a river of blood. "Then fly and get it."

The little man jerks back his head, upper lip retracting in disgust. "Do you know what floats in these waters?"

"Yes, waste that water-Fae should be gathering and fire-Fae should be incinerating!" I don't realize how loudly I've spoken until I notice everyone's face angled toward me.

"Humans need to learn to clean up their own filth."

My temper spikes. "When one is concerned with one's survival—"

"Shh." Phoebus squeezes my forearm. "Let's not start a riot on our first day back."

"I forgot how unfair and senseless Lucins can be."

"Fallon," Phoebus warns. "If you don't settle, we're going to end up in Isolacuori before Tarelexo, and I really, *really* want to soak in my tub for a century and sleep away another before I head out on more adventures with my favorite outlaw."

Fluorescent scales slice through the brown surf, ripping my focus from Phoebus and the injustice of the Fae world I'd been so adamant about returning to.

The flash of pink stops both time and the carousel of my thoughts, but the shriek that resounds over the storm snaps me out of my trance. The woman, who's still attempting to fish out her fallen headdress while a man holds her around the waist, stumbles back, taking her affable anchor down with her.

"Serpent!" she hisses.

The entire row of humans seated near the bulwark scrambles away from the side of the boat, treacherously rocking the vessel.

How deep the Fae have drilled into humans the fear of what lurks in our ocean.

A tusk rises from the water, followed by obsidian eyes set in a head that appears almost equine in shape. When the first band of white flesh appears on the creature's neck, I gasp and tear myself from Phoebus.

Even though Dante publicly nicknamed me Serpent-charmer, I've always hidden my affection for serpents. Now that my origins are known, I no longer need to. I am free to give my heart to whatever beast I desire.

The momentary displeasure that washed over me from being back in a realm of antiquated laws floods right out as I race across the dock and sink onto my knees, arm outstretched, fingers at the ready to stroke the beautiful creature I've missed so deeply.

Minimus's body ribbons toward me, his black eyes never leaving mine. Fresh tears mix with the rain on my cheeks when my skin makes contact with my serpent's slick scales. He presses his face into my hand, and I don't care that brown goop slops down his cheek.

I don't care that a regiment of sprites and a boatload of humans are witnessing my reunion.

I don't care—

"So it's true. Fallon Rossi has dared return."

I whip my gaze off Minimus, who must sense the tremor Tavo's voice causes in me, because his head whirls and his forked black tongue unspools with a resonating hiss.

Tavo, who stands near the prow of a varnished military gondola, gloves his hand in flames.

"Stop!" I yell. "Don't attack him."

"If he lashes out first—"

"He won't." I stroke my hand down Minimus's feather-soft dorsal fins, attempting to calm him. "I swear he won't. Please put your magic away, Tavo."

"It's General Diotto now." Although he lowers his palms, fire still skips along his skin.

I hate that Dante gave this man so much power, even though it could've been worse... He could've made Dargento his new general. After I take in the gilded burgundy jacket that used to grace my grandfather's torso, I cluck my tongue to gather my serpent's attention.

Bracketing his large head between my palms, I whisper, "Go."

Minimus blinks.

I nod to the ocean. "Go."

He chuffs like Furia, as though annoyed by my demand. I'm about to drive his body low with the press of my palm when he sinks like coiled rope beneath the brown surf and vanishes in a flourish of foaming fuchsia.

Goodbye, my darling creature.

I stand just as the ferry docks, bumping into the pier.

"Storm's going to end up flooding me boat," the spiky-eared, gray-eyed boat captain grouses as he blows water out of the hull.

"To what do we owe the pleasure of your visit?" Tavo makes the word *pleasure* sound like anything but.

"I'm not visiting, dear general. I've come home to stay."

The fire has finally gone out of his fingers. "Hmm. So many of you are coming home..." His amber eyes seem to glow redder as he strokes the day-old stubble lining his chin. "Since you come in peace, don't mind the guards that I've enlisted to keep you *safe*."

Even if he hadn't drawn out that last word, I'm fully aware the man is completely unconcerned with my safety. "How long will I need to be kept *safe?*"

"For as long as you're here."

"Forever then?" My voice drips with honey.

His lips flip up into a cruel smile. "Until the day you die, it will be then."

Is it me, or is Tavo picturing sending me into an early grave?

17

Tavo insists on escorting Phoebus and me across the canal. I'm hesitant to get into the military gondola, afraid Dante's new general plans on sailing us past Tarelexo and straight into an Isolacuorin dungeon, but I climb aboard. Although the ship is manned by both a water-Fae and an air-Fae, the boat ride is a rocky one.

"You should sit." Phoebus grips my wrist, refusing to touch my fingers even though the unrelenting rain has washed them clean of Racoccin grime.

"We're almost there." I keep my gaze on the purple awning undulating like Minimus's dorsal fin and the black lettering that reads BOTTOM OF THE JUG.

I can already hear the raucous chatter and bawdy laughter. I can already smell the rich aromas of Marcello's and Defne's cooking and picture the doxies strutting around in their racy getups. The words I plan to have with Giana fizz along my tongue, impatient to leap out.

I know that her intent was to protect me, but couldn't she have told me where Nonna and Mamma were? Why hadn't I insisted on knowing their location? Because I'd been so concentrated on loathing Lore?

When we dock, I tear my wrist out of Phoebus's hold and leap off the boat, then march across the slick cobbles toward the tavern entrance and fling the door wide.

The noise, which wasn't loud to begin with seeing as only four tables are occupied, dies out completely.

I count nine customers.

Nine customers at lunchtime is unheard of. Is a revel underway in some other part of the kingdom? Maybe one to celebrate Dante's nuptials?

The kitchen door flaps open, kicking my pulse up a few notches.

Defne's gray gaze swoops off her tray and lands on my face. "Fallon."

My name gusts through the quiet tavern, as heavy and sticky as the muggy air trapped between the weathered beams and scrubbed floorboards.

I don't miss the dip of her throat or the way her mouth puckers. *Shock.* She's in shock.

I muster a smile and take a step forward.

"Leave."

I freeze. Did she just ask me to—

"Please." She shakes her head from side to side, which makes her wavy, shoulder-length black hair swish over the beige linen bodice of her dress. "Please, Fallon. Leave."

Chair legs scrape as two customers stand. "Something smells rotten," one of them says, pinning me with a razor-sharp glare.

"Please stay, Signore Guardano." Defne holds the platter so close to her that it dents her soft stomach. "Fallon, you're no longer welcome here."

My blood becomes slushy and cold like the waves that lick our shores at the peak of winter. I take a step back, my spine bumping into someone's front.

"What's going on?" Phoebus's voice vibrates against my nape.

"I–I—" My heart is swelling so fast I cannot string an explanation together. I start to turn but pause to scan the room. "Where are Syb and Gia?" My voice is a raucous whisper.

Defne's eyes shut as her throat moves over another swallow. "They aren't welcome here either. You neither, Phoebus."

His hands close around my shoulders in surprise. Eyes stinging, I duck out of his hold and pull open the door. When I step out, I wrench my neck back and shut my lids, forcing the tears to slide back in. The loud thud of raindrops against the stretched fabric awning echoes as loudly as each one of my heartbeats.

"A problem, Signorina Rossi?" Tavo's oily voice slithers through the moist air, basting my strumming eardrums and worsening my mood.

I fling my lids up and glower at him. "No," I lie.

The curve of his lips is so complacent and cruel that I want to punch him in the throat and whistle for Minimus.

Instead, I narrow my eyes on his beady amber ones, hoping that the soldier blowing air from his palms to keep the redheaded general dry runs out of magic.

"Where to next, Signorina?"

"Are you planning on shadowing me, Tavo?"

His smile coarsens but doesn't waver. "My job is to protect the kingdom from people who wish it ill."

"I do not wish Dante or Luce ill!" I yell over the crack and growl of thunder.

Phoebus curls one hand around my elbow and leads me away. "Let's go."

Tavo doesn't follow, but his voice does, "Reaching your house will be swifter by boat."

Although the cobbles are slick and my eyesight blurry from the heat of my disappointment, I prefer to take the long way. I've steam to blow and frustration to shake.

"Did you know?" I snap at Phoebus.

"Did I know what?" His gait is as stiff as the line of his shoulders.

I stop walking in the middle of a wooden bridge strangled by dense vines of honeysuckle. "That we'd be considered rejects?"

"I guessed we weren't going to receive a hero's welcome. We did divide the kingdom, Fal."

"*I* did that. Not you. Not Syb. Not Gia." The rain lashes at my cheeks, plastering the flyaways framing my face to my forehead. "None of you should be banned from Lucin establishments because of me."

"We could've returned to Luce, but we chose to stay."

"You were tossed into Mareluce and carried into the sky kingdom. What choice did you have?" My voice cracks.

"I could've ridden home with Dante, but I didn't, so stop blaming yourself!"

My lower lip wobbles so hard that I have to trap it between my teeth to stop the rising wail from escaping. "Defne and Marcello kicked them out, Pheebs." I croak. "They adore their girls, but th-they—they t-turned them away. My mother and grandmother are gone." My tears tumble, smearing Phoebus's features until he's no more than smudges of green, gold, and peach. "For all we know, our friends sailed to Shabbe."

"They're at Antoni's." He dips his chin into his neck. "Where we should be as well."

My heart catches. "Antoni's?"

"In his new home."

"I want to go home," I whisper.

"Piccolina, no one will be there…"

"I need clothes and—"

His lips press together. "Frankly, I'm scared."

I put on a brave front for my friend. "You heard the sprites. Dante said that we're not to be harmed."

"No, just shadowed."

I manage a shrug. "I was shadowed my entire life."

"Doesn't ease my qualms one bit. Not one bit." He glances down the street, catching sight of a hovering sprite in full military regalia. "I give you one week to come to your senses, and not a minute more. If *anyone* tries *anything*, I'll whistle for Lorcan."

"I doubt he'll answer to a whistle." I try to smile, but the sentiment stumbles off my lips.

Wiping my eyes on my sodden shirtsleeves, I turn to find another winged legionnaire suspended amongst the raindrops behind us and Tavo's vessel rocking at the junction between the canal cinching Tarelexo and the narrower one over which we stand.

Phoebus drapes his arm around my shoulders. "Let's go before we make Diotto's day by perishing of pneumonia."

"You're a pureling, Pheebs. Human diseases cannot touch you."

As he guides me back down the road, I glimpse the faintest streak of black in the eaves of the sunflower-hued house beside us.

I dart my gaze away before I can draw attention to the darkness. *Is someone following us, Lore?*

Many people follow you. You gather quite the crowd.

I don't mean Fae; I mean Crows. Are you having us followed? What do you think?

I think Lorcan Reebyaw didn't listen to me when I told him to leave me be. And I think I'm grateful for his protection, even if it only lasts until Meriam is brought to justice.

I'm still terribly angry with you for keeping me in the dark, Lore.

Because the light has revealed such agreeable things?

You're right. It hasn't. But I prefer to see than stay blind. I prefer to know than be made a fool of.

When have I ever made a fool of you?

Really, Lore? Really?

I think of all the times I traipsed around in the buff before his eyes.

I think of all the relics I brought back to life believing they were just that—*relics*.

I think of how I called him Your Majesty because I assumed it was his name, and he never set me right. Yes, it was to protect his identity, but I gave him everything, and he gave me nothing but evasions and lies.

I've given you back your freedom, Fallon.

And he has, but now I wonder if he returned it to me only because he knew my homecoming would be pitiful.

No, Behach Éan. I set you free because I understood that although you were not a block of stone, you felt trapped, and there is no worse feeling in the world.

The return of my nickname breaks through the cloud cover of my mood and apparently of Lore's, because patches of blue appear overhead.

18

My front door gapes, but that isn't what roots my soles to the cobbles and my heart to my ribs. What makes me freeze are the swoops of red paint that have dried in drips.

Swoops that read *King Killer.*

Fury suffuses me.

Fury against the Fae who desecrated my home.

Fury against Dante, who's yet to set his people straight. Yes, I brought about his brother's downfall, but the dying was all him.

On stiffened joints, I lunge forward and shove my door wide.

Phoebus calls out my name, calls out the words, "Stop! Don't!"

But I don't stop.

My blood becomes as pressurized as the water Nonna would boil in the kettle that sits askew by our disemboweled couch.

Our kitchen has been gouged with more profane language, the windows cracked, the frescoed walls smeared with more cruel words painted in what looks like blood.

Crimson whore.

Crow wench.

Shabbin bitch.

Murderess.

Traitress.

Noxious puddles haloed by flies dapple the honeycomb tiles, and the stench of piss punches up my flaring nostrils.

"Welcome home, Fallon Rossi." Tavo's voice rises over the gentle slap of water and wends through the shattered glass into my throbbing ears.

My gaze cuts to the fiery depths of his irises that sparkle with a smug smile.

"Who is behind this, Diotto?" Phoebus's jaw tics.

"Purelings. Halflings. Underlings. Overlings. I even heard some humans came to pay tribute to the girl who revived the Crimson Crow and his army of obsidian butchers."

Phoebus's tendons strain against his long, slender neck like stretched twine. "Were they punished? Tell me they were punished."

"We believe in freedom of expression in Luce now."

Fucking really? The words stay lodged in my cramping throat.

"You call hate speech freedom of expression!" Phoebus flings his arms in a wide circle while I whirl on myself to take in the very worst of Faekind.

I'm struck by something of greater importance than debating the crude application of this new law. "Were my grandmother and mother—were they still here when the vandals visited?"

"I wouldn't know, Fallon. I was in Tarespagia."

Liar. He was in the south with Dante.

With me.

With Marco's severed head.

"Perhaps you could use your spanking new clout to inquire on my behalf?"

My snide comment is met with a sneer. "You'd be wise not to address me in that tone."

"Or what, General?"

The twinkling amethysts he wears along his peaked ears refract the nascent sunlight.

"You'll brand those monikers into my flesh with your Fae-fire?"

His eyes grow slitted. "Don't mistake me for your savages, Fallon. We neither ink nor score our skin to display what we are."

I don't bother with a retort, for my breath is wasted on this man who believes me a demon. I turn on my heels, sidestep an ochre puddle, and climb the creaking stairs. Every bedroom door hangs off its hinges, giving me an unobstructed view of the chaos inside.

Mamma's rocking chair has been charred and splintered. Nonna's wicker baskets full of medicinal vials have been overturned and their contents smashed. The windows in our rooms have been blown out, the drapes slashed. A motionless bird lies on my bare mattress, its wings splayed like the crow from the Acolti family's vault.

The reek of rot that suffuses the air has me reaching for purchase and sagging the second my palms connect with something solid. I try to harness my breakfast, but every last morsel makes its way out. Once my stomach is empty, I press away from the wall and wipe my mouth with the back of my hand, stilling when I catch the sooty hue of my fingertips.

I raise my gaze, and a blaze as hot as Fae-fire begins to chew my thrashing insides.

"Santo Caldrone." Phoebus rocks back onto his heels, flinging one arm up to his nose.

Lewd drawings of a girl fucking a crow—and not a man-shaped one—darken my walls.

They're vile.

Gruesome.

Appalling.

They destroy my faith in humanity and fill me with a vengeful thirst to punish all those who dared defile my reputation and home.

"Is Dante aware of this?" I speak through clenched teeth, desperately trying not to breathe in the sickly sweet scent of decay.

"He has much on his plate," Tavo says. "And in his bed."

His ignorance of what was done to me doesn't quell my wrath's vigor, but it does temper it, for if Dante knew...

If he allowed this to happen and voluntarily left my house in this putrid state...

Gods, I don't think I could forgive him.

"Clothes." Phoebus wheezes, his arm still smooshed against both his mouth and nose.

I walk to my closet and hook the door with a single fingertip to tug it open, then stare and stare.

I blink back tears of rage before backtracking toward the door.

"What?" Phoebus asks as I sidestep him.

"Let's go."

"What about your—"

"They're gone." I don't add that in their place, someone left me a handful of serpent tusks—one still attached to turquoise scales, another as slender as my pinkie.

Tears filming my lashes, I glance back into Mamma's room, at the shelf upon which she kept her favorite books, love stories I would read out to her. All the books are gone, but something remains on her shelf—the smooth rock with the engraved V I unearthed from one of the dresses I inherited from Mamma when I turned fifteen and outgrew the frocks Nonna would mend and let out so I could wear them another year.

I traipse over and snatch the stone, then give her room a once-over. Like mine, it's been ransacked and soiled. Running my thumb along the grooves in the stone, I fly down the stairs and out the door.

Once I've burst out, I hinge at the waist and breathe. Just breathe.

And then...

And then I finally scream.

My neighbors poke their heads out of their houses, but no one asks me why I'm undergoing a meltdown, because they *know*, they *saw*, and they *sat* on their fucking asses and let it happen.

"Feel better?" Phoebus asks.

Huffing, I straighten. "No. Not even a little."

I hesitated to burn down your house so you wouldn't see what became of it. Lore's voice feels like a warm balm, yet it does nothing to soothe my iced blood.

I close my lids and focus on the breaths sliding in and out of my aching lungs. *Yet you didn't because you wanted me to see, didn't you?*

Oblivion makes one weak.

I trace the V almost manically, thinking of ways to retaliate without stooping to their level.

If you'll allow me, Behach Éan, it'd be my pleasure to restore your honor.

I snort, picturing just how much pleasure he'd take, but that would only poison relations between Crows and Fae. I stride around the embankment toward Tavo's bobbing boat. "Antoni's new house. Where is it?"

"Next door to the Acoltis. Would you care for a ride?"

"No. We'll—"

"We'd love a ride." Phoebus sets his palm on the small of my back. "I'm not risking walking through streets filled with haters and getting socked by a cauldron brimming with animal guts, dead birds, or gods only know what else they're stockpiling in their homes."

I blink up at him. Although it's me the people despise, their abhorrence is so vast that it encompasses all those close to me. "I'm sorry, Phoebus."

"Boat. Now." He shoves me forward. "And you have *nothing* to apologize for. All you did was scratch at the pretty veneer that's coated Luce for far too long. If anyone should be apologetic, it should be our new leader who let this"—the hand not on my back shoots out toward the little blue home that used to be my safe haven—"*carnage* happen."

"Careful, Acolti." Tavo puffs warm air onto a steel dagger before polishing the blade unhurriedly against the fine burgundy of his jacket. "Your words could be construed as antagonistic, and you know where dissenters are sent."

Into Filiaserpens, the lair the serpents established in the fault line that stretches between Isolacuori and Tarecuori. The place where Fae have disposed of their enemies for centuries.

I watch the dagger, wondering how fast I could disarm Tavo and thrust it through his rancid heart.

He must sense the direction of my thoughts, because he stabs the blade back into his baldric and keeps his palm glued to the hilt. "Don't think for a second I'd hesitate to toss you in as well, Fallon."

I raise a harsh smile. "Are you really threatening me with a swim in Mareluce?"

He returns an even harsher one. "I hear corpses sink, not swim."

Shall we find out? Smoke coalesces between the remaining puffs of clouds, ridding me of my smile.

Lore, no! If he kills Tavo, war will break out, and lives will be lost on all sides.

Dante's friend cranes his neck and yells at his men to arm themselves with obsidian.

Go. Please, Lore. You'll only make this worse. Please.

The canal begins to churn and bubble, multihued scales slashing the water.

Suddenly, the warmth of Phoebus's palm vanishes, and he gasps.

I spin to find a soldier holding a steel blade at his throat.

Not just any soldier, though.

Black-haired, tawny-eyed Commander Silvius Dargento. "Call off your pets, or your little friend perishes, Signorina Rossi."

19

Cold sweat drips down the runnel of my spine, and Mamma's stone slips from my fingers. "Stop! Everyone, lay down your weapons! Stop!"

The black smoke splits into five puffs. If I had any doubt that Lore was present, it's gone, for only the Crow king can divide himself into five different entities. Where two of his crows remain poised over Tavo's gondola, the other three carve the air toward me, swirling around my chest, neck, and head, all the weakest spots on my body.

"Release Acolti, Silvius!" The voice that fills the air is one I haven't heard in days, and although it no longer strums my veins, it snips the pressure squeezing my lungs.

"Dante," I gasp as Lore's cool smoke keeps stretching frenziedly over my skin.

My former champion stands astride another military vessel that shines like a jewel against the murky blue canal. The sunray crown shimmers atop his brown braids that lift from the speed the air-Fae surrounding him are using to propel his ship toward us.

"You heard your king," Tavo barks. "Release the pureling, Dargento."

The commander's nostrils flare out twice before he shoves

Phoebus so hard my friend loses his footing and flails forward. His face goes as white as spilled milk as his body tips over the embankment.

I stride forward to jump in after him, but Lore's crows hold me back.

"Let me go, Lore," I growl.

Suddenly, as though someone is reversing time, Phoebus's body lifts. It's only when I see the giant bird pinned beneath his torso, levering him back onto solid ground, that I stop fighting Lore's hold and allow my heart to squeeze back down my throat and into its original cavity.

The second Lore's clinch slackens and the Crow that saved Phoebus soars high, I snap forward and fling my arms around my friend's neck, dragging his big, trembling body down to mine. He's crying, great, racking sobs that paint the whites of his eyes red.

In that moment, I do something I never imagined myself capable of—something I loathed Lore for when he did it to me. I take the decision to stay in Luce out of his hands. *Take him back. I cannot lose him. I cannot*—My mind's voice splinters.

Connor will carry him home, Behach Éan. Lore must pour the command into his fellow Crow's mind, because the mammoth bird who saved Phoebus from a dip in the ocean swoops low.

Before Phoebus is snatched away from me for Cauldron only knows how long, I cup his wet cheeks and kiss his forehead. "I'll see you soon."

He jerks his head free from my palms. "You're leaving?"

"No, Pheebs, you are."

"No." He shakes his head. "Fallon—"

But it's too late. Connor hooks gleaming talons around Phoebus's belt and lifts him.

"Fallon! How could you?" he yells. "How could you?!" His body shrinks, becoming no larger than the yellow balloon Nonna gifted me on one of my birthdays and that slipped from my cake-speckled fingers on our way home from the tavern where the Amaris had treated me to a frosted concoction, ablaze with rainbow candles.

Your turn.

I lower my head and lids. "Not yet. I have to find Syb and the others." I keep my grandmother's name out of my thoughts. I cannot let him see my true intent, or he will whisk me back to his castle and toss away the key.

His citrine eyes gleam as his insubstantial form gains substance. When the dark cloud of a man coalesces into one made of flesh, I hiss, "Shift back. You're a sitting duck."

"Crow, actually. Not the same genus."

I gape at him. "I really don't think now's the time to debate avian species."

A small smile slides onto his mouth as he turns toward Dante. "Good afternoon, Regio. Apologies for dropping by unannounced. With a Crow sentry, no less. I didn't think I'd have to intervene, but your men are decidedly lousy listeners."

An abrasive guffaw escapes through Tavo's parted lips. "The gall of the—"

"Tavo, please head back to the castle." Dante's ship doesn't wade closer. Because he fears the male standing beside me, or is it the zigzagging serpents that make him keep his distance?

Although they've calmed, the beautiful beasts haven't swum off, as though waiting for my command to disperse.

To think I can—*sort of*—command beasts.

"Mind taking the former commander with you, Diotto?" Lore's charcoal-streaked face swings in the direction of Dargento, who takes a nominal step back. "I fear Fallon, who is most wily and stubborn, will obliterate our armistice should he keep hovering."

I snort. *With what weapon?*

Me. He adds a wink that is so at odds with this entire situation—this entire day—that I cannot smother the grin that lifts my cheeks. *I hear I'm a skilled butcher.*

I wrinkle my nose.

Dante must've given Dargento the order to embark with Tavo, because he hops into the berthed boat.

In spite of Dargento's vindictive stare, my pulse slows as they navigate away from the shore. "You should go," I say. "I hear Crows aren't allowed beyond the Racoccin woods."

"Their king is allowed everywhere." Lore's gaze tracks the gondola's trajectory.

"Will the Crow who airlifted Phoebus get into trouble?"

He finally turns his attention back to me. "No."

"How long will you be staying, Fallon?" Dante calls out, his gravelly voice skipping along the liquid expanse separating us.

"Does my visit need to have an expiration date, Maezza?"

Even from where I stand, I don't miss the nerve feathering Dante's temple.

"I hear felicitations are in order." I hold the blue stare that used to enchant me. "Alyona must be bitterly disappointed."

"She was, but her father found her a consolation prize."

Smoke begins to billow off Lore's iron pauldrons.

"Am I allowed to share the wonderful news with Signorina Rossi, Ríhbiadh?"

I frown, glancing between the two men, wondering why Dante is asking Lore for permission.

Lore shrugs. "By all means, Regio."

The sky-blue hue of Dante's irises turns as frosty as chips of ice. "The Crow king has kindly offered to wed the Glacin princess and make her his—what is it you shifters call it again?"

As Lore congenially supplies the term, my stomach bottoms out, and my mouth goes as dry as the arid planes of Selvati.

20

Y ou're—" I try to school the hurt and surprise off my features, but according to Syb, I've the most pitiful poker
face. "You're betrothed?"

Lore watches my expression, studying the effect of the news.

"Since when?" My voice is as thin and brittle as the sweet
almond wafers Nonna would bake for Yuletide.

"We signed the agreement last night."

Last night? He and I had dinner last night! When exactly did
he fly off to Glace to negotiate a betrothal? Before or after his
great big spiel about how Crows mate for life?

The pale oval of Alyona's face, the silver of her eyes, and the
waist-long shock of her white-blond hair brighten my lids, washing away Lore's darkness.

It's silly, utterly silly, but the news of his impending nuptials
feels like a punch to the heart.

Lore's chin dips into his neck as he keeps regarding me. "This
alliance is a great step toward peace."

"I bet." My throat feels as though it's been rubbed raw against
a washboard, along with the rest of my organs. "Imogen must be
disappointed."

"Why would she be?"

Instead of stating the obvious, I ask, "So will you be moving to Glace, or will your fiancée be moving into the sky kingdom?"

I picture her in the room I vacated, fingering the soft fabric of the clothes Lore had sewn for me with her softer fingertips. From what I remember of her body, they'll fit. Will he tell her that they were cut and sewn just for *her*?

Jealousy rears its petty head, and I suddenly regret not stripping every hanger and bringing the clothes with me. Even that atrocious, black feathered gown.

A gentle smile plays on the edges of Lore's mouth. He's surely daydreaming of his little princess, since my thoughts are anything but amusing. "Alyona will remain in Glace for the time being."

So she returned to her homeland... The unrest must've fueled her departure from Luce. Unless it was a broken heart that charted her course back north. After all, she seemed to care a whole lot for Dante. I wonder if she's excited for her impending nuptials or horrified to be marrying a shifter with appendages that could cut her tremendously long Fae life short.

"I need—I need—"

What is it you need, Behach Éan?

I need space to breathe and think.

I need surprises to stop being lobbed at me.

I need to stop caring that other people's lives are chugging on ahead while mine is stuck in limbo.

"I need to go," I manage to say.

"Very well. Allow me to fly you to Antoni's so you do not have to brave the streets of Luce."

"You know me and my passion for promenading."

"Fallon." He sighs. "It's the last time we will see each other for some time. Let me at least ensure your safe arrival at your destination."

"What do you care if I arrive safely?"

The smile warps off his face, and his jaw clenches as though his head is becoming a lump of metal.

"As per our agreement, no one will harm her," Dante, who's yet to command his captain to steer him back to Isolacuori, exclaims.

Lore swings his attention toward his fellow monarch. "Have you seen what your people did to her house, Regio?"

The Fae king's gaze travels over the blue walls that, once upon a time, kept me safe. "I have not." Though his answer doesn't alter the state of my home, it does alter the state of my heart, sweeping away some of the hurt. "I'll see that it is restored to its original state."

"Please also see that all your soldiers keep their distance from my—" Lore so rarely stumbles over his words that his drawn-out pause pulls my eyes back to his. "*Subject.*"

"I'm not your subject." My tone holds no bite. It barely holds any volume. I feel deflated and tired.

I miss Phoebus. I miss Nonna and Mamma, even if they don't—

The rock! I dropped it. I scan the cobbles, but my eyes blaze with so much emotion that the ground beneath my feet resembles a painter's palette. I blink several times, but it does next to nothing to clear my blurry vision.

I crouch and run my hands over the wind-and-salt-buffeted stones, over the coarse grass that somehow found a way to grow in spite of the harsh winds and briny sprays.

What are you looking for? Lore asks through the bond or maybe out loud—I'm not certain.

I'm not certain of anything anymore besides the need to find this piece of my mother and get to Sybille as quickly as possible. "Mamma's rock."

Although no giant wave is closing over me, I feel like I'm about to be sucked so far under that I won't emerge this time unless I have someone and something to hold on to. I crawl on my hands and knees, shaking fingers scrabbling over the cobbles until they connect with a smooth rock. Mamma's.

As I rise, I grip it so tightly that the shallow grooves dig into my palm. "Actually, I've changed my mind about the ride." I need Sybille like Minimus needs the ocean. "If your offer to take me to Antoni's is still on the table."

"Antoni's?" Dante's eyebrows jerk so near each other they almost kiss. "Antoni Greco's?"

"My home is not fit to live in, Maezza."

Although Dante has changed—we've all changed—I don't miss the bob of his Adam's apple. "Ríhbiadh is allowing you to stay with the likes of Antoni Greco?"

"Antoni is a friend. Besides, it's my life. My decisions."

"If you need a place to stay, Fallon, I can find you accommodations in the castle," Dante says.

"No." The gold in Lore's eyes churns as smoke curls off the edges of his broad body. "She'll stay with Greco."

Dante's mouth hooks into a crooked smile. "I thought you trusted me, Lore."

"Do not call me Lore. You're neither a Crow nor a friend, Regio. As for trust, it is earned." Before my next breath, Lore bursts into five crows that slam together to shape one.

"Till our next meeting, Serpent-charmer." Had the nickname escaped any other mouth, I would've scowled, but from Dante, it doesn't sound like an insult. It sounds like an olive branch.

"Will there be another?"

"Many. After all, you've a tendency to stir up trouble, Signorina Rossi."

"Surely that won't merit an intervention from the king himself." I smile at him, and although it doesn't expunge the disappointment of his abandonment, it scrubs away one more layer of my pain.

Bronwen's wrong. Dante and I, we may never be as close as we once were, but I could never end his life.

His full lips bend and separate around blinding white teeth. "Who else is as well equipped to cope with you as I?"

Lore snatches my biceps and hurtles into the sky. We rise so high so fast that my heart bangs against my balled stomach and my ears pop.

The princeling used you, Fallon. Has it already slipped your mind?

I know Lore won't drop me, yet I wrap one hand around the cool metal of his legs, keeping the other locked around my rock. *It has not.*

Dante tilts his face to watch us, and although I hold his stare, I'm soon distracted by the sight of Luce from the sky. Liquid arteries sparkle like streaks of glitter around the twenty-five islands, which grow in width and breadth like the multihued houses and expanses of greenery the farther east we fly.

The same way that your exploitation of my candor has not slipped my mind, Lorcan Reebyaw.

Do not dare cast us in the same boat. Dante and I are nothing alike.

You're both kings. You both love Luce. You're both marrying foreign princesses. Shall I go on? I'm certain I can find many more similarities.

Lore mutters something in Crow that I don't grasp as his body lists forward. Unlike Eefah, he sinks slowly as though to give me one more second to admire the kingdom that, once upon a time, I believed would become mine.

How gullible I was.

As we land, the sprites and Fae soldiers posted beside the apricot walls circling Antoni's property move aside to make room for Lore's giant crow. All have a hand on the hilts of their swords or dart pipes, and all have their eyes on us.

After he's set me down, he bursts into his many crows. *Aoife waits inside. She'll be staying with you for the duration of your visit. As soon as you're ready to come home, let her know, and she'll fly you back.*

I don't point out that his home isn't mine and that I'll surely never want to return now that he'll be sharing it with Alyona of Glace. *Give Phoebus my love, and tell him not to hate me.*

Three of his golden-eyed birds float higher while the larger one, made up of two crows, stays at my side. *If our paths cross, I will.*

Why wouldn't their paths cross? Is he planning on holing up inside his private rooms? Unless he's planning an extended trip to Glace to visit his betrothed.

The questions scroll through my head on a loop as I walk over to the hammered bronze door to knock.

My fist meets air because the burnished rectangle grinds open.

Sybille springs out, my name falling from her lips in a great rush of letters. "Antoni said you were coming, but I thought he was full of shit." The girl who hates hugs winds her arms around my neck and pulls me to her tightly. "Flitter the fuck away before I blow the lot of you into Mareluce."

I gasp at how she speaks to Lore until I notice that it's the sprites she's warning off. I crane my neck, finding that no more black smudges the blue sky.

The Crow king has left.

Sybille grabs my hand and pulls me past the threshold into a hallway made of glass surrounded by geometrically manicured gardens.

"How did Antoni know?"

"Aoife." She suddenly glances over my shoulder while I stare around me in awe. "Where's Phoebus?"

"He's back in the sky kingdom."

"Back?"

I fill her in as we traverse the corridor bathed in sunlight and dappled by the shadows of the sprites buzzing about outside.

"Thankfully, they're not allowed inside. Dante has shown himself rather agreeable, all things considered. Although a lot of his agreeableness has to do with the bargains he made us strike."

"Bargains? What bargains?"

"If we don't keep our mouths shut about his hand in his brother's death, we'll owe him a favor."

"And you all swore an oath?"

She nods.

I dislike how much power that gives Dante over my friends. "I'm sorry."

"'Bout what?"

"That you've all become outcasts."

She hoists a shoulder that makes her yellow sleeve dip. "It's temporary. After enough years of peace, everyone will forget, and life will go back to normal."

Footsteps echo on a floor made of interlocking white and jade marble squares. *Click. Click. Click.*

My eyebrows draw together, because it sounds like the gait of a woman in heels, and for as long as I've known Giana, she's never once worn heels.

And Eefah was wearing boots this morning. Unless she changed her footwear, but she also doesn't strike me as a heel wearer.

Sure enough, it is a woman, and sure enough, that woman is neither Giana nor Eefah.

"Welcome to the resistance, micara."

21

The overlapping, papery, crimson folds of Catriona's dress crinkle as she approaches, her eyes running over my face before wandering lower, over my unfeminine and water-logged outfit. No wrinkle of disapproval mars the smooth skin between her brows.

I side-eye Sybille, who gives my fingers a squeeze before murmuring out of the corner of her mouth, "The upside-down poppy here has decided to aid our cause."

I didn't think my eyebrows could arch any higher, but they now skim my hairline. Granted, I wasn't endowed with a very tall forehead to begin with.

I pull my fingers out of Sybille's to peel the rain-dampened shirt stuck to my chest. "Catriona used the word *resistance*. What are we resisting?"

"Caste tyranny. Fae dominion." The courtesan halts centimeters from where Sybille and I stand, on the threshold of another glorious room, this one boasting a split stairwell that could fit ten fully grown males holding hands.

"Are you working for Lorcan?" I tow my gaze back to Catriona's.

"No." Her rouged mouth tightens, forming concentric parentheses around their corners. I take it she's no fan of the Crows. But if she's no fan of the new king and resisting the other king, then where does she stand?

At my frown, Sybille explains, "We're working for humans. We're working to make Rax safer and salubrious. Lorcan is funding our cause because of a deal Antoni struck with Bronwen ages ago."

I remember Sybille mentioning something about her sister and Antoni's illicit activities in Racocci. I also remember Antoni discussing cutting dust with that Fae guard that very same night.

"What deal?" I finally ask.

"He hasn't shared it with us." Although Sybille's voice doesn't waver, there's something in her expression that gives me pause.

I am so well versed in all things Sybille that I deduce she knows everything about Antoni's deal, but Catriona does not. Does my friend not trust Catriona's intent? Personally, I find the courtesan's enthusiasm to help humans a tad odd considering how readily she transformed the shape of her ears with pointy jewels and how poorly she would address the Amaris' Racoccin maid, Flora.

Deciding to press Sybille for details once we're alone, I ask instead, "And no Fae is aware of your *resistance?*"

"Oh, they're fully aware of our voyages to Rax to ferry over food and construction materials to build them sturdier abodes." Catriona's shoulder-length locks glitter gold in the faerie light spilling off a decadent candelabra mounted with multihued tourmalines.

Sybille rolls her eyes. "*Our? You* knocked on our door *yesterday. You* have not traveled to Rax yet."

"I offered to come, but Antoni insisted he and his companions had everything handled and that you and I should shop for provisions to make this mansion homier." Catriona nods to the house, her gaze stroking over each cornice and cut stone before leveling back on my face. "The estate used to belong to the marquess Ptolemy Timeus. I heard you two were well acquainted, Fallon."

My skin crawls at the sound of his name. Sparks of the night he attacked Minimus score the backs of my lids. "Lorcan bought it off the marquess?"

Sybille's full lips draw open around a blinding smile. "Lorcan bought it from Dante."

"I don't—I'm uncertain I follow." Or rather I'm entirely certain I don't follow.

"Timeus mysteriously disappeared a week ago." Sybille's confession pinches the muscle behind my ribs that had seized up upon learning that I was in the home of the loathed high Fae. "Since the man had no heirs, his estate reverted to the crown. Dante offered to sell Lorcan a bunch of other homes, even offered him an entire island in Tarelexo, but Lorcan insisted on purchasing *this* Tarecuorin estate."

My lashes beat as rapidly as Lore's wings the day he tried to carry me out of the tidal wave's path. Does the Crow king know of my history with the amber-eyed Fae? Did *he* make him disappear? *No.* A week ago, we were still collecting his crows. He wouldn't have risked being exposed to avenge me and my serpent.

Antoni then? After all, this is now *his* house, and he was aware of my twilit spat. But again, the timeline is awry. He was in the south, wrangling the galleon. And it couldn't have been Dante, since he was chasing me across the kingdom.

If I believed in coincidences, I'd deem the marquess's disappearance a stroke of luck. "Why did Lorcan insist on buying this one?"

"Because of the private wharf." Antoni's voice booms across the glass-paned hallway.

I whirl on myself, finding the captain and his two mates rubbing droplets of water from their shaggy manes.

"Welcome to my humble abode." Antoni's mouth is tight as he mucks up his jade floors with boots glazed in mud. After studying me, his blue gaze lifts off my bedraggled appearance and cartwheels around his behemoth home.

"It's grand."

"It's not me. Then again, I doubt my likes factor into Mórrgaht's choices." For someone who used to embrace the Crows' cause, Antoni sounds thoroughly disenchanted.

"I'm sure you could sell it," I suggest when the silence thickens. "It is yours after all, isn't it?"

"My name is on the deed." Antoni's throat dips. "But I neither have the time nor the inclination to relocate. Besides, the ship I was given is too large to dock anywhere other than in Tarecuori, and considering our growing numbers"—he looks between Catriona and me and then tips his head toward the first-floor landing—"we need the room."

I turn to find the telltale smoky haze of a Crow tightening into flesh—Eefah's flesh. "I am apology, Antoni, but I follow orders."

"He's not angry with you, Aoife." Riccio trots up the stairs toward where the new object of his fascination stands, fully formed now. "He just thinks Lorcan sent you because he doesn't trust *him* around Fallon."

My breastbone prickles as I think of the note I shredded before dropping its fragments into the septic tank. Did Lore find the pieces and assume it was a love letter, like I had at first?

"Riccio..." Antoni rolls the *R* in his friend's name, evidently annoyed that the dark-haired sailor transmitted his distrust to one of Lore's trusted Crows.

"Don't know about the rest of you"—Mattia all but jogs to Sybille's side—"but I need a bath."

As he plucks her hand, a taunting glimmer enters her eyes. "I'm not in the business of bathing men, bibbino."

The corners of Mattia's mouth kick up. Because she called him *baby* in public?

When he twirls Sybille into him, pressing his sodden, mud-speckled clothes into her pretty yellow dress, I realize his grin wasn't prompted by the demonstrative nickname. "I believe you're in dire need of a bath now too, Signorina Amari."

"You scoundrel." She laughs, and it loosens the tension simmering between the strange assortment of lodgers.

Thoroughly unlike the shy first mate he used to be, Mattia scoops up a still-laughing Sybille and barrels up the stairs. A moment later, a door rattles shut on the landing above.

Catriona sighs. "Young love."

"Since when do you believe in love, Catriona?" I ask.

She side-eyes me. "You're right. I meant to say young lust."

"Have you been shown to a bedroom yet?" Antoni's question pries my attention off where the latticework railing vanishes into the ceiling.

"Not yet."

"Come."

"I can show her to one, Antoni." Catriona's heels click as she follows him to the stairs. "I'm well acquainted with the house now."

Without turning, he tosses out, "*Now*? Wasn't Timeus one of your most devoted customers?"

Her steps falter while my nose wrinkles. To think that, for half a second, I actually contemplated sleeping with men for coin. I may have lost my faith in romance, but I could never have done Catriona's job.

She perches her slim hands on her hips. "Women aren't given many options to make a living in Luce, so avoid your chauvinistic commentaries, Greco."

His back muscles bunch beneath his soaked black shirt, and he finally looks over his shoulder at the glowering courtesan. "Fine. That was uncalled for. But until you prove your loyalty, you'll have to excuse my suspicions. As for showing Fallon to a bedroom, this is my home, so I'll do it. Fallon?"

I sidestep Catriona and trail him up the stairs. Eefah detaches herself from Riccio's shadow to tail me. Although I admittedly like the Crow that Lore assigned to keep me safe, I don't need

138

her protection within these walls and pause on the landing to tell her so.

"I must keep eye on you."

"But surely not inside Antoni's home?"

Her dark gaze flicks toward the sea captain, then back toward me. "Unless he present, I must be."

I gesture to the leader of the human resistance. "Antoni's right here."

"She's not speaking about me, Fallon." Antoni's timbre is as cool as ice. "She means Lorcan." After a pregnant pause, he says, "He still believes I could alter your destiny."

22

My breath snags in my throat. Is Antoni alluding to me killing Dante? Is he aware of Bronwen's latest prognostic? My thumb relentlessly traces the grooves in the little stone still tucked into my palm.

Antoni's blue stare settles on my wide-eyed violet one. "He still believes that you, Fallon Báeinach, could fall for the likes of an untitled rebel like me."

Although his voice didn't tip in question, the intensity with which he hunts my face for a reaction makes me wonder if Antoni still harbors feelings for me.

"Except he dropped her off here, so he mustn't be overly scared of you," Riccio tosses out as he strides past us down the long corridor paneled in burgundy velvet shot through with gold. "Hey, Aoife, in case you ever get some downtime, my room's the last door down this hall."

"Downtime?" She repeats the word in her strong accent.

Riccio turns but keeps moving backward. "You know, free time?"

Eefah has the graciousness to smile. "I don't think I get much downtime."

Because Lore will be too busy wooing his Glacin princess... The thought lights up my mind like the gold sconces nailed into the wall covering, the ones that barely spill enough light to chase away the shadows.

"Sybille insisted that you get the room beside hers." Antoni wheels around on his muddy boots and treads down the hallway, gait as rigid as his jaw. He comes to a stop in front of the third to last door and pumps the gold handle with more gusto than necessary. "Curtains stay closed. You want light, you go outside in the garden." He sweeps the heavy wood open, granting me entry into a little living area fashioned in every shade of blue and turquoise. "Bed's through here." He pushes apart two carved, wooden panels.

Even the bedroom Lore lent me in the sky kingdom isn't as grand as this one. Then again, Crows lead a much humbler life than Fae. I don't want to find anything that belonged to Timeus beautiful, but as I run my fingertips along the rich brocade backrest of the chaise in the living room, I cannot help but admire the plush richness of it all.

Out of habit, I inspect my fingertips for dust. I obviously find none. After all, the marquess, like all high Fae, had an army of servants. Since I've seen neither hide nor hair of a sprite or a human, I assume that Antoni didn't keep anyone in his employ.

"Where's *your* bedroom, Antoni?"

My question swells the black dots in the captain's eyes until his pupils almost kiss the rims of his irises. "One floor up. Want a tour?"

Eefah doesn't speak, but wisps of smoke lift off her neck and skim the little black feather tattooed on her cheekbone. I've come to grasp Crow's bodily reactions well enough to tell that she's not fond of the captain's offer.

I wonder if she'd outright stop me from going upstairs if I decided to follow him. "I'd really like to bathe and change into some clean clothes."

His pupils retract.

"But maybe later?" I hunger to examine every centimeter of Timeus's home. "Do you think I could—that I could get some clothes? I didn't bring any."

"Sybille and Catriona filled your closet this morning."

I'm guessing I will find only gowns. Sure enough, after Antoni wishes me a relaxing bath and tells me that Sybille will stop by to escort me to supper, I uncover a closet bursting with rainbow silks.

"It is not good idea to go upstairs." Eefah stands in the entrance of my walk-in closet, wide shoulders almost scraping the sides of my doorframe. "Lorcan not like it."

"I don't mean to sound ungrateful, but I don't much care what Lorcan likes, Eefah." I start opening the drawers of the center island, which has been filled with underthings and accessories I would've bled myself dry to own back when I still longed for frivolous things.

"You care about Antoni?"

I jerk my fingers away from a lace choker embellished with sequins, like Catriona loves to wear. "As a friend."

"Only as friend?"

"Yes."

"Then do not venture to his private room."

I frown.

Eefah stares around the oversize closet as though on the lookout for a lurking Crow. "If you want to keep friend, do not go."

I close the drawer a little roughly and squeeze Mamma's rock in my fist. "Are you saying he'd harm Antoni?"

"He does not trust him."

"And yet"—I raise my arms and twirl on myself—"I'm here."

"But so am I, Fallon."

I soak in a scalding bath that reddens the pallor I acquired during my short stay in the sky kingdom. Eefah isn't hovering inside my white marble bathroom, but I've little doubt she's standing guard outside the closed door.

Although I've tried to relax, our earlier conversation runs on a loop through my mind. She's here because Lore doesn't trust Antoni. Since the sky king is betrothed, I cannot imagine his concern is born of jealousy. Lorcan Reebyaw must be worried I won't fulfill Bronwen's new prophecy if I become consumed with reviving an old flame.

After the last soap bubble pops, I heave myself out of the bath and secure a towel around my chest, then trudge over the delightfully heated stone and pick up a gold comb. As I run it through my wavy locks, it strikes me that nothing and no one is keeping me from rekindling something with Antoni.

The mirror before me darkens, and the white marble is replaced by black slate. I blink, but my vision doesn't clear of the sudden obscurity. Water pounds against stone, and steam suffuses the air that I'm panting too rapidly.

I draw my arms through the steam to disperse it. Where in Luce have I—

Oh.

Oh.

I squeeze my eyes shut, willing my body to project itself outside Lore's bathing room.

23

When my lids pull up, I'm still standing inside Lore's bathing chamber, and the male's naked backside is still facing me. I'm tempted to apologize for intruding on such a private moment but get sidetracked by the sight of the water sluicing down the ropy muscles of his calves and thighs and—

I swallow. I don't think I've ever stared at a man's ass, and I'm staring. I try to reason that the Crow king has seen me naked plenty of times. It's only fair that I'm seeing him without his leathers and feathers.

Feeling a tad less contrite, I allow myself to pursue my perusal of the disrobed monarch. It isn't like he's tossing on a towel anyway. Perhaps he hasn't sensed my presence, what with the spray drilling the stone floor in his open shower.

His trim hips and trimmer waist flare out into a V-shaped back with an impressive shoulder span. I deduce that flying, even in Crow form, builds some serious upper body strength. He curves a hand over one giant knob of a shoulder to lather oily soap into his skin, kneading the muscle beneath.

As the filmy cleanser streaks down the runnels between his shifting muscles, my gaze hooks onto a puckered patch of skin beside his spine. I've seen my fair share of injuries from the humans and halflings who've dropped by our house for one of Nonna's healing poultices to know about scarring.

How come the immortal shifter's body bears scars? Each time I freed him from one of the obsidian spikes wedged through some part of his bird body, his flesh knitted back instantly.

Actually, his smoke and feathers knitted back. I have no clue what befell his flesh, since until his five crows reunited, I'd never seen him in flesh.

His spine suddenly stiffens, and his bent neck snaps straight.

I gather he's sensed me.

The comb I'm still holding drops from my fingers and clatters. I jump; Lore doesn't. He merely twists his head to peer over his chiseled shoulder at me. The first thing I notice is the absence of his black face powder. Without it, he seems almost—

Who am I kidding? There's nothing normal or natural about this man. He screams preternatural creature with his glowing citrine eyes and those lethal cheekbones of his. And that nose. Real men don't have such straight, symmetrical noses.

There I go with his nose again. What is my deal?

I clear my throat and tighten my towel. "Um…hi."

Note to self: *wear clothes before exporting body into Lore's realm. Or better yet, stop exporting body where body needn't go.*

When he still hasn't said a thing and I've not winked back into my own bathroom, however many times I try to whisk myself away, I decide to make conversation. May as well profit from this fortuitous meeting.

"Um, the scar on your back…" I shift on my bare feet. "Is it from one of the obsidian screws I removed from your bowl-shaped crow?"

The sky kingdom may have running water like Timeus's house, but it does not boast heated floors.

"You came to discuss my scars, Behach Éan?" The faintest hint of humor gilds his words.

"Do I look like I came to discuss your scars?"

"You look like you came to share my shower."

My cheeks smolder, and I take a minuscule step back even though I don't actually think the Crow king is about to stalk toward me and pitch me beneath the falling water. "I prefer baths. Not that I came to share one of those." I look around, discovering a tub made of the same gray stone as everything else inside Lore's mountain.

It's not oversize, but it seems deep. I wonder if the Crow king ever steeps in it. Birds do so enjoy baths. And...

What am I going on about?

"Lorcan, you know I have no control over where my body goes." I tighten my towel some more, regretting not having slung on a bathrobe.

"Is that the excuse you'll try to feed me if you attempt to visit Antoni's private quarters?"

I gape at him, first in shock and then in fucking fury. How is he so well informed? Last I heard, I was the only one who could speak into Lore's mind. Or can his people communicate with him when they're all in bird form?

"*When* I visit Antoni's room"—I make sure to insist on the conjunction—"I'll have no need to make excuses, since I don't owe you a play-by-play of my comings and goings."

The knuckles on the hand he has splayed on the wall whiten.

Before my next heartbeat, he turns, and although threads of steam still crosshatch the air between us and dark smoke has begun to roil off his naked form, neither do much to hide the full frontal.

After a shocked glimpse of...*everything*, I bounce my gaze back to his clavicle and study it so acutely I could draw it from memory in the steam fogging his mirror. "Would you mind wrapping a towel around yourself?"

"I prefer to air-dry."

My gaze jerks to his golden stare that twinkles as though he finds my predicament thoroughly amusing.

"Besides, this is my bathing room." He stalks closer.

I don't know what soap he's washed with, but it seems to have deepened his thunderstorm scent. Before I can choke on the male, I start breathing through my mouth.

"Perhaps this is my way of proving I mean you no harm."

I glare up at him. "Funny, Lore. Who knew demonic kings were endowed with such a developed sense of humor?"

"Usually, it isn't my sense of humor that women notice when they see me naked or use words like *endowed*."

The heat in his bathroom becomes so stifling that *I'm* suddenly tempted to air-dry.

"As for my scarring, I heal from all wounds, but obsidian leaves a mark upon my skin." Although his gaze is on my face, he drags his fingers across his chest and arms, mapping out all his silvered scars. He even points to ones below his navel, but I don't trail his index finger, too afraid my gaze may stumble across parts of him that are not scarred.

His chest is riddled with imperfections. I wish I were a fan of perfection. I like perfect noses. Why can't I prefer perfect torsos? Why must I find each scar mesmerizing?

My fingers ache from how tightly I'm clutching my towel. "Why is the one on your back so much larger than the others?"

"Because it was inflicted on me while I was whole."

"I don't—" Did someone try to stake him while I was away? No. That wouldn't make sense, since I'm presently the only person who can handle obsidian. "When?"

"Five centuries ago. When Meriam and Costa stabbed me in the back."

"How come you let them come so close to you?"

"Because I trusted them, Fallon." No more soft curves grace his mouth. No more enjoyment kindles his gaze. "He was my most loyal general, and she was like a mother to Bronwen." He sidesteps me to reach his sink, where he picks up a sharp blade and begins to remove the scruff darkening his jaw. "I've learned my lesson."

I study his meticulous movements in the mirror. "Yet you trust me."

He tilts his head to reach the bristly hair on the underside of his chin. I've never watched a man shave, and it's oddly fascinating. "Meriam was never my mate."

My exhale gets wedged on its way out, making me sputter. "Just because I'm your—just because we have a connection—it doesn't mean I couldn't wedge a piece of obsidian through your back."

"You forget that thanks to our connection, I've access to all your thoughts."

"Oh, come on." I roll my eyes. "You cannot possibly access them *all*." *Can he?*

I can, Behach Éan.

I fold my arms in front of my chest, which ticks with annoyed heartbeats. "Then how come I cannot read all *your* thoughts, huh?"

"You could. If you concentrated."

"How?"

The slow scrape of the razor against his damp skin makes goose bumps rise along my own skin as though more than our minds were tied.

"Now, why would I teach a girl who's entertaining bedding another to read my thoughts?"

"I'm not entertaining—" I loose a little growl. "I just wanted to see Antoni's room, which I imagine was Ptolemy Timeus's, and perhaps spit on one of his throw pillows. In case you weren't aware, he was a gods-awful man."

The softest snort escapes Lore. "You're an odd little creature, Fallon Báeinach."

Although it's said with affection, it makes my hackles rise.

"I'm not a creature. I'm a woman, Lorcan Reebyaw. If anyone's a creature, it's you."

The corners of his mouth cant, and his eyes begin to smolder again. And then his big body begins to rattle as though a chill has enveloped his skin, but when I hunt for goose bumps, I find none. At least none on him. There are plenty on me.

"I heard the marquess disappeared." I avert my gaze, because even with a foggy mirror between us, the intensity of the Crow king is entirely too disarming.

Water splashes Lore's blade. When the metal is clean, he sets it down beside his sink. "Did he? How tragic."

"You wouldn't have anything to do with his disappearance?"

"Why don't you tell me, Fallon?"

Even though my gaze is locked on the little puddle forming around the shiny razor, I catch his fingers lifting to his damp locks as he turns toward me.

"If I knew, I wouldn't be asking, now would I?"

"My mind, Little Bird. The answer's there. If you want it, come and retrieve it."

"Am I not already in your mind?"

"No. You're in my bathing chamber."

"But I'm also in mine...right?"

"Right."

"So this isn't one of your memories, Lore?"

"It isn't."

"Is it like when I popped up into your library?"

He nods. "If mates think hard enough about each other, they can project their bodies toward their mate's, the same way they can project words into each other's minds no matter the distance."

"So my body is in two places?"

"Correct, but you can only hold this cellular replication for a short while, so if you want to glimpse the contents of my mind, I

149

advise you to hurry." The gold churns around his pupils, which have become mere pinpricks even though no light shines into them.

Although I'm still reeling over the fact that I can replicate myself, the bathing chamber darkens, and Lore disappears, and in his place, a Fae appears. The one who had me dragged in front of King Marco. Timeus's amber eyes are pitched so wide that there is more white than color in them.

"*Demon,*" I hear the awful male sputter. "*De—*" The second syllable comes out as a wet gurgle a moment before his head topples right off his neck and blood sprays my face. I gasp and blink. When my lids reopen, Lore's head is where Timeus's was right before—

I barrel past Lore and clutch the rim of his sink, the edges of my vision graying and whitening before filling again with color.

Lore stands behind me, his head notched above mine, his bare torso so close that the chill of his skin cools the sweat gathering at the nape of my neck. His palms coast along my biceps, except— except his hands are locked by his sides.

Breathe, Behach Éan. His whispered guidance does nothing to quell the acid scalding my throat. *Breathe.*

One of his hands—his real one and not the phantom smoke he uses in guise of it—wraps around my hair and lifts the short, heavy strands while the other strokes a line from the base of my skull down the rigid line of my spine.

"You killed him," I croak, my throat as raw as Sybille's the morning after Bottom of the Jug's annual Yuletide revel. My friend so enjoys singing louder than the hired bards even though she cannot hold a tune for her life.

His gaze follows the trajectory of his fingers that are gently bumping along my vertebrae. "I did."

"But he died a week ago. We were gathering your crows. So when..."

"You forget that I traveled to Tarecuori to check on Phoebus."

Oh. "Did Timeus—did he spot you flying around and call the sentries? Is that why you—you—" I decide not to finish that sentence, since Lore is plenty aware of how he ended the man's life.

"No one saw me." The smallest smile tugs up the corner of his mouth. "At night, I am no more distinguishable than air."

"Then—I don't—"

"Yes, you do, Behach Éan. You understand perfectly well why I murdered that man." He now thumbs little circles at the base of my throbbing skull, and I let him because—because it feels divine.

Even though my mind is still bursting with gore and shock, I stop to wonder if Lore was a masseur before the Shabbins transformed him into a shifter king.

No, he murmurs into my mind. *I herded sheep.* "I don't like touching people, and I don't like being touched," he adds aloud.

"Could've fooled me. About the *touching people* part." I try my hardest to stifle the little moan that escapes through my barely parted lips, but my hardest is lousy. Hopefully, the still-crashing water eclipses the sound.

Come to think of it, why hasn't he turned off the shower? Did he not finish washing?

"I don't touch people, Behach Éan. I touch *you.*"

"I am people."

"You are not people." His throat dips. "You are my...Crow."

That snaps me out of my daze, and I spin around, disconnecting his hands from my body. Although tempted to remind him that I belong to no one for the hundredth time, I ask instead, "How did you know about my quarrel with the marquess?"

"My stone imprisonment didn't dull my senses." At my frown, he adds, "Have you forgotten where one of my crows was kept?"

In the Regios' trophy room. The one contiguous to the throne room in which my hearing was held.

He watches my round-eyed stare. "I cannot tell if you're terribly angry or terribly touched that I rid Luce of that vile Fae."

I swallow, but it does nothing to slicken my dry throat. "Are you planning on beheading more men on my behalf?"

Lore stays silent, yet his eyes betray his answer.

"You cannot go around separating heads from bodies, Lore. Already the Fae don't trust Crows and call you and your people—" The words on my Tarelexian walls shimmer in front of my eyes. "They call you awful things."

"Do I strike you as a man who cares what the Fae think of him?"

"No. But—"

"As long as Dante doesn't punish his people, I will. It is time they learn to respect."

This cannot end well.

He reaches around me to seize something beside his sink, and the inside of his forearm brushes my bare shoulder. Although I don't shiver, my humid skin pebbles. He rubs what he's lifted—a chunk of coal—between his fingers, then sets it back on a little wooden tray, and his arm, once again, touches my skin. I try to shift to the side, since clearly, I am in his way, but I freeze as he closes his eyes and lifts his fingers to the bridge of his nose, then drags either hand toward his temples, striping his skin.

When his lids pull up, his irises are arrestingly bright. *How I long to paint your face, Little Bird.*

My heart flaps around like a butterfly behind my ribs as I picture him dragging those long, cool fingers of his over my lids to show the world that I am his.

One of *many* of his.

Unlike mine, his chest lifts with unhurried breaths.

"You'll be too busy painting your Glacin princess's face to worry about mine."

To think she will soon stand where I stand.

To think she will gaze upon his golden eyes and silver scars.

The trapped steam of his shower and the roiling smoke of his skin caress my features. This is too much.

All too much.

I don't know why I sent myself here, but I want to leave. I twist my face away from his and shut my eyes and picture the home of the marquess. I visualize the white marble and the gilt-framed mirror. The engraved pebble I propped on my nightstand.

When my lids pull up, I'm back in my body, and another Crow stands before me, lashes as high as Timeus's just before his head dropped from his body.

24

Eefah looses a breath. "You have mate. That's it, yeah? You mind walked."

My first reaction is to *deny deny deny*, but I don't care to lie to Eefah. Not to mention that a blush streaks my face, and my eyes are as glassy as Minimus's.

"Do you have one?" I ask before she can inquire who I'm supernaturally connected to.

She sighs and shakes her head. "No. I still wait. Immy too wait."

I bet I know who Imogen would like to be mated with. Well, he's taken. *By a Glacin princess*, my mind is adamant to toss in.

"But my siér"—I imagine that means *sister* in Crow—"doesn't want bond. She too mated to Crow plight."

I cannot help the snort that steals out of me. "I'm pretty certain your sister would love nothing more than to be mated to Lore."

"Why you say that?" Eefah's mouth rounds with genuine surprise.

"Because she's always with him."

"She part of Siorkahd. That's job. That's why she spend much time with our king. Trust me, Fallon, she not want Lore." She shakes her head, which propels her heavy braid over her shoulder. "Immy too enjoys fighting to love make."

Was her hair and makeup really mussed from plotting Lore's next war?

"Who is mate?"

"I—I—" I bite my lip. "I prefer to keep that to myself."

"Oh. Okay."

She sounds so deflated that I add, "I haven't even told Syb and Phoebus about it."

"You think they not understand?"

"I think they won't understand why I've turned down the bond."

"Turn down?" One of her blackened eyebrows arches. "You can't turn down bond. It's blessed."

"I want to choose, Eefah."

Her lashes beat vigorously as though to clear her eyesight. "Your mate must be very sad."

I shrug. "He's already betrothed to another woman, so he got over it."

Her head rears back. "If he Crow, that not possible."

It takes me a moment to realize that since *I'm* part Crow, I could've potentially been mated with someone who wasn't.

"He not Crow?"

I want her to stop cross-examining me or she'll find out whose mind I can walk into. "Eefah, while we wait for Sybille to come and get me for dinner, can you teach me your language?"

Her nostrils suddenly flare, and I think she's put two and two together—after all, I did admit he was recently betrothed—but then her lips bend into a smile. "I honored to teach you Crow."

Although I'm relieved she didn't guess, the beats of my heart are each duller than the next. I turn away before she can spot the strange upheaval overtaking me.

As I plod into the closet separating the bathroom and the bedroom, I ask, "How do you say *dress*?"

"Dréasich."

"*Dreesseh,*" I repeat as I finger a coral-colored gown with a fitted bodice and a fluted satin skirt. Is it too much for a dinner with a group of rebels? I glance at the rest of the hangers. Except for one rather simple stone-gray frock, everything is over the top.

As I pull down the coral gown, then fish out some underwear, Eefah steps into the bedroom and slides the door closed, affording me privacy. I slip on the silk, grateful that Sybille splurged on such exquisite undergarments, then hoist the dress up and contort my arms to reach all the hooks and eyes.

I'm suddenly struck with the memory of Lore helping me into the gown I wore in Tarespagia, of the ghostly fingers caressing my skin, and a new blush splashes my skin.

I need to get that man out of my head before my body can— once again—project itself toward his, or he's going to start think- ing I *want* to be with him when that couldn't be further from the truth.

"How do you say *shoes?*" I call out.

"Bròg."

"*Brawg.*"

I hear Eefah rifling around as I snare the last clasp. "I have pen and paper when ready. I think it help to see words written."

I hoist up the strapless bodice that does wonderful things for my modest breasts, then select a pair of silver slippers—*brawg.*

I come out of the bathroom and head over to the little living area where Eefah has placed a piece of paper, an inkwell, and a fountain pen. She's traced two words on the paper—I assume the ones she's just taught me even though they look nothing like the way I wrote them in my mind.

"How do you write my name?" I'm relieved to find that my first name is written like I've always written it, then I'm shocked to discover that Bannock is spelled Báeinach. "And my father's?" I discover that Kahol is spelled Cathal, and that his brother, Keeann, is actually written Cian.

I ask her to spell her name and am floored to see that it's not written like it sounds. I ask her to write Lore's name. Although his first name carries no accent, his last name is again full of letters that don't fit with the way I've been pronouncing it.

"And Morrgot?"

She writes it down, and I follow each curl and sweep of ink with raised eyebrows and bated breath.

I've never learned another tongue, and I find it thrilling. "Crow is not an easy language."

"Né. It's not."

The minutes fritter into hours during which Aoife expands my limited Crow vocabulary, and I flesh out her basic knowledge of Lucin. I'm so engrossed by my lesson that I don't hear my door creak open, but Aoife does. She's out of her seat and standing, outlined in dark smoke before Giana has even stepped over the threshold.

The sight of Sybille's sister perforates my elation. Before she can even say hi, I ask, "How could you not tell me that Mamma and Nonna were in Shabbe, Gia? I came back for them."

"You came back for yourself, Fallon."

I don't get up, but I push my chair back and cross my arms. "That's unfair. And untrue."

"Are you planning on helping in Rax? Because if you are, you're going to have to shed the princess dress."

"Your sister chose this dress."

"My sister shouldn't be here either, Fallon. She's not cut out for what Antoni and I are doing. At least Phoebus was sensible enough to stay back."

"Phoebus came with me."

"Where is he?"

"I sent him back because I didn't want him to get hurt."

She scrapes her hands down her face. Her nails are torn and her fingers streaked in gray dirt that she transfers down the sides of her angular face. "You should've sent yourself back."

"Why are you being so hostile?"

"Because I care, Fal. I care about your life. I care about our fight. I care about making Luce a kingdom where everyone has access to everything. Where people are not forced to cut their hair. Where humans aren't treated worse than swine. And where magic can be used without rules or regulations, no matter the shape of one's ears."

"I want the same thing."

She sighs. "I know you do, but you being here, it paints an even larger target on our backs. The fleet of sprites swarming our front door has grown. The number of soldiers inspecting our boat and escorting us across the canals has doubled."

She presses her lips together, stealing a glance at Aoife.

"Not to mention that now we have a Crow in our midst, and Crows aren't allowed in Luce, save for Lorcan. If Aoife is discovered, who knows what fresh grievance they'll hit us with." She tosses a hand in the air. "Knowing Tavo, he'll probably station guards inside our house, which would ruin everything."

"Lore won't let that happen."

"Lore doesn't rule all of Luce yet, dolcca."

Bronwen's newest prophecy echoes between my temples and raises goose bumps over my bare arms. It won't come to that. "My pants will be dry by tomorrow."

"I'll lend you some."

"Dinner is serv— Oh, hey, Gia." Sybille swooshes past her sister in a teal tulle number that makes Giana's mouth pucker.

"How much gold did you spend on dresses?"

Sybille rolls her gray eyes. "I barely made a dent in what Lore left for us to use."

"He left it for us to use on— Never mind. Just don't spend any more on frivolous things, all right?" Giana backs up. "I'm going to shower before dinner. I'll meet you downstairs."

"Santo Caldrone, that one's been tetchy since we landed here. I think the last time I saw her smile was back in the sky kingdom."

"She very dedicated to cause."

"We all are, Aoife," Sybille says.

Although I don't refute this, Giana *has* been working with Antoni on helping Racoccins for decades. Sybille and I, we've just joined their efforts.

"Come. You're going to be floored by the entertainment quarters."

Aoife trails us down the wide stairs, then around them, through a set of mirrored doors that Sybille presses open with a great flourish. The U-shaped space is strewn with candles and tables and sofas and plush armchairs. I count five different sitting areas, because apparently, one isn't enough. As I stare around the garish crimson and gold room, I see Timeus's head roll off his shoulders, and I jerk to a stop, jerking Sybille to a stop in turn.

"What is it?" Sybille, who was explaining that the frescoed ceiling was apparently painted with real gold leaf, quiets and scans the room for danger. "Did you see someone?" she whispers, grip tightening around my arm.

"No." I palm my throat, craving the feel of smooth skin. "It's just—it's just Timeus was a truly hateful man."

"I could not agree with you more, micara." Catriona bustles into the grand room, her gaze stroking over the heavy drapes. Is she picturing them open?

What lies beyond them? The manicured garden I spied from the long glass hallway? I'm tempted to part them to peek, but Antoni was clear about keeping them closed. Not to mention I don't want to endanger Aoife.

Catriona has moved on to scrutinizing her. "You should really wipe the dirt from your face. One, it looks like you've rolled around in the mud, and two, it gives what you are away." Catriona has never been one to mince her words, but her comment is unwarranted.

"It's not dirt," I say.

She flaps a hand. "Yes, yes, it's war paint."

"It's tradition." Smoke curls off my Crow guard's rigid shoulders.

"A tradition that is not very popular these days."

"Catriona, you've said your piece. Now leave Aoife alone."

"Is okay, Fallon."

My skirt isn't ample, so there's no fabric to grab, only fabric to claw at. I claw at it. "Why are you here, Catriona?"

"To aid the cause."

"Except you don't care about humans."

"I care." At my peaked eyebrow, she adds, "In my own way."

"The truth, Catriona."

She adjusts the black velvet gloves she's matched to her black dress, a number that seems to have been created from a single bolt of fabric someone unrolled around her neck and crisscrossed around her body. "Fine. There was no more work to be had at Bottom of the Jug, and my roster of private customers held me accountable by association, so they stopped calling. Since I loathe silence and cannot live on air, I came here."

"You said you planned on helping. May I ask how?"

"I made supper." She gestures to a table laden with platters of food.

"You made—" I gape between the table and the courtesan. I've never seen Catriona lift a finger in the kitchen. "You know how to cook?"

"I am not entirely incompetent."

"Yeah." Sybille releases my arm and walks over to the table, filching a paper-thin slice of fried zucchini. "Should've seen my face when she offered to cook." She puts the crisped vegetable on her tongue, and her eyelashes flutter. "Wow. Catriona."

Catriona hikes up her chin and beams, then bustles toward the table.

Sybille seizes a pitcher of wine and fills a glass. "Who else wants wine? Fal? Aoife?"

Aoife shakes her head.

"I'll take a glass," I say, and Sybille carries one over.

"Catriona?" She offers her the other glass she's carried back from the table.

As Catriona takes it from her, I start lifting mine to my mouth.

"Fallon, wait." Aoife snaps out her hand and seizes the stem.

I jerk, and some wine splashes out of the rim, dribbling down my arm.

"Sorry. I am to taste your food and wine."

I balk. "Why?"

"For protection."

"Protection from whom?" My gaze hops between Sybille and Catriona before arrowing toward the double doors through which Antoni, Mattia, and Riccio are striding, all three sporting embroidered tunics and tapered pants ending in polished cavalier boots.

I've never seen the fishermen trio garbed in anything other than sun-bleached shirts and loose pants, so the sight of them in high Fae regalia is jarring. All they're missing are points to their ears and tresses that reach past their wide shoulders.

Antoni comes to a stop mere paces from me. His gaze slips over my coral dress in a way that makes Aoife tense beside me. "Do you have everything you need?" Although his tone doesn't drip with warmth or gentleness, it's not as biting as it was when I showed up earlier today.

"Yes. Thank you."

Aoife slips the wine into my hand. "Is fine."

That snaps Antoni's attention onto her. "We've no intent to poison Lorcan's precious curse breaker. Please relay that information to your king."

Aoife doesn't nod, merely glances toward one of the sitting areas, and a small smile warps her tense expression. "He hears, Antoni."

My heart fires off a series of quick beats when I spy Lore

lounging in one of the armchairs like a king on his throne, one ankle hooked over his knee, the opposite elbow digging into the armrest, two long fingers supporting the smooth edge of his jaw.

Since I don't remember seeing a throne room during my trek through his realm, I wonder if the shifter king even owns a throne.

No. His golden eyes burn a path straight for me. *For I do not believe that a kingdom is best ruled by sitting on one's ass.*

That spreads a grin onto my mouth. *A bird swing then?*

His lips bend with the ghost of a smile.

"Not that we're not honored by your presence, Mórrgaht"— Antoni sounds anything *but* honored—"but what brings you here?"

25

L ore's piercing gaze comes to rest upon his Crow. "Aoife
needed a rest."

My guardian turned tutor gives him a sharp nod
before heading toward a window and melting into smoke that
coils between sections of the drawn drapes.

"I don't think I'll ever get used to seeing someone shift into
smoke," Sybille murmurs to Mattia, who's got one large arm
draped around her shoulders.

I'm unsure if I'll ever get used to seeing her and Mattia
together, even though they're admittedly quite sweet.

"And none of your *many* other Crows could make the trip to
replace her?" The hard edge has returned to Antoni's voice.

Lore rises from his seat. "Since I can come and go as I please, I
decided to come. Besides, I hear you're harboring a new rebel and
was impatient to make her acquaintance."

Catriona's chest seems to still as the shifter king prowls closer,
circling her once before coming to stand beside me.

"Catriona Madaro, most reputed courtesan in Luce." His gaze
licks up her hourglass figure, from delicate ankle to ruby hair clip,
and although I wear an equally pretty dress, I suddenly feel like a
child playing dress-up.

She rolls her shoulders back. "Lorcan Ríhbiadh, most feared monarch of the sky."

Although I catch Riccio copping a look at the plunging seam of flesh between Catriona's squashed breasts, Lore's eyes return to her face and stay there. "I hear you volunteered to put food on the table."

"I need to pull my weight."

Lore ties his hands behind his back and walks over to the oval dining table, which he lazily rounds, occasionally leaning over to sniff at some fugitive wisp of steam. "Tell me, Signorina Madaro, how does one learn to cook overnight?"

"Overnight? I've been feeding myself for years now."

"With food from the tavern and from the bakery beside your house. Your kitchen has never been used. I took the liberty to check on my way over."

"You had no right to enter my home uninvited." Although she keeps her volume low, Catriona's tone betrays exactly how she feels about Lore's intrusion, as does the rising color in her cheeks.

Lore disregards her disgruntlement and pursues his questioning. "The window was cracked. Did you recently get into a fight?"

Lore? I set my wineglass down on the marble console pushed against the back of one of the many sofas. *Catriona has only ever been nice to me. Is this interrogation truly necessary?*

He holds my stare. *I do not trust the Fae.*

Half-Fae. And you don't trust anyone. I soften my words with a gentle smile.

"If you must know, a sprite was spying on me while I was disrobing. I tossed a book at the glass."

"You read?" Riccio asks.

Her nostrils flare. "*Yes*, I read. The same way I cook." She begins to back up. "I'm done being insulted. Enjoy what I put on the table. I'll see the lot of you in the morning."

As she whirls, I step past Lore. "Catriona, wait."

She halts and glances over her shoulder. "What?"

"Stay. Please."

Her lips pinch. I reach out and touch her hand.

Her gaze slips past me to scan the sea of faces. "Not tonight, but I will see you in the morning."

She slides her gloved hand out of mine and leaves, her shoulder bumping into Giana's. With a murmured apology, she vanishes up the stairs.

"What was that about?" Giana asks, in a fresh getup of pants and shirt.

"She cooks." I nibble on my lower lip as my hand falls back along the folds of my dress. "We were surprised. She took it— *not well*."

"Did you know she could cook, sis?" Sybille steals back her wineglass from Mattia, but he's already drained it.

"I did not, but I'm glad someone's taken up kitchen duty, or we would've ended up eating only raw food." Giana starts toward the table but does a double take upon seeing Lore. "Mórrgaht." She gives him a deep nod. "Will you be staying for dinner?"

"I will. It'll give us some time to catch up."

"I'm starving." Riccio drops into a chair and piles meatballs doused in a pungent tomato sauce onto his plate. When he realizes no one else has joined him at the table, he says, "Hope you don't mind if I start eating." He's already stuffed an entire meatball inside his mouth.

Lore flicks his hand. "By all means."

"We're waiting to see if you drop dead." Sybille sinks into the chair across from Riccio, whose tan has turned as crimson as Catriona's shiny barrette.

"Oh gods, he's choking." I start to take off toward him, but Antoni reaches him first and smacks him between the shoulder blades.

Instead of making the mouthful spill out, Riccio's throat

jostles with a swallow. His complexion remains mottled for horribly long seconds.

"He's still alive. That's a good sign, right?" Sybille says, eyeing the meatballs.

"It depends on the poison." Smoke swirls off the black leather encasing Lore's chest.

I'm not sure when he moved, but he's at present standing in front of me, so close that his smoke skitters over my skin.

Riccio reaches for a pitcher of water. Instead of pouring himself a glass, he drinks straight from the jug. "You're all absolute bastards," he mutters, setting the empty crystal receptacle down so indelicately that it crackles. "Seriously, Syb, what the fuck? Why the underworld would you say such a thing? Why would Catriona poison us?"

"I didn't mean *literally*. I meant it like she'd be awful at cooking." As she fills her stemmed glass with wine, she smirks. "You should've seen your face."

He seizes a meatball and pitches it at her face. She startles when it smacks her forehead before slithering down the bridge of her nose right into her décolleté. "You loggerheaded louse! How old are you?"

As she fishes the meatball from between her breasts, Mattia has the misfortune to snort a chuckle. Sybille whips her head toward him, the mother of all scowls shining through the glistening tomato smear.

Mattia coughs into his fist. "Seriously, Riccio. That was not—" Another chuckle shoots out. He attempts to disguise it as a cough. "Not—" He tries once more to reprimand his cousin but once more fails. Between puffs of laughter, he chokes out, "I'm sorry, bibbina."

"Oh, you're going to be plenty sorry later, bibbino." The way she mutters the affectionate term speaks volumes on whatever plans they had for after dinner.

An entertaining bunch, your friends. Lore's comment makes a smile flip the corners of my mouth. "How do you feel, Riccio?" he asks.

"Fine." He shoves back his dark-brown hair, then leers at Sybille. "Better."

"It's a shame nicer garments haven't given you nicer manners," she mutters.

"Because you think a nice dress—"

"Enough." Antoni seizes the back of the chair at one end of the table and pulls it out. He glances toward Lore, probably debating whether to offer it to him.

He must decide against it, because he sits. Then again, there is another end. Sure enough, that is the direction Lore heads toward, but before sitting, he pulls out the chair beside his and looks at me.

I nibble on my lower lip, realizing that he is making a statement, but Antoni hasn't offered me the seat beside him.

Perhaps I'm being a gentleman.

The fact that he needed to precede his statement by the word *perhaps* tells me all I need to know about the reason behind him pulling out the chair.

Lore's chest seems to grow broader beneath his leather cuirass. *And if Antoni had offered for you to sit beside him?*

This is his house, isn't it?

Lore's jaw is so tight that I expect him to burst into dark smoke and soar off into the night.

Do I strike you as the sort of man who lets another win, especially by default?

You're a king, Lore. You already have everything—a kingdom, loyal subjects, a fiancée. *Antoni has this house—that you bought him—his friends, and this cause—which seems intricately tied with yours.*

Lore's pupils don't pulse; they detonate. *Do you plan on offering yourself to him to make him feel more adequate?*

I don't plan on offering myself to anyone. Before we can create more of a scene than we're already making, I take the seat he's scooted back for me, but I make sure my expression displays what I think of his little cock swinging.

Nothing little about my cock, Behach Éan.

My cheeks smolder with annoyance. *It's an expression. I wasn't— You know what? I've changed my mind.* I start to rise but freeze when Lore picks up my hand and flips it, then holds it to his nose.

Did you cut yourself?

"No. Why?"

"Why what?" Sybille asks, leaning across Mattia to peer at me.

Lore sweeps his tongue over the scarlet smear on the calloused base of my ring finger.

Lore! Although I should've probably been alarmed by the fact that I have blood on my hand, I cannot help but focus on the fact that he's licked my hand. *It's probably just tomato sauce from Riccio and Syb's food brawl.* I try to pull my hand away, but he holds on to it, his cold smoke gliding between my fingers like silk.

It isn't blood.

I cannot believe you licked my hand. My cheeks heat like the desert under the Lucin sun. *Was that necessary?*

He finally releases my hand. *Yes.*

Why?

Behind him, the air darkens, and then those shadows take the shape of two men and one woman. I recognize the woman— Imogen—but not the men. Of course the sky king didn't come alone. He may be the most lethal man in Luce—in the world—but he's a monarch.

They're here for you, not for me. He says this without looking at me.

As Lore finally takes his seat at the dining table, Antoni surveys the three Crows poised behind their king. "What are you play-ing at, Lorcan? Bringing so many of your people will give Dante fodder—"

"Circumstances have changed." Lore unfolds his napkin and sets it on his lap.

"The circumstances being Fallon living here?" Reproach edges Giana's tone.

"No." Lore's golden gaze latches onto mine again. "The cir-cumstances being that Meriam escaped the Regios' dungeon."

The news ices my overheated blood. *Escaped…* "When?"

"No one knows, but the blood on her sigil was still fresh."

"I don't—I thought—" Sybille's spine is straighter than during those endless etiquette classes we were forced to take in school. "Isn't Meriam dead?"

"No." Antoni's answer surprises more than just Sybille; it sur-prises *me*, because the night he and I—

When Lore's gaze sharpens on me, I banish the memory and turn toward Antoni. "I thought you believed her dead."

Antoni's blue eyes lower to the ruffled porcelain edge of his plate. "I couldn't exactly tell you that I knew she wasn't. After all, back then, I hadn't been made aware of your lineage."

Sybille's mouth parts in shock. Since none of the others look surprised, I surmise she was the only one not told of Meriam's undeadness. "What is a sigil?"

"It's the way Shabbins cast magic," Mattia explains softly. "They paint swirly patterns with their blood. That's how Meriam erected her wards."

Sybille blinks as though an eyelash has fallen into her eye.

"Was my—" I still cannot bring myself to call her Mother. "Was Zendaya with her?"

"According to what Bronwen saw the night Meriam kidnapped Daya"—Lore's timbre is as grave as his expression—"Meriam por-taled your mother someplace. Someplace she surely planned on heading to before Marco seized her and tossed her in the palace dungeon. Lazarus was the one to tell me about this underground prison, and I was the one to disclose its location to Dante."

Marco shared Meriam's location with Lazarus but not with his own brother?

Marco murdered his father, Fallon. I've no doubt that if Dante had gotten in the way, he would've disposed of him permanently.

The outline of Lore's body has softened, and shadowy wisps coil around my trembling hand.

I fist my fingers to stop their tremor. Lore must believe I closed my fingers to rid them of his comforting touch, because his smoke glides up my wrist before vaulting back toward his body and firming the broad shape of him.

"Wait." Giana's gray eyes begin to glitter. "If you've found the sigil, does this mean it was erased? Does this mean the wards have come down?"

"No." Lore's answer snuffs out her hope.

And mine.

26

Giana frowns. "But if her blood is no longer fueling the sigil—"

"My Crows tried returning after Dante washed it away, but they collided with a wall." Lore slowly twirls the knife beside his plate.

"She painted elsewhere…" Antoni's theory is all breath, yet I miss no word. "Because she doesn't want the Shabbins to return."

"Why wouldn't she want her people to return?" Sybille asks.

Giana sighs. "Because they'll punish her, Syb. She's locked them on an island for five centuries. Remember when I locked you and Fal in the wine cellar when you were what—eight?—without realizing you two were in there, and I found you the next morning?"

We'd banged our fists against the door while yelling at the tops of our lungs before plopping on the dank floor and settling in for a long, cold night. I remember the feel of fur against my cheek when I awoke to find a mouse nestled against me. I'd petted the little creature, then shooed it off before Sybille awakened, because mice terrified her.

A tiny smile flickers across Giana's tense expression. "You, Syb, looked about ready to pitch me into Mareluce."

Sybille *had* been rather murderous. I'd been too exhausted and relieved to contemplate murder.

Besides, Giana hadn't done it on purpose.

Cellar sleepover aside, I get her point. If the Shabbins ever get ahold of my grandmother...if my father or Lore find her... Gods, they will quarter her.

No if. When. Lore's jaw is so tight and sharp he could probably cleave someone's head off without the use of his iron beak.

"Do you think she's coming after Fallon?" Sybille asks. "Since she hates Crows and all, and Fal is the only one who can 'wake' you?"

Riccio forks another meatball and holds it in front of his lips. "If I'd been held in a dungeon by a Fae, I'd have had way more beef with the Fae than with the Shabbins." He stuffs the meatball into his mouth and chews twice before swallowing it and spearing another.

Mattia snatches the platter before he can do away with all of them. As he spoons some onto his plate, then Sybille's, he asks, "Why keep the sigil fresh all these years? Wouldn't it have been more pleasant to face her people than to be stuck in Fae jail?"

"The wards she created with Costa Regio are the only things keeping Shabbins from coming after her and ending her life." Imogen's nails lengthen to iron talons that clink against the armored breastplate of her fighting fatigues as she clutches her thick braid and tosses it over her shoulder.

"Meriam will not rest until she finds a way to undo us." Lore's voice crackles through the tense air.

"Us?" Sybille asks.

"The Crows." Lore stops toying with his knife and leans back into his chair.

"But you cannot be killed, only *immobilized*, right?" Sybille seizes the jug of wine and fills her cup, then Mattia's, then leans past him to fill mine.

She probably thinks a buzz will help me digest the news that my grandmother's alive and surely hunting both me and Lore.

I reach for the glass, but Lore snatches it from me, then takes a sip.

You could've asked, and I'd have poured you wine, Your Majesty. You needn't steal my cup.

I've no desire to drink or eat Fae food.

Then—my eyebrows bend—*why did you take my glass?*

All your food and wine will be tasted as long as you reside outside the sky kingdom. Didn't Aoife mention it?

She did. As he sets the cup back next to my plate, I ask, *Should you really be the one to test for poison?*

Poison cannot kill me, Behach Éan.

What if someone grinds obsidian into your drink?

My body evacuates it.

The fact that he uses the present tense is alarming. *You've already been poisoned?*

"Fallon can break my obsidian curse."

I startle that Lore reveals this to the others. Shouldn't that sort of information be kept supersecret?

I thought you trusted your friends.

I do, *but* you *don't, so why did you tell them?*

"Oh my gods, Fal!" Sybille's pitch is so high it almost tears a hole inside my eardrums. "You must leave immediately!"

My pulse swells, creating a cacophony beneath my ribs. I cannot leave, for I need to find— I shut down my intent before it can penetrate Lore's mind.

"I agree," Giana says. "Once Meriam's arrested…or killed—"

"Except that this is why Fallon is here." Lore drums his fingers. "She wants Meriam to find her."

Sybille gasps. "Is that true?"

"Do you have a death wish?" Giana hisses.

Antoni bangs a fist against the table. "Why would you let her out of your kingdom knowing she planned on acting like a fucking lure, Mórrgaht?"

Lore's leathers creak as he shifts in his seat. "Same reason you told her where to find the stairs I allowed Cian to build for his non-Crow mate."

I suck in a breath, then swallow so hard my saliva jams in my throat. *You read his note?!*

I read your mind, not his note.

That was private.

So was the existence of that staircase—which I'm having demolished. The same way I should have him—

Don't you dare finish that sentence. I grit my teeth. *You sit here, in part, thanks to him.*

I sit here thanks to you.

I snort. *If I'd known who I was bringing back—*

"Why does Fallon look as red as the meatballs?" Mattia asks Sybille under his breath.

"Because her malefic grandmother is on the lam," Sybille whispers back.

Lore strokes a taloned fingernail down the embroidered table-cloth, shearing the expensive linen like he's sheared the last scrap of my affection and appreciation.

The second Meriam finds me, I will have her paint me in her blood so you can never again enter my mind. My chair legs squeal as I push away from the table and storm out of the living area.

Dead witches cannot cast spells. His voice echoes between my thrumming temples just as I reach my bedroom door.

After I slap it shut, I yell through the bond, *Immobilized Crows cannot murder witches.*

Are you threatening to stake me, Behach Éan?

Better keep your distance.

Although he neither answers nor shows up in my bedroom,

I can somehow feel him smile through the mind link. I doubt he will smile when I head to the harbor market and procure myself an obsidian blade at first light.

I flop into bed, believing that sleep will elude me, what with a churning mind and an empty stomach, but sleep comes and closes over me like a wave. At some point, I wake to find Sybille lying beside me, hands laced over her middle, fingers drumming the stained fabric of her pretty teal dress.

I pluck a lock of hair off my sweaty nape. "How long have you been here?"

No light spills around the edges of the curtains, but the material is so thick, it could be midmorning, and I'd be none the wiser.

As I rub the sleep from my gritty eyes, Sybille turns her head and slides her lips together. "All night."

"Making good on your threat to Mattia?"

"Your grandmother is after you, Fal!" Her voice is so loud it clangs against my barely awakened eardrums. "Your grandmother—the *evilest* witch of all time—is after you!"

"I'm aware."

"That's all you have to say? You're aware?"

"What more do you want me to say?"

"That you're sorry for not telling me! That you're heading back to the sky kingdom immediately!"

"I'm sorry for not telling you, Syb."

"Go on…"

I fluff the pillow beneath my head. "I thought Lore wanted to keep the fact that she was alive a secret. I didn't know the others knew."

"The others *can* and *have* apologized for keeping me in the dark. I'm still waiting for you to speak the second half."

"The second half of what?"

"Of what I asked of you earlier. To return to the sky kingdom immediately."

My chest prickles. "No."

"You are."

"Never."

"She is out there, just itching to murder you."

My hands curl into fists beneath my pillow. "You don't know that, Syb."

"I don't—" She scoffs. "You can break Lorcan's curse, which will make him unstoppable. Honestly, I'm surprised Dante hasn't put out a kill order on you. If I were him, I'd murder you on the spot."

"Glad you're not him."

She shoots me an eloquent side-eye.

I smile; she doesn't.

I sigh. "I imagine he isn't aware of the extent of my curse-breaking abilities."

"Well, the moment he learns, he'll—"

"Kill me?"

"Yes."

I chew on my lower lip. "If he kills me, Lore will kill him. If Dante were up to no good—which I truly pray isn't the case—he'd go after Lore first, then after me."

"Is that supposed to reassure me?"

"Look, Syb, I cannot go back. Lore can pluck every thought from my mind. Can you imagine if your thoughts were no longer private?"

"He can see into our minds?" Her mouth and eyes gape. "I thought he could only put images into them!"

I reassure her that the seeing bit only applies to his Crows.

"Can Crows see into his?"

"No."

Her brow rumples. "Last night, it felt like the two of you were carrying out silent conversations. Can *you* see into his mind?"

Since I don't want to lie to my friend, I elude the question.

"What time is it?"

"It's time for you to tell me what the underworld is going on between you and Lore."

"Nothing is going on between us. He's engaged. Haven't you heard?"

She flips onto her side to better scrutinize my face. "How do you feel about that?"

"I've no opinion on Lorcan's betrothal."

She snorts. "That's funny coming from someone who has an opinion on everything."

"Fine. Although I believe this game of thrones and alliances is ridiculous, I could not be gladder that Lorcan will soon have a wife. Once married, he'll have no more time to eavesdrop on my thoughts."

Even though I keep my gaze steady on hers, the rising corners of Sybille's mouth suggest that she's not buying my earnest declaration. And *yes*, it is earnest. I'm fucking ecstatic at the prospect of having my mind all to myself again.

Sybille parts her lips, probably to pursue her little inquisition, but a succession of hasty plinks shears off her reply and draws her attention to the curtained window.

I think it must be a Crow and toss my legs off the bed to stand before they let themselves in. When the sharp raps start anew, I hook the heavy fabric and peek outside. My visitor isn't feathered, but he is winged. With a sigh, I drag the curtain open.

Sybille treads over to where I stand, bare toes poking out from beneath the hem of her dress.

The sprite's mouth moves as though he's bitten off a chunk of soft caramel. I tap my ear to signal that I cannot hear him. His lips part wider as he resorts to shouting. The glass must be thick, because I still cannot make out his words.

"Syb, can you understand what he's saying?"

"Nope."

I try to unlock the window but cannot find the latch. "How do you open this thing?"

"You don't," comes a voice from behind me.

I spin around to find Imogen standing on the threshold of my bedroom.

"As for what he says, Dante Regio wishes an audience with you."

I fold my arms across my torso. "And I suppose your king has sent you over to stop me from going?"

Her dark eyes taper. "I've actually come to escort you. On the orders of *our* king."

27

The large hammered bronze doors clang shut behind Sybille, Imogen, and me. Even though I tried to talk Sybille out of coming, she claimed I needed a buffer, what with my tendency to always speak my mind.

Gabriele stands aboard the military gondola, waist-long blond hair blowing in a soft breeze that smells like summer-soaked honeysuckle. I'm glad Dante didn't send Tavo or Silvius Dargento, for if he had, I might have pushed both overboard.

Gabriele's gaze tracks my approach before lifting to the five feathered giants eddying above me like a storm cloud. Their bodies cast shadows upon the swarm of nervous sprites escorting me toward the sturdy dock and the thickening crowd that white-garbed soldiers hold back.

Antoni's new black ship lists over the turquoise Tarecuorin waters, berthed beside a varnished gondola packed with silken pillows—Ptolemy Timeus's. Although childish, I have half a mind to hop aboard and toss every pillow into Mareluce. Since I am trying my best to act dignified, I shelve my juvenile revenge for later.

The tension is so thick that it makes the bowl of grapes Imogen insisted I eat—after testing one—bounce around in my stomach.

"Signorina Rossi." Gabriele inclines his head.

"Signore Moriati." I incline my head back.

Unlike Tavo, Gabriele does not insist I call him by his new title: Commander.

I pinch the fluid skirt of the gold dress composed of a mix of silk and glittery chiffon and step aboard the military vessel without touching his proffered hand. I settle at the back of the ship with Sybille and a glowering Imogen, whose presence aboard sends the four soldiers manning the boat pedaling backward.

Although not the most frightful Crow I've encountered, Imogen does carry a murderous clout that makes me glad not to be her enemy. As the gray-eyed captain powers us away from Tarecuori, Gabriele braves the frightful Crow to come stand beside me.

"You have tits of steel, Fallon," he murmurs.

Since he does not glance at my cleavage, I imagine it's an expression. "Because I returned?"

"Do you know how many people want you dead?"

"Do *you* want me dead?"

"However convenient, no. I do not. Thanks to you, I've become commander of Luce." A blond strand flogs his forehead. He presses it back behind his peaked ear. "Why *did* you return? Did your winged king not treat you well?"

"I returned because I've lived my entire life in Luce. This is my home."

The tainted walls of my house light up the backs of my lids. I blink them away, focusing instead on the powerful body of the emerald serpent that's jumping in the foamy wake of our vessel like a child playing hopscotch.

Although threads of sparkling magic vein the palms of two soldiers, neither hoses the beast with their fire. If one so much as tries, so help me gods—

"Why did you wake them?" Gabriele's platinum gaze is set on the circlet of giant crows.

Since I prefer he not find out about my foolish prophecy go-getting, I say, "Because I wanted to meet my father."

"Is he one of the crows trailing us?"

"No, he's searching for my mother."

"The Shabbin one?"

I don't bother acquiescing.

He lowers his gaze to the cobalt fault line that runs from Tarecuori to Isolacuori. "I was not aware Crows could swim."

"Swim? I suppose they can float and paddle well enough, but they're far better at flying. What does swimming have to do with my mother?"

"I heard Meriam killed her before Marco and Justus managed to trap her. I heard she tossed her own daughter's exsanguinated body into Filiaserpens."

I jerk my attention to the seam in the ocean floor. "You heard wrong." My heartbeats are so strong that each feels like a punch to the ribs. "Meriam portaled her someplace."

"Someplace in Luce?"

"My father has yet to find her."

Unless he's made progress on his quest?

I glance toward Imogen for an answer, but her full attention is on the solid gold wharf shimmering like the rest of the royal isle.

Imagining Lore is nearby—in some form or another—or at the very least eavesdropping as he does on the regular, I ask for an update. When he does not give me one, I surmise he's either not listening—*for once*—or doesn't know.

As the boat slows, Gabriele asks, "Don't the wards magnetize Shabbin blood?"

"They do." The surface of Mareluce is so placid that it looks as though a god has taken a hot iron to it.

"Then she must be in Shabbe."

"She isn't." I turn to stare at the stately male. "Lorcan believes Meriam may have bound her magic."

"Like she bound yours?"

"Meriam didn't bind mine. My mother did." Or another Shabbin witch. Unless it *was* Meriam?

Lore never did say who stripped my blood of its magic. Granted, I never asked.

Who bound my powers, Lore?

I wait for him to answer.

And wait.

When we dock, the sky king still has not answered me. I surmise that he must be out of range or busy. Perhaps he's in Glace, wooing his princess and her father. After all, he's not only marrying a woman; he's also marrying her kingdom.

To think that she will become queen of Luce…

Well, of a significant part of the land.

To think she will hold the title I once believed was meant to be mine.

"So tell me, why am I being summoned, Gabriele?"

"For a diplomatic lunch." Dante's voice reels my gaze toward where he stands on the quay, shimmering like a Fae idol in his golden tunic and sunray crown.

Here I'd believed he'd elect a more sober outfit than his brother's. "Good morning, Maezza."

"Morning has come and gone, Fallon. Just like your grandmother." He's replaced the gold studs lining his peaked ears with graduated black diamonds…or are they chiseled obsidian?

"So I hear."

He neither edges closer nor does he proffer his hand. Then again, why am I expecting Dante to offer me a hand? He's king now, and kings offer nothing to anyone.

I can just imagine Lore grumbling that my judgment is harsh, but the sky king does not complain. He does not speak a word, which reminds me of the night in Tarespagia when his voice disappeared from my mind for excruciatingly long minutes. Terror that something had happened to him had seized me then. Anxiety seizes me now.

What if I'm here because Dante has staked his enemy and is looking to do away with me next?

I should've listened to my friends and stayed tucked away in Monteluce.

What am I going on about? If Lore had been immobilized, his people would be as well, and none have turned into statues.

Still, I try to sense his heartbeats, but I do not know how to tune in to his pulse. I'm about to ask Imogen, whose body steams as though she were about to burst into her bird form, before remembering what asking would reveal. Unless all Crows can sense their king's heartbeats? I decide to assume he's all right, since no bird-shaped stone is plummeting from the sky.

"That is some crazy-ass ship." Sybille gestures toward the giant white vessel flying the Nebban flag. The hull is so shiny and white, it seems crafted from polished marble, but stone would sink, even if a whole fleet of air-Fae blasted air against it day in and day out. "I wonder how many coats of paint it takes to make it so white."

"No paint." Gabriele ogles the ship like Tavo eyed the doxies at Bottom of the Jug. "It's fashioned from a material manufactured in Nebba."

"What sort of material?" Sybille asks as she steps onto the wharf.

"A mix of different things." He lists them all, but the only two that stick are the pulped wood and heated natural gas.

Again, he offers me his hand.

Again, I don't take it as I shuffle past Sybille toward the Fae monarch who seems to have grown taller. Surely an illusion caused by his crown.

His eyes slowly drop down my body, tracing the panels of shimmering fabric that wrap around my slight curves—sheer around my collarbone, arms, and legs, opaque everywhere else. "I'm honored you wore my gown."

"*Your* gown?" I cock an eyebrow. "I wasn't aware you owned dresses, Maezza."

His pupils shrink before distending, like his mouth. "I see your stay in the sky kingdom hasn't done away with your sense of humor. I was afraid you'd be returned as stern as the rest of Ríhbiadh's flock."

"*Returned*? I'm not some abject present Lorcan is sending back." Not that I've been much of a gift.

"That's not—" The fragile smile that lifted a corner of Dante's mouth tips back down. "Not how I meant it, Fal."

"Fallon. You lost the right to use my nickname the day you left me behind on that mountain and stole my horse. Which I want back. Where is my beautiful stallion?"

An entire minute slips by before he murmurs, "On the barrack island."

"Please arrange for him to be brought to Antoni's house."

Dante grinds his jaw at my demand. "Gabriele will see to his safe return."

The king and his commander exchange a look that makes me add, "Alive and well."

"The fact that you believe me capable of sending you a dead horse out of spite makes me wonder what brainwashing you incurred in Lorcan's realm."

"Unlike in Luce," I say, "Crows do not brainwash their people, Maezza."

Sybille stares at me with eyes so wide they've usurped a full third of her face. "Fal…"

Dante interrupts whatever she was about to hiss at me. "I invited you here to make amends for how we parted and what was done to your house. I did not convene you so you'd spit on my kingdom and call me a monster, Fallon."

My ribs clench at his rebuke, and I lower my gaze to his tall boots that have been waxed to a high shine. "You're right. That was unfair."

For several breaths, we just stand there—me gazing at his feet and him gazing at my downturned face. How far we fell when he rose.

Dante must forgive me, because on a sigh, he crooks his arm. "Allow me to escort you to the stone veranda."

I glance up to check that it is me he's asked. When I find his blue eyes leveled on my violet ones, I feel even worse for my earlier scathing comment. I dislike this girl I've become, so bitter and sour, who seeks the bad in people before rummaging for the good.

As I thread my arm through his, I murmur, "You really hurt me, Dante."

He turns quiet for almost a full minute. "The gown I was alluding to earlier was the one I bought you for Marco's revel."

My lashes reel high.

"The one you wear resembles the one I had sewn." His Adam's apple rises and falls as he tracks the flutter of fabric that parts around my bare legs with each step. "I thought—hoped—you'd remembered and that it was the reason you wore it, the same way I hoped you'd come back"—he licks his upper lip and lowers his voice to add—"for me."

Dante never factored into my reasons for returning to Luce. "Are you happy?" I ask him.

"Happy?"

"Yes. Happy. Are you happy to sit on a throne and marry a princess?"

"I would rather marry another princess."

The memory of the pallid Glacin shrivels my heart. "Perhaps it's not too late to swap with Lore."

Dante's forehead puckers before smoothing. "Fallon, I'm not speaking of Alyona."

"One of her sisters then?"

He halts. "I'm speaking of you."

My heart holds as still as the both of us. "I'm not a princess."

"Your great-grandmother sits on the Shabbin throne."

"Last we talked, you called Shabbe an island."

He shrugs. "When you have a common enemy"—his gaze wanders over my shoulder—"you find your views shifting."

"Are you speaking of Meriam?"

He nods.

"How did she escape?"

His attention returns to my face before wandering up the shell of my ear to the little hoop outfitted with the ochre crystal. "I believe Lazarus let her out, even though Lorcan refuses to hold the healer accountable."

azarus?! As we traverse gold bridge after gold bridge, Dante's absurd theory runs on a loop inside my mind.

The giant Fae wanted Marco gone, not Lore. By freeing Meriam, he'd be dooming Lore's reign, and he seems to appreciate Lore, so that makes no sense.

"What is being done to retrieve Meriam?" I ask.

"I've tasked Dargento and several legions of sprites to sniff her out."

I swing my gaze off the olive tree grove. "You must be kidding. Silvius?"

"Yes. Silvius."

"The male wants me dead."

"The male also wants to be reinstated in my regime. He will not harm you."

I snort.

"What?" Dante's jaw stiffens in annoyance.

"He may not harm me himself, but if he does find Meriam, he'll assuredly lead her to my door and hand her a dagger."

"I've sprites watching over you, and I've granted Lorcan permission to send some more birds into my lands. I fathom you are currently better guarded than I. Not to mention that it'll keep

Dargento busy and away. Isn't that what you want?"

"What I want is for him not to exist," I mutter under my breath.

If Dante hears me, which he must—not only is he a pure-blooded Fae, but he also stands mere centimeters from me—he doesn't ask why I want the man dead. Either he does not care or he does not want to get involved.

As we walk up shimmery stone steps, past a carved archway, I'm momentarily pulled out of my glumness by the splendor of the columned veranda with its garlands of yellow vines in full bloom and the rosette cutouts in the pale stone.

Dante comes to a stop and slowly drops my arm. "Fallon, I'd like you to meet my betrothed, Eponine, and her father, King Pierre Roy."

My attention swerves off the stonework and onto an ornate dining table. Sybille, who trekked through Isolacuori beside Gabriele, bumps shoulders with me.

"Santo Caldrone," she murmurs. "We're lunching with two kings?"

My Crow vigilantes dive beneath the arches. Where some perch on the balustrades, others rise to the tall stone eaves and pace the air. With a squeak, Eponine releases the gold wineglass she'd been lifting to her painted mouth.

Although the goblet doesn't shatter, the large terra-cotta plate it hits cracks, and a crimson splash lurches from the goblet's rim, splattering the burgundy velvet she wears. The servants, who haven't seized up at the sight of my feathered companions, jump to attention, wet and dry cloths at the ready.

Unlike Eponine, her father does not make a sound, but the harsh lines of his face visibly sharpen. As he surveys my assigned guards, I survey the Nebbans who sit across from each other.

They look almost identical, what with their twin green eyes and narrow faces, matching brown hair shot through with various shades of gold, slender noses and tall foreheads that one has adorned with a crown of golden thorns and the other with a jeweled headpiece.

Sybille drops into a low curtsy. When she sees I haven't followed suit, she tugs on my wrist. I don't sink into a reverential squat, but I do incline my head toward father and daughter.

Although I cannot see much of Eponine since she sits, the triangular shape of her torso baffles me. Until I recall Sybille explaining that Nebban women use corsets to crush their rib cages so a man can encircle their waists with his hands. I hope Eponine isn't planning on making Lucins adopt such a barbaric trend.

A round-eared woman with chin-length hair dressed in a white sheath pulls out the chair beside King Roy and nods to me. The fine hairs along my arms rise, because I don't care to sit so close to the man nicknamed the Butcher of Nebba, but refusing will cause tension, and I want to keep the peace.

Besides, women are allowed to be soldiers in Nebba, so perhaps the man's reputation is unmerited.

As I tuck myself into the proffered chair, I launch right into that subject. "I hear you let women into your army."

"You hear correctly." Pierre Roy turns in his seat, the emerald tunic he wears barely creasing as he turns. Although centuries-old, the monarch's skin is unlined.

"*All* women?"

"All those who wish to fight for Nebba."

"Even halflings?"

"Even humans, Mademoiselle Rossi." He tilts his head, his gaze slinking over each one of my features, as though he'd never looked upon such an exotic face. Save for the hue of my eyes, nothing about me is exotic. "Just like your king."

I look past Pierre at Dante, who's lowering himself into the seat at the head of the table between father and daughter. "You're allowing women into the army?"

Dante halts midsquat, palms flat on the table.

Pierre leans back. "I didn't realize you still considered the Fae monarch your king."

My faux pas hits me at the same time as Sybille's foot. Why the Cauldron did my mind hop to Dante when Roy mentioned my king?

"I don't have a king," I end up saying. "I have a queen. Have you ever met her, Maezza?"

"I had the chance to meet Priya once. When the wards fell two decades back, she paid me a visit to discuss an alliance. I turned her down."

"May I ask why?"

"She suggested we join forces to take down the Regios, but the only thing I wanted, she wasn't willing to give."

"What thing did you want?"

"A Shabbin wife." His gaze slicks across my face. "From her bloodline."

My spine prickles. Yes, he added the word *line*, yet all I heard was the word *blood*. Although it isn't uncommon for a king to want to wed someone of his status, I sense his desire to marry someone from my bloodline has everything to do with the strength of my lineage's magic and nothing to do with rank.

"I hear Meriam is a free agent," I suggest sweetly, and also…how practical would that be? "Perhaps you should find her, Your Majesty?" I turn toward the Lucin king. "Would I be too forward in supposing that you'd assist your future father-in-law in his search and"—since the term *rescue* doesn't seem fitting, I swap it for—"*capture*, Dante?"

My suggestion is met with a stony-faced expression on Dante's part. Pierre, on the other hand, seems quite amused.

"I know for certain you'd have Lore's backing, Maezza." I wonder if Lore's listening. "Come to think of it, it would make for great alliance building."

Eponine coughs, and since she's setting her wineglass down, I imagine the bubbly liquid went down the wrong pipe.

Pierre slings one arm around the sculpted back of his armchair, swiveling more fully toward me. "We've got a real little diplomat on our hands, Dante."

I glance toward Dante, whose jaw is slowly ticking. I wonder why my suggestion perturbs him. Shouldn't he be enthusiastic for any and all help in finding the runaway witch who surely wants him dead by proxy? He may not have imprisoned her himself, but like Mattia suggested last night, she must have a bone to pick with every member of the Regio line.

"But I have to wonder"—Pierre tilts his head—"why go through all this trouble when Priya's great-granddaughter sits at my side?"

29

Pierre's words stiffen my posture to the point where, when I shift on my seat, my skeleton creaks like old floorboards. "Oh, you don't want me, Your Majesty. I'm out of order."

Pierre's attention falls on my palpitating carotid. He better not be imagining slicing it open to harvest what runs in my veins.

"I've zero magic."

When he doesn't look deterred, I plant my elbow on the table and hunch, then seize the flaky bread roll beside my plate and squash it between my fingers as I carry it up to my mouth. "And I'm horribly uncouth. Unfit for any and all regal events."

Before I can take a chunk from the bread, Imogen seizes my wrist and takes a bite. Since she doesn't drop dead, I sink my teeth into the roll.

"Just ask Sybille," I say around my mouthful of bread. "She claims I was raised by a den of serpents."

Is it me, or have Sybille's eyes grown so round they've spread to other parts of her face?

I make sure to add spittle. I personally find few things more disgusting than spittle. "Meriam, however, would be a great match." I slug down a loud gulp of water—*after* Imogen tastes it— then pound down the rest of my bread and wipe the buttery flakes down the front of my dress. "She's had training, what with having been Dante's grandfather's concubine."

Although he's watching me eat, Pierre's face doesn't contort in repugnance. "Delightful, aren't you?"

Eponine coughs again. This time, since she's not gulping down wine, I think she may be coughing to cover up her horror that her father would find someone like me delightful.

A smile tightens Sybille's features. "She has her moments." Clearly, she doesn't believe this is one of them.

Pierre's smile only firms up.

I drain my water, then set the empty goblet back down beside my wineglass, which is being filled by the same halfling who tucked my chair under the table. "No wine for me, thank you." I need my wits about me.

The halfling pauses midpour and glances at Dante as though to get his take on my liver's fate. When he flaps his fingers, she backs up and circles the table toward Sybille.

"What a change you've brought upon our world, Mademoiselle Rossi." Pierre's gaze flicks between Imogen and the giant black birds dotting the stone veranda. "I'm surprised, though, not to find Ríhbiadh at your side."

"He's a busy man."

"We are *all* busy men."

I've hit a nerve. *Finally.* I persevere on my streak. "Except you, sire, haven't been dead to the world for five centuries and twenty some years."

I expect the male to scowl and hoist his chin as the high and pointy so love to do, but instead, Pierre grins again, teeth as white as his ship's hull. "Lucin women are so delightfully spirited, in contrast to the proper dullards we raise in Nebba. Apologies, Dante. I did try my best with Eponine, but her mother, rest her soul, tried harder."

My head rears back at how he's just insulted his daughter *and* dead wife in the same sentence. Granted, Eponine has yet to say a word, so she could very well be dull, but Pierre's her father. Fathers have a genetic obligation to find their offspring extraordinary.

He turns toward Dante and nods. "You were right."

My attention volleys between the two kings. "About?"

Pierre tips me a smile that makes me want to scrub my skin raw with salt. "That I'd enjoy meeting you, my dear."

"Why in the world would you enjoy meeting a scazza like me?"

"Because Nebba needs a queen."

My heart misses a beat. Is he saying what I believe he's saying?

"If you stopped murdering your queens, Pierre, you'd have no need for a new one."

I whip my head in the direction of the deep voice that's just spoken.

Lore stands at the head of the table, directly across from Dante, strapped to the gills in iron armor. "You invite me to lunch yet don't save me a seat, then attempt to marry off one of my Crows to an enemy king? Where are your manners, Regio?"

Dante holds himself as stiffly as the collar on his gold tunic. "I was told you were in Glace."

"I was. Vladimir's daughter sends her love."

As he gestures for a seat to be brought out for the third king, Dante's cheeks hollow. "Have you selected a date and place for your nuptials?"

"Vlad and I are still ironing out the terms of our alliance." Lore sinks into the seat between Sybille and me, the air dark with the shadows of the extra guards he's brought with him. "Have you and Eponine set a date for your nuptials?"

Dante works his jaw from side to side. Since he's yet to touch the flaky roll on his bread plate, I imagine it isn't food but annoyance that bastes his tongue.

"They'll be wed within a fortnight." It's Pierre who answers.

"How wonderful. I'll be sure to keep that week wide open in

order to attend the festivities. Faerie weddings are oh so joyous. And speaking of weddings." Lore leans back in his chair. "You will have to hunt for a wife elsewhere, Pierre, for Miss Báeinach's hand is not up for grabs."

Pierre's eyes slant. "Whyever not, *Lore?*" The man is decidedly afraid of nothing. "Is she spoken for?"

The sky king's pupils shrink. "Until the wards fall, Fallon's place is at my side."

"And once they've fallen?" Pierre asks.

I stare at Lore so hard that I manage to slip into his mind and hear him hiss, **So will you.** Since he's looking at Pierre, I imagine his thoughts are directed at the Nebban king and not at me.

"Once they've fallen, she'll be free to choose her fate."

"Wonderful." Pierre is making buds bloom and wilt in the floral centerpiece.

I stare around the table, pulse swelling my tongue and chest, and am about to blurt out that I've no desire to marry anyone, especially not the man known as the Butcher of Nebba, not even if he flings a trussed Meriam at my feet. But then I take a second to actually reflect on it.

A trussed Meriam would be the answer to most of my prayers and all of Lore's.

Don't you dare, Behach Éan.

But I do. "Deliver Meriam to Lorcan, and my hand is yours for the taking, Pierre Roy of Nebba."

The silence that follows my declaration is so complete that I can hear the breeze ruffling the feathers of my Crow guards and the grinding of Lore's molars.

Or is it his talons curling against his armrests that emit the sound?

30

Pierre is the first to move, glancing at his upper arm with a furrow between his brows. Since I doubt he's checking for lint on the green velour jacket that he wears over his high-collared black shirt, I assume he's wondering why my bargain didn't bind to his skin.

Fallon, Lore growls.

I pretend not to hear the seething monarch beside me, who is heaving more smoke than the bonfire I attended back in Rax the night Bronwen sent me on my wild-goose—pardon—*crow* chase.

"Why didn't your bargain prick my skin?"

"Because I'm not Fae?"

"Crows and Shabbins are capable of bargaining," Pierre says. "Any magical being is."

Huh. Well, that answers one of my many, *many* questions. "Then it's because my magic is bound. But you've my word."

The Nebban king glances away from his arm, one eye a little squintier than the other. "Except I'm unfamiliar with the worth of your word."

"Isn't the worth of my blood what matters anyway?"

Fallon, for Mórrígan's sake, stop baiting the male. We've no need for him.

I pay him no mind. "The faster we find Meriam, the faster my veins will bloat with magic."

Sybille wheezes as though she's inadvertently swallowed a large insect. Dante and Lore are both as silent and still as the stone pillars surrounding us. And Eponine…she's blinking at me with eyes as large as Minimus's.

"Mademoiselle Amari"—Pierre rests his forearms on the mosaic table—"what is your friend's word worth?"

Sybille startles at being called upon to testify to my character a second time.

I shoot her a pleading look that I hope screams *Play along. We need Meriam.*

"Fallon has never reneged on a promise." I'm about to blow out a sigh of relief when she adds, "However, do you really wish to marry a woman who will, one day, be capable of shifting into a bird with iron appendages? If I were you, sire, I'd leave her to Lorcan."

What.

The actual.

Underworld?

"Ríhbiadh?" Pierre snorts. "He's marrying Vladimir's daughter, is he not?"

"He certainly is," I say perkily.

Sybille holds my stare. "What I meant to say was I'd leave her to whichever *Crow* wants her. Or Shabbin, since I hear iron doesn't affect them."

A curl of Lore's smoke slithers across my collarbone. "You'd require Priya's approval to marry her great-granddaughter, Pierre. *And* the approval of Fallon's father."

I brush the shadows away, smooshing down the goose bumps they've carried along. "The only approval he'll need is my own, Mórrgaht."

"Tell you what, Mademoiselle Rossi. I'll have a contract drawn up for your approval. Once I've collected your signature—in blood—I'll put my best trackers at your disposal, and we will scour the three kingdoms for your grandmother. Does that suit you?"

"It does."

Lore's shadows slink over my skin again, but this time, they press down so hard, they feel like palms. "I cannot wait to inform Cathal of your desire to marry the man who is poisoning our oceans, Fallon."

I was about to break my vow of using the bond in order to yell at him for touching me, but his words freeze the roar before it can roll from my mind into his. "What does Lore mean by that?"

Eponine picks up her glass of wine. "I believe he's referring to the substance that counters the salt in our waters."

A memory worms itself to the surface of my mind. Dante once told me that the Isolacuorin canals were treated daily with a chemical manufactured in Nebba that thins out the salt density.

She tips her metal goblet to her maroon-hued lips and downs the contents. With a hiccup, she adds, "Father's lead scientist has managed to make the chemical self-regenerating." She presses dainty fingers topped with matching lacquer against her spasming lips.

Pierre's jade eyes harden along with his expression. "Take away my daughter's wine. She's had enough."

Because she's shared sensitive information, or because he deems her too inebriated?

"I thank you for your consideration, Father, but I will keep my cup." Eponine no longer hiccups. "And full at that." She taps the rim. "More."

The carafe-toting halfling hesitates.

"You are my servant, Liora, not his. Now serve."

Dante keeps quiet as though he knows better than to intercede in the Nebbans' conflict.

Pierre leans over the table and whispers something in Nebban to Eponine that makes the fine hairs along my nape stand to attention.

I fold my napkin and place it on my decorative presentation plate that is painted over with grapes. "How exactly does this salt-blasting compound regenerate?"

Pierre retracts his gaze from his daughter's and turns it back toward me, but it's Lore who answers, "The chemical feeds on the salt instead of merely destroying it."

Eponine readjusts the jeweled headpiece that graces her forehead. "At the rate the compound is being dumped, our oceans will be salt-free before Yuletide. Can you imagine? If I were you"—she taps the side of her nose as though to impart a secret—"I'd start designing swimwear, as every Fae and their great-grandparent will take up swimming."

I frown. "There'll still be the matter of the serpents."

She snorts. "Because you think serpents can—"

"Eponine, can you go check on what is taking the cooks so long to deliver our food?" Dante's tone is ice.

Silence stretches like boiled sugar between the two—scalding and tacky.

Finally, her chair is pulled back and she gets up. "Why certainly, micaro." She wobbles, which elicits a grumble from her father. "Got up too fast."

I'd heard rumors Eponine was a bit of a shipwreck. Although I don't much care for gossip, the future queen seems to live up to her reputation.

"Signorina Amari, accompany me to the kitchens, will you?"

"I—"

"She's our guest, Eponine," Dante says.

"But I need a crutch," she whines, "and she's the perfect height."

Sybille blinks up at Eponine. "I...um—"

"We'll only be gone but a minute. I'll make it worth your while, Bibble."

Bibble? My nerves are so shot that a grin drapes across my lips.

"My name is actually Sybille," I hear my friend mutter as she stands, and my chest spasms. *Not the time, Fal, not the time,* I chide myself, focusing hard on the painted grapes on my plate.

"I'm sorry about your pets, Signorina Rossi," Eponine says.

My hilarity withers. "My pets?"

The future queen of Luce winds her fingers around Sybille's forearm. "Your serpents. I may not be Shabbin, but I do care about the balance of our world." She wobbles as she heads toward the stairs.

"Perhaps you should care more about your own balance." Pierre looks about ready to hurl her onto a Crow's beak.

Although his voice is low and she gives no reaction, I've no doubt she's heard him. After all, her ears are pointy.

"Why is Eponine sor—" My palm rises to my lips at the same time as my heart rises into my throat.

Serpents cannot live without salt! By ridding our oceans of salt, Dante and Pierre will also be ridding them of serpents.

"You cannot do that!" I blurt out.

The soldiers in forest green shift closer to Pierre. Are they worried I'll spring out of my chair and claw his face out with my very human nails, which, granted, are sharper than they've ever been but still not as useful as iron talons?

"We are kings. We can do anything." Pierre polishes his crown of golden thorns with a long thumb. "Besides, we will be augmenting the supply of potable water."

Still care to pledge yourself to this man? Lore's mild tone sparks my already fiery temper.

I shoot a glare his way. **Why don't you worry about your own fucking betrothal?**

His mouth bends with the murkiest smile, one that says *Look at you breaking your vow never to speak into my mind again.* Or maybe his warped lips say *Enjoy lying in the filthy bed you've just made for yourself.*

"What are your thoughts on this salt-blasting compound, Mórrgaht?" I snap.

Lore presses his chair back as though to stand, but he doesn't. He merely hooks his ankle over his opposite knee and reclines in his seat, settling in. "Crows have no need for salt or serpents, so it matters little to me."

"Except"—I match his smile with a frigid one of my own— "you've need for me still. You said so yourself."

"Only until Meriam is found." Wisps of darkness rise from his iron pauldrons. "Which should be soon thanks to Dante, who's put his very best trackers on the job. How fortunate that our ambitions align." Lore's gaze wanders toward the Lucin Fae king, who sits erect and quiet on his chair. "Both of us desiring a wardless world. How spectacular it will be once the Shabbins roam free." Lore plants his elbow on his armrest and rests his chin on two curved, iron-tipped fingers. "Right, Regio?"

Why does it feel as though Lore is taunting Dante?

The embellishments in Dante's braids clink as he squares his shoulders. "Who isn't eager for Shabbins to roam freely once more?"

Um...*him.*

When serving girls approach, balancing plates covered by gold cloches, I tear my attention off the goading monarchs.

If the food is here, then why aren't Sybille and Eponine?

Dread begins to froth behind my breastbone as I scan the castle grounds for two women in fancy gowns. Did the Nebban princess really take my friend to the kitchen, or did she lead her into some dungeon?

31

A s our decorative plates are swapped for ones topped with food, Lore says, "Actually, Pierre, questing to retrieve Meriam aside, a marriage with Fallon would prove an advantageous alliance for our two monarchies. If you're still interested in binding yourself to Zendaya's child, we can work on drafting a proposal after lunch."

"I'm very interested." The Nebban king's eyes slither over what he can see of my face, which is not much considering I've swiveled fully toward Lore to better glower at him.

Unlike you, I didn't actually have the intention to bind myself to someone for personal gain. I press out of my chair. "I'm afraid the heat is making me feel faint. Thank you for this enlightening get-together, Maezza. Where do you suppose I can find Syb and Eponine?"

Dante brackets his plate with his forearms, slender braids rushing over his gold jacket as he looks left and right. "That is an excellent question. Guards, where have the women gone?"

"To the healer's," one of the white-robed men announces. "The princess was feeling under the weather."

Dante clicks his fingers. "Escort Signorina Rossi there, and see that she is given something to counter her lightheadedness."

Pierre rises from his seat. "Mademoiselle Rossi." He shoots me a smarmy smile as he takes my hand. "Such a pl—"

A dark shape coalesces between Pierre and me, all at once springing his fingers off mine and forcing my body to fall back.

Black swords slide out of scabbards just as deafening caws resonate throughout the stone terrace, tightening my marrow and detonating my pulse.

The darkness surrounding my body is so thick and absolute that I assume all five of Lore's crows shield me, even though I'm not the target of those obsidian blades.

"Stop! Everyone stop!" Dante shouts. "I will not have blood spilled on my terrace. We have a treaty, which I intend to uphold. You want to fight, you fight on Nebban soil, but Luce remains neutral. Pierre, Lore, call off your warriors *now*!"

It takes several heartbeats for the Nebban guards to sheath their weapons. And then a few more heartbeats for the Crows to land and Lore to reform.

He no longer sits, though. He stands. Right in front of me, his body outlined in smoke. "You are not to touch Fallon Báeinach." His neck rotates slowly as he takes in the rest of the Fae as though to extend the sentiment their way.

"I wasn't going to bleed her, you raging buzzard," Pierre grumbles.

The gold fabric atop my heart palpitates. Oh my gods, was that his intent?

The man is a psychopath, so who the fuck knows? Now get out of here before you throw yourself at more monsters and strike more foolish deals.

My head rears back as though he's slapped me, and my fingers ball into fists. *I was only trying to help our common endeavor, so screw you, you condescending, feathered ass.*

You've helped grandly. Now, go back to Antoni's, and I beg you, from this point forward, avoid playing games with rules you're unfamiliar with, for I've enough on my plate.

The fucking nerve of him! I'm fucking *here* because of him! As I turn to storm off, I use the mind link one last time. *Make sure my marriage contract is financially advantageous for me. I've never had much coin, and I hear Pierre Roy is loaded.*

Lore's armor creaks as he turns his neck just enough to toss me a withering stare.

Although tempted to toss out a few more demands just to spite him, it would be petty, and I pride myself on not being that. So I fist the glimmering material of my dress, and trailed by a livid-faced Imogen, I storm down the terrace steps.

When a cloud of sprites forms over my head, I spin around. "Dante, call back your air fleet!"

"They're for your protection, Fallon."

I gesture to the five crows that drench the sprites in darkness. "These birds are seeing to my protection, so it's truly overkill." I linger on the flagstone path, waiting for Dante to give the order that would prove he isn't using his men to keep tabs on me.

Although it takes several heartbeats before he speaks, he does end up commanding his airborne squadron to see me to the Isolacuorin harbor and then leave me in peace.

"Thank you."

"Don't thank me, Fal. They truly were for your protection."

"My protection from whom, Dante?"

"From those who wish my brother still sat on the Lucin throne."

"Wouldn't it be wiser to keep them around yourself then?" My comment puckers his lips, even though I didn't mean it to be grating.

"I suppose you're right," he finally concedes.

"Enjoy your afternoon, Your Majesties."

As I head toward the healer's with my Fae and Crow escorts, I stare at the golden slippers I picked to match my dress, at the pointed toe caps fashioned from mirrored leather and the thick straps adorned with decorative gold spikes. I thought them beautiful, but now they remind me of Lore's eyes, which I do not find pretty in the least.

His patronizing words ding through my mind. "Foolish deals, my ass," I mutter under my breath. I may have been punching above my weight, but I was trying to punch. Shouldn't that be worth something besides scorn?

I feel Imogen's stern gaze on my cheek. I've no doubt she thinks me a silly fool also.

"Roy has had eight wives," she says. "And he's murdered each one of them."

"Did they not run the castle to his liking?"

"That should not be a reason to murder your spouse."

"Cauldron," I grumble. "I was jesting, Imogen."

"You joke about assassinations?"

I swirl on her, my mood as raw as my nerves. "You're right. It was in poor taste. The man's a fucking monster."

"Yet you offered yourself to him?"

"I'm immune to bargains, and I only suggested it to get more manpower in our search for Meriam. I swear, sometimes it feels like I'm the only soul on this earth who cares to find my runaway ancestor. Shouldn't everyone be more worried that she's on the loose? Shouldn't Dante mobilize *all* his troops? Shouldn't Lore—I don't know"—I toss my hands in the air—"do something more than crash Fae lunches and plan his wedding to a foreign princess?"

Imogen's black gaze tapers on my puffing cheeks. "You should not underestimate our king."

"*Your* king. Not mine." Nails digging crescents into my palm, I streak off ahead of her.

"I suppose you're right. Until you wear our feather on your cheek, you're not a true Crow."

I grind my teeth but decide not to engage, for I've nothing

to gain from debating the value of inked skin. "Has my father returned?"

Although Imogen stares straight ahead, I don't miss the pulse of a vein at her temple. "No."

"Is he still searching for my mother?"

"No."

"Then what is he—"

"I'm not at liberty to discuss him with you."

"He's my father, Imogen. I've a right to know—"

"You're neither a Crow nor part of the Siorkahd. You have no rights. If it were up to me, we wouldn't be wasting what little manpower we have on protecting a flighty girl who'd rather have peaked ears."

"Cauldron, tell me what you really think," I grumble.

"I just did."

I pick up my pace. "It's an expression. And for your information, I'm perfectly content with the shape of my ears."

We traverse two more bridges in wrought silence.

It isn't until we come around a leafy bend that Imogen addresses me again. "When Lorcan returns later, he may be willing to answer your questions."

That would entail sitting down for a chat with him. "I'd rather sail to Nebba with Pierre."

She hisses, and I think it's because she mistakes my irony for truth, but her attention isn't on me. It's on the two Crows who broke away from the wreath above our heads to slam down on the footpath we're traveling.

As they morph into men, my pulse takes off like a comet, streaking across my rib cage. "What's happening?"

"Better keep your distance, for we've instructions to pierce your heart if you come within breathing distance of Fallon," one of my guards growls.

I cannot glimpse who stands behind the wall of brawn and

iron armor, but I'm guessing it must be Dargento. Unless it's my grandfather? Could Justus have finally surfaced, or is he resting at the bottom of Mareluce, being snacked on by serpents?

In the narrow space between my guards' bodies, I catch a flash of amber eyes and narrow face. "I'm not here for the Shabbin cunt. Not today anyway."

Cunt? I wonder what Dante would do if I marched over to the prissy turd, snatched the steel sword from his scabbard, and skewered his neck? Would he hold Lore accountable or just me?

"Such dignified creatures, Fae," Imogen mutters under her breath. "I cannot wait until Lore reclaims our kingdom."

As Dargento sidesteps the Crows, giving Imogen a wide berth, his scalding stare latches on to mine. "I will have to report your comment to the king, corvo."

"By all means, communicate my sentiment to your monarch. You can be certain I will be doing the same about the slanderous expression you used to qualify Fallon."

Dargento smirks. "You've threatened the Lucin crown. I merely used a part of Fallon's anatomy to refer to her."

"And I'll back the commander, for I've heard it all," a sprite who hovers too close adds, puffing out his chest.

I raise an eyebrow. "Commander?"

"A slip of the tongue." The sprite smiles, displaying teeth that seem too wide for his tiny mouth. "Although I've no doubt Silvius will earn the title back. Moriati is too soft for the job."

I cannot imagine that Dante would ever replace Gabriele with the vile Fae who lingers beside Imogen, a cruel smile slashed across his mouth. "Until our paths cross again, Signorina Rossi."

"I'll be sure to pack some steel for our next run-in." I sweeten my tone to add, "*Prick.*"

Dargento's palm drifts toward the ruby-encrusted pommel of his sword that looks a mighty lot like…like—

I fling my gaze back up to his face. "Where did you get that sword?"

Dargento's fingers freeze just above the faceted rubies. "I pried it off your grandfather's dead body. I didn't think he'd have any more use for it considering one needs a head to command a hand, and one of your beasts wore his on its tusk."

Each pulse of my heart feels like a stab.

Justus is dead.

A serpent killed him.

I wait to feel a wave of relief clap over me, but it doesn't come. Perhaps it'll come later. "A shame another of my beasts didn't adorn their tusk with your head."

Dargento's grin grows in cruelty as he backs away.

As soon as the foliage fences him off, Imogen barks at the soldier leading us across the isle, "How much farther is your gods-damned healer?"

"Just over the next bridge," the man replies, voice as tight as the lines of his body. Although he doesn't touch his own sword, his gaze keeps flicking between my Crow guards.

"Did you know my grandfather was dead, Imogen?" I ask as we start up again.

"No." Imogen mutters something about being led in circles.

Since everything in Isolacuori is round, from its five islands to its canals, I'm guessing we are walking in circles. But it is true that we've walked for quite some time. Perhaps we really have been taken for a loop. Why, though? To annoy us?

I trip, then come to a standstill.

What if they didn't take Sybille to the healer?

What if—

"We've arrived." The soldier points to a wooden one-storied structure with stained glass windows and a door bearing the sunray insignia.

Imogen shoves it open.

The second my gaze lands on my friend's black hair and mint-green dress, I breathe out a sigh of relief. Perhaps my worry was unwarranted, yet I cannot help how antsy I felt.

"Fal!" Sybille exclaims, startling the Nebban princess, who is inspecting the dusty vials lining one of the many shelves.

I frown, wondering why Sybille is propped on the exam table and Eponine is the one walking around. And where is the healer?

From the tight press of both women's lips, I fathom I've interrupted a conversation. "Ready to go home, Syb?"

"Yes." She hops off the exam table. As she bustles toward me, she looks over her shoulder at Eponine. "We'd be honored to attend your gilding revel. Thank you for the invitation."

My jaw slackens. The princess's gilding revel? Sybille better not have included me in the *we*. There is no way in Luce I'm attending festivities to celebrate the arranged marriage of my ex-lover and his tanked-up Nebban princess.

"I hope the healer finds herbs to help soothe your headache," my friend adds before turning her attention back to me.

As soon as the door shuts behind Sybille, I ask, "She's invited you to her gilding revel?"

"She's invited *us*—you, me, my sister, Catriona—as well as whichever Crows guard you that day."

Imogen's dark eyebrows slant. "I will have to run this invitation past—"

"No one," I say, "since I do not plan on attending."

"Oh, come on, Fal. Dante apparently wants to keep it super exclusive. Just family and closest friends. And we get party favors. *Regal* party favors. Which means *jewels*." Sybille flaps her eyelashes.

"Syb, we haven't returned to Luce to paint Fae gold so they may live an even more gilded life!"

"Let's discuss it later."

"No. Let's not."

She pats my forearm as though I were being childish.

"Actually, Syb, we totally should discuss it later. I cannot wait to hear what Giana thinks of attending the Regios' gilding revel. I bet she'll be *oh so* enthused."

32

When Sybille mentions the revel over dinner that evening—a dinner that the boys don't attend, having
elected to spend their evening moving merchandise
in Rax—Giana glares at her sister as though she was nuttier than
the fruitcake Catriona baked and that I've single-handedly demolished, after Aoife tasted it and gave me the go-ahead to eat it, of
course.

"Gods, Syb, what went through your mind to accept?" Giana
hisses.

Sybille raises both her palms and blows air against the
keys of the grand piano in Timeus's living room, making it play
discordantly.

I smack my palms over my ears, but Sybille catches one of my
wrists and yanks it down. "She said she knows where Meriam is."

"Where?" I ask at the same time as Giana snorts, "And you
believed her?"

"Unlike you, sis, I don't assume all purelings are evil." My friend
trusts too easily, and yes, I'm aware I'm the pot calling the kettle
black, but I like to think that my avian pilgrimage has taught me a
modicum of discernment.

Giana's head rears back as though Sybille has slapped her, but the only thing Sybille slapped are those damn piano keys that are starting to give me a headache.

"As for where," Sybille continues, "Eponine has conditions."

"Of course she does," Giana mutters.

"She'll tell us if Lore agrees to"—she raises one hand to her neck and mimics a knife slash—"her father the night of the revel."

I must've stopped breathing, because my lungs are cramping.

"Why the night of the revel?" Giana asks.

"Because the whole fam's going to be bare chested. In other words, not a scrap of armor." Sybille momentarily stops hammering the piano with her wind magic. "Have you never attended one, Gia?"

"No, Syb. I tend to stay away from inane pureling ceremonies. When did you attend one?"

"Last Yuletide with Pheebs. It was for one of his third or fourth cousins."

I'd been supposed to go as well, but the ceremony took place in Tarespagia, and Nonna forbade me from traveling to that part of the kingdom without her. Although she never outright said why, I sensed it had to do with running into Domitina— the daughter who turned her back on us when Nonna picked Mamma and me.

As a matter of fact, upon their return, Phoebus and Sybille reported that my aunt had been amongst the guests. They also reported that Nonna was as sweet as custard in comparison to that woman. Since Nonna was many things but sweet, I took it Domitina was wretched. Yet, naive me had held out hope to be proven wrong. My visit to my great-grandmother's estate had efficiently squashed that hope.

Xema and Domitina were plain horrid.

"Catriona, you've been to the palace several times." I turn toward the courtesan, who is sipping her tea quietly, pinkie raised like a pureling. "What can you tell us about Eponine?"

"She despised Marco." With a curl of lip, she adds, "I wouldn't be surprised if she loathes Dante as well."

"Oh, she definitely does," Sybille says.

Giana scrapes back her springy curls. "But that doesn't mean she likes Shabbins and Crows."

"Perhaps, but I think"—Sybille goes back to filling the living room with brain-numbing noise—"it's worth going. Even if no king culling takes place."

Bile bastes the inside of my mouth.

"Butttt…" Sybille drags out the last letter, dragging out the beats of my heart in turn. "We may be able to get her drunk enough to learn what she knows without spilling blood. How about we invite her to the house—"

"No." Aoife shakes her head. "Lorcan will not accept."

"Perhaps he can pay Eponine a visit?" Giana must be biting the life out of her cheek, because it dimples. "It would save us all time and energy."

Or that.

My vigilante's gaze flits dizzyingly fast around the bow-shaped room as though hunting each polished corner and gilded crevasse for an eavesdropping sprite. "What if trap?"

"Her claim to know where Meriam is?" Sybille glances at Aoife, who's elected to stand in spite of my insistence for her to sit.

Ever since she arrived this afternoon to replace her sister, she has acted incredibly edgy. When I asked if anything was the matter, she shook her head and attempted to smile to put me at ease. But her attempt was paltry and did nothing to quell my worry.

"Invitation to revel. Maybe she hope ambush Lore and Fallon." Aoife's paranoia speeds up my pulse.

"She really hates her father, Aoife." Sybille keeps pulsing air against the piano, filling Antoni's house with the strident cacophony necessary to camouflage our conversation.

"What does hating her father have to do with anything? She can hate him *and* hate Crows and Shabbins."

Giana's retort makes Sybille's jaw clench. "She wouldn't offer to hand Meriam over if she hated Shabbins."

"Hand over?" Giana snorts. "She *claims* to know the witch's hideout."

"Why do you have to be so fucking negative all the time?"

"Realistic, not negative. Besides, if Eponine is such a fan of Crows and Shabbins, why didn't she go straight to Lorcan with her information? Why come to you?"

"Because Lorcan is fucking terrifying, sis." Sybille all but yanks the strand of hair she's playing with.

"No move and no invitation until Lorcan is informed of situation, okay?"

Sybille rolls her eyes. "I wasn't planning on heading back to Isolacuori tonight."

"Will he stop by tonight, Fallon?" Giana's question tightens my neck.

"Why would I know his schedule?"

Giana stares at the fingers I'm drumming against the armrest. "Aoife, can you shift and ask him through your mind link?"

Aoife nods and shifts, and then her black eyes glaze over, resembling twin billiard balls. Two full minutes later, her feathers melt back into skin. "He no answer. Fallon?"

"Yes?"

She drops her voice. "Can you try?"

I stop tapping the armrest. "Can't shift, remember?"

"I meant mate way." She touches her temple. "Immy says you—"

The sound of Catriona's porcelain cup clanking into its saucer cuts off Aoife. "You married the Crow king?"

"What?" My cheeks warm from the sudden surplus of blood that swarms into them. "Of course not. Why in the world would you jump to such an absurd conclusion?"

She pushes a blond strand behind her ear. "Isn't that what mate means to Crows?"

"You don't have to be lawfully married to be mates. But that's beside the point, since I'm not Lorcan Ríhbiadh's mate. I'm not anyone's mate." I shake my head with great verve. "If I were, he wouldn't be getting hitched to another woman, now would he? Crows are very attached to their mates, since they only have the one."

Sybille has stopped trouncing the piano with her air magic. I really wish she'd start it up again, if only to drown out the colliding beats of my heart.

Aoife regards me a long time from beneath lowered lashes. "Fallon says truth. No Crow with mate would marry other person."

"What happens if a Crow gets a mate after he or she marries?" Although I doubt Sybille's asked this to take the heat off me, I cannot help but feel grateful.

Aoife's lips crook with a forlorn smile. "They will always choose mate."

Sybille's lips pop as wide as her gray eyes. "So they will leave whoever they married?"

"Yes. Very sad, but is impossible for mates to live apart." Aoife's dark gaze returns to me, and although I haven't known her all that long, I don't miss the quizzical look she ferries my way.

The one that says *I'm not convinced, but I'll play along for now.* Or maybe that is not what her eyes say at all and I'm merely being paranoid.

Wanting to steer the conversation away from the subject of mates for good, I ask, "What are your thoughts on the gilding revel, Catriona?"

"It may be tedious, but the party favors will surely be worth our yawns."

Sybille's eyes glitter as though she were already unwrapping some precious trinket.

Giana gets to her feet. "I think you'd be a fool to risk your life for a party *or* a party favor."

"Why don't you go murder someone else's buzz," Sybille grumbles.

"Instead of calling your sister and Fallon fools, you should applaud them both, for it takes courage to join a battle." Catriona says this pleasantly enough, but I don't miss the irritation scenting her tone like rose oil scents her skin.

"Is it courage that also brought you to our doorstep?" Giana flings back her way.

Catriona lowers her gaze to her hands, which she is wringing in her lap. "No." Her glossy mouth puckers before smoothing. "It's cowardice."

The woman who's always filled Bottom of the Jug with her jubilance and beauty seems suddenly so small, as though the brocade couch upon which she sits is gobbling her up, one kilo of flesh and satin at a time.

After Giana leaves to *clean the kitchen since no one else can be bothered*, I go sit beside Catriona and gather her hands in mine. A shudder goes through her at my touch.

"You're not a coward. Cowards don't willingly join a bunch of outlaws." I will the drooping corners of her lips to lift, but all my words do is filch a tear from the woman's mossy eyes.

Catriona squeezes my hands once before slipping them from my grip and getting to her feet. "Time for me to retire."

I know her well enough to realize that it isn't fatigue that tows her from the room but modesty.

She pauses in the doorway, one dainty hand clasping the sculpted wooden frame, the other kneading the skin over her heart—or rather rumpling the sky-blue satin of her halter dress. "I may disagree with Gia often and on everything, but perhaps you should—" Her throat jolts with a swallow that makes her lids slam shut and her nostrils flare.

"I should what, Catriona?"

"Perhaps you should head back to Monteluce, micara." Her voice is no more than a choked whisper. "Perhaps you should keep yourself hidden until Meriam is found."

As she rips her hand away from the frame, I don't miss how hard her jaw contracts and how energetically she massages her chest—like someone reneging on a claimed bargain. Except no dot—that I'm aware of—glows on her chest. I would've noticed one considering her propension for low-cut, sheer frocks.

Which, come to think of it, she hasn't been wearing…

The doorbell chimes before I can ask Sybille what she thinks. Because the hour is late and the boys all have keys, my heart jounces into my throat.

"I go check who here. Wait." Aoife pivots sharply.

After she leaves the room, Sybille asks, "Was it me, or was Catriona acting really strange?"

Goose bumps pebble my skin. "She totally was."

Before we can dissect what could be the matter with our blond housemate, Aoife's voice plinks off the glass and jade stone entrance hall. "Fallon! For you."

Frowning, I rise to my feet in time with Sybille and head out of the living room. Aoife shifts to the side, revealing Gabriele.

He stands on the threshold of our house, and at his back…

My heart trips over itself at the same time as a whinny cuts across the torchlit air.

33

The gold silk of the dress I've yet to slip out of snaps around my legs as I race to the front door. I'm about to burst out onto the street and throw my arms around Furia's neck when I freeze.

The horse behind Gabriele is dun-colored, not black, and scrawny in girth and height, with vines laced around his muzzle and neck that it keeps trying to shake off. It lifts its head as I approach, nostrils flaring and brown eyes widening in alarm.

No, not eyes. *Eye.* Singular. The other socket is concave.

What's happened to this poor animal?

"That's not my stallion, Gabriele." I don't reach out, unsure of why he's come to my door with this horse.

"I'm aware."

The horse whinnies and shakes its head, then rears back and attempts to lift itself onto its hind legs, but the soldier who tethered the vines around the animal yanks so hard, it drives the horse down onto its knees.

When the vines begin to dig into the animal's coat, reminding me of the day Nonna strung Minimus up over the bridge, I pounce forward and smack the soldier's wrist to clip his magic before he lacerates the frightened horse's flesh.

"Did you just assault me, Serpent girl?"

"I tapped your wrist. Hardly an assault, but hey, take it up with your commander if your ego's bruised." I hold out my hand for the animal to sniff. When its velvety nose pulses against my palm, I raise my other hand and stroke the areas on his neck not tangled in vines. "Why did you bring me this horse instead of Furia, Gabriele?"

The new commander of the Lucin army shifts on his shiny boots, his gaze running over my hands and the somewhat calmer creature. "Furia fractured his leg on the way down the mountain."

"He's been immobilized?"

The soldier I tapped—not hard enough, unfortunately— snorts. "That's one way of saying it."

Dread pulses at the back of my throat. "What is that supposed to mean?"

Gabriele's front teeth sink into his thinner bottom lip. "We had to—we had to—"

Sybille frowns. "You had to…"

"I'm sorry, Fallon," he murmurs. "He was limping. We had no choice."

My throat burns. "Are you saying—" I swallow to ease the burn, but it only enflames my throat some more. "Are you saying that you put him down?"

Gabriele drops his gaze to the carpet of white and jade marble behind me. "His leg was fractured."

Heat swamps my lids, while the rest of my body is racked by shivers.

"You could've brought him to a healer! Or to an earth-Fae who knows their way around poultices."

Gabriele flinches. "He couldn't walk."

The dun horse's hot, brisk breaths warm my icy fingers. "So, what? This horse is supposed to be some sort of consolation prize?"

"No. Dante wanted me to tell you we set Furia free in the mountains, and although we did set his soul free—"

"If animals had souls," huffs the vine wielder I am seconds away from pushing into the nearest canal.

"That's enough!" Gabriele's cheeks flame with annoyance. "I didn't want to lie to you, Fallon. It didn't feel right. As for this filly, I brought her because she's unfit for the army, and Tavo ordered she be put down. I thought—" He rams a hand through his long, unbound hair that's acquired quite a few knots. "Maybe I thought wrong, but I thought that maybe you'd like her. That maybe she'd like you." His throat bumps over another swallow. "You know, because—because…"

I do know. *Because I'm Shabbin.*

Tavo rises to the top of my Fae hate list like cream atop boiling milk.

"Remove your vines from *my* horse," I snap at the soldier.

Gabriele expels a deep sigh, and although he looks beat, he manages to smile.

The soldier, though, doesn't smile. He scowls as he reels in his magic. "Better grab the lead rope, Serpent girl, or I'll have to lasso the damned beast again."

"You lasso my horse again, and I will lasso *you*. To a serpent." I speak this so very sweetly that it takes the pointy-eared male a second to grasp my threat.

Once he does, his narrow nose flares as wide as the horse who is dancing in place, still unnerved by the presence of her two-legged bully. "Commander, you cannot possibly let her get away with menacing a pure-blooded member of the army?"

Gabriele watches me steadily. "If you care to punish a Crow under Ríhbiadh's protection, by all means, Pietro, try your luck, but I prefer to keep my head attached to the rest of my body."

The Fae turns as satisfyingly pasty as the moon beating down on his face.

"Thank you, Gabriele. I'll remember your kindness, and I'll make sure Lore hears of it." I turn back toward the soldier. "As for you, my offer of riding a serpent has no expiration date." I punctuate my menace with a smile, then lead the horse past the large copper front door, down the hallway, and into the living area.

"Um, sweetie, I don't think we should keep the horse *inside* the house."

"We're not." I haul open the forever-drawn drapes, then unlock the glass door that leads out to the garden and tug on the filly's rope.

She rears back, knocking over the piano bench. The loud thwack makes her bound forward and hit the doorframe.

"Quiet, sweet girl," I murmur, keeping my gaze steady on her spooked eye.

I wait until she's calmed before leading her out onto the jade terrace, toward what resembles a miniature Fae temple. As I get closer, I realize that it is, in fact, a place of worship complete with columns, an altar, and a domed roof showcasing murals of the four Lucin gods.

Such a pious man Timeus was... Too bad religion didn't improve his character.

Under the painted portico, I remove the filly's rope, and although she stamps the stone nervously, she allows me to circle her. The fur on her rump bares a burn mark, and a seeping wound on her neck makes my teeth tighten.

"I'm sorry about horse, Fallon." Aoife stands beside me, her gaze rolling over the darkened sky, forever in search of a threat.

I wonder if she means Furia or this mistreated creature. Perhaps both.

I'm tempted to rouse Catriona and ask her if she can concoct a remedial poultice, but having earth as one's element does not make one a healer, especially when one's ears are round. Not only was Nonna pure-blooded, but she once told me it had taken her decades to understand plants and hone them into potions.

The filly flicks her ears when I circle back to her head. I'm about to ask Sybille to fetch a healer when I remember the bead on my earring. Although I've no clue if it'll work on animals, it's worth a shot. I rub the amber between my fingers until a paste coats my fingertips, then, seizing the rope so the horse doesn't pounce away, I touch the wound lightly.

The creature seizes and throws her head, but I hold her steady, comforting her with a quiet apology.

Before my very eyes—my very *stunned* eyes—the filly's flesh seals. The horse still dances in place, but she must sense I wish her no harm, because she holds her head perfectly still.

"What should we call you?" I whisper.

"How about Arina?" Sybille cocks her head toward the horse's coat. "Since she's the color of cornmeal."

The horse chuffs.

"We have a horse now?" Antoni's voice startles the filly, and the rope blisters my palm as she springs back.

The sea captain stands beside the door we've left open, arms crossed, brown hair mussed, jaw and clothes smudged with dirt.

"We have a horse," I say with a smile.

I like that he used the pronoun *we*. She won't ever replace Furia—no being is interchangeable—but I'll love her with all my heart nonetheless.

"Her name's Arina!" Sybille hollers back. "Speaking of cornmeal, we should probably get her some food. I'll go check the pantry to see what we have." As she bustles back into the house, as excited as on Yuletide mornings, Antoni steps closer, stopping only when the side of his arm brushes along the side of mine.

"How did we come in possession of this one-eyed creature?"

I slide my teeth against one another, my jaw as painfully tight as the organ behind my ribs. "I asked for my stallion back, but he didn't make it home. So Gabriele brought me Arina."

The horse's eye, like Aoife's, rolls incessantly between Antoni and me. She whinnies and attempts to pull away.

"Hold out your hand," I instruct him.

He does, and Arina sniffs his palm. It takes her a few seconds, but soon, she begins to calm. I'm about to unclip her halter so she can roam freely when Sybille bursts back into the doll-size temple, frightening her with her vigorous enthusiasm.

She plucks a carrot from her basket and holds it out. Arina sniffs at the air, then at the produce, and then her large teeth snap the orange stick in half, making Sybille titter and proceed to feed her a month's worth of vegetables.

As the food vanishes into Arina's belly, I remind myself that we are no longer struggling to afford produce. That we have gold aplenty.

Antoni's knuckles graze my own. I lower my gaze to his hand, then bring it back up to his and find his blue eyes on mine.

I'm about to pull my arm closer to my body to avoid fanning Lore's aversion to the sailor but decide that the sky king doesn't get to dictate who I touch. Besides, he isn't even here. "How was your day?"

"Long. And yours?"

"I met Pierre and Eponine of Nebba."

"Where?"

"In Isolacuori. We lunched."

"Lorcan let you go off to Isolacuori?" The hollows beneath Antoni's cheekbones puff and sink like Arina's.

Aoife has inched closer as though she's aiming to press herself between Antoni and me. "Mórrgaht wanted her meet Nebban king and see what vile man he is."

"Why?" Every one of Antoni's features harden. "So that she'll be on board the day he decides to lop off his head?"

I startle at his contemptuous tone, then stare past the columns of the temple at the cobalt sky. Although no sprite flaps overhead and we stand a ways from the tall hedges enclosing this manicured garden, nothing seals our conversation from eavesdroppers.

"Are you very attached to Pierre's head, Antoni?" The bored timbre makes my neck snap straight and my gaze slam into the man who is leaning against one of the columns, eyes lowered to the spot where Antoni's hand and mine connect.

I should move aside, if only to protect my friend, but I keep my hand exactly where it is.

"Not particularly, Mórrgaht."

"Then avoid questioning my decisions."

The sailor crosses his muscled arms.

"I received your message. Let's talk inside the house."

Antoni's lips thin, and then he jerks his head with a nod and strides back into his home.

Lore doesn't follow immediately. Instead, he stares at Arina who, after gobbling down everything Sybille had to offer, is now snuffling my friend's shoulder and cheek as though to locate some secreted carrot. Sybille's ensuing laughter carves into my dark mood, alleviating it a little.

"Where did this creature come from?" he asks.

Between giggles, Sybille says, "Tavo was about to put her down because of her missing eye, but Gabriele saved her and brought her here to make up for killing Furia."

I squeeze my eyes shut a beat.

"Sorry, Fal. I didn't mean for it to come out so rashly."

Once I've gotten ahold of my feelings, I reel my lids back up. Although I don't want to look at Lore or engage him in any way, I keep the promise I made to the new commander. "Gabriele's one of the good ones. Whatever happens, whatever you do, spare him."

The moonlight slashes Lore's face, painting it white and black and gold. I cannot tell what he's thinking and shift my gaze away before I can fall into his mind. I'm done smudging the lines between us.

I catch the twitch of his fingers and the metallic nails elongating from his cuticles. "I heard you had questions for me."

"You heard wrong."

"So you aren't interested in finding out if Lazarus freed your grandmother?" *And if Eponine can be trusted?*

I side-eye him. "Dante mentioned you're not holding him accountable. Have you changed your tune?"

"No."

Although not overly anxious, I'm reassured to hear that Lazarus hasn't betrayed the Crows.

Hasn't betrayed *me*.

"As for your second query—"

"I don't have a second query."

"I'll come find you to discuss it once my meeting with Antoni adjourns." Lore backs away before melting into the shadows.

My jaw aches from how hard I clench my teeth. How relentless can one person be?

Once Arina has settled, I head up to my bedroom and attempt to sleep, but every creak outside my door makes me startle, and every brush of a branch against my window ignites my pulse.

I end up lying awake all night—for nothing, since Lore never shows—and yawning through the next day. Although I wonder what Antoni and he discussed, when I ask the sailor over supper the following night, he remains tight-lipped.

And moody. Gods, he is moody. He mustn't have gotten much sleep either.

I trail after him when he leaves the dining table, and Aoife trails after me, but she's kind enough to keep her distance.

"Antoni, stop."

He keeps pounding up the stairs.

"Godsdammit, Antoni."

He finally stops and spins around. It's so sudden that I smack into his chest. His hand snares my bicep, keeping me from tumbling down the stairs and breaking my neck.

"Do you really care so little about me?" His rough murmur scrapes across my furrowed brow.

"What? Why would you ask that? Why would you even think such a thing?" I stare into the blue depths of his eyes and catch the hard shine of his frustration.

"Because, Fallon. Because." He tucks a piece of my hair behind my ear, inspecting the waning crystal on my hoop.

"Because what?"

His touch is warm yet gentle in spite of his many calluses, which, unlike mine, have not begun to soften. Probably because of his Racoccin activities that I so wish he'd share with me.

"Let me come to Rax. Let me help."

His Adam's apple rolls up and down twice before he says, "Rìhbiadh would kill me, wouldn't he, Aoife?" He doesn't break our stare as he addresses my Crow guard.

Her lack of answer is answer enough.

I grit my teeth. "I wouldn't let him."

His lids slide shut, and his hands drop away from my body.

"Antoni, please let me help."

When his eyes open, his irises have deepened to the indigo of night. "The best way you could help is by leaving."

"How would my leaving help you?"

He starts up the stairs again.

"Antoni, how—"

"Because I'm a man, Fallon. A man with cravings, and what I crave belongs to another. That's why!"

I clutch the handrail as he storms up the rest of the stairs, his footsteps loud on the buffed stone but not as loud as my heart. "I don't belong to anyone!"

Again, he stops. "Gods, Fal, you're his mate. His *fucking* mate." He does not speak loudly, yet his words feel as though they resonate through all of Tarecuori. "I cannot compete with that." And then he's gone.

And I am left to contend with the aftermath of his announcement.

"Immy was right."

"No. Antoni's mistaken."

I've become familiar enough with Aoife's facial expressions to know that she doesn't buy my grumbled answer.

"I need wine." I trundle back down the stairs, shouldering past her.

What I also need is to throttle Lorcan Ríhbiadh for spilling a secret that, in part, belongs to me.

Especially since he's betrothed! It's fucking unfair and fucking rude.

Since I cannot throttle him at the moment, I will drink away my anger. That seems like a solid plan.

On my way to the cellar, I bump into Catriona. Not literally. Not like I bumped into Antoni. It's our paths that collide, not our bodies, even if she pants like we'd collided into each other at terminal velocity.

When she spots Aoife over my shoulder, her chest only pumps harder. Though my mind whirs with murderous thoughts, I've enough mental wherewithal to wonder why Catriona looks as though I've caught her doing something wicked.

34

The pulse point in Catriona's neck throbs so hard I worry her heart may derail.

"Are you all right?"

"Yes. Absolutely. You just spooked me, that's all."

"Is that really all?" Aoife voices the question that sits heavily on my tongue.

"Yes. That's fucking all, corvo."

"Don't reduce Aoife to what she is, Catriona. It's unnecessary. I know times are tense, but we all live under the same roof, so let's try to get along. That goes for you too, Aoife."

Catriona's mouth tightens. I've no doubt Aoife's too. I don't glance over my shoulder to find out, though.

I keep my gaze on Catriona's shrunken pupils and pulsating lips. "What were you doing down here?"

Her eyes tighten on mine. "If you must know, I was cleaning the kitchen."

Odd, considering Giana mentioned no one but her ever tidied the kitchen.

"Hmm." Aoife steps in front of me and clutches Catriona's wrist, lifting it between two fingers. "Seems like you forget put away knife."

I take a small step back at the sharp shine of Catriona's blade. "I heard loud voices." She tears her hand from Aoife's hold and falls back a step. "You may not be able to grasp this, Aoife, but I've no talons to rely on if our house is breached by ill-willed Fae."

"You have magic, no?"

"I'm a halfling. Which means that my magic is half as potent as a pure-blooded Fae's. What good will twigs and flowers do if I'm attacked by a ball of fire or drowned on dry land?"

"What good will knife do against fireball or water in lungs?" Aoife counters.

She has a point, but so does Catriona. I understand her need to wield something sharp.

"You can put that knife back, Catriona. No ill-willing Fae has penetrated Antoni's domain."

"Then what was all the shouting about?"

"Nothing." The briskness with which I say this hikes up one of her eyebrows. "I just had a disagreement with Antoni over something."

"I'm glad. Not about your disagreement but that we're all safe." Her arm falls back alongside her body as though the knife suddenly weighs a ton.

For a long second, none of us move or speak, but then Aoife slices through the thick silence. "You should put knife back before you injure someone."

"How clumsy do you believe me to be?"

I decide to defuse the tension by bringing up the reason I came down to the basement in the first place. "Would you happen to know where the cellar is?"

"I do, but we're not allowed in there."

"Says who?"

"Giana and Antoni."

"Are they afraid we'll drink all their wine?"

Catriona snorts. "There aren't only bottles of wine behind that armored door, micara."

"What else is there?"

"Do you really think they trust me?"

I look toward the stairs, debating whether to seek out Antoni or Giana and ask them point blank what lies behind the door. Which one would be more likely to tell me the truth without the use of salt? I want to earn their secrets, though, not muscle them off their tongues.

"I've wine in the kitchen, if that's what you're after." Catriona turns her attention toward Aoife. "I was headed back there to put away this knife."

"Lead the way."

I follow, and so does Aoife, even though my Crow guardian looks like she'd rather eat worms.

Actually, she probably enjoys worms very much.

My nose wrinkles until Aoife murmurs into my ear. "Careful, Fallon. She acting suspicious."

I nod. "I'll be careful."

We finally penetrate a room covered with creamy white tiles and outfitted with massive, blackened hearths. Copper pots in all shapes and sizes fringe a high rack, glimmering orange in the dimmed lantern light. The space is tidy—vegetables tucked into wicker baskets, eggs piled high in a wire one, cheese wheels wrapped in cloth, and jar upon jar of oils and spices aligned in neat rows.

If only Defne and Marcello could see this kitchen...how they'd love it.

The pop of a cork carries my gaze back to Catriona.

"What drives you to drink?" She pours out two glasses. "The words you had with the sailor?"

Aoife seizes one of the glasses and tastes it before handing it to me.

"Something like that," I mumble as I raise my glass.

"So what are we toasting to?"

"To men butting out of our lives."

She sighs long and deep. "What a quixotic sentiment."

"In Lore's realm and in Nebba, women have freedom. It's only a matter of time before Dante catches up and applies this to Lucin women. Right?"

"After all he's done, I'm surprised you still hold the youngest Regio in any esteem."

"You've heard?" Which one of my friends broke their bargain to Dante?

"Yes. Beryl likes to talk."

I choke on my gulp of wine. "Beryl?"

Catriona presses a golden lock behind her ear.

Still coughing, I lower my glass. "Beryl knows?"

A frown dents the milky expanse between her shapely brows. "Well, she was *there*."

My chest prickles, because Beryl was definitely *not* there when Dante bargained with Lore to kill his brother. Unless she was hiding behind some rock, but last I heard, the woman was a courtesan and not a spy.

Catriona tilts her head. "Why does it feel as though we are talking about two different events?"

Because we are, Catriona… "What did Beryl tell you about Dante?"

The courtesan studies the bubbles popping at the surface of her wine. "Forget I said anything."

But I cannot. "Please tell me."

She sighs. "It isn't so much something that was said but something that was done." I'm thoroughly confused, and it must show, because Catriona adds, "We courtesans cannot afford to turn down royals. We've too much coin to gain."

"She slept with him?"

She watches the effect of my conclusion, her pretty mouth bending with pity. "Whatever a Regio wants, he gets."

"And he wanted Beryl?"

"He also wanted you."

My heart feels like a rock inside my chest. "He said nothing ever happened between them."

She lifts the glass of wine to her mouth and takes a slow sip.

"What exactly happen?" Aoife's confused stare sears the side of my face.

"Let bygones be bygones."

Again, I should, but I want to hear the depth of my first love's deception. "Dante called on her, or Marco sent her to his brother?" Catriona sighs my name, but I cut her off with a snapped, "Just tell me."

"Dante sent Tavo to fetch Beryl and sail her to the barrack island for him. He sent for me once, but I knew how enamored you were with him, so I pretended to be all booked up."

I don't even love the man anymore, yet my heart fucking chips.

"She said he was a terrible lay, but as courtesans, we're paid to endure the selfish whims of our customers, so it didn't much matter." She glances toward Aoife as though hesitant to add the next bit out loud. She must decide I must be fine with Aoife knowing, because she adds, "I can only imagine that it mattered to you."

"You know?" My toneless voice ricochets dully across the tiles.

"You visited his tent in broad daylight, micara. All of Luce knows."

My heart hammers the ribbing of my dress.

What a mistake that had been.

What a mistake Dante had been.

I drain my glass and take it to the basin full of sudsy water that Riccio must've fired clean, because the water is limpid. I submerge the glass, then pull it out and watch the bubbles snake down the sides as I upturn it on the drying rack.

"Thank you for the wine." I cannot look Catriona in the eye as I say it, not because I'm embarrassed but because I'm ashamed that a man I've no consideration for and who evidently has never had any consideration for me can still affect me so.

With Aoife hot on my heels, I return to my bedroom. She thankfully doesn't try to speak to me. Doesn't even wish me a good night as I slide my doors shut and swap my pink day dress for the short white one I wear at night—a lacy number that feels as smooth as water against my skin.

I expect another sleepless night, but I must sleep, because I'm sitting at Bottom of the Jug with Dante and Lore, discussing Meriam, while an apologetic-looking Beryl straddles Dante's lap. I turn fully toward Lore just as a girl slides onto *his* lap. And not just any girl but the princess of Glace. As much as the sight of Beryl and Dante disgusts me, the sight of Alyona languidly running her delicate fingers through Lore's black hair while whispering sweet nothings into his ear makes me want to commit murder.

Some part of me is aware that the scene is a figment of my imagination, yet my dislike of the Glacin princess takes on a whole new dimension. One that makes me soar out of my nightmare and plummet back into my darkened bedroom.

I'm about to feed the flame of my bedside lantern to vanquish the darkness when the fine hairs along my arms rise, because someone is watching.

35

As quietly as possible, I twist around and squint into the obscurity until I lock eyes with the figure seated in the armchair in the corner of my bedroom.

Pulse a mess, I grumble, "Fucking Cauldron, Mórrgaht," then grip the edge of my nightgown and yank it down over my lace underwear before tussling with the sheets until I succeed in drawing them back up my body. "Has no one ever taught you that it is impolite to watch someone sleep?"

Lore drops his elbows on the tufted armrests and manspreads. The male may not possess a throne, yet sits on every chair as through it were one. "Had pleasant dreams, Behach Éan?"

My heart holds still as I ponder whether his question is meant to be conversational or taunting. Did he mind walk into my subconscious and toss in Beryl, Dante, and Alyona, or did I do that? I still don't really understand how it all works.

"How long have you been sitting here?" I end up asking.

"A while."

"Creepy much?" I mutter. Then again, watching me sleep seems to be a favorite pastime of his considering the number of times he's done so in the past.

"I came to discuss Eponine."

I slide my lips from side to side as he baits me to ask for more. "Fine." I sit up in bed, keeping the sheets tucked snugly around my body. "Why don't you step outside so I can get dressed?"

"Dressed? To go where?"

"To talk."

"I wasn't aware one needed to wear clothes in order to talk."

"You're just bursting with humor tonight."

"I'm bursting with many things. Humor is not one of them." The twin gold orbs extinguish for a moment. "Just stay put and talk, Fallon." He sounds so exhausted that I indulge him.

"How's Phoebus?"

"I thought we were discussing Eponine."

"We will, but first I'd like to know how my friend is."

The glow of Lore's irises burns a path through the darkness. "He's enduring his daily torture sessions with great aplomb."

"Funny." I press my lips together. "Does he hate me?"

"Even though he swears he'll never speak to you again, he misses you greatly and is counting the days until your return."

My heart fires up a series of erratic beats, because I don't know when that'll be. Soon, if Eponine isn't attempting to lead us astray. "Can the Nebban princess be trusted, or is she as despicable as her father?"

"Few people are as despicable as King Roy. As for whether she can be trusted, she dislikes both Dante and her father. The enemy of our enemy is our friend."

"So we should attend her gilding revel?"

"We?"

"Didn't Aoife tell you? We were both convened."

"She may have mentioned it, but I've been a tad taken by other…*things*."

Things or person? I force my mind not to even creep to Glace.

"Enlighten me, Fallon. What is a gilding revel?"

"A pre-wedding ritual where gold paint is brushed over the

betrothed's skin as well as their family members' to wish them a happy fortune."

"Faes and their tawdry rituals."

"Are you telling me that Crows don't have bizarre mating rituals of their own?"

"We have rituals, but we do not trim each other's bodies in gold."

"Do you roll around in mud?"

I catch a flash of teeth. "We are crows, not hogs. As for Eponine, if you feel like gilding her and her future mother-in-law, then by all means, attend the party."

"Men are painted too." My eyebrows slide nearer to each other. "Am I not allowed to ornament Dante or Pierre?"

"No."

"Why not?"

"You know perfectly well why I don't want you brushing paint over those two men."

"Because you think they'll use the proximity to prick me and collect my blood?"

His pupils tighten. "There's that."

I picture Pierre striking me with a dagger and flinch. Giving my head a small shake, I say, "I wouldn't actually go there to paint anyone. I'd be going because she said she knows where Meriam is. However, she'll only tell us if you agree to"—I drop my voice to the faintest murmur—"kill her father."

Leather creaks and fabric rustles as the sky king unfolds his legs and rolls his neck.

"Giana thinks it's a trap."

"And what is your opinion?"

My eyes are slowly getting used to the obscurity, and I manage to make out more of him. "I don't trust my judgment anymore."

"But you trust mine?"

"I trust that you want to keep me alive. At least until you pin down Meriam and Bronwen figures out how I break your curse for good."

"She has."

Surprise makes the sheets slip from my fingers. "How?"

"We need Meriam."

"Meriam is the key?"

"Meriam is the key to many things." His gaze draws low on my body.

I stare down to find my nipples poking through my chemise. Since his senses are far keener than my own and my nightgown is on the sheer side, I grip the sheets and tug them back high. "How's my father?"

"Busy."

"Too busy to pay me a visit?"

"He doesn't know you've come down to the Fae lands."

Well, that explains his silence. "What is keeping him so busy?"

"I am."

"You're keeping him busy so he doesn't find out I've left your kingdom?"

"I know this may come as a surprise, but I prefer my neck talon free. The news of our mating link has already made me slip from his good graces."

"Except you're engaged to another. That must've reassured him." When Lore doesn't say anything for a protracted amount of time, I ask, "You've told him about your upcoming nuptials, haven't you?"

"Naturally."

"Have you decided on a date?"

"No."

"Why not?"

"Are you in a rush to see me married, Fallon?"

The question sounds innocent and yet feels loaded. But loaded with what? "Will the ceremony take place in Glace?"

"The location has yet to be decided."

"What exactly has been decided?"

"Come home, and I'll give you all the answers you desire."

Home... I don't have a home. I've got places I sleep and store clothes—clothes that aren't even mine—but I don't have a place to call my own anymore.

I nibble on my lip. "Speak them into my mind so no one overhears."

"Except you no longer want me inside your head."

"I may not want you there, but for the time being, we still have a connection, so you may as well make use of it."

He grows quiet again.

"Lorcan, please don't keep me in the dark."

"You want answers, you come home."

"Stop calling it home! Your nest is not my home."

Fabric tears. Is he gouging something with his talons? "And Antoni's house is?"

"No."

"Then why in Mórrígan's name are you staying here?"

"You know why. I'm trying to find Meriam."

"Because you think she'll just knock on your door? Come on, Little Bird. I know you're smarter than that."

"Actually, you think me a fool." My eyes sting.

"Fallon..." he murmurs on a sigh.

"And yes, I realize telling Pierre I'd marry him in exchange for his help was impetuous, but that doesn't give you a right to shit on me *or* on what I'm trying to achieve. Now, unless you have anything constructive to add, show your fucking self out of my bedroom."

He shoves a handful of hair off his face. "I gave Aoife and the rest of my guards the night off, so you're stuck with me until sunrise."

He must've lost a whole bunch of brain cells from all his shifting if he thinks I'll allow him to spend the night in my bedroom. "I'll go sleep in Syb's room. She'll keep me safe."

"She's with Mattia. That would surely be awkward."

"I'll go to Gia's."

"She's gone out on an errand."

"At this time of night?"

"Rebels don't keep office hours."

I disregard his jibe. "Then Catriona's—"

"I do not trust that female."

I toss my hands in the air. "Then I'll go to Antoni's. You trust him, don't you?"

"Not with you."

Provocation makes me push the sheets off my legs and rise. "What do you fucking care, Lore? You're about to get married."

"Do not go to his bed, Behach Éan." His voice is as sharp and low as the snap of one of his great wings.

"Why? Are you afraid that I'll distract him from his task?"

Lore's edges blur, then something cold and smooth presses into my front, forcing my knees to buckle and my ass to hit the bouncy mattress.

"Why are you so adamant to keep me from him? Do you know something I don't?"

After his crows have regrouped in the armchair, he says, "I know many things you don't."

"Does he want me dead?"

"No."

"Then I don't see the problem with me seeking out his company—"

"You've got me. You've no need for him."

"Except I've an itch to scratch, and you're someone else's fiancé, so your company is rather pointless."

My comment must catch Lore off guard, because he turns lethally quiet, but his silence lasts only a few heartbeats. "You've got hands, Fallon. You've no need for Antoni's."

It takes me a second to recover from the shock of his answer.

"Besides, he's left the house with Gia and Riccio."

"How convenient that no one with a cock is available."

His leather armor creaks again, and although it's surely my imagination, I think I hear his molars gnash.

"But hey, you're right. I've got ten functioning digits and a fucking *splendid* imagination." I lie back in bed. "I'll just conjure Antoni's tongue and scratch my own fucking itch. You may want to step outside. I wouldn't want to make you uncomfortable." My tone is viciously brittle.

"I'm not leaving your bedside, Behach Éan, but I applaud your creative attempt at making me flee."

Of course he doesn't take me seriously. "Fine. Stay for the show. Watch me fantasize over the man you're so desperate to keep me from, the Cauldron only knows why."

The Cauldron and himself. And maybe Bronwen…

What if Antoni alters my future? What if she's seen something—

"Go back to sleep, Little Bird."

His dismissal sparks my rebellious streak. I'm not going back to sleep as long as he sits in my bedroom. I'm probably not going back to sleep at all considering how alert I feel. So I decide to make him squirm and show him that I'm not some gutless child full of silly plans and sillier threats.

36

A s I lower my hand down my body, I glower at Lore, willing him to explode into his five crows and flap out of my bedroom.

He doesn't.

Damn him.

I close my eyes and conjure the sailor's face, then slip my index and middle fingers beneath the silken lace and swipe at my sex. I haven't pleasured myself in what feels like months. It probably has been months.

After all, I was sort of busy these past few weeks.

Also, I'm not very good at it.

Concentrate, Fallon, I chide myself.

I hook Antoni's face and drag him back to the forefront of my mind. "Don't hesitate to peer inside my head, Mórrgaht."

Something creaks. Perhaps the arms of the chair Lore sits in. Perhaps his neck.

Wood splinters. The chair it is then.

I picture Antoni sitting on the pier in front of Bottom of the Jug the night he suggested I follow him into his boat's cabin. In hindsight, I should've taken him up on his offer. It may have changed things, but I can only imagine for the better. It would've spared me from sleeping with a selfish and disingenuous Fae.

Dante's face ruins what little heat I've stoked between my thighs.

I think about Antoni again, about his blue eyes and brown hair and tanned skin. I think of how hard he pursued me and how hard I resisted him because I was so blinded with love for a princely prick.

Another piece of wood splinters. I can only imagine that Lore has penetrated my mind and is displeased with the reel of images I'm showing him.

"Don't you wish you'd flitted away when you still had the chance?" I keep working my fingers, but no heat builds. I could be wiping down dirty tables at Bottom of the Jug for all the pleasure this is bringing me.

My jaw squeezes as tight as my heart. I try one last time, but the backs of my lids fill with another face—one adorned with a small feather tattoo and too-bright eyes. A sharp tingle shoots up my core and warms every corner of my body.

Before Lore can catch me thinking of him, I jerk my hand from my undergarment and turn onto my side—the side Lore is not on—and bury my burning cheeks into my pillow.

My attempt at making the Crow king squirm has epically backfired. The only one squirming is me. Why in the three kingdoms and one queendom did this feel like a sensible idea?

The armchair creaks again, but not like someone is destroying it...like someone is getting up. The carpet swallows the footfalls of the Crow king, but I nonetheless hear him pad closer in the silence of my bedroom. And then I feel him even though he doesn't touch me—neither with his shadows nor with his flesh.

"Go away, Lore. I'm not in the mood to fight."

The air churns, and I think he's finally listened to me, but when I crack my lids open, I find him crouched beside me, his golden eyes fastened to mine.

"I'm not in the mood to fight either, Little Bird." He reaches out and tentatively pushes a strand of hair off my face, untangling it from my clumped lashes.

"Please, don't."

"Don't what?"

"Don't do that. Don't stroke my face as though I were some child."

"Trust me, that is not how I see you."

Why must he be so confusing? Why must I be so confused each time he is near?

His cool fingers linger beside the crease of my ear. "Fallon, I—" A series of rapid plinks on my window makes him heave an annoyed breath and mutter, "For focá's sake…"

He stands, towing the sheets over my skimpy chemise. I'd thank him for covering me up, but my throat is too tight with embarrassment to produce words.

"Don't go anywhere."

I'm not sure where exactly he's expecting me to go. To Antoni's bed? If my failed onanistic performance proved anything, it was that I turned that male down for a reason, and that reason wasn't my obsession with Dante.

Lore's pupils shrink, and his mouth flattens. I think he's about to growl something when the plink of metal against glass comes again, and he strides around the foot of the bed and wrenches open the curtains.

One of his Crows is treading air. Lore steps aside with a nod. Instantly, the bird dissolves into smoke that slips through the closed window before firming back into a woman.

"What is it, Imogen?" His voice is low and rough but a different kind of rough than when he was addressing me. Instead of a velvety rasp, his timbre is grave.

Imogen murmurs a rapid-fire series of words in their tongue that all elude me. What doesn't elude me is the reaction Lore has

243

to her words.

Every one of his features turns bladed. "You're certain?"

"Tà, Mórrgaht."

What is she saying *yes* to? What's happened?

"Focá," he mutters again.

I prop myself up. "What's happened?"

Imogen casts my chemise a long-suffering look. What exactly does she wear to bed? Full-body armor?

Lore's gaze flicks to me, and the corners of his eyes crinkle just the slimmest bit. "Your wish has come true, Fallon. I need to depart immediately."

My heart starts and stops, starts and stops. I blame its irregular pattern on whatever bad news Imogen has brought with her.

Lore must command Imogen to leave the bedroom, because she steps into the living room and shuts the door while he pulls the curtains tight again.

"What happened?"

He returns to my side of the bed and sits on the edge of the mattress. "Two Crows have gone missing."

"Missing? Where?"

"In Nebba."

"What were they doing in Nebba?"

"What do you think they were doing in Nebba?"

I assume it has to do with that noxious chemical Pierre is sprinkling into the ocean. "So you think Pierre had them... *immobilized?*"

"That's why I need to fly to Nebba, Fallon. To feel out their location. But I don't believe Pierre would have staked them or imprisoned them. After all, that would be an act of war."

"And what you're doing in Nebba isn't?"

"We aren't harming any Fae." He covers the hand with which I'm torturing the sheets.

Although the only thing that should matter is the news of his missing soldiers, his skin becomes my single point of focus. It is so very smooth. The exact opposite of my own, which still bears the brunt of years of manual labor.

I bet Alyona's hands are like satin. I picture them twining through his hair like in my dream and grit my teeth, then attempt to steal my hand from beneath his before he can feel the hardened skin on my palm, but he clasps my hand.

And then he carries it up to his face.

I hold my breath, because I don't know what he's doing.

And then I hold my breath for a whole other reason. His nose is traveling up the length of my middle finger, the one I used to—to—

When he reaches the tip, his eyes close, and he inhales a long, slow breath, and although it's physically impossible, it feels like he's just siphoned out all the air from my lungs.

When his eyes open, his pupils are so dilated that only a thin ring of gold remains. He carefully sets my hand back on the bed.

This time, it's *his* hand that shakes and mine that has grown steady. "Stay away from Antoni."

That is all he says. No *please*. No explanation as to why he so wants me to keep my distance from the sailor.

I'm leaning toward a prophecy of some sort that'll make me stray off my Bronwen-beaten path. "Why?"

"Because the sailor's more useful to me in Luce than he'd be in Shabbe."

My mouth gapes. Is he truly threatening to ship Antoni past the wards if he touches me? "You've got a fiancée, Lore!"

One who'd undoubtedly disapprove of the pathetic little show I just gave her betrothed.

Before I can react, he seizes my wrist and guides my hand back under the sheets. I'm so shocked by his move that by the time I try to resist, he's towed my hand well past my navel.

He leans over to murmur into my ear, "Your show wasn't

pathetic, Little Bird. You were just thinking of the wrong man." His fingers slot through mine and bend until his blunt nails are flush with the lace covering my dark curls. "Well, right up until you stopped."

My breath snags in my chest as he presses his palm a little more firmly against the back of my hand, forcing my thighs to part around our clasped hands.

"When I stroke myself, it is you I picture, Fallon. Always you," he rasps. "Only you."

I choke on my next inhale, then proceed to wheeze when the blunt nail of his middle finger digs into the lace until my lips part for him. He runs the tip of his nose down the side of my neck, and I shiver so hard that goose bumps burst over my skin.

What little dignity I'm still in possession of makes me yank our hands off my underwear and out from under the sheets. "Stop." I snatch my hand from beneath his and cast my eyes on the flickering wick of my lantern that casts the sky king in more shadows than light. "Don't toy with me, Lore. It's unfair to your fiancée, and it's unfair to me."

He sighs. "As soon as I return from Nebba, you and I will have a little talk."

"We have many little talks."

One side of his mouth quirks up. "Well, we're due for another."

"About?"

"About us, Behach Éan."

Us. There is no us. There's only him and Alyona.

He studies my face, probably studying my thoughts.

"I'm not interested in being the other woman, Lore."

I don't miss the corners of his mouth tipping up right before he shifts to smoke and merges with the shadows of my bedroom.

I'm serious, Lore.

You looked it, Behach Éan.

I cross my arms at his reply.

Reminded me a lot of your father, actually. You've the same vertical groove between your eyebrows when overtaken by the desire to throttle me.

I raise my hand to my face and, sure enough, feel the slim indent between my gathered eyebrows. It's silly, but the comparison eases my disquiet.

You can imagine how often he's wanted to strangle me, seeing as the skin between his eyebrows is permanently grooved.

Another gust of warmth envelops me.

Your mother called it his "resting crow face." He wasn't fond of the term, but he was so fond of her that he took it in stride. What he did not take in stride was when I made use of the expression.

An unexpected bubble of laughter ruptures the tight seam of my lips.

Such a lovely sound. I request to hear it more often.

Request, huh? I shake my head, a smile digging into my cheeks. *You're giving my sanity whiplash, Lore.*

I wait for his answering quip.

And wait.

As silence stretches between us, I sink into my pillow and wonder if he's already reached Nebba. And then I wonder if he's located his missing men.

The sun rises and sets twice, and although I ask whichever Crow is stuck with me for news, I'm not given any.

By day three, I've grown so worried that I've bitten my nails down to the quick. Not even my daily strolls through the garden with Sybille and Arina have helped vanquish my anxiety. I start imagining horrific scenarios and inspect my guards daily for signs of obsidian gangrene.

On day four, I leave Antoni's home and wander the Tarecuorin harbor marketplace arm in arm with Catriona in the hopes that my grandmother will decide to show herself—she doesn't—but someone else does.

"Fallon Rossi, just the girl I came to the mainland to find!"

37

Long brown hair whipping in the midday breeze, Eponine stands at the bow of a gondola lacquered with so many coats of varnish that it reflects the tall forehead she's adorned with an amethyst circlet.

My guards—two in skin and two in feathers—box me in as the vessel docks and royal guards, some in white and some in forest green, spill onto the Tarecuorin wharf.

"You came to the mainland to see *me*, Princcisa?" Although I do not bow, I do nod as Eponine walks toward us in a gown that seems fashioned from real wisteria clusters. Only the sequins that glimmer amidst the blooms betray the fact that they are made from ribbon and taffeta.

"I've booked us an appointment at my favorite tailor."

I momentarily find myself hoping it's the same tailor who stitched the dress she is wearing, for it is by far the loveliest thing I've ever laid eyes on, but then I snap out of my shallow contemplation, because I cannot imagine the princess is that desperate for companionship that she'd seek me out for a shopping spree.

She probably came to discuss the gilding revel and find out if Lore is willing to do the deed.

"You're not too busy to come shopping with me, are you?"

Eponine stares between Catriona and me, her gaze lingering on the golden-haired beauty whose arm is still wound through mine.

"Not busy at all, but I'll need to stop by my house to fetch my purse."

"Nonsense. This dress will be courtesy of the crown. It's the least Dante can do after all *you've* done for him." Eponine casts a conspiratorial smile my way that makes my spine prickle. Is she referring to helping him seize the throne?

I shudder as the memory plays out behind my lids.

Eponine misinterprets my shudder for a refusal. "I won't take no for an answer."

"I won't say no then." I paste on a smile I try terribly hard to feel and decide to purchase the most expensive fabrics so Dante's purse takes a beating.

"Will you be coming as well, Katya?"

I arch an eyebrow. "Katya?"

Catriona flinches at her butchered name but doesn't correct the future queen, so I do.

"My apologies, Catriona. So many women have warmed my former fiancé's bedchamber that I have a hard time keeping your names straight."

"No harm done, my lady. It is, after all, *just* a name."

"But I should've remembered yours." Eponine tips her head to the side, one finger running over the sequined edge of a petal. "You were Marco's favorite."

Catriona's arm stiffens, or perhaps it's mine that stiffens.

"I doubt that man had any favorites," she ends up saying.

"Well, he talked about your talents. All. The. Time. Thank the Cauldron I'm not the competitive sort, or it would've greatly vexed me."

We gather quite the mob as we linger in the middle of the street. Usually my presence outside Antoni's home is noted with a mix of disgust and fear that drives most Fae into whichever shop they stand nearest. Today, all linger in the open, eyeing their future queen and the birds outfitted with iron appendages that darken the broad, sunlit stretch of cobbles.

"You saw Marco often?" I ask as Eponine turns to have a word with the head of her guards.

Catriona's glossy lips thin. "You don't turn down a king."

"You turned down a prince."

"Because you cared for him. Had you cared for Marco, I may have pretended to be busy."

"So you didn't like him as more than a customer?"

"No."

The swiftness with which she answers eases the knot forming in my chest. I don't want to doubt our friendship. I've enough doubts about everyone else. Am I still tempted to slip her salt at dinner tonight and reiterate my query? I'm ashamed to admit that yes, I'm very much tempted. Since Fae households don't stock the seasoning, I'll have to dip my hand in the ocean and collect the residue once it dries or purchase some off a vendor on the sly.

"Shall we?" Eponine nods to a lemon-yellow boutique that I've only ever walked past, even though Sybille has tried time and again to coax me inside.

Originally, I hadn't dared enter because I hadn't come to the Fae lands to shop. But then another reason kept me on the sidewalk—the sneers of the pointy-eared Fae running the boutique.

Today, they don't sneer.

Today, they gape.

The Tarecuorin whose family has owned the shop for centuries keeps rolling her lips, clearly bothered by my presence... or is it my guards that make her uncomfortable? Although they all shift, they are just as frightening in skin as they are in feathers. Except for Imogen and her sister, Lore has saddled me with gruff males who look as though they pick their teeth with faerie bones.

A chorus of "Buondia, Altezza" rings throughout the tailor's as every attendant and their customers drop into curtsies, expensive dresses rustling and tinkling as they do.

Only Eponine is greeted. Apparently, Catriona and I aren't worthy.

"We've come for our fittings," the future queen announces, even though I doubt anyone requires an explanation.

I do find myself wondering what sort of dress she's planning on wearing, since a gilding revel necessitates next to no clothes. After all, how are guests supposed to paint the bride's body if it's covered? I don't ask, of course, for that would reveal I've never attended a gilding revel, which would in turn reveal I'm not the type of guest invited to such a party.

The owner takes us up one flight of stairs, to a space almost as grand as Timeus's living room, complete with varnished hardwood flooring, aquamarine velvet poufs, and silver wallpaper to match the semicircle of standing mirrors.

"I sent for Sybille and her sister," Eponine says as she takes a seat on one of the poufs. "Shoes! I forgot to bring the shoes I intended to wear. Catriona, would you mind heading to Francanelli and purchasing the stardust sandals for me, the ones with the tall spiky heels." It isn't a question; it's a command. One that makes Catriona's jaw clench. Eponine either doesn't seem to care or doesn't seem to notice. "They know my size."

One of the female attendants extends a platter of crystal flutes brimming with sparkling gold wine. "I can go, Altezza," she offers.

Eponine snatches a glass, paying the woman's offer no mind. "And, Cati, get yourself a pair and put it on my account. It's the least I can do."

Catriona's eyes flash a brutal shade of green at the nickname Eponine has just flung her way, but she dips her head and abides by her future ruler's directive.

The platter of drinks is extended my way, but I shake my head.

Once she's retreated through a door built into the wallpapered wall, Eponine murmurs, "You shouldn't trust that woman, Fallon."

I assume she means Catriona. "Why do you say that?"

"Because she'll do *anything* for coin."

"Like most people in Luce."

"I'd still be wary of her if I were you."

"I assure you, I'm wary of everyone. Even of you."

A smile quirks her lips, which are painted the same hue as her amethyst circlet. "As you should be. You are, after all, the most loathed person in Luce. Word has it you're even more loathed than the sky king."

"So I hear."

She flicks her gaze around the room as though to ascertain that no one stands too near. "But not as loathed as Meriam." She tips the glass to her mouth and takes a long swallow, keeping her eyes on mine.

I wait for her to say more. When she doesn't, I ask, "Do you really know where she is, Princcisa?"

"Please, call me Eponine. And I do, but my knowledge comes at a cost."

My heart pounds so loudly that I can feel it palpitate in my tongue. "I was told of the cost."

"And?"

"It will be done." Sure, Lore hasn't agreed to it—yet—but do I really need him? Obviously, he'll have a strong opinion on my decision to take this project upon myself, and his opinion will go something like this: *You're not actually contemplating murdering the king of Nebba yourself, my foolish little bird?*

"Wonderful." She downs the contents of her glass, then taps one pointy nail against the etched crystal to indicate she desires a refill.

Something scratches at the walls of my mind. "Who'll rule Nebba?"

"Why"—the princess's eyes glitter like the wine being ferried back her way—"*me.*"

My heart slowly twirls as I picture a woman rising to such a position of power. "What about Dante?"

"What about him?"

I side-eye the pointy-eared female attendant replenishing Eponine's flute, waiting until she scampers away before asking in a hushed tone, "Will you take him with you?"

"Gods, no. I'll leave him to Luce and the women who want him." She wriggles her long, arched brows. "I hear one of these women might be you."

My heart twinges. "Once upon a time, but gods, not anymore."

She tilts her head to the side, which sends her long, silken hair cascading over her shoulder. "For what it's worth, you're far more interesting than that frigid Glacin scarecrow. If I thought you had any interest in women, I may have invited you to rule at my side, but I sense your heart is already taken."

A blush scampers across my cheeks at her perspicacity.

She places her hand on my knee and squeezes my leg, then raises her glass. "To the future queens of this world, Signorina Rossi." With a wink, she adds, "To us."

My spine prickles at her toast.

Is she referring to our agreement to remove her father from power or to me sitting upon a throne of my own?

"Eponine, you swear to never poison our oceans?"

"On my life, Fallon."

I suddenly wish bargains could adhere to my skin, for I want this one inked in magic. As an ebullient Sybille bursts up the stairs, sallow-faced sister in tow, I begin to plot how I will go about murdering a king.

Gods, who have I become?

My mind whispers, "*King killer.*"

I hush it, choosing another qualification for myself.

One that doesn't make my stomach convulse: "*Queen maker.*"

38

A familiar Crow finally shows up the next day.

That Crow isn't Lore.

Still, I'm glad to see Aoife, especially when she brings me a bottle of Crow wine to make up for her prolonged absence. Although she owes me nothing, neither wine nor her company, I'm glad for both.

Asking her about Lore's whereabouts is on the tip of my tongue, but I swap my query with one that won't make her wonder why I care that he hasn't come to visit. Just because he hinted that we were due for a talk doesn't mean he's in a hurry to have one.

He's a king with much to do.

Of course, my mind hops right over the missing Crows and goes straight to Alyona. I catch myself hoping that he isn't doing her. If he is, it would make our talk very short.

I close my eyes and attempt to steady my thrashing heart. I may be Lore's mate, but I've no claim on him, especially since I rejected him.

"Adh fin," Aoife says as she scratches the sheet of vellum between us with the tip of her fountain pen.

I give my head a rapid shake to bring myself back to the here and now.

"Aww fion," I repeat, trying my best to mimic her pronunciation.

"Sky." She points to the word *adh*, then underlines the word *fin*. "Wine."

Of bloody course, it's not pronounced the way it's written. What would be the fun in that when one can pepper vowels at random with accents and declare that the coupling of two consonants creates an entirely new one?

"Crows are such devious creatures, Aoife."

"Why say that?"

"Because…" I tap my own pen over the vellum, sprinkling it with ink. "If anyone comes across a written note, there is no way they'd make heads or tails of the contents, since Crow doesn't sound like it's written."

She smiles, and there's pride in that smile. "I do not know if that was intent, but I hope it was."

Although far from fluent, my knowledge of Crow has expanded thanks to Colm, a bear of a man who happens to be as sweet as cotton candy. When Aoife didn't show, I asked if he'd dispense the lessons. Thanks to him, I can now compose short sentences. Sybille too, since she usually stays for my daily lessons.

Unless Mattia is home. Then she deserts me. I suppose I would desert me too, considering the quiet sailor is apparently a god in the sack, caring more about her pleasure than his own.

My chest prickles every time she tells me, not out of jealousy but out of disappointment that my one and only experience was so…disenchanting.

However hard I attempt to repress the thought, I cannot keep myself from wondering if Dante didn't bother pleasuring me because I wasn't worth the effort. After all, he neither needed to impress nor seduce me.

I shake these glum thoughts out of my mind as Aoife explains how to conjugate verbs in the present tense.

As she dips the pen in the inkwell, I finally cave and ask, "Have the missing Crows still not been located, Aoife?"

"They were found long time ago."

Both of us startle at the answer. I'm guessing not for the same reasons.

She slaps her palm over her mouth. "Me and big mouth."

If they've been found, then why hasn't Lore returned like he promised he would? Well, more like threatened he would. Why hasn't he answered any of the questions I've tossed into his mind? Why hasn't he let me mind walk? Gods know I've tried.

I swipe the tip of my tongue over my teeth, reasoning that he's possibly *just* found them. Done with assumptions, I ask, "When?"

"When what?"

"When did he find them?"

"I not supposed to discuss Crow matters here." She crinkles her nose.

"Here or with me?"

"Here. You Crow, so you fine to hear."

Although it warms my heart that she, unlike her sister, considers me one of them, I cannot help but lean back in my chair and cross my arms. "When were they found, Aoife?"

"Why matters?"

"Please tell me when."

She sighs. "The night they disappear."

Her confession loosens the knot of my arms, making them flop onto the armrests.

That was…that was five days ago!

I grip the wood so hard, it's a wonder I don't pulverize it like Lore did to my bedroom armchair the night I—

The night I thought—

The night I—

Gods, I cannot even think of that night without wanting to scream.

Aoife's brow furrows. "Why so upset, Fallon?" Her voice is soft like Marcello's when he was trying to lead Sybille away from the brink of a tantrum.

Although I'd prefer to worry about him and Defne, my mind and heart are wholly focused on Lore.

Since I cannot tell Aoife about his ~~promise~~ threat of a long talk, I say, "I just expected him to check on Antoni and the rest of the rebels, that's all."

"Oh. He busy in Glace. Finaling alliance." Again, she smacks her palm across her mouth. "Shoot. I not supposed to talk about that too."

After starting and stopping a great many times, my heart turns quiet. What is it they say about insanity? Oh right, it's doing the same thing twice while expecting a different outcome.

I fell for Dante, and he jilted me. I will not fall for another man whose promises and actions diverge.

I harden my heart, turning it into a block of obsidian that no one—especially a Crow—will ever be able to soften.

She mistakes my murky mood for confusion. "We need Glacin army, Fallon."

"How do you say *ass* in Crow?"

"Animal or body part?"

"Body part."

"Tàin."

I repeat the word, and spittle flies out of my mouth because it is positively guttural. "*Tawhhn*." Such a fitting sound.

A crooked smile bends her lips. "Should I be teaching insults?"

"Oh, you should. I want to learn them all."

"I do too!" Sybille exclaims, bustling into the room, a large, glossy shopping bag swinging from her arm.

"You picked up our dresses for the gilding revel?"

"They weren't ready yet." At my frown, she says, "Eponine

agreed to meet for dinner, but she insists we all wear headpieces. You know, so no one can identify us."

I cannot help but wonder if by *us*, she means me. After all, I'm enemy of the kingdom number one, and she is the crown princess. We may have gone shopping together, but we were inside a boutique. Hanging out in public is a completely different story.

"Catriona fetched them from the shop. This one's for you." She plops the shopping bag on the table.

Aoife reclines in her seat. "Dinner?"

I seize the bag. "Yes, dinner."

"Did Lorcan approve?"

Although I hate lying to Aoife, I say, "He did. He said it was a wonderful idea to speed things up on the Meriam front."

Aoife frowns.

"By all means, shift and ask him, Aoife. Then again, now may not be the best time if he's in Glace and all."

She puckers her mouth as she obviously mulls my suggestion over.

"He's the one who suggested headpieces, by the way," I add tritely.

One of Sybille's eyebrows rises high, but a look at my livid face makes her go with it. "Want to see mine?"

"I would love to see yours," I say with great enthusiasm.

Sybille overturns her shopping bag, and out spills a fluorescent pink wig attached to a crystallized mask. "They're genuine tourmalines," she explains as though she saw me thinking the word *crystal* and just had to set me straight. "And look at the length of the hair!" She holds it up, and the pink strands unspool like Minimus when he's about to dart away. "I've always dreamed of growing my hair long."

I pluck mine out from the bag and gently unfold the silk paper, then stare at the strange but beautiful creation. The waist-length platinum hair glitters as though threaded with diamonds, and the filigree gray mask looks crafted from pure silver. It really is a thing of beauty.

Aoife sets the pen down, splattering the paper with more droplets of sapphire ink that expand as they soak into the vellum. "So you will wear scary thing on your head to go to meal with queen?"

Sybille blinks in shock. "*Scary?* These are glorious." To demonstrate just how so, she plops hers atop her head.

"You look like lampshade." Aoife gestures to the desk lamp.

I cannot stifle the laugh that erupts from my mouth, because Timeus's brocade lampshades fringed with crystals are indeed a dead ringer for what Sybille is modeling.

"Aoife's right, Syb." Giana stands in the doorway, arms folded. "Instead of spending— How many gold coins did you pitch away this time?"

"None. The headpieces were a present from the princess." Sybille pinches her lips together as she removes the headpiece and sets it down with the tenderness of a mother setting down her newborn babe. "We all got one. Even you. Catriona dropped it off in your room."

Giana's lashes rise so high they skim her brow bone. "Why?"

"Because I managed to convince her to go out for a girls' dinner tonight at Terramare, that's why."

"It was Lore's suggestion," I add, because the sky king can make no bad decision in Giana's eyes. Unlike Sybille and I.

Giana stares between Sybille, Aoife, and me. "Was it?"

"Absolutely." Sybille nods, laying it on a little thick.

Before Giana can call our bluff, I say, "It's really too bad we couldn't have hosted the dinner here, but I understand that we cannot have her sniffing around the cellar."

Giana sucks in a breath and swings her attention to Aoife, but Aoife misses the look because she's busy gawping at me. I deduce my handler is on the insiders' list while I am, well, *not*. Thankfully,

Sybille is not only dating an insider but also incapable of keeping a secret from me, so I'm up-to-date on all things resistance.

"You cannot tell anyone about what's inside, Fal. I mean it." Giana's complexion has turned the same gray as the dirt streaking her jaw and neck.

"I would *never*, Gia." Who would I even go blab to about Antoni's stock of pixie dust, or whatever it is they call the drug the human rebel Vance manufactures in Rax? "Plus, I'm immune to salt."

"I'm sorry we kept it a secret, Fal, but Lore didn't want you involved."

"I bet," I grumble. "I am, after all, so *dreadfully* unreliable and childish."

"Fallon." Giana sighs. "That's not—"

"You said so yourself the day you left the sky kingdom, Gia."

Sybille sets her hand on my shoulder and gives it a soft squeeze. "Eponine's picking us up by gondola in two hours. You may want to bathe, sis."

Giana scrubs a finger through the dried mud graying her pointy jaw, then peers down at her no-frills white shirt and sturdy canvas trousers—both caked in Racoccin muck. "Come get me when it's time." And with that, she retreats into the hallway.

"Syb, can you help me pick out a dress?" I get up so suddenly that I knock my knee into the underside of the table. The dull throb matches my mood.

Sybille snatches my hand and hauls me from my chair before marching me out of the living area, through my bathroom, the door of which she slams shut, and into my closet. "What the actual fuck?" she hisses. "Lore?"

"What about him?"

She sticks one hand on her hip. "You do realize that if Aoife can get through to him, he's going to tell her the dinner wasn't his idea."

"So?"

"So I'd prefer not to be gutted."

I roll my eyes. "He would never dare gut you."

Although she's still breathing hard, clearly not convinced, she says, "Did something happen between you and him while I was gone?"

"I haven't seen him in days, so no." The male cannot even be bothered to mind stroll, which just goes to show I haven't crossed his mind once.

"Okay, so what the underworld is eating at you?"

"Absolutely nothing."

Her eyebrows writhe. "So learning to speak insults in Crow was—"

"Educational." I rifle through the plethora of gowns, the wooden hangers clinking jarringly.

Sybille tilts her head to the side and gives me a look. "You can lie to everyone else, Fal, but not to me."

I study the pleats of an indigo chiffon gown so hard I've no doubt my forehead becomes just as pleated as the dress.

"What happened with Lore, Fal?"

"Nothing."

"Nothing, huh?"

"Yes. Nothing."

"So it has nothing to do with the fact that he's in Glace?"

"How do you know where he is?"

"I heard Antoni mention to Mattia that Lore couldn't help because he was visiting the Glacins."

More like visiting a certain Glacin…

"What I can't wrap my head around is why in the world he's marrying Alyona when clearly, he's—"

"She has a kingdom to offer him." My fingers have grown so tight that the dress slips off the hanger and puddles at my feet.

"And you a queendom."

I hinge at the waist and scoop up the feather-soft cloth. "What do you think of this dress?"

Sybille sighs. "So we're really not discussing the serpent in the room?"

"Not tonight."

"But tomorrow?" In a hushed voice, she asks, "Tomorrow you'll finally stop lying to me and to yourself?"

I neither nod nor shake my head.

"I really wish salt would work on you," she grumbles. "Oh, the truths I'd pry from your stubborn tongue."

"Speaking of salt… Did you buy some?"

"Obvs." She fishes a small pouch from in between her breasts and drops it into my open palm.

As I close my fingers over the truth serum, my bathroom door flaps open, and Catriona barges in. "I've changed—" Her palm lies flat against her heaving chest as she comes to a stop in my closet. "My mind!"

Sybille's eyebrows hook up. "About?"

"I want…the silver headpiece." A sheen of sweat glosses the courtesan's forehead. "Orange…doesn't match…my dress."

Sybille snorts. "You gave yourself heart failure over a headpiece?"

Catriona's green eyes meet mine in the mirror. There's something large and almost possessed about them. "You don't mind, do you, micara?"

I turn toward her, raising a soft smile that does nothing to blot out her anguish. "Of course I don't mind."

She jerks up her hand that's strangling a tawny masterpiece. "Here."

"I left mine on the writing desk."

A single bead of sweat travels down her bobbing throat and stains the high collar of her dress.

I place my hand on her forearm, meaning to give it a squeeze when I feel it tremble. "Catriona, is this really about some head-piece, or is something else the matter?"

Her pupils grow and shrink. Grow and shrink. "You know I'm superficial to a fault."

My eyebrows knit. "Except you're not."

"My nickname was the Puddle of Tarelexo."

I balk. "What are you talking about? I never heard anyone call you that."

"Sybille has."

Sybille plucks the blue gown off the floor and lays it out on the central chest of drawers. "Dargento considered us all as dirty and shallow as puddles, Catriona."

"Dargento is a fucking fool and a disgusting excuse for a human being," I growl.

Catriona's gaze dips to the blue fabric. "You're going to rob everyone of breath in that dress."

I don't know about everyone, but certainly myself. That corset boning looks torturous. I snap my attention off the dress and refocus on Catriona. "Mark my words, one day, I will murder Dargento." How I wish he'd been the man Bronwen saw in her vision…just for confirmation's sake.

Her lips flex over a murmur. Although not a hundred percent certain, I think she says, "May you succeed where I failed."

Catriona tried to kill Dargento? When? Why? Did he hurt her? As she spins away, I call out her name, but she doesn't turn back.

"She said she tried to kill him, right?"

"I didn't hear." As we stare at the empty door that she closed behind her, Sybille says, "She's probably on her monthlies. Mine started two days ago, and you know how we're all in sync from living atop one another." She nods to my bathroom. "I stocked your bathroom with some disposable, wadded cotton pads. Did I mention they were disposable? Meaning we don't have to wash them and reuse them."

Although still worried for Catriona, I cannot help but return Sybille's contagious smile. "This may come as a surprise, but I am aware of the meaning of disposable."

Sybille proceeds to tell me how she's planning on finding a way to make them affordable, so halflings and humans have access to them. After all, we're the ones without servants to do our bidding.

As I listen to her rising excitement, I roll the salt pouch between my thumb and forefinger. Sybille and I have always menstruated at the same time, and my monthlies haven't come yet. What if Nonna's drink, the one that smelled and tasted like Racoccin water, wasn't effective?

I drop my eyes to my stomach and pray to every deity that it's as barren as the Selvatin desert, because if—

No. My grandmother knew what she was doing. Fae and humans came to her from far and wide for herbal decoctions.

For the first time in my life, I wish to bleed.

39

My stomach hasn't stopped churning since Sybille left to get ready.

Although I insist I'm not hungry, Aoife has gone downstairs to fetch me food. That was her one stipulation: that I eat before leaving so that she doesn't have to worry about anyone slipping me poison. The platter of food she returns with turns my stomach some more.

At my grimace, she says, "Please say you having thoughts about going tonight, Fallon?"

The only things I am *having thoughts about* is Catriona's strange behavior and the possibility that I may—

No.

I will not let my mind wander there.

I eat six measly bites of food. Each goes down like plaster. I drink a full glass of water, but that does little to wash down either the food or my nerves.

I spend several minutes struggling with where to stash the pouch of salt, electing to squash it between my breasts, since pureling clothing doesn't include pockets, and although I know my way around a needle and thread thanks to Nonna, it's too late to create a secret pocket in this dress.

I suppose I could add a cloak, but that may raise eyebrows and spur a search of my person, and my person does not want to be searched. My person wants to toss salt into the princess's wine, learn her secrets, then either storm my grandmother's hideout with Aoife and my guards or go to Lore with the information and watch his view of me change.

It shouldn't matter, but I hate that he finds me impulsive and naive. I want to prove him wrong.

I want to prove the world wrong.

I jump when someone knuckles my bedroom door but relax when I catch sight of Sybille in her fluorescent wig. "Ready, babe?"

I stick the orange wig on my head, readjust my breasts, then the shoulder piece Sybille insisted I wear. It's an odd thing, fashioned from indigo lace and fringed with sapphire-colored beads. According to my friend, shoulder accessories are an incoming trend in pureling fashion.

"I know tonight isn't for fun, but gods, we make hot spies. We'll have to do a masked evening with Phoebus. He'd absolutely love it."

Cauldron, how I miss my friend. Selfishly, I wish he were here, because life is just not as bright without him.

He's safe, I remind myself as I link arms with Sybille and head down the stairs.

I expect to find Catriona, but only Giana stands there.

"Aoife"—she tenders her sky-blue wig my guard's way, and is it me, or is her arm shaking?—"something came up. I know you were thinking of flying, but I'd feel better if you stayed right beside these two."

"*These two?*" Sybille scoffs. "Gods, why must you make us feel like children?"

"Because you *are* children." Giana runs her palms down the sides of her face and expels a long, long breath. "To me, you will always be children. That's just the way chronology works. Wait till you have almost a full century on someone."

I suddenly cannot wait to turn one hundred, not to be older than everyone else but because if I do reach that number, then that means I wasn't killed off by some Shabbin or Crow hater.

What will Luce look like in a hundred years?

What will Luce look like next year?

Giana's lips bend, but the curve vanishes almost as quickly as it appeared. "Please, Aoife."

My Crow guard pinches the wig as though it were deeply soiled underwear.

"She'll need to wear a dress"—Sybille gestures to my guard's leather and iron armor—"or everyone will know what she is, which will alert the Lucins to Fallon's presence amongst us. We're supposed to be anonymous."

Aoife scowls at the blue hair. "No dress."

Taking pity on her, I head to the coat closet beneath the stairs and unearth a red silk cape that must've belonged to Timeus, because first, it's huge, and second, I cannot picture any of the boys wearing such a garish garment. Yes, their wardrobes have improved, but their preferred clothing palette remains basic—white, black, navy, and gray.

Although Aoife grumbles, she dons the cape and wig. As we exit through the living room, she looks at the sky and mutters many words. Crows may worship Mórrígan, but they don't pray like the Fae, so I assume she's verbally flipping off her fellow guards.

The terrible friend that I am cannot help but laugh at her irritation.

"I will revenge for this," she huffs under her breath, shooting me a very Imogen-like glare, which is hard to take seriously considering her lurid accoutrement.

"I'm sorry," I whisper between more puffed laughter. "It's nerves. Just nerves."

She hoists her chin a centimeter higher. "You lucky I like you, Fallon."

My hilarity turns into a gentle grin. "I *am* lucky."

Aoife sighs, and her glower transforms into another look altogether—one I may have called smug had it graced anyone else's face. "I will still revenge," she proclaims.

"Get in line."

"In what line?" One of her eyebrows rises over the upper rim of her mask.

"It's an expression. It means there are a lot of people who also want revenge." Honestly, some days, I can hardly believe I still breathe considering the number of people who want me buried in Filiaserpens.

"We protect you, always."

Or rather until the day Lore has no more use for me. Which could potentially be tomorrow if all goes according to plan.

"I go check boat. Colm and Fionn wait with you."

Although not members of the Siorkahd, they're high up in the sky kingdom's military pyramid and mates to boot, so Lore rarely assigns them to different tasks.

As Aoife marches down the moonlit path, her red cape flows behind her like a river of blood. The comparison jars me so deeply that I fling it wide. I don't want to think of a bleeding Aoife, because a bleeding Aoife would be my fault.

Just as she reaches the gate that leads out to the dock destined for smaller vessels, an arm winds through mine...a *shaking* arm.

I glance toward Sybille, whose gray eyes are as wide as the holes in her pink mask. "What is it?"

She closes her eyes and inhales a deep breath that makes her nostrils flare wide. "Antoni's missing."

40

My eardrums begin to buzz. "Missing?"

"He sent Mattia and Riccio to gather more supplies earlier this afternoon, and when they returned—when they returned, he was gone." Sybille's voice is a fragmented whisper.

"Perhaps he went to run an errand of his own?" My suggestion falls flat to my own ears.

"Perhaps. Giana went to Rax to meet the boys to help them look."

"Does Lore know? Is he also looking?"

"Imogen came to get Gia."

It does little to appease my thundering heart. "We should—" I lick my lips that feel as dry as paper. "Maybe we should—"

"Gia said that we need to stay the course to keep the Lucins 'distracted.'"

By Lucins, I imagine she means Dante's soldiers. We may be cloaked tonight, but the princess is amongst us. Surely, many guards will be present.

I jump when Arina snuffles my neck, so lost in thought that I neither heard nor saw her clop toward us.

I reach the arm not strangling Sybille's around the filly's neck and give her head a long squeeze and a quick scratch over her scarred skin. She lets out a soft, satisfied whinny. When my fingers begin to fall back alongside my body, Arina pushes her velvet muzzle into the crook of my shoulder until I give her another scratch. Even though I know her blind trust in me has everything to do with my Shabbin blood, it never fails to make my heart flutter.

Sybille clucks her tongue, and our horse darts her head toward the hand my friend holds up. Her intent is to pet the newest member of the resistance, but Arina is wholly uninterested in a caress. She's probably expecting a treat, since Sybille and I did spend our morning attempting to teach her tricks using quartered apples.

"You little scoundrel, you just like me when I have food, huh?" Sybille murmurs, and although she attempts to smile, a shudder steals it right off her lips.

Her mind, like mine, is full of dark thoughts, because Antoni's cause doesn't benefit the crown. At least not the Fae crown.

"I'm sure he just got lost in the tunnels," she murmurs.

"The tunnels?"

Sybille's mouth rounds. "I meant in Rax."

"What tunnels?"

"Shh."

I drop Sybille's arm and round on my friend. "What fucking tunnels?" I hiss even though I'm half tempted to scream.

Sybille doesn't keep secrets from me. Or at least I thought she didn't.

"Fal, I swear I will tell you everything I know when we get home, but please drop it for now, or you'll get them into more trouble than you did by moving into the house."

My head rears back as though Sybille has slapped me.

"Merda," she mutters. "I didn't mean it like that. You know I love having you around."

The beads threaded in my orange wig begin to clink together. I take a small step back from my friend, a whole slew of emotions roiling through me—betrayal, shock, but also guilt. I knew my presence was inconvenient—both Giana and Antoni have made it clear time and again—but I hadn't realized just *how* inopportune.

So as not to *get them into more trouble*, I snap my lips closed and march out of the garden.

After tonight, no matter what happens or what I learn, I'll leave.

If my house was rehabilitated like Dante promised, I'll move back in there. Of course, the odds of Lore accepting *that* living situation are laughable. I expect he'll cart me right back to the sky kingdom. I take comfort in the fact that Phoebus is there, although he'll probably want nothing to do with me for a while.

My musings jerk to a stop like Arina, whose single eye grows so wide, the brown iris floats in a sea of white. "What is it, girl?"

She releases a low whinny that shakes her entire body. My spine tingles with alarm, and for a brief moment, I consider heading back inside. But if this is to be my final contribution to the Meriam retrieval movement, I wish to make it count.

"Ladies." The all too familiar voice flattens my heightened pulse. *Tavo.*

That explains Arina's behavior. She must've smelled the manwench who wanted to slaughter her because she was born flawed.

I reach out to pet her between her pricked ears, but Tavo's voice echoes through the darkness again, and she rears back and tosses her head, scattering the purple blooms I threaded into the plaits I gave her while we promenaded through the gardens earlier. She pivots on her haunches and canters off, engulfing herself in the marble temple that Sybille and I filled with hay.

I hope life goes on after death just so that Timeus's spirit can glimpse how we transformed his home. He would undoubtedly perish anew.

What little delight this contemplation brings me is tram-
pled by the long once-over Tavo gives my body as I climb aboard
Eponine's gondola. The male hates me and everything I stand for,
so why must his eyes wander?

"Evening, Serpent-charmer," he murmurs. "Or, should I say,
Nebban-charmer?"

"I wasn't aware generals doubled as cruise directors," I reply,
passive-aggressive as always in his presence.

The male's amber eyes flare red in the lone lantern light that
illuminates the embankment. "Dante's betrothed has asked that
you sit beside her."

"An honor." I step around the upholstered bench occupied
by a stiff-backed Catriona and sink onto the triangular couch
festooned with golden throw pillows upon which sprawls the
future queen of Nebba—if all goes well—or Luce—if all does
not go well.

Her green gown is threaded through with so much gold that it
gives the luxurious satin a mirror sheen. "Apologies. I didn't know
Dante would saddle us with Diotto." She regards me from over
the rim of her wineglass, and even though Eponine and I have met
only twice before, I comprehend her look, the one that says that
Dante does not trust us if he sends his general.

I can feel Sybille's eyes on me as she steps into the gondola
and takes a seat beside Catriona. I don't look her way, partly out of
annoyance and partly because I'm wholly focused on the courtesan's fingers. Or more accurately on the buttons she keeps toying
with that run from her navel to her neck. Here I was expecting her
to wear a grand and colorful gown loaded with gems and sequins.
Although made of crushed velvet, her black dress is more conser-
vative than the ones worn by my former school teachers.

"I wasn't aware that only silver suited black," I say as Eponine
and Sybille exchange pleasantries.

At Catriona's frown, I gesture to her dress.

"I was going to wear red." Her usually dewy complexion is wan in the moonlight.

"Then I suppose we should switch. Silver will better suit what I'm wearing."

"Too late." Her fingers fall away from the black-pearl buttons, folding over one another in her lap. "We're already out in the open."

How convenient... "We're still tethered to the embankment. It would take but a minute to swap."

"No." She doesn't yell the word, yet it pops out of her mouth almost brutally.

All right then... I drop the subject so as not to make a scene. Catriona will only back herself further into a corner if Eponine gets involved. Not that Eponine is listening. She's too busy laughing at something my *friend who does not trust me* has said and that I've missed.

The gated entrance to Antoni's garden—*park*, really—clangs behind Aoife. As she locks it, her head turns toward the sky, and she nods. Is Lore here, or is she nodding at something Colm just told—

The seam of my lips firms, because she isn't in bird form, so her fellow Crows cannot communicate with her. Only Lore has that ability, which means he must be present. But if he was present, wouldn't he command her to abort the mission he never encouraged in the first place? Still, I hunt the darkness for the familiar golden pinpricks, but I see neither Lore's eyes nor any giant bird circling above. I lower my gaze without making contact through the bond and refocus on Aoife just as she steps into the boat. It rocks, and she flails, catching herself on the varnished bulwark. At her guttural slew of hissed words, the gray-eyed gondolier goes as stiff as the long oar in his hands.

He must realize he has a Crow aboard.

Beads clink in Eponine's black headpiece as she reclines. "Diotto, fetch my friends some wine."

The general tenses, surely considering the task beneath him. The white smile that Eponine casts him says she's singled him out for the job specifically for that reason. Naturally, this makes her leap up in my esteem.

Although I don't feel like alcohol, I do feel like watching the redheaded Fae do my bidding.

It's all the more satisfying when the boat rocks and the wine sloshes onto his hand and soaks into his burgundy sleeve. His head whips up, and he lobs an insult at the gondolier, who's scrambled off the port side of the gondola.

"Serpent." The air-Fae nods to the rippling water.

I twist around and hinge over the bulwark. In the transparent water beneath us glimmer two scaled beasts—one as blue as my dress and the other as pink as Sybille's headpiece...and *scarred*. Although tempted to fan my fingers through the water, the whole point of our masks is to preserve our anonymity. Since no pureling in their right mind would stick their hands in the ocean, I keep them flush with my cushioned seat.

"Those beasts better not rock the boat again." Although Tavo says this quietly, the menace in his words rushes through the lantern-lit darkness toward me.

"You lay a finger on them, Diotto," I murmur loud enough for him to hear, "or touch them with your magic, and I will see that a vital part of you is shortened. With steel."

Silence follows my threat.

But then Tavo's mouth curves into an ugly grin. "You strike me with steel or with a serpent, and I get to strike your friends with obsidian, so I'd be careful about issuing threats. Unless you care to start a war? I suppose that would make the Crimson Crow all too happy. He'd get to raze our kind and call it revenge."

"Fallon, I carry you home. Please." Even though the air is dark, I don't miss the curls of black smoke drifting through the red silk of Aoife's cape.

"Né. Fás." *No. Not yet.* Answering in her tongue makes her eyes widen behind her mask.

After getting over her shock, she grumbles, "Ríkhda gos m'hádr og matáeich lé."

Although I don't understand everything, I grasp the essence, thanks to the expression "mattock lé"—*murder him.*

I smile as Tavo walks around the bench to hand me the half-filled flute. Aoife snatches it from his fingers, startling the general, who retracts his hand so fast I expect to find bleeding gouges. Unfortunately, his skin is unmarred.

"Gondolier, if I'd wanted to bob, I would've invited my friends to join me in my private pool."

The man jerks at Eponine's censure, then tentatively steps up onto the port side and, peering over the edge of the boat, dips his oar. Another serpent must've glided under the boat, because he steps back down into the vessel and uses his air magic to propel the boat forward.

"Will someone please get the bard to sing songs that do not involve dashing men risking their lives to save silly damsels?" Eponine sips her wine, observing the *pop-pop* of Tavo's jaw.

I try to catch Catriona's eye, but the courtesan is staring fixedly at something behind me. I turn to find a vessel, identical to ours, filled with a similar crowd. Here I imagined this would be a quaint affair, but apparently, Eponine has more female friends than I presumed.

She leans in to murmur, "They're all decoys. You'll notice they have the same-colored headpieces as we do."

Her comment turns my attention away from the other vessel and the water that stretches between us, frothing over the roiling bodies of the serpents.

"Well…" The mouth she painted black to match her headpiece twists. "Except for Catriona's. She probably paid the saleslady extra to be the only one with a metallic headpiece."

My heart misses a beat, because the platinum wig was supposed to sit on my head.

Catriona doesn't seem to have heard Eponine, focused as she is on the glowing Tarecuorin estates we slip past as the thick-waisted bard riding on his very own gondola serenades us with his honeyed baritone.

Although the world may believe the courtesan's posturing, she is not. Which raises the question: why did she step under the spotlight destined for me?

Whose attention is she looking to garner?

41

ybille glances our way before refocusing on the bard gliding beside us. More than once, she's joined her voice to the man's. Although his ears are as round as hers, he wrinkles his hooked nose and hikes up his soft chin as though her singing were the vilest sound he's ever heard.

Granted, Sybille *is* slightly tone-deaf, but if her participation merits anything, it's enthusiasm. It takes guts to sing out loud.

As I stare at her, the word *tunnel* spirals around my mind. I nudge Aoife in the ribs to get her to bend over and murmur, "News from Imogen?"

"Why?"

"Antoni," I say simply.

After a protracted blink, her long throat moves with a swallow, and she shakes her head.

I raise the wine to my lips reflexively. When the sweet taste hits my tongue, it reminds me of the pouch lodged in my cleavage. How will I fish it out without anyone noticing?

The answer comes in the form of an ivory tusk. I'm going to have to entreat my beast to shake the boat again, anonymity be damned. I grab a miniature cheese puff from the golden platter set between Eponine and me and lift it to my mouth. Ever attentive,

Aoife seizes it and takes a nibble. Once it passes her poison test, she hands it back. I pretend to take a bite before sliding my arm over the side of the boat and spreading my fingers.

For a moment, nothing happens; but then the gondolier hops off his raised platform, cursing a blue streak. My heart beats so frantically that I worry all of Luce will hear the salt crunch between my squashed breasts.

Suddenly, water sprays onto the deck, and the gondola seesaws. Aoife squats just as a gust of water splashes Catriona in the face. The courtesan's complexion, which was already uncharacteristically pale, grows even whiter until it all but matches her platinum mask.

I palm my pounding heart, fingers creeping toward the seam between my breasts. I freeze, because Tavo is staring at my hand.

Merda.

Sybille also stares, silver gaze a little strained, a little pained. She shoots back her wine. "My glass is empty, Diotto."

She holds out her cup toward the general, surely taking immense pleasure in the fact that he's serving *us* for once.

The second he swipes it from her fingers, her eyes cut to Eponine, and she smiles. "Want to hear a story about a certain someone?" She nods to Tavo.

"Always."

Sybille crooks her finger, and Eponine changes position to bring her head closer to my friend. I dash my fingers between my breasts and pinch out the pouch. My hands shake so hard that it tumbles onto my lap. The second I clasp it, my gaze vaults back to the gondola passengers.

Only Aoife catches my lackluster stealth.

Catriona is too busy staring upward, fingers wound so tightly around the stem of her crystal goblet that her knuckles are white. Her distress gives my chaotic pulse and blundered scheming pause, and I consider dropping salt in her glass first, but Eponine is target number one.

I dip a nail under the silk strings and loosen the knot, then spread the pouch open. As Sybille spills a long-winded tale into Eponine's ear, Tavo's eyes narrow on their bent heads, tapering on Sybille's mouth, which she's painted the same pink as her headpiece.

I pinch some salt, then envelop the pouch in the gauzy chiffon of my dress and scoot toward Eponine. "What did I miss?"

"Oh, to have been a fly on the wall of your tavern that night," Eponine muses, lips bent into a smile that is blinding in comparison to the black hue of her mouth.

My gaze surfs between her green eyes and the glass she holds aloft. Sybille leans forward again and drops her voice, which forces the princess to tilt her head to offer Sybille better access to her ear. Heart walloping my rib cage, I raise my fingers to the princess's wine and release the truth-telling flakes just as a laugh booms from her mouth and she swings her arm. Wine sloshes from the rim.

I measure the amount left—three sips—then worry the salt may not have had time to dissolve. As Eponine reclines back against the throw pillows, her eyes meet Tavo's, and she smirks.

"Not much to shorten with steel, I hear."

Tavo flinches, and although I positively loathe the male, I cannot help but feel a little bad that the story Sybille chose to relay involved his anatomy.

"I'm not often glad to have been born a woman, what with the automatic lack of consideration that comes with our gender, but at least we've no need to worry about what sits between our legs."

The general's face turns a shade of vermilion that surpasses that of his hair and eyes and almost matches the burgundy of his uniform.

To put the man out of his misery, I shoot my glass upward. "I'd like to propose a toast."

I wait for Eponine and Sybille to lift their glasses, then call out

Catriona's name. My voice jerks her, which makes the embellishments in her wig tinkle.

"To the women who deepen our days and brighten our nights."

"Such a pretty sentiment." Eponine raises her glass to her mouth.

The ligaments running down the length of my throat tauten when her nostrils flare. Can she smell the salt?

My gaze wants to go to Sybille's but remains fixed on Eponine, who still hasn't drunk. *Come on. Come on.* My heart begins to tremble as hard as the rest of me. *Come the fuck on.*

When her eyes flick to mine, the blood drains from my face. *She knows…*

Oh gods, she knows.

She tilts her glass and drinks. As she licks her lips clean, her nose crinkles.

All right, so perhaps she didn't know, but now she must.

She holds out her glass to Tavo, rings sparkling on each one of her fingers. "Change my glass, Diotto. The serpents have flicked seawater inside."

If she really believes the serpents responsible for the salt, why is she staring fixedly at me?

After he takes her glass, she leans back into the cushions and strokes the velvet tassel on one of the cushions. "Better ask your questions before it wears off."

My heart comes to a screeching standstill. "I'm sorry."

"Are you?"

"Yes. I don't like to steal secrets, but I cannot wait another week to know." I swipe my tongue over my lips, then lower my pitch so that only she will hear it. "Where is my grandmother?"

"In Shabbe."

I startle, until I grasp she is speaking of Nonna. "Meriam. I meant Meriam."

She crooks a finger my way, and although I'd prefer to keep my distance, I inch closer. "Near."

"How near?" My voice judders like the rest of me.

"In Luce."

"But where?"

My heart beats six times before her mouth finally shifts over words that firm my decision to leave Antoni's home, but not in favor of the sky kingdom.

No. I must go west, back to the land of beaches and jungles, to the land guarded by women who wear the name I used to believe belonged to me as well. Here I'd hoped never again to cross paths with the terrifying Xema Rossi…

Still reeling with the knowledge that my return to Luce wasn't all for naught, I touch Eponine's knee. "I'll see that you still get what you desire."

I set aside my resentment toward Lore to transfer the confession I coaxed from her lips into his mind. **Xema Rossi hides Meriam.**

I don't expect a *Well done, Little Bird*, but I am hoping for some sort of response. An *I'll send some birds to check out her claim.* When no answer penetrates my mind, I realize that he must not be present after all, and a touch of…*something* corrodes my joy.

"Will you stay through dinner now that you got what you came for?" Eponine's question steers my mind off Lore.

I conjure delight I'm no longer feeling, even though, like she said, I did get what I came for. Why is joy so fleeting? "I'd like nothing more than to dine with a future queen, if said future queen is still willing to break bread with me?"

A smile creeps across her mouth. "Turn right!"

My brow furrows, because turning right will lead into Tarelexo.

"I want to see where the other half lives. Where *you* lived."

I forget all about my shame and edginess then, because I haven't returned to my home since Dante promised to have it restored.

Has he?

What will the sight of my house do to me if he hasn't?

42

Although most of Eponine's face is hidden behind her mask, I don't miss the slight curl of lip that grows as we wade deeper into Tarelexian waters, as the houses narrow, slumping against one another like exhausted children.

"Is this your first time in Tarelexo?" Sybille asks the Nebban princess.

"It is."

Her answer doesn't surprise me, because purelings usually stay away from Tarelexo. Apparently, their keen sense of smell is overwhelmed by the troughs filled with dirty water that fleck our islands.

"It's...colorful."

And it is. Although peeling and faded, our homes look like a painter's palette. As I track the trajectory of her gaze, I realize she is speaking of our hand-washed laundry that flaps in a gentle breeze.

Unlike the high and pointy, we don't have an air-Fae at our disposal to dry our sheets. Not to mention restrictions still exist on our—on halfling magic. The realization that I still identify as such startles me.

"Do you miss your neighborhood terribly?" Eponine strokes

up and down the stem of the glass she's had refilled so many times that Tavo has already retired three jugs.

"In all honesty, no. I miss the people there, though. I miss my grandmother and mother. The ones I grew up with, not the...others."

"Obviously." She clinks her glass with a nail that is as black as her lipstick. "My cup runneth empty."

Sybille slides me a wide-eyed stare that says, *That woman's liver must be cast in metal.* Or perhaps her eyes ask, *Am I forgiven?*

As Tavo fills Eponine's cup, his amber gaze settles on mine. "Will the serpents require more wine as well?"

"Excuse me?"

"I've noticed much of your wine ends up overboard."

"Because the gondola keeps rocking, and I'd rather the wine spill into Mareluce than onto my lap and soil my lovely gown. Living in Tarecuori has given me airs of grandeur."

Sybille cannot contain her snort.

"I agree." Eponine presses away the long black strands of her wig. "Diotto, the gondolier is terrible. I want him replaced before our trip back across the channel."

"That wasn't—" I nibble on my lip. "The serpents aren't making his job easy, Princcisa."

"No job comes without its challenges." She watches me for a couple silent minutes as though daring me to contradict her or to press the issue.

Since I did not join her tonight to debate the merits of overcoming challenges, I turn my gaze toward the cramped islands I grew up on. Amidst the wild blooms and crawling vines, spider cracks vein the facades. When we reach the westernmost island, I sit up and grip the side of the boat.

Though many times I've wanted to travel across the bridges of our kingdom to check if Dante had made good on his promise, my Crow minders refused to let me venture out of Tarecuori, where the streets are wide and easy to guard.

Now, as we slide beside my little blue house, I am glad they kept me in Tarecuori, for I'm uncertain how I would've reacted had I traveled back to my house sooner.

Although no light glows inside, moonlight drips off the shattered panes and drifts across the dusty rooms, catching on the walls reddened by slurs. What little faith I still had in Dante vanishes like dew under a burning sun.

When the gondola turns, revealing the side of my home facing Rax, Aoife hisses, and I clamp down so hard on the bulwark that I expect it to splinter, but I'm not superhuman. Not yet. The only thing that splinters is my cool when the vile words graffitied in black beside the wisteria vine sear themselves onto my lids.

"*Crimson whore.*" Eponine reads this out slowly. "Your home, Catriona?" Her pleasant tone makes the quiet courtesan bristle.

"Mine," I murmur between barely separated teeth. "Dante promised to have it restored."

A smirk plays at the corners of Tavo's lips. "We're still trying to find the culprits. He would like to teach them a lesson. Also, he prefers not to dip into the kingdom coffers so as to avoid being flooded by demands for handouts."

My desire to bring the general's shortcomings back up tickles the tip of my tongue. It's only the press of something filmy and hard against my hand, coupled with the onyx eyes blinking at me from a bright pink face, that quells my rage. I relax my fingers and glide them down Minimus's tusk before knuckling my gentle beast's cheek.

His lids slip shut, and he rattles in pleasure, which makes him snap his tail and spray oily canal water onto Aoife and Sybille. Where my Crow friend doesn't react, Sybille wrinkles her pert nose and grumbles a "yuck," plucking a piece of seaweed off her décolleté.

I may have laughed were it not for the fact that I'm still a tad salty about her secret keeping.

"I wasn't aware I was marrying into such an impoverished family," Eponine says. "Nebba will be more than happy to foot your renovations, but please do carry on with your search for the culprits, Diotto."

The general's cheeks hollow. "I will bring your offer to the king."

"Oh, it wasn't an offer." She looks around at the rest of us. "Did it sound like one?"

Her compassion heightens my guilt of having dosed her drink.

As we finally sail away from my desecrated house, I steal my hand from Minimus's reach and finger the string of the salt pouch that is still nestled in the folds of my dress. I want Catriona's secrets almost as much as I wanted Eponine's, and I debate whether to spell her drink now or at the restaurant. Considering how distracted the courtesan is, I doubt I'd even need a diversion.

I watch her watch Tarelexo as the bard intones a new song, a melody I barely decipher over the drum of my thoughts.

When the gondola glides in front of the Tarelexian wharf and the purple awning of Bottom of the Jug comes into view, I glance toward Sybille, whose thin throat keeps tossing down swallow after swallow. I press away the lingering shreds of my annoyance and reach over to clasp the hand she's buried in the folds of her white-and-pink dress. She jumps at my touch, but once she realizes it's me, a pained smile dashes the downturned edges of her mouth, and she grips my hand tight.

I cannot imagine how heartbreaking it must be for her to be within walking distance of her parents' home and yet be unwelcomed. I imagine Nonna and Mamma will want nothing to do with me once the wards fall, but I keep hoping that I'm wrong, that they won't shun me like the Amaris shunned their daughters.

Bottom must be terribly quiet, because the bard's song makes what few customers loiter inside swivel their heads toward the canal. In one of the windows, Defne appears, toting a steaming casserole. After setting it down, she too looks out the small glass panes. New lines frame her eyes and mouth. Lines put there by me. By what I brought down on to those closest to me.

Does she recognize us beneath our masks and wigs? Does she see our hearts breaking over the chasm that stretches between us? Although it would hurt if the Amaris never forgave me, it would hurt far more if they never reconciled with their daughters.

When the flapping purple awning slips out of view, Sybille squeezes my hand and upends her wine.

I tip my cup into hers, and she drinks my ration. "They'll come around," I murmur softly.

She flashes me a grief-stricken smile. "From your lips to every god's ears."

"What am I missing?" Eponine asks.

As Sybille explains the situation, I go back to studying Catriona. She seems elsewhere, lost in her mind. Her gaze keeps flicking between the rooftops and sidewalks. I wonder what she is watching for—Crows? Sprites?

If only I'd sought her out before this boat ride instead of spending a useless hour dwelling on the fact that my monthlies have yet to come.

The heat of Aoife's gaze scores my cheek. I swivel my attention to hers. Although no words pass between us, I don't miss the flutter along her neck and the tension crimping what few features aren't obscured by her mask. It seems no one is quite serene tonight.

My own sentiment of victory has long withered, superseded by a dread that coils around me like thorny nettle.

"What a lively neighborhood." Eponine's observation snips my gaze from Aoife's and my mind off whatever hangs in the dark.

"It used to be livelier." Sybille's gaze tracks the scraggly throngs of sunburnt, overworked, and turbaned people who tread our cobbles and wooden bridges. "I cannot believe this is your first time in Tarelexo."

"Marco didn't want me traveling through his kingdom. He probably feared I'd form an opinion on how he treated the lower castes."

"And have you?" Does she hear the strain in my voice?

"I've opinions on everything and everyone." She stares at Catriona when she says this.

I want to defend my friend, but she *is* hiding something. If only I knew what...

Although the courtesan's shoulders square beneath all the black she wears—an indication that Eponine's taunt didn't go amiss—she merely keeps gazing at the rooftops that are growing taller and brighter as we travel back east, toward the pureling side of the capital.

"Are there restrictions on halfling magic in Nebba?" I ask, genuinely curious.

"The only restrictions that exist apply to both purebloods and half-bloods. Magic cannot be used to cause harm, though it must be said the law regards claims of self-defense issued by pure Fae with much more lenience than claims issued by half-Fae."

"So anyone can use magic to facilitate day-to-day tasks?" Sybille's eyes have grown in volume and presently fill the entirety of her mask's eyeholes.

"Absolutely. They're even encouraged to do so. Anything to increase productivity."

"Maybe I should move to Nebba," Sybille says on a sigh.

Eponine smiles. "We'd be glad to have you."

I wonder what Lore's views are on the subject. Will he put restrictions on Fae, or will he encourage the use of magic as well?

Something gleams in the night sky, and I think it may be the Crow king's eyes, since no other Crow has metallic eyes, but I'm wrong.

It isn't Lore.

It's the tip of an arrow.

One that is sailing straight for our gondola.

43

A oife, shift!" I shout. "Princcisa, watch out!"

Eponine has already encased herself in a tangle of vines, but my friends have yet to coax out their magic, so I launch myself off the divan, arms extended in order to bowl them both down.

As I flatten them against the deck, I gasp. Not from the impact of falling but because something bit the back of my thigh. A glance over my shoulder reveals an arrow protruding from the delicate indigo. Although the rush of adrenaline coursing through my body nulls the pain, when I shift my leg and the arrow doesn't fall, I imagine it's nicked more than the folds of my dress.

Are more missiles about to rain down on us? Did I bring this upon these women?

Merda, merda, merda.

I hear Tavo shout at the gondolier to change course and the princess shriek through her cocoon of branches. Has she been hit? Who was the archer's target?

The boat rocks, and water sloshes over the low rim, drenching my back, just as the air darkens with massive wingbeats that blunt out the stars and lanterns. Spine-tingling caws erupt in time with brassy shouts. Both echo against the choppy canal and smooth limestone walls.

"Syb, are you okay?" I ask.

"Watch out!" Gray eyes as wide as twin moons, Sybille grips my nape, yanking my body down just as another arrow whizzes over us.

I don't dare move as I wait for the attack to end. My pulse has become such a violent thing that it distends my throat, and I cannot catch my breath.

"Is it over?" I croak, since Sybille is facing up.

"I th-think s-so." My friend is trembling so hard that it shakes my body.

Levering myself on one forearm, I reach around myself and pluck the arrow out. I almost black out from the scalding pain, but the whimper that falls from Catriona's lips keeps me alert. Tossing the arrow aside, I whirl my attention toward the courtesan just as another soft mewl falls from her lips.

A scream claws its way up my throat as I stare in horror at the arrow embedded in her cheek.

"We need a healer!" For all the horrible things I think of Tavo, his enlarged gaze and waxen complexion tell me he's in just as much shock as the rest of us. "Tavo, did you hear me?"

He jerks a nod.

I crawl nearer to Catriona, the back of my leg burning like a mother. The courtesan's eyes glitter like the shards of the wineglass that shattered beside her shoulder.

Cauldron, the pain she must be in...

Although conscious that this might make it worse, I pull the arrow out, and blood spurts from the wound and flows in rivulets down her beautiful face, soaking into her silver wig.

I bracket her jaw between my shaking palms. "Catriona?" My gaze flicks to the wound on her cheek, where, beneath the blood, I catch the white of bone.

"Oh my gods, is that—is that—" Sybille's aborted question vibrates through my orange wig and thudding skull.

Tears finally spill over the reddened rims of Catriona's eyes, beading beneath her mask. "I'm...sorry." Her murmur is all breath, but I'm so close that I catch her words. "I didn't want to..."

To what? *Sorry* for what? I want to scream but can hardly regulate my breathing.

When Catriona's mouth shifts again and I don't hear what she says, I tear off my mask and wig.

"What did you say?" I manage to croak.

"You shouldn't...have returned."

Sybille's earlier words scroll across my lids, the ones about me putting everyone at risk by coming back. They crack my chest wide, because *I* was the one being targeted.

These women were attacked because of me!

Catriona's scarlet mouth parts, and I think she's about to shape more words, but she coughs and mists my collarbone and neck with droplets of blood.

Her flesh is hot beneath my palm and feels as though it's swelling. Sure enough, her cheek has grown puffy. And bumpy. Welts are forming around the wound and spreading. Her mask has become so tight that it cuts into her skin.

I fling my gaze around, noticing we've docked and a crowd has formed around us. "Where's the healer?"

Tavo stares down at me dumbly.

I'm about to implore the Crows to find a healer, since the Fae are incompetent, when another idea lights up my mind. "Tavo, glove your hand with fire to cauterize her wound!"

Catriona moans. "It burns."

Yet Tavo hasn't touched her with his magical flames.

For two point one seconds, I consider rolling us into Mareluce and getting Minimus to lick her wound with his miraculous tongue, but what if my serpent snatches the courtesan and swims her into his lair?

As I shove my hair back, my fingers collide with my earring. How did I forget about Lazarus's crystal? I rub the pollen-colored bead between my fingertips until I've ground it down to almost nothing and my fingers are coated in its sticky residue.

Catriona watches me, her eyes growing glassier, her complexion paler, her face so distended and full of welts that I'm momentarily torn from the here and now and propelled into the vision that Lore once sent me of the boy who ate the poisonous moss lining the riverbed.

As her skin brims over the silver mask like proofing dough, I rub her open wound, biting back the bile basting the back of my throat when my fingers encounter bloodied tissue and hard bone.

A million questions throttle my mind—*What is it you were sorry for? What did you not want to do?*—but the sight of her lips inflating into red buoys steals them all away.

With my free hand, I try to tear off her mask, but the thing is stuck. "Tavo, a knife! We need to cut her out of this thing!"

She lies so still that I root around her swollen neck for the pulse point at the base of her jaw.

My heart stutters, because I feel nothing save for rutted flesh. "Catriona?"

In spite of the terrible swelling, the wound in her cheek is gone.

"Catriona!" I will her lashes to flutter and carry her lids back up. I will her mouth to open around a breath or a moan or a grumbled *micara*.

"She's gone, Fallon." Tavo stands over me, eyes a terrible shade of amber.

"But…but…no. She's healed. I healed her." I begin to pump her chest to jump-start her heart.

Come on, Catriona. Come on.

"Stop," Tavo says.

But I don't stop. I cannot stop. Stopping means giving up, and I'm unwilling to give up on her.

"Too late, Fallon." Hands slip under my arms and pull me up.

I stumble, but Aoife bears my weight, steadying me. "Aoife, no. I healed her."

I try to break away from her, but I've no strength left. I tremble so hard that I almost go down as she maneuvers me toward the dock upon which Sybille and Eponine stand, surrounded by a thickening clump of Lucin soldiers. Makes sense, considering we've docked on the barrack island.

Two Crows in skin haul me up. They must sense my knees will buckle, because they keep their hands on my biceps.

"Why did she transform into a beast?" Eponine's waist-long brown hair is damp with sweat and sticks to her scalp and pumping chest.

"Poison." Tavo's voice is low, yet I hear his word.

After shock comes anger. "Who did this?" I yell. "Who fucking attacked us?" The crystals and chains of my shoulder piece have shifted and hang around my neck like limp seaweed, shivering with each one of my chaotic heartbeats.

The air in front of me heaves with smoke that sharpens into a man.

A man with radiant yellow eyes that sear a path straight into my skull. "Drop the archer."

I frown, until I understand that I'm not the recipient of Lore's words.

A body—presumably the archer's—tumbles from the sky, thumping into the slats so hard that the wind-beaten wood splinters.

I suck in a breath as the person flops onto their back, revealing a head inked with brown swirls and blackened teeth unlocked around a moan. My shocked gaze traces over every fanned-out dreadlock and the dozens of beaded strands that hang around the woman's neck like a noose of her own making.

A hiss catches behind my teeth, because I remember this woman…this savage. I remember when she swung before me on her liana. I remember when she and her friend Lyrial bartered for gold and more gold before raining arrows over me.

Did she come down from her mountain to finish the job? Is that why she attacked me?

Ice chips flood my veins as I'm again reminded that Catriona is dead because of—

No. She's dead because of a bargain she struck with a gutless man.

I fling my gaze up to Lore's, confused. "I don't…" I swallow, but the lump in my throat is so jagged, I end up choking for breath instead of finishing my sentence.

"Fuckin' feathery demons." The savage spits at Lore's feet.

Holding my breath, I watch the glob of saliva slither down the toe of Lore's black leather boot, waiting to see how he'll react. I'm not alone in staring. Eponine, Sybille, and every soldier in a one-kilometer radius stare.

Only Colm and Fionn, who bracket me, don't bother, their eyes too busy roaming the sea of white uniforms.

Tavo crouches, inspecting the hennaed woman sprawled before him. "What brings you to the capital, wildling?"

She turns her head and narrows her gaze on Tavo. "Nostalgia for the rainbow houses of yonder."

Tavo's jaw sharpens. "How about the truth?"

"How 'bout you ask your commander?"

"Gabriele?" I sputter.

The female's gaze lands on me, and her upper lip hikes up in a hiss. "Well, if it ain't the whore who got my friend's arm chopped off."

Lightning forks across the sky, brightening the Fae and darkening the Crows.

Tavo glances up at me from beneath a hooked eyebrow just as

Lore bursts into smoke. A second later, a scream rends the air and metal clinks as every soldier on the island brandishes his sword.

When he reappears before me, Lore's talons drip blood, which he casually wipes against the black leather ensconcing his muscled legs. "Hurry the interrogation, Diotto, for the next time that savage speaks poorly of my Crow, I will be removing her tongue. Considering she no longer has hands to write a confession, it may prove impractical."

At the sight of her mangled wrists, Tavo loses what little color he'd regained, while Sybille and Eponine lose the contents of their stomachs.

If my insides weren't frozen in both terror and shock, I may have thrown up or screamed myself.

The apple in Tavo's throat rolls up and down a few times before he manages to ask, "Gabriele asked you to shoot arrows at who?"

In between ferocious pants, the wildling snarls, "At the silver-haired one! He paid me to stop her heart."

My hand crawls up to my throat and clutches it as a soft sob tears itself from my heart. Catriona sacrificed herself to save me.

As Lore scrutinizes my damp lashes and pallid cheeks, thunder growls, vibrating the wooden dock upon which we stand.

Why would Gabriele want me dead? Did Dante command him to have me murdered? Wouldn't Tavo have known?

Something doesn't add up.

"What color hair did the commander have?" My voice is so hoarse that my murmur gets lost in the medley of loud invectives swarming the barrack island. *Lore, ask her—*

My thoughts become garbled as fire crawls up and down my thigh, which has become gummy and—

Oh, Cauldron, no. I hinge at the waist and claw at my skirt, hitching it past my knees.

No, no, no.

Someone hisses.

Focá. Lore is suddenly standing before me, his face as pale as the bloated leg that looks as though it should be screwed onto another body.

Oh gods, I'm going to perish like that boy... Like Catriona.

My life begins to flash before my eyes. I see the women who raised me, the man who fathered me, the friends who loved me. I see golden eyes and black feathers and smoke. So much smoke.

You cannot die, Lore grinds out.

Except I can.

I'm not immortal.

A tremor shoots through the ground beneath my feet, unsteadying me further and pitching my body against Lore's.

Although fear claps my heart, it's guilt that overwhelms me. Guilt that I've doomed Lore and every Crow who's protected me since I ventured back into Luce. *Lore, Meriam is in Tarespagia! Xema Rossi is hiding her.* As ground and sky rumble, as wind and rain lash at our faces, I seize Lore's biceps and yell, "Go find her!"

He clasps either side of my face as the world around us continues to blur and shudder.

I focus on his eyes, on the pinpricks of black adrift in an ocean of gold, and I wonder if they will be the last thing I see before the poison takes me. They're very nice eyes, long-lashed and glittery, and kind—*sometimes*.

Say goodbye to Luce, Little Bird.

How cruel and so very tragic. Must he remind me that I'm dying?

But then he finishes his thought, and I realize he isn't telling me to bid adieu to life.

For tonight is the last time you will see the Fae lands until they fall to us again.

44

The stars darken, and so do the lights of Luce as we climb into the raging storm.

This body of mine has become so inflamed and stiff, I want to use the talons Lore has wrapped around my limbs to pierce my skin.

Lore beats his great wings, soaring higher, and although I strain to stay alert, the pain radiating from my wound flares and fleeces me of consciousness.

I gasp awake, but my scream is muffled by something soft. I think it may be a pillow, but it's so wet it could be a sea sponge. I try to twist around, but all I manage is to turn my head.

"Lore?" My mind feels fuzzy, yet I'm lucid enough to wonder why he is the first person I call.

Because he was the last person I saw?

Fingers sail through my hair. "I'm right here, Little Bird. Right here."

"Where is—" A cry rips the word *here* from my throat when what feels like twenty blades flay the back of my body open.

"Shh." The fingers keep stroking, cool against my scorching scalp.

I squeeze my lids tight as another breaker of pain rolls through me, and fire and ice collide inside my bones. *Is raising the dead one of your powers, Lore?*

Why? Did you want me to revive the wildling so you could kill her again?

What? I'm so stunned by his answer that I momentarily forget about the pain, but then it comes rushing back, and I grit my teeth and curl my fingers into the bedding. *I think I'm dying.*

Would I ever let that happen?

You may control many things, Lorcan Ríhbiadh, but you surely cannot control the rhythm of my heart.

I control all that belongs to me, Behach Éan. His voice is both hard and soft, sharp and supple.

My heart belongs to you?

It's always belonged to me. I'm hoping that soon you'll understand this so you stop wasting its precious beats on males who aren't me.

I snort into my pillow. *You are most delusional, Mórrgaht.*

My pain softens suddenly, and my mind wanders, drifting as though it's grown wings, as though I were riding atop a Crow and soaring through the bright blue.

I want so much to live and wander the world.

And fly. Oh, how I long to fly, and not as a spirit. I add this in case the Cauldron is listening and cares to grant me my wish.

I swear to you, Fallon Báeinach, that you will live, wander, and fly.

Another one of your empty promises?

The fingers slow. Halt.

Fire suddenly erupts in my veins, stealing what little respite I'd gotten, and I fall.

But I don't fall alone. Someone falls with me, and although I cannot see the person's face, his thunderstorm scent coils around me like the frostbitten threads of his magic.

I'd have preferred to fall with anyone else—well, almost anyone else—but I've neither the energy nor the willpower to press this perplexing man away.

⌒

Raised voices rouse me.

My head hurts. My muscles ache. My veins burn. Every part of me is sore.

I feel as though I've been strapped to a writhing serpent and set on Fae-fire by a dozen purelings while rabid beasts feast on my entrails and humans use me as a dartboard.

"You said the poison was out! It's been *days*! Fucking days!" *Lore.*

"The poison is out, Mórrgaht. I've drained it." *Lazarus.*

"Then why the fuck is she still bleeding?"

Even though darkness is towing me under, I force my lids to open. A candle shivers on the nightstand beside me, beads of wax gliding down its creamy stalk like teardrops.

A knock sounds, followed by Imogen's voice saying something about Cathal and Lore shouting back something about *Daya* and *Nebba*.

Is that where my mother is? My eyebrows bend, but that hurts my head, so I level them out. Silence.

Then footfalls pad toward me, leather creaks, and a pair of golden eyes snare mine.

Under the faded streaks of his makeup, I catch shadows bruising Lore's eyes. *How do you feel?*

Like I got shot with a poisoned dart, then healed by knife-wielding barbarians who then, for good measure, decided to roast me in a hot cauldron. Am I close?

One corner of his mouth twitches.

More importantly, though, do I look as horrid as I feel?

His shadows stream over my cheek. *You look beautiful.*

My heart misses a beat because...*what?* But then I roll my gummy eyes, because of course, he'd find my flesh attractive at the moment. *I forget birds of prey have a thing for carrion.*

His eyes spark. *I assure you, you do not resemble carrion.*

I twist my head to peer over my shoulder and see for myself, but his smoke grows denser, obscuring the sight of my body. *If I don't resemble rotted meat, then why are you blocking my view?*

Although the candle flame still shivers over his face, it no longer casts him in light. Then again, he's pooled so much smoke over me, there isn't much of him left to illuminate. **You still need to heal.**

How bad is it? And please don't lie.

Try to sleep.

The spectral version of Lore unfurls.

How bad, Lore?

When he doesn't answer me, I grit my teeth, and then I pull them apart to call out Lazarus's name. He may be gone, but in case he isn't, I'm hoping the healer will offer me a straight answer.

"Yes, Fallon?"

I start with the more pressing question. "Will I live?"

"Yes." I appreciate his lack of hesitation, even though I'd appreciate it even more if he stepped into my line of sight so I can scrutinize his expression.

The pounding between my temples resonates through the rest of my body and rattles my bones, and although I'm surely imagining the oozing sound, I cannot help but wonder whether my wound—*wounds?*—are hemorrhaging. "Am I bleeding?"

A slow beat of silence rolls through the room. I can only imagine Lazarus is looking at Lore to figure out how to answer my question.

"The truth, please."

"We had to make a couple incisions to release the pressure

that built beneath your skin, then pack the wounds with crystals." The room is so quiet that I hear him swallow. "Your body is still fighting the infection."

I feel he is keeping something from me, but I'm not sure what. "Have the crystals ceased working?"

Again, the room—which I still don't recognize—grows deathly quiet.

"They've all absorbed. We're trying to gather more crystals."

I let the information settle.

"Nebbans don't possess Shabbin crystals," Lazarus goes on. "And Glacins have turned over what little stock they had."

"And the Lucins?" I wonder out loud.

"The Lucin supply, which I diligently kept track of until I left, has mysteriously vanished."

Thoughts fester. Has it really vanished, or does Dante not want me healed? I dislike this theory almost as much as the wildling who shot arrows at me.

I wonder if she lives, but then remember Lore mentioning something about bringing her back to life. I wonder who killed her.

Imogen. After the savage confessed to the identity of the man with whom she had dealings.

It wasn't Gabriele, right?

It was not.

Although relief seizes my body, so does a fresh wave of anger and murderous intent. As soon as I'm healed, I will unalive Dargento. *Unless—*

He still breathes. The smoke around me thickens as whichever remaining crow of Lore's dissolves.

I slide my chapped lips from side to side, ambivalent as to whether I'm glad or annoyed by the news.

Not for long, though. I've sicced my best trackers on him.

"It's just a matter of time before the Lucin hoard is located." Lazarus finally steps into my line of sight. "After all, Our Majesty has offered Dante the assistance of his people in the recovery of these missing crystals."

I imagine that assistance isn't quite what Lore offered.

My teeth begin to chatter. Although my skin is feverish, I feel as though I've slipped into a canal in the middle of Yuletide. "La-La-Lazarus?"

The large healer inclines his head. "What is it, Fallon?"

"Have you tried to get the serpents to heal me?"

The old man runs a hand through the silver hair that's come loose from the knot in which he's bound it. "No." He stares at the shadows reassembling into the shape of a man. "We were afraid salt would anger your lesions."

My temples prickle, this time from a memory on a past conversation. "Isn't salt the antidote?"

"Only when the toxin is ingested. Not when it's in one's blood."

I try to roll onto my side...and succeed. The effort feels monumental. So much so that stars dance at the corners of my vision, threatening to tip me right back, but I bolster the pillow beneath my torso.

I finally catch sight of my surroundings, and my cheeks warm at the realization that I am in Lore's room, the one I've only ever mind walked through. Which means I must be in his bed.

"Take me to the ocean."

The Crow king crosses his arms in front of a black top that clings to the many muscles that contour his chest. "No."

"I'm not asking." I move my gaze to the window, to the darkness lacerated by lightning beyond. "Don't you want your curse breaker to live?"

"You're alive."

I narrow my gaze on his. "Don't you want her not to suffer?"

"She may suffer more if seawater gets into her wounds."

"Why must you outshine me in the stubbornness department?"

A minuscule smirk tugs at his stern expression.

"I'm presenting you with an almost guaranteed solution to get me out of your feathers and bed. Why in the three kingdoms and one queendom aren't you jumping at the chance?"

Why do you assume I want you out of my feathers...or my bed?

A crushing blush mottles my skin. On the upside, if all the blood in my body is currently lodged in my cheeks, my wounds must've stopped weeping. Right?

Lazarus stares between us, his amber eyes filling with a knowing glint. "Well, that explains why Our Majesty's been acting particularly feral."

My face gets so hot that I almost ask Lore to smother me with his cold smoke.

Lore now grins, which does make him look slightly unhinged. Out of every Crow in existence, why did the Cauldron shackle me to the mad one? Couldn't I have been paired with a more gentle-tempered specimen who didn't feel the visceral need to fight my every decision...especially my better ones?

Lore raises an imperious brow. *Shackle?*

Lazarus sighs. "Mórrgaht, perhaps you could take her down to the beach and see if a serpent will come. None may even swim up, what with the unending storm you've unleashed upon our poor kingdom."

Deciding I may snag more crows with honey than vinegar, I add, "If you take me for a swim, I will stay up here and leave raiding Meriam's hideout in Tarespagia entirely up to you."

The healer blinks. "Tarespagia?"

"Lazarus, fetch Fallon a quill and a piece of vellum please."

As the giant Fae vanishes through an archway into an adjoining room—I imagine an office of sorts, possibly the library I showed up in during one of my mind strolls—I ask, "Are you really going to make me write this promise down?"

"Absolutely."

"In blood? Like Pierre?"

"Unlike Pierre, I prefer to keep the blood inside your body."

"How considerate of you."

The male prowls closer to my bedside—technically, *his* bedside—and drops into a crouch, legs splayed wide, elbows propped on his thighs, fingers twined in the wide gap between. "You may think me a monster, and perhaps fighting monsters has turned me into one, but as you said, you're shackled to me, Little Bird."

I puff a breath out of the corner of my mouth in frustration. "I didn't *say* it. I *thought*—"

"Do you know what that makes me in regard to you?"

I sigh. "My ball and chain?"

His mouth tips. "That makes me *your* monster. The one who will fight off all the others in order to keep you safe."

In a moment of rare pragmatism, I ask, "And who, do tell, will keep me safe from *you*, Lorcan Ríhbiadh?"

My words are met with a dusky smile that heightens the fever in my blood and the throb everywhere else.

45

After penning my promise to remain an alacritous jailbird in ink, Lazarus makes Lore step out of the room so he can help me dress. My skin is so tender that he selects a black robe—presumably one of Lore's considering the belt ties lie at my hips and the hem drags on the floor.

I hiss as the fabric grazes my open wounds that extend in hyphenated slices from the juncture of my shoulder blades down to my left ankle, the longest cut being on the back of my thigh.

I wonder how Dargento and the wildling met. While he was chasing after me? And then I wonder how much coin Dargento offered the wild Fae to remove me from the world? And who fronted him the money? Dante? He may not want me healed, but does he desire me dead?

Thinking of Dante pitches me back into my walk-in closet at Antoni's and the conversation I had there with Sybille.

Right before we pad out into the stone hallway, I turn my gaze up to the gentle giant whose eyes look as bloodshot as Lore's. "Lazarus, may I ask you a *medical* question?"

"Of course, Fallon."

"Is there a way to tell whether I—whether I'm—" I battle back my shoulder-length locks that are in dire need of a brush.

"Whether you're…?"

I drop my voice. "With child?"

The ancient man blinks, his gaze roving to the closed door. Does he think I've lain with Lore?

I'm about to set him straight, but the truth is so pathetic that I let him run with his assumption.

He gestures to my stomach. "May I?"

I'm not quite sure what he's asking permission for, but I nod. He kneels before me, opens my robe, then presses one of his peaked ears against my abdomen. Anyone else and I would've burned with embarrassment, but Lazarus doesn't inspire that feeling in me.

After a few excruciatingly long seconds, he rises back to his feet. "Your womb is empty."

"Thank the gods." Actually, *thank Nonna.* Thank that awful decoction she made me ingest.

A soft smile sprouts on his haggard face. "I suppose we should thank the gods you haven't made that man a father yet. Considering how disposed he is to raze the world for you, it begs the question… What would he do for his child?"

My frenzied pulse deepens the ache at my temples. "It wouldn't have been his," I confess in order to put an end to his assumptions. "The sky king is all but married, and it isn't to me."

"But aren't you"—a deep furrow appears between his graying eyebrows—"aren't you mates?"

"No."

"I thought—"

"I'm just his curse breaker."

Lazarus stares steadily at me, and I stare steadily back, because averting my gaze would hint at a lie, and I don't want him spreading his theory to the rest of the sky kingdom.

The healer's forehead pleats, smooths, before pleating again.

I've confused him. *Good.* "Thank you for saving my life, Lazarus."

He rolls his lips. "Glad I could be of service, Fallon, but please avoid getting shot or knifed or drowned, for my ears are now bare." He gestures to them, to the twin columns of hoops that no longer hold remedial stones.

"I penned this promise earlier."

As he takes my arm to lead me out of the bedroom, he asks, "Who told you Meriam was in Tarespagia?"

"Eponine. I salted her wine so she'd spill her secrets."

He draws open the heavy door and bears my weight as I hobble toward the air hub where a giant crow with golden eyes awaits. "I wasn't aware you two knew each other."

"In spite of what many may think, my trip to Luce wasn't for pleasure."

His knotted eyebrows tell me that it is *exactly* what he'd thought.

Lore crouches so I can climb onto his back. Once astride him, my forearms sink into his soft feathers as I harness his neck.

Hold on tight, Little Bird, he whispers as he takes off for the beach I don't have many fond memories of. For good reason. After all, I was almost gulped down by the ocean.

I'm hoping to make new memories tonight.

Better memories.

Memories where a kindly serpent swims up to me and licks the nightmarish wounds that stick to the black robe like a clew of thirsty leeches.

Although the air is heavy with moisture, the clouds have scattered, revealing a moon as thin as a fingernail clipping.

Lore flies me down slowly, wings never once retracting. Although impatient to reach the white-crested ocean, I'm grateful for the gentle descent, because I doubt my trembling arms would've survived a nosedive. Around us, other dark shapes eddy through the air. More Crows, I presume.

When we finally land, Lore dissolves into smoke. I shut my

eyes, preparing myself for a face full of sand, but all I get is a face full of cool shadows that harden into a solid chest full of heartbeats. As I reel my lids up, I find I am standing with my face cradled in the slope of Lore's neck, the tip of my nose against his pulse point and my cheek pressed into the hard ridge of his collarbone.

I arch my spine to pry my body away from his—well, as far away as his arms will allow. "You can let go."

The breeze ruffles his black hair, tossing it into the golden eyes that are inspecting me, assessing whether I am indeed fit to stand on my own two feet. "And have a serpent swim away with you? I think not."

I sink my teeth into my lower lip and glance over my shoulder at the ocean. "Do you really think they'd try to carry me down to their lair?"

"The only thing I really think is that this plan is madness and that I'd prefer not to have to wrestle you out of their hold like the last time one took a liking to you."

I sigh, but it comes out all choppy because of my chattering teeth. "Fine."

I pivot, forcing his hand off my waist and onto my elbow. Although I try my hardest not to put any weight on him, a bolt of pain shoots up my shin and thigh and does away with both my balance and breath.

Lore curses low in his throat, shifting his hold on my body. He's so well acquainted with my injuries that he manages not to touch them. Another few strides and I am knee-deep in the ocean.

I hiss at the sting of salt but push through the pain before Lore can decide to whisk me back to his bed.

The chilled seawater laps at my warm skin, drawing goose bumps to the surface. I hold my breath as I stride in deeper, as the salt saturates the robe and chews into my injuries.

Lore is muttering something under his breath. Something about ridiculous plans.

"Has your voyage to Glace made you forget that they are my specialty?"

He grows quiet at my mention of Glace. Or perhaps it's the memory of the cold front that settled between us the day he told me to stop playing games I didn't know the rules to.

"You will never let that go, will you?" The salted wind snaps Lore's black hair against the hard lines of his face.

I side-eye him. "I'm quite proficient at holding grudges."

"You're also quite proficient at forgiving men who don't deserve your forgiveness."

I press my lips together, returning my gaze to the ocean that is as agitated as I am. "I've not forgiven Dante."

I take another step and another until the water rises over my chest and balloons my robe. I'm aware I will need to remove it so the serpents can have access to my wounds, but I decide to keep it on until one arrives. The astral light may be thin, but Crows have exceptionally sharp senses, and even if Lore has seen me naked more times than I care to remember, I'd prefer not to flash him a nipple.

"Great Mórrígan, you are like nectar to them," he murmurs.

"Beg your pardon?"

He nods his stubbled chin to the tusks slicing through the surface like shark fins. From the size of them, I take it I'm in the company of full-grown serpents. I drop my hands to the knot of my belt and untie it, then maneuver it off my arms with Lore's help.

I slip it back on so that it now parts at my back and covers my front.

Lore's long fingers glide up my long sleeves and wrap around my wrists. "May this work," he murmurs, just as the beasts reach us.

Their black eyes rise over the waterline. I shiver, for they are huge, and although I know they mean me no harm, it remains daunting to bathe with such monstrous creatures. Lore watches them, hissing when one attempts to nudge him away from me.

His fingers tighten almost painfully around my skin as he stands his ground and growls at them to heal my wounds.

The serpent hisses, his long black tongue smacking Lore's cheek.

I cannot stifle the laughter that rolls up my throat at the sky king's stunned expression, nor can I quit giggling as his gaze tightens on mine.

"Your mother would just love this."

"Seeing you get assaulted by a sea creature?"

"That too, but I meant seeing her daughter swim with the beasts she so loves. Knowing you found your way to them and them to you."

His eyes glow in the darkness, bright like his wet skin. I concentrate on them as the giant scaled bodies weave around us, dorsal fins caressing my aching flesh. Suddenly, both stop twisting and the ocean turns quiet. I glance over my shoulder to make sure they haven't left just as the larger of the two sweeps his velvet tongue against the cut between my shoulder blades.

My fingers dig into the roiling muscles and sinews of Lore's forearms because, holy Mother of Crows, that hurts. A second tongue ribbons across my ankle before rising up the length of my shin and thigh.

I close my wet eyes and concentrate on my breathing.

"Enough." Lore begins to pull me out of the ocean.

"What are you doing?"

"You're in pain."

My lids pop open. "No, Lore. I'm not in pain."

"You're crying."

"Because I'm moved by the compassion and magic of these beasts who the Fae so fear." I steal one of my hands out of his grasp and skim my fingers over the orange coils within my reach.

The serpent rattles and licks my skin faster as though to remove every last scratch on my body.

Lore frowns. I steal his hand from where it found new purchase on my hip and carry it to the serpent's body, then press his long fingers against the creature's dorsal fin, which is as soft as crow feathers. The serpent rattles again, which makes Lore suck in a breath.

"It's their way of showing gratitude."

"It better be."

I frown up at him. "Why do you say that?"

"Because our kind rattles to attract their mates."

My grin deserts my face. "That's surely not— Serpents cannot shape-shift, can they?"

"Do you really believe I'd let them lick you if there was anything human about these beasts?"

I'm too flustered by his answer to even breathe out my relief. Lore spins me, my feet slipping against the fine grains of sand, then runs his knuckles down my spine.

"What are you doing?" I choke out.

"Inspecting that their job is done."

"It is." Just as his fingers reach the dimples over my ass, I catch his hand and pull it away. "You could've just asked."

Why ask when I've hands to feel?

Because I don't care to be felt up by a man whose fingers will feel up someone else in a few hours.

I wait for him to deny this, but all he does is sigh against my neck, his warm breath adhering to my salted skin.

He grips my flapping robe from behind and belts it snuggly around my waist. "Come. You need to eat and rest."

Although one of the serpents has retreated, the other hangs around as though waiting for the opportune moment to snatch me away from the other predator in the water. I reach over and scratch him around his ivory tusk, eliciting another rattle, one that reminds me of what Lore said about crows rattling.

I do not wonder if he's rattled for Alyona. Nope. The thought absolutely doesn't cross my mind, because it's absolutely none of my business.

I stroke the serpent's head with so much gusto that I end up submerging him. The creature just shakes harder before popping his head back out and sweeping his forked black tongue across my jaw, coaxing a smile from my cold lips.

Lore is still working on my belt. Each time his nails skim one of my ribs through the thin fabric, I hold my breath. Each time his fingertips dent my waist, I push my breath out. I sound like the women in labor who'd come to Nonna for a dose of her home-made pain relievers. How their eyes would shine as brightly as their sweat-slicked skin when the medication took hold. As I'd held their hands through their spasms, I remember wishing that I'd been born with green eyes so that I could've grown medicinal plants like the woman I so admired.

The woman who lives an ocean away.

I stare in the direction of Shabbe as Lore adjusts my belt, now that he's finally finished tying it. Not that I'm in any rush to step out of this starlit ocean, but how long does it take a person to belt a robe? One that is presumably his?

Just making sure no part of your body will be on display when I fly you back. Speaking of... "Would you prefer to sit astride my back or hold my talons?"

"I'd prefer to walk."

"Not one of the options I just presented you with."

I work my lips from side to side.

"Shall I have one of my people retrieve our treaty, Little Bird? The one that promises me your unremitting cooperation?"

I give my new serpent friend a final pat on the head, then turn toward the gray cliffs that rise toward the ebony sky like a sunflower seeking the sun, winged figures darkening its crevasses, watching, waiting.

I raise my hands. "I'll hold your talons."

The male tips me a satisfied smile before morphing into the most frightening beast in the kingdom and carrying me back into his nest where I've agreed to stay.

Willingly.

What little freedom I had dissolves like smoke, but when the smoke clears, Catriona's beautiful face burnishes the backs of my lids, reminding me that this cage of stone and glass is a haven and not a prison.

A place where evil cannot penetrate.

When we land, I inhale deeply, scoring myself with the scent of this place—this unlikely home.

The only one I have left.

46

Lore starts walking in the direction of his rooms but stops when I don't follow.

I wrangle back a stubborn lock of hair that insists on falling across my face. "I thought we were heading to the tavern." The lock springs out from behind my ear. I suddenly wish it were longer, not because of Lucin fashion but so that I could bind it in a tight braid.

"I assumed you'd want dry clothes."

I look down at myself, at the black robe that sticks to every nook and cranny of my body and puddles water at my feet. "Right. Yes. That'd be preferable."

Will I be handed another ill-fitting robe, or will Lore have someone fetch me something in my size? Of its own accord, my gaze wanders to the door at the end of the darkened hallway. I imagine he's given the room away. Probably had it prepared for his new bride.

"All your clothes are still in your closet."

My pulse trips. "My closet?"

"The one in your room."

"My room?" I repeat like a dolt.

"Yes." He holds my stare as he rolls the hem of his wet shirt and squeezes the excess water. "*Your* room, Fallon."

The reason that he hasn't given my room to anyone else hits me hard and fast. What need would Alyona have for a room of her own when she'll surely be sharing her husband's? My stomach churns and churns. I'll have to put in a request for a room on the other end of the kingdom.

"Come." He tips his head toward my door. "You're going to catch a cold."

The idea of catching a cold is laughable, yet I don't laugh as I stride through the darkness alongside the quiet king.

Once I've crossed the threshold of my borrowed room, he tells me he'll be right back. I stare around me, and although little has changed, it feels entirely different. It's too quiet and somber and neat. I'm no slob, but the sheets hug the bed without a crease, and the pillows are plumped to perfection. Even the knit coverlet rests in a too-perfect rectangle at the foot of the bed.

As I travel toward the closet, I reach behind me, ready to struggle with the intricate knot Lore tied, but find it loosens with the gentlest tug. I peel the waterlogged fabric off my skin and drop it into the laundry chute so I no longer have to lay eyes on it. Although not imbued with terrible memories, it belongs to a man who does not belong to me.

After showering, I wrap myself in a towel and pad over to the closet that is smaller than the one in Antoni's Tarecuorin house but packed with just as much finery, albeit in muted shades of creamy white and bluish black. The brightest garment inside is an indigo shirt that reminds me too acutely of the dress I wore the night I got shot.

How many days have slipped by, I wonder? Does Phoebus know I'm here? And my father? Is he back? And Sybille?

I clutch the doorframe of the closet as the avalanche of questions topples over me, blurring the row of garments. It suddenly feels like too much of a feat to get dressed, but then I remember

Lore saying he'd be back, and I'd prefer not to make towel-wrapped chats a thing.

I finally press my exhausted body away from the doorjamb and grab a simple white sheath that feels finer than Timeus's sheets. Shapeless as it was on the hanger, I assumed it would be comfortable, and it is, but the scoop neck is so low, the material droops past my breasts.

I tug on the sleeves, attempting to hoist the neckline up, but I only succeed in covering one half of my body. "How the underworld is this dress supposed to be worn?" I'm about to pitch it off and replace it with a matching pant and shirt set when I sense the air shift and fill with the scent of twilight and clouds.

I swiftly tuck both my breasts in and pinch the material at the front before emerging from the closet to find Lore wearing his usual leather trousers, long-sleeved black top, and charcoal stripes. Although impossible, he looks as though he's just woken up from a restorative nap, while I look like life beat me to a pulp. My complexion is so sallow and greenish and my muscles so shrunken that I could pass for a stick insect sporting a toga and a toupee.

Lore's lips twitch. "You have the dress on front to back."

Ah. I backpedal into the closet and twist it around. Although the back tumbles past my shoulders, the neckline is finally decent. "You knew that because you happen to have the same one in your size?"

"I don't wear night frocks to sleep."

No wonder it looked comfortable... Since I cannot exactly show up in the tavern in nightwear, my fingers skip over the rows of hangers to find a dress to slip over the white sheath. "So what do you sleep in? Leather pajamas?"

"I prefer to feel the silk of the sheets against my bare skin. It's refreshing when one needs to wear armor and leather as often as I must."

I should not picture him tangled in his bedsheets. Absolutely should not. On the plus side, the visual that flashes behind my lids chases away the greenish tint of my skin, replacing it with a mix of mollusk pink and ladybug red.

"Don't bother adding layers. I've called for supper to be brought to us. The tavern is rowdy at this hour, and I thought we could both do with a little peace and quiet before your father flies back from Nebba to assassinate me."

I pop out of the closet, slightly out of breath. "Why would he assassinate you?"

"I allowed you to leave the sky kingdom and meet Pierre of Nebba. Not to mention that you were shot with a poisoned arrow."

"Except none of that was your fault."

Lore's easy smile collapses on a sigh. "I also may have sent him on a merry chase around Nebba for your mother. That will tip his mood for the worse. He may never forgive me."

"So my mother is not in Nebba?"

"I believe your mother is with your grandmother." He ambles toward the unlit stone hearth and grips the frame, staring at nothing.

Not nothing.

At ash.

I've never lit a fire and don't remember ashes graying the stone floor, which means someone's been using this room.

"Phoebus comes to sit here most afternoons to read the books I lend him." Keeping his back to me, he gestures to a low coffee table stacked with a hodgepodge of leather-bound novels.

"Does he know I'm back?"

"Don't you think he'd have been here if he had?"

"Unless he's mad." I approach the table and kneel to browse the titles.

Five books are in Lucin, but two are in Crow. Has his knowledge of the bird tongue improved so much that he can now read a book in their language?

As I trace the accents peppering a word made up almost exclusively of vowels, I mumble, "Granted, his grudge holding isn't quite as impressive as Syb's. Is she— Did she come back?"

"She decided to stay with Mattia." He must sense my disappointment because he adds, "She wanted to help find Antoni."

I wish she'd returned with me, but I understand. "So he hasn't been found?"

Lore stares to the side, toward the little window overlooking Mareluce. "Not yet."

"Do you think his disappearance was an accident?"

"I don't much believe in accidents." Moonlight gloves the straight line of his nose, the strong pane of his forehead, and the hard cut of his jaw.

"So you think he was ambushed?"

"Yes."

My heart rate spikes. "Do you think he—he—" I cannot get myself to finish the sentence.

"I don't think they'd have killed him, but I have no connection to him, for he is not a Crow, so I cannot sense his pulse." He wets his lips, and although he does so unintentionally, it gusts heat low in my belly.

Why couldn't Mórrígan have blessed Lore with a porcine nose, a reedy mouth, and a few boils? It's the least she could've done considering the immeasurable power she gave that man. It's simply unjust for the rest of us.

He stares over his broad shoulder at me, one hand resting on the tall stone mantle, the other relaxed at his side. "You find me pretty, Behach Éan?"

His question makes my finger skitter off the embossed title full of accents and apostrophes. "Fishing for compliments is beneath a king."

"Alyona finds me hideous. Her exact word was *bestial*."

My first reaction is *What? How?* But that would just blow

air up his ass, so I brush off the subject entirely and flip distract-
edly through a book, refocusing on our earlier conversation. "You
believe Meriam is holding Daya prisoner?"

"I believe Dante is holding *both* prisoner."

My hand jerks off the book, and the leather binding settles
with a muted thump over the silken pages. "Dante? But he's... I
thought he believed she'd escaped his dungeon and was running
amok?" Even though I now know she isn't running amok. "So
he knows she's in Tarespagia? Is he the one who locked her up
there?"

Lore drops into a crouch, grabs logs from a metal hamper, and
tosses them atop the cold ashes, making them puff and scatter. He
then seizes some brambles, tucks them over the logs, and picks
up two blackened rocks that he snaps together over the dried
branches until a spark forms.

"Lore?" My voice has gone up a full octave. "Are you saying I
went to Luce for fucking nothing?"

He finally sets the rocks down and rises from his crouch.
"Don't swear."

My eyes bulge as I lurch to my feet. Invigorated by my fury,
I swing around the table and poke his chest with my finger. "Are
you *fucking* saying I went to Luce for *fucking* nothing?"

His pupils shrink. "You got to see your friends, adopt a horse,
and meet Eponine of Nebba. I would hardly call that *nothing*."

I stumble back a step. "You knew?" I hiss. "You knew all this
time that Meriam wasn't on the loose?"

"Fallon, do you really believe I would've let you wander around
the Fae lands as bait to lure a witch who damned my people and
her own? Why are you so angry?"

"Because! Because I feel like a fool, Lorcan. On par with the
day I learned you could shape-shift into a man!"

"Why?"

"Because!" My anger vibrates against the wooden rafters and

bone-smooth stone. "Because…" I give a humorless laugh. "How many people know?"

"Only the members of the Siorkahd."

"So not Antoni?"

"And Antoni."

"What about Riccio, Mattia, and Giana?"

"I believe they were told since they helped excavate the tunnels under Rax."

"The tunnels he vanished in?"

"Correct."

I drag my hands down the sides of my face. "Wait. My father is a member of your circle, yet he's looking for my mother in Nebba?"

"It's possible I told him that Marco traded her for that salt-blasting compound."

My arms fall into a tight fold, and I grin. "Wow. Forget furious." My broad smile turns into a cackle. "He's going to pluck you like a pheasant."

Lore crosses his own arms, expression tinged with amusement.

"Oh, you are in such deep shit." Tears drip from the corners of my eyes.

Lore leans against the mantle, a smile curling his mouth. "I'll just have to distract him with the news that you propositioned Pierre of Nebba."

My laughter sputters like my good mood. "To find Meriam, Lore. Not because I had any romantic interest in the vile male. Unlike you, I'm not jumping headfirst into a profitable marriage to better the fucking world. Now get out of my room. I'm feeling suddenly exhausted and appetite-less and in no mood to talk to the likes of you."

"I wasn't aware that ensuring your safety was such a horrid thing."

"You kept me in the dark, Mórrgaht. Which means you don't

actually trust me." I press my lips together. "If you did, you would've let me in on your big secret. You would've let me help solve it."

He presses away from the mantle and stalks closer to me. "How exactly would you have helped? By rekindling your friendship with your little princeling in the hopes he'd let slip in which part of the tunnels he and Justus moved Meriam?"

I suck in a breath. "My grandfather?"

"Justus isn't your grandfather." Lore's rough tone spikes my temper.

"I fucking know that."

He seizes my chin, his thumb pressing into my lips, denting them.

I bite down on his finger, hard, before spitting and twisting my head so he cannot stamp my mouth closed. "Keep your fucking fingers off my body or I'll chomp them off. And don't you dare comment about my word choice. If I want to curse, I'll fucking curse."

He growls a long string of words in Crow.

"Is Justus Rossi even dead?"

"No."

Of course he isn't. And of fucking course, Lore knew. He knows fucking everything where I know fuck all. Well, besides the fact that Meriam must be in the tunnels beneath Tarespagia.

"The tunnels span from Isolacuori to Monteluce."

"Eponine said she was in Tarespagia, so they must run farther west."

"Eponine lied to you."

"That's impossible. She ingested salt."

He sighs. "Salt doesn't affect the Nebban elite, because for years now, they've been ingesting the compound they dump into the ocean."

My jaw unhinges before snapping shut with a click. "You could've at least told me that much."

A knock sounds on my door, and then Imogen steps inside, holding a platter of food I want to take from her hands and dump on Lore.

She exchanges a couple words with him that I—*again*—don't understand because my knowledge of my father tongue is still too basic. Which is obviously why they use it.

He expels a slow breath. *We'll talk when I return.*

Don't bother.

I assure you, it's never a bother. He strides toward the door Imogen is holding open now that she's deposited the platter on my bed.

The door shuts, and I think I'm finally rid of him when a frosty draft winds around my body and forces my neck to tip back. I glare at the lambent eyes staring down at me from a cloud of writhing smoke.

Your safety is my paramount priority. You may not approve of how I go about it, but know that everything I do, I do to protect you.

I don't unfold my arms even though my desire to claw at his icy shadows burns strong. *So you're marrying Alyona to protect me?* I mutter through the mental bond, which I again wish we didn't share.

I wrench my head from his grip and storm into my bathing chamber, slamming the door shut behind me, then walk to my sink and study my reflection in the speckled mirror over the sink. My face is distorted with so much anger that I barely recognize the girl beneath the ire.

The girl seemingly not worthy of her own mate's trust.

Best of luck to Alyona.

May he drive her just as crowshit crazy as he's driven me.

47

After scarfing down all the food Imogen brought to my bedroom—grilled vegetables and a plethora of cheeses that taste completely different from the ones back in the Fae lands, thanks to the addition of salt—I curl onto the armchair in front of the still roaring fire and pick up a book.

And I read.

And read. I don't understand three-quarters of what my eyes are deciphering. Nevertheless, I push on, inferring the meaning of a lot of things and learning new words in the process. I'm two hundred pages into a thousand-page historical tome titled *RAHNACH BI'ADH—Kingdom of the Sky*—when the lavender of dawn washes over Luce.

I manage to flip through three more pages before my lids collapse and I black out.

When I awaken hours later, the sapphire ocean is flecked in the gold of the setting sun. I rub the grit from my eyes, then the dried trail of drool on my chin. And then I wrestle my chaotic hair back and blink around the room.

And *everything* comes back to me.

Catriona.

The arrow.

Lazarus.

The serpents.

My fight with Lore.

I pick up the heavy book that's toppled beside the armchair and smooth out its silken sheets, then place it reverently atop the others.

Over the scent of the cold fire, I smell the brine of the ocean and the mineral scent of the mountain I'm now confined to. I smile to myself, because I'm not shut inside Monteluce alone.

As I shimmy off the broken-in armchair and stretch my neck from side to side, I decide I'm ready to seek out Phoebus and endure his dissatisfaction. I contemplated going out to find him last night, but I was so stinking furious and focused on me that it wouldn't have been fair to reconnect with him when I couldn't have given him one hundred percent of my mind and heart.

Tonight, he will be the sun to my planets, the moon to my tides, the—

Clearly, I've energy to spare. Which I suppose is not a terrible thing to have before going into battle to reconquer a lost heart.

I toss on a new dress, an opaque gray frock that clings to my chest but not to my waist or hips. It probably should be belted, but I can't be bothered to crush my waist. Besides, I have a friend to conquer, not a lover.

When I sweep open my bedroom door, I startle Aoife, whose fist was poised to knock. I smile at her. "Hi."

"I come to check if you alive." Her eyebrows scrunch as she studies my expression. "You look…"

"Happy?"

"I was going to say determined." She tilts her head as though a new angle may give her a peek into my intent. "To do good or no good?"

"When am I ever up to no good?"

"Last week. When you lie about Lorcan saying good idea to wander in open so you trick Eponine."

"It's been one week?"

"Tà, Fallon. I thought you dead and say goodbye to all friends for my final voyage." Her face is stark white beneath her black makeup, and her eyes shine with what I soon realize are tears.

A wave of shame and guilt closes over me at the stress I put this wonderful, sweet woman under. "Oh, Aoife." I take her hand and squeeze it tight. "I'm so sorry I lied. I didn't mean to cause you so much grief."

"Ha fios."

"I know you know, Aoife, and I know apologizing won't erase all I did, but I hope you'll find it in your heart to forgive me."

She expels a deep sigh and squeezes my fingers back. "I not angry with you. I angry with myself. I knew Catriona wanted harm you, and I didn't do what I should do."

My fingers drop away from hers. "What do you think you should've done?"

"Make her leave Antoni house. Make her talk."

"The fact that you didn't may very well have saved my life."

"How so?"

"Dargento would've found another way to hit me. Catriona may have owed him, but she was strong enough to drag her repayment out. She was brave enough to wear the wig that was supposed to grace my head." My heart lets out a dull beat. "She sacrificed herself to save me."

"She should've killed Dargento instead of sacrifice herself. Sacrificing is coward way out."

My head rears back. "That woman died because of me. *For* me. She was not a coward."

Aoife's mouth puckers. Clearly, she doesn't share my opinion, but she's gracious enough not to debate this further.

"I was on my way to find Phoebus." I stare into the hallway beyond her. "Do you know where he might be?"

She looks toward my bedroom windows at the quickly darkening sky. "At this hour, you probably find him in baths."

I frown. "And you know Phoebus's bathing schedule how?"

"The baths are public hot-water pools. You not heard of them?"

"No."

"I heading back to my room. They're on way. I show you."

As we walk side by side, Aoife is uncharacteristically quiet, but so am I, both of us reliving our shared time in the Fae lands. At some point, she nods to an archway that is extra-wide as though built to accommodate a soaring Crow. Perhaps that was the intent of the architect who built this kingdom in the clouds.

"Take stairs down, and you find baths."

As she walks away, I call out, "When's our next lesson?"

"You want lessons still?"

"Absolutely."

"Tomorrow?"

"Tomorrow sounds perfect." Even though I'm a little down, I wrangle my lips into a smile, which I keep in place until she turns the corner.

Once she's gone, I pluck up my skirt and start down the stairs. It takes almost five full minutes to reach a grotto heaving with steam, chatter, and many, *many* naked bodies.

It is both disconcerting and mesmerizing. Sure, most Crows are waist-deep in water, but many are lounging around the many basins, just yakking it up—naked.

Does Lore hang around here also?

I stare around the pools for a tall blond with pointy ears. Phoebus should be easy enough to spot, what with his light-colored mane, but it's dark, and there are *many* pools and many large rock formations separating them.

The noise level suddenly plummets, and I realize why when

hundreds of eyes turn toward me. I take a minuscule step back, deciding it best to wait for Phoebus where people are clothed, but then I see him, and I stop retreating because the look he casts me...

It shatters my heart.

48

Phoebus's beautiful face is warped in anger, dejection, and disappointment. All feelings I put there. All feelings I was expecting, yet the sight of them isn't any less jarring.

I plow through the steam to reach where he stands by the wall with a towel slung around his neck.

"You're back," he says, and his tone is so flat that it makes me want to cry.

"I'm so sorry, Pheebs, but I was scared."

He folds his arms in front of his bare torso. "So you shipped me back without my consent?"

"You were safer here."

"Not your decision to make, Fallon. Not. Your. Decision."

"I know." I push my hair back, but the humidity makes it cling to my cheeks. "And I feel horrid."

"If you'd felt horrid, you would've returned sooner and apologized."

"I was trying to find Meriam."

He turns. "Not interested in your excuses."

I try to circle him without getting blasted by the ropes of water jetting from the wall. "Pheebs, please forgive me."

"Why should I?"

"Because I'm your oldest friend."

"I've made many old friends. Centuries old, for that matter."

"I meant our friendship is old, not—"

"I know what you meant. Still not interested. Go back to your *other* old friends, none of whom you sent back to this mountaintop."

"Pheebs."

"Don't *Pheebs* me." He raises his face and shuts his eyes, letting the water sluice over his clasped lids and rigid jaw.

My pulse quickens. I deserve his anger, but I refuse to let it fester. They say actions speak louder than words, so I step behind him and hug him, pressing my cheek against his shoulder blade.

I hope my hug will clang through him. "I love you and will forever shorten your name."

He doesn't toss off my arms. I take it as a good sign.

"Please find it in your squishy heart to forgive your favorite maiden."

"Maiden?" He grunts. "You're almost a doxy."

I pinch one of his nipples.

"I like my nipples pinched, even though I prefer when they're pinched by much larger hands."

I wrinkle my nose and laugh, but then I stop laughing and just keep hugging him. "I love you, Pheebs. I love you so much."

A sigh lifts his hard chest, and then one soft hand lands on my forearm and squeezes it. "Say you forgive me?"

Slowly he turns in my arms and cups either side of my face. "I love you too, Piccolina. As for my forgiveness, you— Actually…" His mouth curves with a devious smile. "You're going to have to grovel. *A lot.*"

My heart twirls slowly—two parts relieved and one part alarmed.

"What are my friendship and forgiveness worth to you?"

"Everything."

"Fabulous." His grin broadens, lighting up the green irises

that look so much lovelier on him than they look on any other earth-Fae.

Except for Nonna.

"First things first, you will disrobe and join me in the baths."

I gulp. "What?"

"You said you'd do anything. The first thing I want—since I just got here and want to hear all about Luce—is for you to macerate in this delightfully tepid water with me."

I unbind my arms from around his waist and gape at the naked crowd. "I...um...I—"

"Let me help you out of your dress. Which, by the way, resembles a paper bag without the leather corset that goes over it."

"I didn't find a corset."

"Did you look for one?"

"I preferred to look for you."

"At least you're wearing Crow clothes." He cocks an eyebrow. "Which begs the question... How long have you been back if you've had time to stop by your room for a change of clothes?"

"Apparently, I've been back a week."

"A week?!" He sputters.

"I woke up only yesterday."

"All right, you lost me."

"I was shot with a poisoned arrow while sailing around the capital with Eponine."

"I'm sorry...*what*?"

"Syb and I attended a lunch in Isolacuori where we 'bonded' with the Nebban princess."

Phoebus blinks. "I'm sorry, what?"

I repeat all the words I just said, then add a few: the Meriam carrot Eponine dangled over us, which led to the shopping trip, which led to Sybille's boozy dinner idea, which led to the boat ride and the arrow through my thigh.

I'm about to tell him about Catriona but stop talking because his jaw keeps dropping and dropping, warning me that my friend's brain is nearing dangerous overload.

"A royal gilding revel? You scored an invite to your former lover's gilding revel?"

"Not just me."

"And you planned on attending?"

"We did, until the wildling fiasco."

"Gods, who are you and what did you do with my Fallon?"

I smile at being called his Fallon, but then my smile fades because I think of Catriona's spoiled life. Dargento's bladed features float across my friend's beautiful face. However much I don't want the former commander to intrude on my reunion, until his heart stops beating, he'll forever be present.

I sigh. "I've more to tell you."

"I bet, but let's talk while we soak." He nods to the fabric clinging to my body. "Dress off."

"It's already ruined. May as well swim in it."

"You've got nothing half the people around here don't have."

I glance around the steam-filled grotto. Although Crow females aren't as voluptuous as Fae, they're *all* strong. I'm both soft and bony, a conundrum that perplexed the seamstress in charge of my measurements for Eponine's revel.

Even though I reminded myself that I was attending the party to murder a king, my cheeks had reddened at her remark.

"Pheebs, I—" I push away a lock of hair stuck to my cheek.

"You what?"

"I—I'm not comfortable getting naked in front of"—I bite my lip—"so many strangers."

"A body is just flesh, Fal. Well, feathers for some, but at present, it's predominantly skin, and we're all made of skin."

I gnaw on my lip.

"You're beautiful, Fal. For a female." He winks.

His attempt to put me at ease does nothing to settle my heart.

"Piccolina, no one will judge you. Get rid of your blasted insecurities."

"That's not—"

"Really?" He tilts his face so low that his chin looks like it dents his long neck. "Look me in the eye and tell me that's not the reason you're not shedding your frock."

"You're right. It is." Resolve makes me snatch the hem of my dress and pull it up and over my head.

"Good girl."

My cheeks burn as the moist air envelops my bared skin. I kick off my slippers, then, tongue swiping incessantly at my lower lip, I hook my thumbs into the band of my underwear and roll them off.

⌒ℓ⌒

"I can't believe I'm bathing naked in public." My awed whisper is gulped by the hiss of steam and splash of water.

Phoebus has his head propped on the stone lip of one of the smallest pools. "Doesn't it feel divine?"

The water is so hot that it does feel delightful. "So now that you've heard all my news, tell me about a certain stormy, tavern-running Crow."

He smiles. "Not much to tell yet, but I believe I'm slowly eroding his scowls with my unparalleled charm."

"Unparalleled charm?" I laugh, and gods, it feels good. "How I've missed your extravagant ego."

"And I've missed your mercurial character."

I flick water his way, but it falls long before splashing him. "Where have you been sleeping?"

"Lorcan made me the owner of a bedroom not too far from here."

"And how have his people been treating you?"

"With a mix of caution and kindness. More kindness than

caution. And his mother has been teaching me to grow plants *without* magic."

"Do you miss using your magic?"

"I do." He raises his head. "But life without magic isn't so terrible."

I trail a perfect curl of steam until it disintegrates into mist. "That's because you know you'll get it back the second you leave this place."

He's quiet for a long moment. "I cannot believe Dante pretended Meriam was free."

His comment jiggles the metaphorical knife the men in my life have planted inside my gut.

"I also cannot believe Lorcan hasn't made the Fae king sing. I wonder what he's waiting for."

The blade goes in deeper, because of course, Lore hasn't shared *that* with me. I glide my palms over the silken surface of the water, hating my constant state of cluelessness.

"Lore is surely biding his time for a reas— Hi." Phoebus grins so wide that I assume his Crow heartthrob must've arrived.

I glance over my shoulder, a greeting at the ready, but my words wither, along with my nascent smile. Although a male of shifting faith stands behind me, that male is not Connor.

49

L ore's gold stare pins me to the rock seat I've been propped on for the better part of the last hour. "Enjoying our amenities, Behach Éan?"

"I should...um..." Phoebus clears his throat. "Start getting ready. You know how long it takes me to do my hair."

I blink away from Lore's face toward Phoebus, who's wading to the far side of the basin. "Do your hair? *Seriously?*" I hiss. "Wait."

"No, no, you stay." He's already circling Lore, who's blocking the narrow passageway.

I am absolutely not staying behind with a fully dressed monarch whose body is steaming just as profusely as the water pruning my skin.

As Phoebus climbs out, I hop to my feet, forgetting that the level is waist-deep and that I am currently putting my breasts on display for all to see.

Not that there's anyone looking.

Not that there's anyone here.

Where is everyone?

Gone. Lore's monosyllabic answer knells between my temples.

When I feel his eyes on my chest, I sink back down to my neck. I'm aware he's already seen my breasts and that they're really not something to write home about, but popping up in his bedroom naked and stripping in front of a few dozen strangers has apparently not rid me of my self-consciousness.

"You have a tub in your bathing chamber, Fallon."

I bristle. "I was looking for Phoebus, and Phoebus wasn't in my tub. I didn't realize I needed a permission slip to use the public baths. You know, what with them being *public* and all."

His outline wavers some more but not his scowl. His scowl remains unyielding and in perfect focus.

"Bad day at the office, Mórrgaht?"

He stretches his neck from side to side, eliciting cracks I hear over the slap of water. "I've had worse days."

"Such a positive man." My voice is as tight as a rubber band and snaps against the water and stone.

"I'm sorry I kept secrets from you, and I'm sorry I stayed away."

"I don't give a flying fuck that you stayed away."

His eyebrows draw close. "Your tone says differently."

I laugh a very ugly laugh. "Please." I roll my eyes. "You were busy; I was busy. How's Alyosha? All moved in?"

A half smile cocks up one corner of his mouth, and it makes me want to stab him in the eye.

In *both* eyes.

"Good thing we meet in the baths then. Fewer chances of me being staked."

Gods, how I hate that he walks so freely into my mind. "What makes you think I don't have the weapon hidden on my person?"

His eyes dip to my body that the muggy, dark air is hopefully blurring. "I'd imagine, depending on the blade's sharpness, that carrying it on your person would be rather uncomfortable."

A blush seizes my cheeks, because I'm fully aware Lore isn't hinting at it being strapped to my thigh.

His eyes shimmer at my discomfiture.

Tàin.

That half smile of his grows brighter. "You've been enhancing your vocabulary, I see." One vambrace drops to the floor.

"What are you doing?"

"I'm in dire need of a bath."

As the second vambrace hits the floor, I toss his words back at him. "You have a tub in your room. Use it."

He's already unstrapped his armor and is gliding it over his head. "I haven't bathed here in centuries."

When his fingers clasp the hem of his skintight black shirt, I whip my gaze to the stone lip of the basin and scuttle toward it. "Hold your crows. I'm leaving."

"Why?"

I gape at him. "Because, Lore."

"Because...?" He draws the shirt up slowly, revealing his ladder of abdominal muscles peppered by scars.

Again, I avert my gaze. "Because I need to get dressed for dinner. Please turn so I can get out."

"Dinner won't commence without me."

"*My* dinner will." I scrutinize a chink in the rock wall. "Turn."

"Why so adamant to get away?"

A growl vibrates up my throat, and I slam my gaze back on his. "Because I'm all bathed out."

"You're all bathed out, or you're frightened to soak with me?"

"*Frightened?*" I roll my eyes to emphasize how *not* frightened I am. "Are you planning on shredding my skin with your iron talons?"

"This may come as a surprise"—he tugs on the ties of his leather trousers—"but I'm no fan of bloodbaths."

I attempt to map out an exit that doesn't involve circling him, but the only other way past Lore is scuttling up one of the boulders, and doing so slick and naked is truly not ideal. I decide to wait for him to step into the pool, then I'll swim past him and climb out.

The lazy smile that draws up one corner of his mouth makes my spine prickle. I cross my arms and scowl as he pulls off his boots excruciatingly slowly.

"Should've bathed in bird form. Would've been quicker."

"I believe that pleasurable things should never be rushed."

"You find undressing pleasurable?"

He just keeps smiling as he hooks the waistband of his pants.

I turn my glare toward the boulder keeping me corralled in this pool. Why did Phoebus have to lead me so deep into the grotto? *Right.* Because I insisted on sitting in the most secluded area. Damn him for listening to me.

The water ripples as Lore gets in. I side-eye him, briskly at first, to make sure he's decent. Once I've established that he is, I turn fully toward him. I wait for him to move to the side so no parts of our bodies brush on my way out of the basin. I may be slight, but I'd have to be missing a few major bones to weasel past him without our limbs connecting.

If only he weren't so…*massive.*

Unbothered by my desire to escape, he sits and cups water, dribbling it over one ropy shoulder, then over the other. Every one of his movements is deliberate. Calculated.

Surely calculated to madden me.

"Water's warmer thataway." I nod to the far side of the pool where the water is the exact same temperature as everywhere else.

"How fortunate that I prefer cooler water."

"It's cleaner also."

"May as well stay put, or I'll just make it filthy."

I grind my teeth.

He wants to play it that way? *Fine.* Keeping my eye on him, I move forward, then hunt the slender divide to his right and to his left, trying to decide which exit is wider.

I dart right.

He sprawls.

"Seriously?" I grumble.

"A problem?" He drapes his arms on the stone ledge, taking up more space. All the space.

I back away to regroup. "Unlike you, I'm incapable of flying—"

"A shame."

"—so unless you want me to scale you, move."

His golden eyes spark like a predator who's trapped his prey. "By all means…scale me."

The nerve of him! "Fine."

I don't miss the stunned flutter of his jaw as I shoot to my feet and plow forward. I smack my hands against his left shoulder and stick my foot on the submerged stone ledge he sits on. When the stone shifts beneath my foot, I realize—with horror—that I've stepped on his thigh.

My foot rolls, and I lose my balance, but before I can smack backward into the pool, he hooks my waist, and I land astride the hard thigh I mistook for the bench.

Perhaps for the first time in my life, it isn't the fall that rattles me but the landing. My pulse strikes my ribs and neck, making both vibrate so hard that ripples form around my body.

As I squirm to scoot off his lap, Lore spreads his fingers and clasps me, not hard enough to bruise but hard enough to make me feel like a fish caught on a lure.

The black dots in his eyes throb just as hard as my pulse. "Don't move."

His husky growl makes me go stock-still and scan the darkness for a threat. When the muggy air doesn't move with more than steam, I murmur, "Why?"

His lids close, and his nostrils flare. If we were about to be attacked, he wouldn't be closing his eyes, which means—

Something grazes the side of my knee, and…oh my gods, are there eels in these pools? I'm not intrinsically scared of eels, but I

OLIVIA WILDENSTEIN

heard they can shock a grown male with a flick of their tails. I'm
in enough shock as it is at the moment.

When I feel it brush up against the side of my leg again, I yelp
and plunge my hand under the surface to bat it away, wondering
why Lore doesn't seem the least bit perturbed by the feel of something slithering so close to his—

I freeze just as my palm connects with—

Lore shudders, and because our bodies are connected in many
a place, the tremors shoot into me and make me rattle as though
I were part serpent. I jerk my hand back out of the water, feeling
the imprint of his...of his...

"*Eel?*" Lore supplies.

My face burns, and although his mouth bears just the faintest
hint of a smile, mine bears a full-fledged scowl.

"Forgive me, Fallon"—the thumb pressed to the bottom edge
of my rib cage traces the curve of my bone—"but it's been over
five centuries."

"Since someone's referred to your junk as an eel?"

The crow master doesn't just smile; he laughs, and the vibrations of his laughter shake me from heart to eyelash.

I hold my breath, then pulse it out. "Lore, this is…" I grab at
the fingers hooked around my waist and attempt to pluck them
off my skin when his thigh moves and—holy Mother of Crows.

This is what, Behach Éan? He shifts again, and the pinpricks
of heat turn fiercer.

"It's… It's…"

His muscles contract, hardening, sharpening, and then ease
before contracting anew.

Holy fucking Cauldron… "You need to"—I bite my lip to
avoid panting—"stop. Lore. Stop."

"Why?" His husky voice fans across my jaw.

When did his face get so close to mine?

He moves again beneath me, and my vision goes white as

338

though the grotto has magically filled with a thousand flames. I smack his hard chest with the palm that touched—that touched a part of him I had no right touching.

You're my mate, Fallon. He slides his leg against me like a man honing his blade on a whetstone, and the friction blanks my mind. *My body is yours to touch, just as your body is mine to touch.*

His words drop like pebbles into my mind, sinking deep, embedding themselves in my marrow. "Lore," I croak. "It's not right. You're—" *Not mine.*

His mouth touches the underside of my chin, and the arm wound around my waist tightens, scooping me in closer, dragging my clenching center over the steel of his thigh. In some distant recess of my brain, I am screaming at the rag doll that I've become to stop riding a man's leg.

A married man, no less!

Vows mean something to me. They should mean something to him.

If I come on his lap, I'd be no more dignified than the entertainers at Bottom of the Jug. Shame pelts my thrumming spine. "Lore—stop!"

He stops, but it's too late, because the wiry hairs peppering his thigh brush against my agitated nub and undo me.

50

I weep as I climax. My tears may fall quietly, but my shame is deafening, as deafening as the clap of my abrupt pleasure. I clamp my teeth over my lower lip to keep it from quivering.

What have I done?

I am disgusted.

I am disgusting.

"I'm sorry," I croak, even though he's partly to blame. After all, if he hadn't pinned me to his lap…

If he hadn't moved his leg…

"Fallon, look at me." He pushes a strand of hair off my cheek, tucking it behind my ear.

My lids remain sealed, because I cannot look at this man I used as a scratching post. Keeping my eyes shut, I push against his chest, but my body feels like an overcooked noodle. My elbows collapse on themselves until the rest of me sags as miserably as my mood.

"Let me go, Lore."

"Not until you look at me."

When I feel his cool fingers chase the tears on my cheeks, I swivel my head to remove it from his reach. "I don't want to look at you." If I look at him, it'll make all this real.

He sighs. "Fine. Don't look at me, but listen to me."

"Don't try to tell me that what just happened between us isn't wrong because we're magically bound to each other. You're married—or about to be—and although you may not have sworn a vow of chastity to Alyora, I will not—I will not desecrate your future union."

"Just her name then?"

My eyes pop open. "What?"

"It's Alyona. Not Alyosha. Not Alyora."

I growl at the fact that he is choosing to focus on spelling instead of on what we've done.

He drags his blunt nails down the slope of my neck. "Fallon, I'm not sure why you think I've married the Glacin princess, but I've not wed her, nor do I ever intend to."

I side-eye him, eyebrows bending. "Aoife said you were finalizing your alliance."

"My alliance with her father. I never intended nor suggested marrying Alyona. Vladimir assumed I'd want to because that's how Fae establish alliances."

"But Dante said—"

"Again, an assumption."

My mouth gapes. "But you let me believe it!"

"Only because I thought it was helping you come to terms with the fact that rejecting one's mate is physically and emotionally impossible."

The hinges of my jaw creak open some more.

He presses another wet strand of hair off my face. "Unless I become a forever Crow, I'm afraid you will be stuck with me eternally, mo khrá."

Mo kraw... I assume it means *my crow*. Since Lore doesn't correct me, I run with that translation. "So you're *not* betrothed or wed?"

"No."

I catch the strong bangs of his heart in my palm. "You were never betrothed?"

"Not even for a minute."

"You asshole." I slug his shoulder, injuring my knuckles on the ridiculous knot of muscle and bone. "I cannot believe you let me run with it."

He seizes my hand and carries it to his mouth, sliding his lips back and forth over my skin. "Don't injure these pretty fingers." He sets my hand on his neck, then drops his hand back under the water and cups my knee before gliding his hand up my leg. When he reaches my backside, he gives it a pinch and rasps, "And don't call me an asshole."

"Or what?"

His fingers spread on my cheek, then begin to rub my skin.

"You'll spank me?" I say with a snort.

The smile he raises is pure, delicious evil.

Oh my gods, I'm right on the mark. Because I've never been spanked, I stare at him slack-jawed. Slack-jawed *and* turned on. How can I be turned on by the threat of corporal punishment?

He kneads my cheek with a little more gusto, and a moan slips through my parted lips. I think Lore could pluck my eyelashes out one by one, and I'd find it pleasurable.

"Mórrígan, the thoughts that go through your head." He expels an amused breath. "There'll be no uprooting of lashes."

My heart must've changed consistency, because it no longer feels very solid. It feels as though it has begun to drip through my ribs. "So you're unattached?" I ask around another moan.

"I'm very much attached."

That puts a cork in my mewling. "I didn't mean to your cause. I meant amorously."

"I also meant amorously. I am attached to my mate, Fallon." The steam glistening on his face scrapes down his black makeup. "I am attached to *you*."

"Magically. Not amorously. Gods, you cannot possibly *like* me. I've worked so hard on being a complete cow to you."

His lips twitch. "And I was impressed with your dedication. At times, I almost believed it would take an act of great valor to conquer your heart."

"You've not won my heart, merely my attention."

His chest lifts with a theatrical sigh. "An act of great valor it will have to be then."

I find myself smiling until something shifts behind him. Something that ends up being a curlicue of white steam. It does serve to remind me that we're in a public place.

"No one will come." He cups my cheek to steady my twisting head. "I've stationed guards upstairs and told them to bar the entrance to all."

I swallow, wondering if they all know I'm down here.

He traces the shape of my mouth with his thumb. "How Mórrígan has blessed me."

Although he may rethink this once he *really* gets to know me, I do store away this pretty declaration that makes him sound as though he's hopped straight off the pages of one of Mamma's books.

Granted, he is from another century. Several centuries, for that matter. "How old are you?"

"Going on seven hundred."

Seven centuries... As old as Xema Rossi. "You look rather svelte for such an old man."

His citrine irises glitter.

"If I ever become immortal, will I stop aging like you?"

The glitter turns flat, and his thumb stops stroking my lower lip, denting it instead. "You *will* become immortal. Don't ever doubt this. And yes, once immortal, you will forever stay the age you are at when you come into your powers."

Speaking of immortality... "I'm still mad at you for not telling me about Meriam."

He reclines as much as one can recline when one is sandwiched between a rock and a hard—all right, *soft*—place. "I didn't tell you immediately because I wasn't one hundred percent certain Dante was lying. After all, he took a salt oath in front of me and proclaimed she'd escaped." His fingers sketch arabesques on my submerged skin. "It wasn't until the Crows I sent to Nebba reported back that the high Fae were ingesting the same compound they've been pouring into the ocean in order to immunize themselves against salt that I understood Dante had lied to my face."

"Does he know you know?"

"He does now." At my arched eyebrow, he continues, "He's sealed all three Racoccin tunnel entrances that Antoni and his crew managed to blast open."

"So Antoni is stuck in the tunnels with my grandmother and mother?"

"And Justus Rossi and whichever other poor sod Dante sent down into the earth to guard the women."

Underground. They're all right under our feet. "How do we get them out?"

"*We?*"

Right. I signed a contract to stay put. "You."

He clasps my chin between his fingers to bring my eyes to his. "Fallon, it's not a punishment."

"Ha fios."

The smile that rises over his face at my use of Crow feels like watching the sun break over the horizon and unleash all its color and light. "What a gift it is to hear you speak my tongue." He noses the side of my neck, and Holy Cauldron, my bones turn to dough. "Can you make more sentences?"

"I can." And I do. And although my pronunciation is awry and my sentence structure still poor, he smiles at me with such pride that heat scores my heart.

"Make sure to speak in Crow when your father returns."

"To distract him from murdering you?"

"Did you read my thoughts, Little Bird?"

"Actually, I didn't."

"Do you wish to read my thoughts?"

"Does the serpent wish to swim?"

With a slow smile, he draws down his walls, and I peer inside his mind, and oh the things I see. All of them involve our bodies disrobed and entwined.

A blush touches my cheeks when I pull out of his mind, growing when I realize that I'm still straddling him. I go to slide off, but his arm bands around me to keep me in place.

Allow me to hold you a moment longer, Behach Éan. You've no idea how long I've waited to touch you. As he speaks into my mind, his submerged hand strums up and down the runnel of my spine.

Although I stop moving and consent to his caresses, my conscience pesters me about how poorly I'm behaving. If Nonna were here, the points of her ears would shrivel from shame.

"You've touched me plenty of times," I point out.

"Not in this form." With a sigh, he says, "Soon enough, we'll have to get out of this pool and return to real life."

"What will *real life* look like now?"

Lorcan Ríhbiadh brings his mouth closer to mine. "Like this, Little Bird." He erases the gap between us, fusing our mouths and gripping me bruisingly tight.

Like a human high on sprite urine, I go from shock to ecstasy in a single heartbeat. And… Why must I think of sprites and urine at this moment?

Lore chuckles against my mouth, because as always, my thoughts spill into his. *Twice now that you've mentioned sprite urine.*

I swear I've never tried it. I nip at his lip.

He hisses, so I pull back, but he slides his fingers through my hair to cup the back of my head and drive my mouth back onto his.

If you ever do, you'll do so around me.

I curl one hand around his nape, feeling the play of tendons beneath my fingertips. *Weird ask, but all right.*

I will not have you high around anyone but me. He sweeps my body closer, allocating new heat into that part of me that had somewhat calmed and cooled.

To think I was going to give him the silent treatment...

He kisses the hinge of my jaw, then slips my earlobe into his mouth before rasping, "You, Fallon Báeinach, are incapable of staying quiet when I'm around."

I roll my eyes, but then he begins to move his leg again, and a moan drops from my mouth.

Gods, who knew a leg could be so...so...

Erogenous? he suggests.

Versatile.

His gentle snort coaxes a grin from my lips and fills my chest with warmth. As he leans back, his amusement transforming into something else...something akin to rapture, I widen my knees, and the side of it bumps into what I assumed was not attached to his body earlier. How did I ever mistake something so rigid and thick for an eel?

His eyes spark, then gleam as he guides me up and down the length of his thigh. With each stroke, my brain goes the way of my heart, liquefying, and my organs rearrange themselves inside my softened body, my heart sinking into that place between my legs that Lore is tormenting so very wondrously. I find myself locking air into my lungs before gasping it out.

Although we sit in a grotto, surrounded by stone and steam, it feels like we are melding into each other under a star-filled sky. The gathering heat arches my spine and makes my head fall back. Never in my life has anything felt like this. Gods, if it had, I'd have spent more time in bed riding my hand or someone's lap.

Lore growls. *Behach Éan, from this point forward, the only lap or hand or face you will be riding are mine. Is that clear?*

My cheeks burn just as ardently as my sex at the mention of his face.

Yes, my face. His fingers crush my skin—in the best way—as he grinds me against him. *My nose. My tongue.*

I sputter as he uses said tongue to lick a line from my clavicle to my chin.

Mórrígan, how jealous I am of my own thigh. He kisses back down the column of my throat, his perfect nose grooving my humid skin.

My vision goes sparkly black, and my blood converges in that one place he's been titillating since I attempted to climb over him.

Best.

Botched.

Endeavor.

Ever.

This time, as I unravel against his thigh, as my heart swirls and blurs the contours of everything around me, as his arms band possessively around my waist and his mouth grazes my pulse point, I don't weep.

I exult.

51

L ore studies my upturned face, and although he does not touch me with his fingers or mouth, his dark smoke laces around my neck before gliding over my kiss-swollen lips.

We reached my bedroom door several minutes ago—me dressed in Lore's black shirt that falls to midthigh and Lore wearing only his leather pants and boots—but we've yet to part ways.

Lore, until we're both certain of what exactly this is, can we keep it between us?

One dark eyebrow arches so high that it gets lost behind a lock of mussed, damp hair.

"What?" I whisper.

He readjusts the unbound armor slung over his wide shoulder. *Nothing.*

You are clearly thinking something.

Am I?

I narrow my eyes on his, then startle when I catch the tail end of a contemplation. "I *whispered* your name. I didn't scream it."

Right?

At the rise of another cocky smile, I fathom that I may have gotten a little carried away. *So your guards may be aware, but can you ask them to keep what they heard to themselves?*

If this is the only thing that stands between you and your happiness, Behach Éan, then let's pretend we are only friends.

We were never really friends, so I'm not sure how believable that will be.

Fine. He looses a long-suffering sigh. *Back to enemies it is then. It was fun.*

I cross my arms. "Fun? I honest-to-goodness loathed you many times over. Especially when you confined me up here."

Yes. He bobs his head in the direction of the studded door. *In that horrid cell full of minuscule windows that you couldn't fit through. What a grievance you endured.*

"You can be so insufferable." I snatch my sodden dress from his hand.

As I turn toward my door, Lore steals my hand and lifts it to his mouth. *My temperamental little bird.* He kisses my knuckles one by one. *In my mind, there isn't even a sliver of a doubt as to what this is, but I will ask my birds to bite their tongues until your qualms dissipate.* He flips my hand and licks a languid line from the center of my palm to the inside of my wrist. *Till the sky is darkest, and I can taste you everywhere.*

I stand planted in front of my door like one of Nonna's medicinal shrubs for a solid minute after he retreats to his rooms, gaping after him. And then I am gaping at the inside of my hand, at the glistening trail that reminds me of the one leftover by the snail that took up residence in my palm a long-ago summer day when I'd been supposed to help Nonna harvest herbs from our narrow planters but instead had found myself playing with their diminutive inhabitants.

Dress dangling in the crook of one arm and fingers closed around Lore's strange show of possession or affection, I pump the door handle of my bedroom, squeaking when I catch sight of someone lounging upon my bed, a book in hand.

"Oh my gods, Pheebs," I hiss at him as I clap my door shut and toss the sodden gown on the foot of the bed. "You almost stopped my heart."

He pitches the heavy book aside, and it sinks into the pillowy comforter. "How was your soak?"

At his eloquent smile, I avert my gaze, studying the gilded accents gracing the title that shimmers gold against aged brown leather. "Fine."

"Second rule of friendship: one cannot give a stock answer after best friend forfeits a delightful moment of relaxation so one's friend can spend quality time in the buff with a hot male. It's just not allowed. Had I been in there with Connor, I would've given you a play-by-play of every minute of our interaction."

I bite my bottom lip, which still tastes of Lore's kisses. "Everything said in here remains between us."

"That's the third rule of friendship: what is said between friends remains between friends."

"Are you penning a manifesto of some kind?"

"Not at the moment, but perhaps I should spread my wisdom."

I smirk.

He rolls out of bed and swaggers toward my closet. "I picked out your outfit."

Upon seeing him emerge holding a gauzy black dress and a scrap of black lace, I gulp. "I—"

"—will put it on immediately. It's perfect, Phoebus darling."

I take some offense that his impersonation of my voice is squeaky. "I don't sound like that, do I?"

"When you whine."

"When do I *ever* whine?"

"You're whining right now."

"I haven't even said a word about the dress!"

"On the inside, you're saying many words."

I snort.

"Don't pretend like you don't have an opinion on the gown."

"I was just going to point out that it was sheer, which will allow everyone to see everything. And black. I don't usually wear black. Black is for funerals."

"What color do you think you're wearing at the present moment, sweets? Yellow?" He nods to Lore's top. "As for black, it's the color of Crows. Besides, you agreed to my terms. If you prefer to pick another outfit, then by all means, browse away, but know that you'll have to pick another friend, and best of luck finding someone of my caliber."

I cannot help the grin that overtakes my face at his dramatic declaration. "Fine. Dress me like a first-class harlot."

He hesitates for a second. "Fal, even with tawdry makeup and tits spilling out, you could never look like a harlot. Besides, I checked, and the bodysuit beneath will cover all those essential bits that you're saving for the eyes of a certain handsome, lethal king."

My cheeks warm, and my heart takes flight.

"And no, I am not referring to Dante."

My mind hadn't even wandered Dante's way.

"Now, tell me everything."

I wrinkle my nose and squeeze my lids shut.

"Piccolina, I assure you, nothing you did down there will shock me."

I am fully aware of Phoebus's breadth of experience. Most of Luce is. Keeping my eyes shut, I confess, "I stumbled onto his lap."

"Clever. I may recycle your trick."

My lids reel up. "It was no trick, Pheebs. I was trying to climb out of the pool, and I slipped."

"A shame you didn't stumble onto his cock. He looks like he's in possession of a substantial one. Not that size matters *all* that much, but..." He wrinkles his nose. "Was your target his penis but it was too small?" Phoebus appears suddenly so anxious that I cannot help the laugh that bubbles out of me.

"My target was neither his cock—which would've been, I assure you, *unmissable*—nor his leg. My target was the exit."

"It's a much better story that you fell into his lap because you thought falling onto his giant penis was too forward."

"Forget that friendship manifesto. You should write erotic booklets, Pheebs."

He blinks, and his eyes acquire a glazed sparkle. "That is a brilliant idea. Almost as brilliant as awakening the Crows. Gods, life was dull before they flapped back into Luce, wasn't it?"

Life may have been dull, but it was safe. Now nothing is secure, save for this kingdom in the clouds.

"Back to you tumbling onto Lorcan Ríhbiadh's lap."

Since Phoebus is like a sprite with a coin, I know he will not stop asking me until I tell him everything, so I do, and by the time I'm done, he's finished doing up my black gown.

As I stare down at my legs that are on full display thanks to the sheer material, I ask, "We are going to dine at the tavern next door, right?"

"Yes."

"Are you sure this is appropriate? The last time I went, everyone was wearing battle armor and pants."

He points to himself, to the fluid black trousers that sit low on his waist and the soft white shirt that shows off a good portion of his torso. "Am I wearing armor?"

"No, but you're a Fae, and I'm a Crow."

"You're also a Shabbin, and from the book I'm reading about Shabbe that Lore lent me from his private library—you can thank me later for my thorough research—Shabbins favor silken, barely there gowns. They weave most of their material from the iridescent excretion of a land mollusk. Fascinating, isn't it?"

Worries that I am underdressed flee my mind. "Incredible."

Phoebus heads into my bathroom and returns with a block

of black clay, the same that Lore rubbed between his palms. "And now for the finishing touch."

I shake my head. "Pheebs, no. I'm not ready for that." My reasons for refusing to apply stripes have changed. I used to associate them with picking sides. Tonight, I've realized it is a privilege earned, and I haven't earned it yet.

"Lorcan will appreciate it, and so will your father."

"He's here?"

"I heard the guards mention he was flying home."

Home... Is that what this place has become to Phoebus?

"It's just makeup, Piccolina."

Except it's not.

Phoebus settles on darkening my lash line with the black paste stuck to his fingers. After he blackens his own lash line, making the green pop, Phoebus takes my arm, sweeping me out of my bedroom and into the hallway. Although we don't cross paths with many Crows, the few that we pass gape at the two of us as though we were one serpent short of a den. As I feared, everyone is dressed in battle leathers, while the two of us are dressed for a stroll in Tarecuori.

"Will Lore be joining us at the tavern?" Phoebus asks.

"I don't know." I tug on the sides of the plunging V, attempting to stretch the unyielding fabric to cover more of my skin. "He's meeting with the Siorkahd. Why? Did you want to dine with him?"

"Who wouldn't want to dine with that man? But no, I'm asking because I'm so looking forward to witnessing his expression when he lays his eyes on my handiwork."

"Have you taken up a craft I'm not aware of?"

Phoebus snorts. "Although Connor's son is teaching me to engrave, I meant *you*, Piccolina. You can thank me by bringing me breakfast in bed tomorrow. If, that is, you're not still tripping and impaling yourself on a certain Crow's colossal—"

"Say one more word, and I will murder you in your sleep." Between clenched teeth, I add, "That way, I will be spared from lugging a breakfast tray your way."

He pats my hand as though that were the silliest threat I'd ever issued. "Come. I have a usual table."

My skimpy dress becomes the least of my concerns as we wind around diners to reach the far wall along which stands the smallest table in the tavern, a little round one right beside the bar.

It's set for one.

"I thought you said Crows were being friendly."

He pulls out the chair. "They are. What's with the bent brows?"

"Your usual table has one chair." Not even a bench. "*One* plate. *One* glass."

"How observant you are, Signorina Báeinach." As he tucks me in, he leans in close and murmurs, "Perhaps you will observe that my usual table also has an unobstructed view of the bar."

Although I understand what he is implying, I cannot shake my concern. "Are you eating alone?"

"No. Sometimes Lazarus joins me. Sometimes Bronwen."

"Both Fae!" My exclamation drags many a stare our way. Or maybe they were already staring in our direction.

"Aoife stops by for tea daily. Usually to complain about you."

I cannot even bring myself to react to what is obviously meant as a taunt.

"And at closing time, Reid will share a drink with me."

Hearing that he has *some* Crow company somewhat reassures me. "Reid?"

"Connor's son. The one teaching me stone engraving. We've become unlikely friends," he explains, just as the man makes his way toward us, holding a chair aloft. "He's the only half-Crow left in Luce, since all the others either were killed or fled to Shabbe."

"Killed?" I blink at Phoebus.

But it's the light-haired Crow who answers, "We leath'cinn aren't immortal. Well, those of us with a human parent."

I take it that *lehken* means half-Crow. I also take it that Reid is not including me in the *those with a human parent* group.

He sets the chair down for Phoebus, then lingers beside our table, hands on his narrow hips. "You were not aware, daughter of Cathal and Zendaya?"

"Fallon. Daughter of Cathal and Zendaya is a bit of a mouthful. And no, I was not aware. What about the progeny of Fae and Crows? Are they immortal?"

Phoebus sighs, scooting himself under the tiny table. "Fae and Crows cannot conceive children. Conflicting blood. Crows have too much iron, and iron poisons Fae."

My mouth parts. Gods, I know nothing.

Right as Connor's son begins to turn away, I call him back, "Reid, right?"

"Yes."

"Thank you for keeping my friend company."

Pink streaks across Phoebus's cheekbones. "You make me sound like some abject runt."

Not my intent.

"Your friend has many interesting stories." Reid's jaw isn't as square as his father's, and his skin is a much lighter shade of brown, like his hair, yet there is a lot of Connor in that face.

"I'm certain you must have plenty of your own."

"Not yet." A tepid smile slides across his mouth. "But hopefully I will get to make more stories this time around. If our king can keep himself in one piece, that is." He reaches for something behind the bar—an extra plate and goblet. "A feat when one's curse breaker favors the Fae lands."

My spine stiffens at his quietly delivered affront. I'm tempted to engage, but Phoebus clasps my knee under the table and gives his head a little shake.

Reid backs away. "I'll go fetch you some food."

"No meat or fish," Phoebus instructs. "And not too much salt, or I'll be spilling way too many secrets again."

Reid nods before finally turning away.

"I do not favor the Fae lands," I mutter once it's only the two of us.

Phoebus cocks his head to the side.

"I don't, Pheebs. I only went there to find Meriam."

"A task you could've left for immortals to oversee."

"I assumed, when I left here, that my grandmother was on the run and that she'd run straight for me."

"Piccolina, if she'd been on the run and had run straight for you, what makes you think she wouldn't have run you through?"

"If she'd wanted me dead, she would've killed me already."

"Unless she couldn't kill you at the time."

I frown. "The woman created a magical barrier with her blood, Pheebs. She kidnapped my mother. Her *own* daughter." I don't tell him about Gabriele's belief that Meriam would've killed Zendaya. I'm afraid that speaking it aloud will somehow make it true. "Do you really think that someone as powerful and twisted as she is would have the least bit of trouble murdering another?"

Phoebus's eyes are glazed in thought. "I meant that maybe she struck a bargain or something that kept her from killing you."

"With whom?"

"Marco?" He shrugs. "Who knows?"

I blink at my friend.

"I'm just thinking out loud. Maybe no bargain was struck."

"If Meriam struck a bargain with Marco," says a gruff voice, "it'll have expired."

The apple in Phoebus's throat climbs as high as my pulse as I spin in my chair to face the man I haven't seen in two weeks.

"You left the sky kingdom, ínon?" My father's growl flutters my lashes.

"I...um...will—" Phoebus vaults out of his chair. "See what's taking our food so long."

I allow Phoebus to escape, since that's clearly his intent.

"I'm going to kill Lore," my father says through barely separated teeth.

I'm about to spring out of my seat to latch on to my father's arm before he can go hunt Lore down when black shadows congeal between us and firm into a man-shaped shield.

"A feat many have failed at, Cathal," I hear Lore quip beneath his breath.

My father's large fingers close around the sky king's neck and flex. "I trusted you, and you let her leave the sky kingdom?"

"And she's returned." I'm honestly not sure how Lore is keeping his cool. "Now unhand me before I break your nose for what, the fourth time?"

My eyes go as bulbous as my father's. *You've broken his nose three times?*

All in good fun.

You've a strange definition of fun... Before any bone breaking can occur, I speak up. "I forced Lore to let me go, Dádhi."

My father glances over Lore's broad, fuming shoulder at me. His hand drops, not because he's released Lore but because the Crow king has dissolved into black vapors that knit back in the very same place a moment later.

As Cathal's heavy arm flops back along his side, the buckles on his vambrace clink against his chest plate.

"And I was the one to encourage her, Cathal." Bronwen steps into the tavern on Cian's arm.

"You encouraged her?" Lore seems to grow more rigid in spite of the wisps of smoke leaching off him.

My father spins around to face Bronwen and barks something crude in Crow, which I fathom must mean "Why in Mórrígan's name would you do that?"

"She needed to leave."

"She needed to leave?" Lore repeats in a tone that makes the air feel as solid and chilled as a block of ice.

I'm admittedly surprised. Here I'd assumed Lore had been kept abreast of Bronwen's latest prophecy.

His gaze whirls to mine, ramming into me with a force that makes my heart take refuge behind my spine. "What new prophecy?" he growls, and although his rage should really alarm me, his timbre has a completely different effect.

Not the time.

Not the time.

"Did you just—" Cian looks between Lore and me, his eyes growing wider and wider. "My niece is your mate, Lore?"

52

I f someone were to drop a pin in Adh'Thábhain, the whole of the sky kingdom would hear it plink. That is how quiet it's become.

Phoebus, who retreated behind the bar when my father swooped into the tavern like a bat from the underworld, mouths, *"Mate?"* Or maybe what he says is "Merda." Both would be appropriate.

With a sigh, I murmur to Lore, "Well, I guess the crow's out of the bag."

Lore tips me a very unamused look over his shoulder. *What fucking prophecy?*

The coward that I am drops the hot potato on Bronwen's lap. Technically, it's her prophecy, so she gets the honor of telling everyone about it. "I'll let Bronwen fill you in."

"Speak, Bronwen!" Lore's command raises the fine hairs along my arms.

"I foresaw that Fallon needed to return to the Fae lands to end Dante Regio's life." Her tone is so placid you'd think she was commenting on the weather. "Only then will Luce be returned to the Crows."

Thunder cracks outside the stone portholes, and lightning shreds the black sky.

"Over my dead body," Lore growls.

Good thing you cannot actually die, Lore.

He sends me another withering look over his shoulder, one that does not hit me in the same place his earlier one did. I may like the man worked up, but I don't like him angry.

"Are you mad, Bronwen?" My father is so livid, he could surely pulp bark with his jaw. "My daughter is not going after the fucking Fae king!"

As they all begin yelling at each other in Crow, Phoebus crooks his finger at me. I slide out from behind the table and sidle close to the bar, opposite where he stands.

"I'm sorry, *what?*"

"Bronwen can see the—"

"I'm not talking about the prophecy, Fal. You're Lore's *mate?*" he hisses as he thumbs open a bottle of sky wine and pours himself a very full glass.

I reach over the bar and pluck it, so he pours himself another. "I swear I was going to tell you, but I was waiting to decide if I wanted the link."

He dribbles wine outside the cup. "*Waiting to decide?*"

Connor hands him a kitchen rag, but Phoebus is in too much shock to notice the tendered cloth, so the Crow tosses it on the spill before moving back down the bar to sliver some cheese.

"A mating link isn't some new fashion trend, Piccolina. It's something sacred. I may not be a Crow, but even *I* know that."

I bite the life out of the inside of my cheek.

"Oh my gods, if you're the Crow king's mate, then that makes you—"

"His friend whose mind he can penetrate at will." The words whiz through my lips like that demented Fae tribe's arrows—swift and soundless.

"—queen."

"I'd have to marry him, and I'm not there. I'm not really any-where at the moment. Well, besides in this tavern with you and"—I glance over my shoulder—"a lot of livid bird people."

Phoebus trails my gaze. "I like drama, but this is a lot."

Is he referring to my father's anger, Lore's mood storm, or Bronwen's prophecy? Not that I'd forgotten about the proph-ecy, but the reminder that I'm destined to end someone's life—someone I know well, no less—chills me to the core. Then again, that man is a big, fat liar.

I press my back to the stone wall and take a gulp of my wine. "Dinner to go?"

"I'll see if Connor can wrap some things up for us."

"Just grab the wine and—"

Do not even think *about leaving.* Lore's command makes me jump.

Wine sloshes over the rim of my cup and splashes the V of bare skin between the black material.

Lore's citrine gaze heats as he follows the downward descent of the crimson droplets but then cools as Bronwen says, "It's already in motion, Lore. It cannot be stopped."

He whirls back on my aunt and takes a step in her direction. "Watch me stop it, Bronwen."

Forks of lightning streak the blackened sky that groans like the floor beneath our feet.

"If you kill Dante, Mórrgaht, you will doom us all. And this time, not for a handful of centuries or a couple of decades but forever." No tears tumble from Bronwen's eyes, yet they gleam like the newly formed knobs atop a juvenile serpent's head. "He knows how to turn you into a forever Crow."

Hisses erupt around the room.

"How the fuck does he know?" Lore's voice is low yet some-how resonates over his people's dread.

"Meriam told him."

Imogen approaches Lore, berthing herself right beside him. "She refused to tell Marco yet told his brother?"

I'm well aware Aoife's sister is part of the Siorkahd, but must she stand so close?

Even though my petty jealousy should really be the last of his concerns, Lore takes a step sideways, adding distance between their bodies. *If you stood at my side, Fallon, no other would.*

You've two sides, Your Majesty.

"Yes, Imogen, Meriam told Dante in exchange for her freedom. Little did she know he would withhold it."

Imogen's mouth puckers. "Forgive me, but I find it out of character that she would strike a bargain without ensuring—"

"The Nebban-made substance my nephew has started ingesting hasn't only made him immune to salt *and* iron; it's also made him immune to bargains." Bronwen's words snap on the tail end of a lightning bolt.

My eyebrows bend, because I remember King Roy's surprise when my bargain failed to sink into his skin. Aren't they imbibing the same chemical?

I'm about to ask why it would affect people differently but lose my train of thought when my father asks, "What if *I* kill him? What happens then?"

"*Any* Crow who attempts to kill my nephew will be turned into a forever Crow, Cathal. The Cauldron has shown this to me." Her eyes shut for a moment, and she burrows her face against Cian's chest as though to reassure herself that his heart still beats. "He's been collecting Meriam's blood."

The tavern goes deathly quiet as every Crow in attendance contemplates their humanity…and mortality.

"To do what with it? Cast spells?" My vocal cords feel as snarled as wind-tossed hair.

"No. To baste his weapons," Bronwen explains. "If the mixture of Shabbin blood and obsidian enters a Crow's heart, it rids them of their humanity."

Making them forever Crows...

Come to me, Little Bird. It will help me think. The fingers of Lore's right hand unspool from their hardened fist. **Fallon, take my hand.** When I don't move toward him, he adds, **Please.**

It isn't so much the *please* that makes me pare myself off the rock wall at my back and approach but the weariness in Lore's tone. And perhaps also the desire to fence him off from Imogen.

I know Crows cannot die of strokes, Lore, but seeing how purple in the face my father is, I believe it may be safer—for all our sakes—not to hold hands? My unsettled nerves make this come out as a question.

Lore must take pity on my father, because he doesn't spear his fingers through mine. Nevertheless, his dark smoke coils around my fingers and wrist before wrapping around my waist like a cashmere stole.

"It has to be Fallon." Bronwen's declaration makes every single person stare at me. "It is what the Cauldron wants."

"What about what I want?" Lore all but roars, his shadows hardening and chilling, turning to frost against my pebbled skin. "What *my mate* wants?"

My father's eyes glitter with fury. "Crow blood runs in my daughter's veins, Bronwen."

She inhales a deep lungful of her mate before turning her scarred face back toward us. "As long as Fallon's magic is bound, obsidian will not affect her."

Lore's outline darkens. "I'll get Vance to do it. That man will do anything for coin."

"Vance is human," Bronwen counters, "and humans are weak."

"What if a Fae"—Phoebus's cheeks grow pink when everyone's attention presses against him—"k-kills—

"Don't even think about it." I shake my head.

"I suppose a pure-blooded Fae could stand a chance—"

"No!" I all but shout at Bronwen before the insane seed can take root in Phoebus's mind.

Bronwen stares in my direction, and I stare back. My anger is so potent that I've no doubt it leaps off me and into her.

"If a Fae—other than one you're attached to—can do away with my nephew, then *perhaps* you and Lorcan can steal away to Shabbe to break his obsidian curse. I'd need to ask the Cauldron."

My eyebrows scrunch. "*Shabbe?* I thought we needed to find Meriam to break his curse."

"Your grandmother has nothing to do with—" Bronwen stops talking so suddenly that I suspect Lore or Cian have asked her not to spill more secrets. Because a Fae is present...or because I am?

I turn toward Lore. *Please tell me.*

Lore's eyes close briefly. When they reopen, they burn a path straight into Bronwen's skull. "If Fallon and I head to Shabbe, we'll be stuck behind Meriam's wall." His smoke thickens like the icy mist that rolls over Tarelexo in the dead of winter. "I will not abandon my people."

"Then you will doom them all, for if a single one of your crows falls to obsidian dipped in Shabbin blood, you will never be whole again, Mórrgaht."

"Oh my gods." I take a step back, because I have Shabbin blood, and yes, at the moment, all of it is contained in my veins, but I will not risk—

Your magic is bound, and unless I'm mistaken, you're in possession of no obsidian stake. To everyone else, Lore says, "I will use a sword to remove his head. I was good with swords once upon a time."

"You'd risk all our lives?"

"You give me too little credit, Cian."

"I did not mean to slight you, Lore." My uncle drags Bronwen closer even though little space exists between their bodies. "But my mate has finally found a way to remove our weakness. It's been a collective dream of ours for centuries, and your unwillingness to heed her words baffles me."

Rain lashes at the mountain, filling the cavern in which we stand with the sound of a thousand drums. "I took an oath, Cian." Lore's gaze cycles around the room, over the wide-eyed black stares fastened to him before stopping on the door that leads to the rest of his kingdom. "An oath to guide and protect each one of you until you decide to live out your days as forever Crows. What sort of king would I be if I hid behind a magical wall and let you fend for yourselves?"

Colm shakes his head. "You cannot call it hiding when—"

"The Crows who took refuge in Shabbe still cannot shift," Lore rasps. "My call does not carry through the wards."

"I stand with Cian and Bronwen," my father says.

"Of course you do, Cathal. Your daughter would be safest in Shabbe. In truth, I should send her—"

You're not sending me anywhere.

Lore's mouth thins. *I could not anyway, for I am too selfish a man.*

The sky king is many things: impossible, controlling, possessive, infuriating—

Do I have any redeeming qualities?

You're nicely muscled?

He must not have been expecting that, because in the middle of the storm he is waging both outside and inside his realm, his mouth curves with a smile destined only for me.

I'm so lost in the white glow of his teeth and honeyed shine of his eyes that I fail to register that Lore's smoke has turned into an arm and a hand that are towing me into the body attached to them. The realization sets my cheeks ablaze.

Like you said, Behach Éan, the crow is out of the bag.

"Fallon?" My father's voice tears my gaze from Lore's.

"I'm sorry, Dádhi. What?"

"Pack your things." He whirls on his tall boots.

"Pack my…"

"I'm flying you to Shabbe." He's already striding toward the tavern's exit.

Lore must yell into my father's mind, because the huge man stalls in the doorway and glares over his shoulder.

"You may be my king, but she is my daughter, Lore."

"And you may be my closest friend, but she is my mate, Cathal. You will not take her away from me."

I pull away from Lore and stick a hand on my hip. "I'll remind the two of you that I'm endowed with both an opinion *and* a voice." The twin glowers they hurtle my way make my chin lift a fraction.

"Which she will not be using." Phoebus clasps his wineglass between whitening knuckles, a grimace scoring his pretty face. *Please*, he mouths.

But I use it. "Until Meriam is bled dry, I will stay here."

My father's dark eyes simmer with rage. "You set even a toe outside the sky kingdom, ínon," my father says, "and I'm carrying you to Shabbe. Is that clear? And, Lorcan, find someone else to send on your fool's errands to Nebba, because I'll be staying right here with my daughter. It's about time we bond." My father's smile is rather terrifying. "I'll be by to pick you up at sunup, Fallon." As he becomes one with the darkened hallway, he adds, "I recommend you get to bed soon. And alone."

Oh. My. Gods. My father did not just say that.

Body temperature near combustion, I look up at Lore, who is simpering at the blackened space that used to house my father's body. I try to press away from the sky king, if only to allow fresh air to sweep around my skin and into my lungs, but there's no give to Lore's hold.

How can you smile at a time like this?

Lore's gaze falls on my mouth. *The most magnificent woman in the room belongs to me, and everyone, including herself, is finally aware of it. How in the world could I not smile?*

I wet my lips with my tongue. *Because this woman's father wants to delimb you. As for belonging—*

You are mine, mo khrá. The same way that I am yours. From now until the end of time.

His declaration of everlasting love not only steals my breaths but also my heartbeats. They tumble from my chest into my bloodstream, then press against my skin, desperate to penetrate Lore and gather inside his fierce heart.

His thumb sweeps across the indent at my waist. *We should get you fed.*

I blink out of my daze, puzzled by his change of subject, until I hear the riotous gurgle of my stomach.

You will need sustenance before we retire.

"You mean before my morning excursion?"

I'll see that you are fed before then as well.

His insinuation makes everything inside me blaze hotter.

He commandeers a larger table and has a mountain of food set before me. Well, before all of us—Phoebus has made his way back to my side, and a few more members of the Siorkahd have taken seats. Only my father, Cian, and Bronwen departed.

Although Lore drinks, he doesn't eat. He merely strokes up and down my spine with his fingertips, which earns me a rather dour look from Imogen, who sits across from us. In the past, I would've labeled it jealousy, but she seems more upset with me than anything. A lot like Reid.

"Reid?" Lore's murmur smacks my lobe.

I pretend not to have heard him by asking the man beside Imogen—Erwin—about life in Nebba, since that is where he and my father were stationed for the last few days.

What has Reid said to you?

Nothing, Lore.

Clearly. I guess I will have to ask him myself.

I clap his leg to keep his ass glued to the bench. *He said he hopes you will stay whole.*

And...

How do you know there's an and?

There's always an and *with you.*

What is that supposed to mean?

That your interactions are often layered. Now tell me, Little Bird, what else did that boy say?

I hold his golden stare but let go of his leg. *He suggested I abstain from heading back to the Fae lands so I don't put you in harm's way.*

Is that all?

It is.

He tilts his head to the side as though an incline will help him pluck Reid's insinuation from my brain. It must, because he stands. *Excuse me.*

Lore, please...

Do you prefer the Fae lands, Fallon?

Once upon a time, I did. So you see, he wasn't entirely wrong.

Perhaps, but he was out of line. I will not have anyone speaking to my—

I'd prefer they speak honestly.

He interrupts Erwin's monologue, which I'd meant to listen to, and nods to the entrance. "A word."

You swear you'll leave Reid alone?

Although he grinds his jaw, he does end up acquiescing. "Thank you."

Aoife, who arrived at the same time as my silent altercation with Lore began, gapes in absolute wonder between the king and me. "I hope it will not take as many centuries for me to find mate."

As she and Phoebus discuss if there's a way to *speed things up,*

HOUSE OF POUNDING HEARTS

I follow the movement of Lore's lips, attempting to make out the quiet words he is having with one of the men who went missing in Nebba for a few hours. However hard I concentrate, though, my espionage is useless, for he's not speaking Lucin, and I'm still far from fluent in his tongue.

Which reminds me... "How do you say *crow* in Crow, Aoife?"

"Chréach."

"*Kreyock?*" My eyebrows bend. "I thought— So what does *kraw* mean?"

"Khrá?" Aoife smiles. "Where you hear that word, Fallon?"

My shoulder blades tighten. "Why?"

Phoebus grins so wide I'm seized by the sudden urge to smack his pec, because that smile is totally at my expense.

"I heard it nowhere. Forget I asked." I drown the sudden spike of my pulse in my wine.

Aoife's eyes glitter just as brightly as the garland of glass lanterns over our heads. "Khrá means *love*."

I flip my gaze over to Lore, who is staring right back at me, one corner of his mouth tugged up. **Ready to retire...mo khrá?**

53

y cheeks are still flaming, yet it's been a full minute since Lore suggested we leave together and called me...called me...

You haven't even eaten, I deflect.

I will.

When?

When we get to my bedchamber.

Should I make you a plate?

I've an appetite for something other than food.

I choke on my sip of water, then hack up what feels like a lung.

"You all right there, piccolo serpens?" Phoebus taps my back.

I snatch his goblet of wine, since mine is empty, and upend it.

We're not going to war, Little Bird, only to my bedchamber.

I know this, yet it feels like one and the same.

Lore sighs. I'm not sure if he does so out loud or in my mind, but his expelled breath is so strong that it feels as though it fans across my flushed skin. *Come. I'll walk you to your room and then depart for mine.*

My pulse skips over a beat at the out he gives me, and although my skin still feels hot, a glance at my collarbone shows my mottled complexion is finally receding. "Pheebs, where is your room?"

"Mine? Aren't you more interested in knowing where—"

I flick his bicep before he can finish that sentence. "I want to know on which door to pound after I'm done *bonding* with my father."

"Cathal made it back?" Aoife asks.

"Oh yes." Phoebus replenishes the glass I set back down. "And he's in a jolly mood."

"It's great honor for him that daughter is mated with—"

"Phoebus was being sarcastic, Aoife." I finally hoist myself from the bench. "My father is *not* in a pleasant mood. I'll let Phoebus fill you in since he so loves to gossip."

"What slander!" Phoebus sputters, which brings a smile to my mouth, the first in a while. "But she speaks true. I do live for gossip."

After Phoebus explains where he sleeps, I drop a kiss on his cheek, then wish Aoife a good night before slipping around the tables toward the doorway where Lore waits, calm and steady, the outline of his body in perfect focus.

Blood rushing beneath my skin, I stride past him down the hallway. Why does this feel like a walk of shame? Shouldn't walks of shame involve daylight, rumpled clothes, and smudged makeup? Lore follows me in silence—a silence that isn't altogether uncomfortable, if not a little nerve-racking.

We cross paths with no one, and when we reach my closed door, we stand facing each other like earlier. Unlike earlier, though, there is no playful banter being exchanged. No smirks either.

We are both still like a forest before the storm, except the storm Lore unleashed over Luce has ended, whereas the heavy air between us crackles with new beginnings.

"I never want you to feel as though I'm cornering you, Fallon." His features are feverish in the darkness—his irises lightning bright, his skin luminescent like the moon, his lips glossed as though he's just dampened them with his tongue.

I take a step nearer, aligning the tips of my shoes with the polished toes of his boots.

"What of me cornering you, Mórrgaht?" My pulse bangs against my skin, against my eardrums, against my bones. "How do you feel about that?"

His shadows unspool and wrap around me, dragging me infinitesimally closer. "Petrified."

Although the tension in my body is at an all-time high, my arm is steady as I raise it to his neck, and so are my legs as I roll up onto my toes and kiss the smirk off his mouth.

The scent of wind and night thickens, swirling off him and into me until I am so full of Lorcan Ríhbiadh that oxygen does not manage to worm its way into my lungs. Yet I cannot find it in me to unfasten my mouth or my body from his. I've plunged headfirst into his darkness and am sinking fast, my pulse rippling, my ribs tightening, my stomach clenching.

Lore cups my cheek with one hand and the small of my back with the other and smothers what few particles of air remained between us.

How did I ever think I could resist this…this magic? But mostly, why did I spend even a second trying? At times, I am baffled by my stubbornness.

Lore gently thumbs my jaw, parting my lips wider and sweeping his tongue into every corner of my mouth.

I sigh, and he consumes the sound before pulling away.

Breathe, he instructs.

I'd rather kiss you.

And I'd rather not asphyxiate my mate. Especially so early on in our relationship.

My lungs burn as they inflate with not only air but with a laugh.

He presses open my door. "Now, go inside and rest. Knowing your father, he'll have energy to spare in the morning."

My laughter becomes air, which becomes a tight press of my lips. I'm not ready for this night to end. Not when it was just beginning.

Lore's pupils shrink as he, I imagine, reads my thoughts. Sometimes, I wonder if he has any more space for thoughts of his own what with absorbing all of mine.

His lips curve into a slow smile. "I assure you, I have many thoughts of my own, Little Bird."

"Prove it."

"Step inside my mind." He lowers his lids. When he reels them up, his irises are lambent.

My vision whitens as I not only penetrate his mind but drop into it. And I see myself through his eyes, the flush of my cheeks and the sputter of my pulse point, my widening violet eyes and my reddened mouth.

I turn, and I am there too but dressed differently and galloping atop Furia. I spin again to find ghostly hands fastening the laces of the gown I wore in Tarespagia. And then I catch water beading over my collarbone and collecting in its hollow and a thumb pressing into it gently, tipping my head back, back, back before lapping at the glimmering drops.

Everywhere I look, I find myself, and I feel him watching me, thinking of me, feeling me.

I shut my eyes, extricating myself from this disorienting and heady blend of memories and fantasies. "They're all of me," I murmur in wonder. "Gods, you must be terrible at your job."

He frowns. "And how, do tell, have you reached this conclusion?"

"You cannot possibly be any good at ruling a kingdom if all you do is daydream of me."

His black eyebrows jolt, and then his mouth splits open around one of those rare laughs that stirs every fiber of my being. "I assure you, when I need to rule, my mind becomes a frightful place, full of rigor and gore."

I must make quite the grimace, because he runs the pad of his thumb over the divot between my brows and the rumpled bridge of my nose. "Remind me to keep out."

"Consider it done. Now go."

I hold out my hand.

It takes him a moment to grasp my intent. Actually, he must not grasp it, because he takes my hand and carries it up to his mouth. Before he can kiss my knuckles or lick my palm, I curl my fingers around his and draw him into my bedroom.

"Once upon a time, Lore, you told me that we were just beginning." I glance over my shoulder as my words settle into him. "So let's begin."

54

My bedroom is dark save for the slashes of moonlight across the hand-tufted wool rugs that dapple my smooth stone floors and the lone candle bleeding firelight beside my bed. All the other candles Phoebus lit have puddled on their brass holders.

I'm glad for the darkness, for the light reveals all, and there's much I'd prefer Lore not to see yet—the first being the slenderness I've acquired, the second being the blush smothering my face.

"I love when your cheeks pinken. Especially when I'm the one to paint them that color. As for your body, Fallon"—he tugs on my hand, twirling me into him, then settles both hands on my hips—"I've been painfully attracted to you since before Mórrígan decided that I, a man with a heart of steel and talons tipped in blood, could be worthy of such a sweet mate."

My chest tightens at his declaration, yet I roll my eyes. "Please. I'm many things, but sweet isn't one of them."

He slides one of his hands to the small of my back while the other travels toward my front, circling my thigh, leaving behind a ring of frost that grows hot in his wake. His palm lifts until only two fingers remain in contact with my skin. He walks them toward the slit in my skirt and kicks it open.

I drop my gaze just as his hand penetrates beneath the black chiffon. A heartbeat later, the same two fingers that parted my skirt settle over the taut opacity shielding my most intimate region.

I hold my breath, waiting to see and feel what he does next. In some recess of my brain, I think I should touch him as well, but I'm loath to lose what little pressure he exerts on my center.

His fingertips curve around me, stilling on where the fabric is embarrassingly wet.

He leans over until his mouth is flush with my ear. "There is no greater turn-on than to feel your body priming itself for mine." As he hooks the damp fabric, he licks up the shell of my ear toward the naked gold hoop.

My lungs are so cramped and my heart so wild that when his cold knuckle connects with my heated flesh, a tremulous moan escapes my mouth. One that turns into a choked mewl when he closes his fingers around the crotch of my bodysuit, driving his knuckles into me.

"I cannot decide whether to snap the fabric or use it."

I imagine he means to sop up the additional wetness coursing from me.

"And deprive my mouth of drinking from you?"

Oh.

My.

Gods.

Between his dirty confession and the slide of his knuckles, the whole of me burns as though lit from within. How can he keep alluding to wanting to put his mouth *there*? He surely cannot desire such a thing.

"I desire nothing more."

"Why?" I choke as his knuckles crest higher, hitting a particularly tender part of me. "Why would you want to do *that*?"

He stops teasing me and straightens to peer down at me. "Mo khrá, why *wouldn't* I want to do that?"

"Because... Isn't it"—I wrinkle my nose—"foul?"

"Foul?" He pivots his hand, extends one finger, and dips it into me.

The shock of the intrusion is quickly replaced by a delicious fullness. My lungs seize, and his name leaves my mouth on a gasp. He tows his finger out, and at the very same time as he noses the column of my throat, he sinks his finger back inside my heat. A full-body shudder takes ahold of me and doesn't let go.

"You've already ensnared me, Behach Éan. But rattle away."

"Is that...is that why...I'm shaking?"

"It is, mo bahdéach moannan."

Mo badock meanan. "What does...that mean?"

"My beautiful mate."

When he removes his finger, it feels as though I've lost an essential part of myself. The sensation of emptiness only worsens when he releases the fabric he pulled away from my flesh and it settles against me with a snap.

My frustration must score itself across my face, because he murmurs, a lilt to his tone, "What an impatient little bird you are." He raises the fingers that were on me—*in* me—to his mouth, extending his middle finger, the tip of which glistens as though he's dipped it in honey. When he laves it clean with the flat of his tongue, I can hardly draw breath.

"Honey. That is *exactly* how you taste, Fallon."

The air grows as stiflingly hot as the pulse of blood beneath my skin.

Lore moves the finger he's licked clean back beneath my skirt, shifts the black fabric aside, then sinks not just one finger but two inside me. After pumping them twice—*fucking* only twice—he deserts me again.

I narrow my eyes.

"Now, now." He chuckles softly, because he knows his teasing is driving me close to tears. "Stop pouting, Behach Éan, and open that pretty mouth of yours. I want you to understand why I plan to spend a great portion of my life between your legs." He holds his fingers in front of my mouth and waits.

And waits.

Is he really expecting me to...to...to—

"I will not touch you again until you taste yourself."

"Here I thought a man like you would be above blackmail."

"My love, a man like me lives to coerce and confound. Now open wide."

So I do, and he presses his fingers into my mouth with a languor that slicks my juices over every millimeter of my tongue. And nope, I don't understand the appeal. I mean, the musky sweetness is not the absolute worst thing in the world, but I've tasted far better things, like beinnfrhal and the liquor they squeeze from the fruit's thin skin; Lore's mouth—I adore the taste of his kisses; and Montelucin cheese—gods, the addition of salt to curd is otherworldly.

He shakes his head, then leans over and replaces his finger with his tongue and licks every dark corner of my mouth as though to rid me of the flavor he put there. *More for me.*

As he plunders my mouth, I think of the one and only time I put my mouth on a man. I don't want the memory, and from the growl that lashes my mind, neither does Lore, but it surfaces in spite of my best efforts to drag it back into the boxes of souvenirs my mind holds.

I wish I could toss away the key to that particular box.

I hated my first time, and I'm suddenly worried I may hate my second time also. What if I hate the act? What if it hurts? I don't want it to hurt.

Lore pulls away, and those molten eyes acquire a cold shine. "Let this be the one and only time we discuss your first time, Fallon."

"I don't—I'd prefer not to—"

He thumbs my cheekbone. "I'd prefer not to either, but you need to know that if it hurt, it's because he was a selfish prick who didn't bother readying your body." A nerve twitches beside his eye as though this conversation is killing him. "It's not the conversation that makes me angry but the man who put this fear in your eyes. You've nothing to be afraid of. *Nothing*. And if at any point you experience *any* pain, you tell me to stop, and I will fucking stop. You hear me?"

I gape at him, a mix of humiliation and affection swelling beneath my breastbone.

He cups my burning cheeks, tilting my head higher. "Do you trust me?"

"Yes."

"Good." His hands fall to the straps of my dress, and he thrusts them off my heaving shoulders.

As the deep black V of fabric collapses down my arms, freeing my breasts, I ask, "Do you trust me, Lore?"

His eyes flick off the tightened peaks of pink flesh pointing at him. "You are my mate, Fallon."

"I've been your mate for some time now, but you didn't trust me before."

"You're right. And it was small of me, but being an ancient ruler apparently didn't prepare me for the bitterness of your rejection." He coasts his palms down my arms, hooking the fabric and dragging it lower.

The bodysuit is so tight that it sticks to my waist.

"What was the name of the woman who spoke ill of this body?"

"*What?*"

"You mentioned someone had the audacity to make you doubt how spectacular you look."

"I'm pretty certain I never mentioned this. At least not out loud."

"Give me her name."

"Lore, she doesn't matter."

"Anyone who hurts you matters a great deal to me." He sets his long fingers on either side of my rib cage, and thumbs pressing into the twin runnels framing my abdomen, his hands climb back up the length of my torso, halting beneath my breasts.

"You make me feel beautiful. Shouldn't that be all that matters?"

His pupils shrink in their metallic pools. "I'll let it go this time, but if anyone ever makes you feel less, mo khrá, I will ruin them. With or without your consent."

"I doubt anyone will dare. You are quite fearsome."

He smiles as though that was the greatest compliment I could've ever paid him. "Now, where were we? Oh yes, I was going to use this marvelous dress"—he lowers his lips to my collarbone and licks a line from one end to the other—"to fleece you of more sweet nectar."

55

As his mouth kisses one sensitive nipple, his hands seize the stretchy sides of my bodysuit and tug them up. I hiss as the fabric quarries my intimate lips. He lifts his head to peer up at my crimped brow, his breath warming the coolness of the kiss he applied to my pebbling flesh.

He pulls on the suit again, and the fabric moves against my wet flesh, digging against the throbbing nub. He presses an open-mouthed kiss to my other nipple, then flicks the tightened bud with his tongue, stealing a ragged breath from my lungs.

My hands land in his silken locks just as he begins to rock the fabric. When he flicks his tongue against my nipple, more air hisses between my clenched teeth.

"Lore," I gasp, tugging on his hair to drag his head away before he can bruise my too-sensitive flesh. "I'm not sure I like my breasts touched."

He lifts his head and kisses the bone between the swells of creamy flesh. "We can explore that some other time."

"Thank you." I must be close to my monthlies, because I feel like weeping that he listens to me.

"Please never thank me for listening to you, Little Bird." He kisses my mouth with such tenderness that a tear spills over and beads down my cheek.

When it hits our joined mouths, a rumble forms in his throat, and his fingers close so hard around my bodysuit that he yanks it against my crease, all but lifting me off the floor. I suck in a breath at the sharp burn that he follows with a frenzied seesaw that hitches up my pulse.

I will murder Dante.

After you murder my clit?

He stops so suddenly that a yelp tumbles from my mouth.

Don't stop.

I feel his brows bend as he tentatively starts using the fabric to titillate my skin again. The rhythm soon makes my head fall back and my back bow, and I'm reminded of when he started a fire, clicking and rubbing those two stones together. He's kindling a fire now, inside me, igniting flames that scamper into my stomach and billow up my spine.

"Santo Caldrone, Lore…" My lashes flutter closed against my cheeks. "What are you doing to me?"

Waiting for your body to put out the fire.

"Wh-what?"

He gently releases the sides of my dress and smooths the material along my hips. If he plans on hooking the straps back onto my shoulders and calling this a night…

Laughing softly, he plunges one hand through the part in my skirt and palms my sex. "What a good little bird. So drenched." He caresses me over the fabric, and I mewl because I want more friction, more, more, more. "Shall we take this off?" He must've grown his talons, because something bitingly cold and sharp shears the sopping textile.

And then Lorcan Ríhbiadh, master of the skies and rightful king of Luce, drops to his knees and takes both my hands from where they lie restlessly at my sides and carries them to his head. "Hold on to me, mo khrá."

I fist his hair just as he seizes the sheer black material and tears the front clean off the bodysuit, leaving me standing in nothing but a stretchy black scrap of fabric that sits around my waist like a maladjusted garter belt adorned with a tail.

Talons retracting from his fingertips, he grips one of my knees and hooks it onto his broad shoulder, atop the leather cuirass he still wears while I wear close to nothing. I list, clutching his hair so tightly I worry I may rend it like he rent my gown.

Before I can even find my balance, he angles his face, parts my swollen lips, and presses his mouth to my center.

The first swipe of his tongue immobilizes me. The second pulls whimpers from my throat and vibrations from my limbs. The third...the third undoes me. I grip his head while he grips my thighs, and I shudder so hard that my bones liquefy and I sink onto his face like molten wax.

He suckles my throbbing clit, flicking it time and again with the tip of his tongue as I come down from whichever overworld he sent me soaring toward.

So fucking sweet.

Hearing him speak steadies the chaotic beats of my heart. Here I was, worried I'd smothered him. What a shame that would've been, considering how gifted he is with his tongue.

His lips curve against my engorged core as he sets down the foot he hooked around his shoulder and gives that most phenomenal square centimeter on my body a final kiss.

As he leans away, he wears the laziest, smuggest, shiniest grin. "I hope I will forever be able to impress you, Behach Éan." He tongues his lower lip that glistens with me and makes a sound low in his throat that makes my stomach clench.

Coming on his thigh was something.

Getting lapped at by a male seemingly intent on ridding my body of moisture is something else entirely.

As he unfurls his tall, broad body as indolently as a curl of smoke, my heart pounds. I am terrified and excited—terrifyingly excited—of what is to happen next.

He snares my gaze with his as he flips a lock of hair out of his eyes. "There is no need for terror. There is no need for anything further tonight—"

I press up on my toes and squash my lips to his to shut him up, because the man has seen to my pleasure thrice, and I've yet to touch him. I taste myself again, this time on his mouth, but instead of wrinkling my nose, it drives me wild with want. I want to sample him. To mix our flavors and create one that will be uniquely ours.

After I've squirmed out of the ruins of my dress, I curl my fingers around the hem of his shirt but cannot tear it off because of the added leather breastplate. I press away to study his armor. His smile grows incandescent as I struggle and scrabble with the myriad of straps.

I shoot him a death glare that transforms his smile into that deep laugh I usually love, but I'm a woman on a mission at the moment, and that mission is to peel away all Lorcan Ríhbiadh's layers so that he stands bare before me.

I drop my gaze to his waistband, a devious smile tipping up my lips when I catch sight of laces.

Those should be easy enough to undo.

"You deal with the top"—I drag my nails along his midriff, and his laughter sputters—"I'll deal with the bottom." Before rolling down his trousers, I palm the bulge straining against the leather.

Lore curses, not once and not softly. As I knead him with one hand, I pull on the leather laces. Sadly, they don't magically rid him of his pants. Looser now, the material fills out, his bulge swelling as though there was more cock than met the palm.

I know he's large, for I felt him drift against my knee in the baths, but I'm wholly unprepared for what lies in wait behind the smooth leather.

56

Holy Mother of Crows, what am I supposed to do with *that*.

I stare at the veined, bobbing beast that stares right back at me, and I feel like weeping the same way it's doing, because I want to make Lore feel good, but I will surely expire if I put that in my mouth.

"Fallon"—my name is a rough murmur on his lips—"you do not have to—"

I roll my fingers around his impossibly long, stiff length and pump, robbing him of speech. His eyes are wide and locked on where my tanned fingers connect with his pale flesh, tipped with an almost violet head that puffs out in a way Fae cocks don't.

Phoebus, my go-to encyclopedia on all things Crow and sex, explained to me as we steeped in the warm baths that Crows cut a thin strip of skin off their sons' appendages at birth and feed it to the Cauldron to show their allegiance to Mórrígan. Apparently, Shabbin men observe the same rites.

I find its mushroom shape oddly alluring.

How fortunate, for this will be the last cock you will ever touch or look upon until your very last breath.

I look up at him, a smile blowing away my former anguish. *My first is to be my last. How thoroughly ironic.*

His eyebrows pull so taut over his eyes that they dent the skin between them. "I beg your pardon. Your first?"

"Remember your first crow? The one Phoebus dislodged from the Acolti vault?"

"Yes?"

"Remember when I touched you...*there*?"

It takes several seconds for a smile to crest over his frown, but the moment it happens, I know he remembers me fumbling with his iron crow and pressing on the faint depression between his legs. Yes, in bird form, nothing dangles, but gods, how foolish I'd felt believing it to be a switch to a mechanical clock.

To this day, I'm still torn between utter mortification and silly amusement, but tonight, as I kneel before Lore, I choose to view this strange event as comical. "That was the first time I fondled a man."

Although Lore's eyes glimmer with mirth, it's the fondness with which he gazes at me that makes me dart out my tongue and lick the dewy bead before it can trip off his swollen head.

My lashes flutter because he tastes like salt and storms, like the ocean and like the sky—my two favorite places on our beautiful earth. Where my flavor didn't light up my palate, his makes me sigh and tongue him for another hit.

Give me your eyes, Little Bird, he rasps as he loosens his breastplate with white-knuckled fingers.

I look up at him, gently pumping his cock while sweeping the new dampness that forms at the tip. He curses, his fingers slipping off his armor's straps before grasping them with such force that I fear they will not survive.

Angling him up so I can reach the root, I flatten my tongue on his silken flesh and drag it from one end of him to the other.

Lore goes preternaturally still. He doesn't even attempt to remove his armor. He simply stares and stares, and instead of degrading like my first time, it feels empowering. I may be on my knees, but I have all the power.

I tighten my fingers around him, and that precious part of Lore that I hold in my palm seems to grow thicker still. Instead of my tongue, I give him my mouth, and I take him as deep as my throat will allow. When I begin to gag, he drops his hand from his armor to knuckle my taut jaw. The caress is so sweet that it floods my heart, making it feel too large to be contained by my chest. I'm about to suck him deeper when he dissolves into smoke, only to reappear crouched before me.

"I don't want to spill myself into your mouth, Little Bird. Not tonight." He cups my chin, his thumb tracing the shape of my lips.

I swallow because I know what he wants, and my stomach writhes as though filled with a thousand serpents. Before the fear can settle, he scoops me up into his arms and carries me to the bed, sweeping the lone book Phoebus left behind onto the floor.

"There will be no pain. This I swear."

Considering he's never penetrated himself, he cannot possibly be certain of this. I attempt to calm my nerves as he pitches aside his armor and the shirt he wears beneath. His boots come off next and then his pants, until he stands gloriously naked before me, a work of art shaded in gray and gold.

The moon gloves his torso, catching on every brick of muscle and highlighting the trail of black hairs that thickens beneath his belly button. I track their spill to that daunting cock of his that is still erect, pointed straight at me, a weapon made of veined skin.

As he climbs onto the bed, I hold my breath, gasping it out when he stops midway up my body to spread my knees and lean down. At the press of his mouth against my curls, at the stroke of his tongue between my folds, I choke out his name.

Just ascertaining that you're still wet, mo khrá.

I'd assure him that I was if I could get my mind to focus on crafting words, but the only thing it manages to craft are moans of devotion to the male carrying me back into the starlit sky with only his tongue.

My spine arches as my blood thickens and converges in that swollen nub he is striking. When he whispers into my mind how exquisite I taste and how his tongue is so coated with me that he will be savoring me for days, I fracture into a million floating cells no more substantial than those clouds he calls over Luce whenever his temper gets the better of him.

He finally scales the rest of my body, dragging his weeping tip along the inside of my leg, painting my skin with his desire. When he stops moving, his cock flopping heavily between my thighs, he nudges my nose with his, then presses a featherlight kiss to my parted mouth before evaporating into his vaporous self. Wisps of his cool smoke glide between my breasts and around my neck, and then...

And then his icy shadows glide between my hot folds, and although they don't firm, they expand and thicken, stretching me ever so slowly.

"Skin, Lore," I moan. "Shift back so I can touch you."

Not until I'm certain your body will tolerate mine.

I hold my breath as the frosted breadth of him burgeons.

Can you endure more?

"Yes," I breathe out, and his shadows unspool, shouldering into my walls. My hands rise only to fall through the cool mist spread thinly over my body. "Skin...please."

He finally indulges me, his shadows brightening into firm knolls and jagged trenches. My teeth sink into my lower lip as he fills in and out *everywhere*.

"Too much?" he rasps.

"No." I grip his ass to keep him from dematerializing, and although bliss softens the edges of my lucidity, I'm painfully aware that not even I have the power to hold on to this man if he decided to leave. "Stay."

On me.

In me.

With me.

And he does, his golden gaze gleaming as he carves himself deeper into every corner of my being. ***From now until the end of time, Behach Éan.***

My heart tightens, storing each feverish beat before releasing them all at once.

He tows his hips back, drawing himself out. When only his tip is buried, he flexes his ass and sweeps in deep, glancing against each one of my walls.

Although his body was made for the sky, it moves like the ocean, a swell that rolls in deep, dashing itself against my shores before retracting like the tides.

He grazes my lips with his, keeping his touch soft, soft, soft, as though to counter the punishing pumps of his hips. "Pain?" His eyes are half-lidded, half-crazed.

Raking my nails up the runnel of his spine that is as taut and slick as a rain-soaked mooring rope, I whisper, ***No, mo khrá.***

As my words register, he freezes, and then he slowly blinks. And then his mouth crashes down against mine, and he pistons his hips. Heat builds everywhere our bodies connect, a glorious burn that ignites my flesh and inflames my core.

He pulls his mouth from mine, and I lament the loss, but my lament is cut short as his torso ripples off mine and he hooks one of my legs to curl it around his waist.

Hand splayed against the underside of my lifted thigh, gaze pinned to mine, he whispers, "Ha'rovh béhya an ha théach'thu; ha'raì béih."

Although his timbre is low, his words imprint themselves into my mind, each foreign syllable and strange consonant roll-ing into me in time with his hips—*haroff beya an ha thock thoo; haray beh.* "Tell me…what it means."

That until I met you, Little Bird, I was merely living; I was not alive.

My pulse surges as emotion seizes my lids and lungs. I lift one trembling hand to his cheek and caress the small feather inked beside his eye before tracing the smudged line of black that frames his glowing eyes.

My thumb stills and my lips part around a shocked gasp as he rams in so deep, a lightning bolt of pleasure skitters across my marrow. I scream his name, which makes him curse and accelerate his thrusts until a shudder overtakes him, and he roars like a beast released from his cage.

The beast I released.

My beast.

Tremor after tremor rattles his big body, wringing a hot gush that must breach my walls for the way my blood warms.

Yes, Behach Éan. He turns his face and kisses the center of my palm. *Your beast.*

A bead of moisture rolls off the tip of his nose and drips into my mouth. I swallow, intent on absorbing more of this man, all of this man…this mate who's enveloped me in his dark gusts and drenched me in his relentless affection.

Your monster.

But monsters in stories never get happily ever afters, and if anyone deserves one, it's the male still buried inside me.

Bronwen's prophecy echoes between my temples. For once, I neither feel guilt nor revulsion as I contemplate ending Dante's life, only intractable resolve.

As always, Lore sees the images foaming behind my lids. "We will find another way. Do not even entertain the thought."

But I do.

How could I not?

57

I am dragged from slumber by the heavy raps of a fist against my door. It feels as though the knuckles are banging against my skull.

"Wakey, wakey, ínon."

"Focá," Lore grumbles against my temple.

My lashes spring up, and heat blisters my skin as I scramble toward the edge of my mattress, praying my door is locked before remembering that Cathal can morph into smoke.

Dawn hasn't even fucking broken, Lore growls.

A glance at the sky beyond my window confirms that the sun has yet to rise. For all I know, I fell asleep minutes ago.

"I am two minutes away from letting myself in, ínon."

"And I am two minutes away from pulping his face," Lore grumbles.

Merda. "I'm up! Just getting dressed." I try to sit up, but Lore tightens the arm and leg he draped across my body before we fell asleep, caging me into the hard crook of his body. "Lore," I scold.

"I'm not ready for this night to end, Little Bird."

I'm not either, but I want to build something with my father.

Lore sighs, and his cold breath flutters my snarled hair. *Fine.*

Let's go seize the day. He runs his palm along my hipbone before pinching my ass cheek.

I turn my head to side-eye him for the pinch. He smiles before taking my mouth in a toe-curling kiss and rolling me on top of him. Every muscle in my body screeches in protest at being jostled.

Oh, this is going to be a long day. I think I may cry if my father suggests a promenade through the kingdom.

My father! Merda. I flatten my palms against Lore's chest and press against him to pry my torso from his. The movement makes us both groan, but I suspect for very different reasons.

"While I wait for you, ínon, I'll go discuss something with Lore. Come and find me in his rooms when you're ready."

My eyes grow wide. "You have to go," I hiss. "Immediately."

But Lore bends one arm and pillows his head on it, all the while shooting me the laziest smile. His morning wood digs into the crease of my ass, and even though I'm pretty certain I have second-degree cock burn from the four times we made love last night, my core— that little vixen—revs right up, turning nice and dewy.

When his gaze drops there, as though to survey the odds of a quickie, I growl, "Don't even think about it."

His gold eyes snap to mine. "You do realize I'll think of little else." His fingers close around my buttocks and squeeze, then loosen before squeezing again.

My mouth parts around a deep moan, because the male has the absolute *best* hands.

I thought I had the best tongue, he murmurs as he kneads my sore muscles again. **And *nose*.**

They're all tied, I manage to choke out, wondering if more than two things can be tied. Why am I even dwelling on this? Who the underworld cares?

Lore grins as he continues to massage my knotted muscles. What I wouldn't give for a full body rubdown instead of— I smack his chest.

"Such a violent little bird," he murmurs dramatically.

"Stop sidetracking me and go meet with my father to buy me time to"—a sniff at my skin makes me swap the word *dress* for the word—"shower."

I grip both his hands and tug them off my skin, then whimper as I scoot off him, because damn…it isn't only my muscles that ache. *I think you shattered a few essential organs,* I whisper into his mind as I hobble toward the bathing chamber.

Lore laughs.

Tàin, I grumble, glancing over my shoulder to make sure my sentiment registered.

His chuckle turns into a smug grin that makes me stop my mad crawl toward the bathroom and reach out toward the nearest wall to avoid stumbling and shattering more organs and bones. In all my years on this earth—which, granted, haven't been copious—I've yet to set my gaze upon a sight as arresting as the naked king sprawled on my bed, cloaked only in pale moonlight and the vestiges of his makeup.

"My father is waiting," I remind him and myself. "You shouldn't keep him waiting."

"Tell me…what do you suppose he'll want to discuss?"

"The next move in your Meriam recovery mission?" Even as I suggest it, I know that will not be the focus of their conversation.

Lore rises from the bed in one fluid movement that has all his muscles rippling, and then he's walking toward me, hard cock bobbing, and the bruised walls of my reproductive organs clench and dampen.

It would really help if you could shift into your crows right now.

How would it help? When he reaches me, he's still in skin, and I'm still helpless to move.

"It would help me concentrate on what I'm supposed to do," I mumble.

393

He slides a bent knuckle under my chin to tilt my head, then presses a kiss to my already parted lips. *Your father is still standing in front of your door. He knows there's only one place I'd be, and that's right here, with you, Behach Éan.*

My gaze shoots to the studded wood that suddenly seems too thin.

He'll stay out, for there are some sights a father prefers not to see.

I tow my gaze back to Lore's.

I advised him to stroll the hallway and reflect on how lenient I was with him when Daya finally accepted their mating bond.

The reminder of my mother crushes my crackling nerves. "I hope she's alive."

Although Lore's golden gaze drifts to the door, I don't think he's seeing it. "I hope so too, Little Bird."

It strikes me that it's the first time he's sounded unsure of her fate, and his uncertainty carries Gabriele's words to the forefront of my mind.

She cannot be dead.

I *will* her not to be dead.

Showering takes longer than expected, because after cleaning me, Lore dirties me anew. I hadn't thought my body could take it—take *him*—but apparently my body can endure a lot. And enthusiastically at that.

It's laughable that I feared having sex with this man.

As I finish tying on a pair of high-waisted, pearlescent pants over a snug white top that feels woven from clouds, I find myself grinning and impatient to wake Phoebus to tell him how wrong he was about kings being selfish in the sack.

My smile wanes when I remember that Sybille won't take part in this conversation.

Since Lore is keeping my father company, I'm not awash with guilt when I take a few extra minutes to tidy up my room. I make the bed until it looks less battlefield and more place of slumber, then do away with the telltale battle Lore waged against my dress, discarding it in the laundry chute instead of the wastebasket. Even if I don't succeed in mending it, I want to hold on to it, for objects contain memories.

Like Mamma's rock…

My fingers close around air, because the engraved rock sits in Antoni's home. Although it exists in the same land as I, it feels an ocean away. As far from me as the two Rossi women I miss with all my heart. I touch the window, watching as dawn pinkens the horizon and gilds the Queendom of Shabbe.

Though I wish they were here with me, I'm grateful they're safely tucked behind the wards, for war is coming. It hangs over Luce like the mist rolling off the gray rock of Lore's mountain. I spend a second longer gazing at the sun rising over the distant pink shores before finally exiting my bedchamber to face my father.

He and Lore stand in the hallway, discussing something in low tones. I read their bodies to decipher the current mood. My father's posture is stiff, his features tight. Although Lore isn't quite as relaxed as he was after our shower, when he senses me approach, he raises a smile.

My father's dark gaze tracks my approach. "Good morning, daughter," he says in Crow.

"Álo, Dádhi," I reply in his tongue.

A weary smile crimps the corners of his mouth and eyes. He may have retired early, but the shadows smudging his blackened eyes speak of a short night, perhaps even shorter than my own.

"So where are we off to?"

"Moath'Thábhain."

Mof hawben. My mind manages to translate the second word: *tavern.* I'm unsure what the first one means, though.

"*Moath* means north," Lore says. **It's on the other side of the kingdom.** "I told him you've yet to venture that far."

Excitement stampedes up my spine but stops and teeters as I remember my trek with Phoebus across this kingdom. "We're not walking, are we?"

"You do not care to stretch your legs, ínon?"

"Um...well, um..." I snag my lower lip and gnaw on it.

Lore shakes his head at Cathal as though he can read the man's thoughts, but the only thoughts Lore can read are my own. What he's reading is my father's temper, which is written all over his face.

"You woke her too early, brother."

"And you kept her up too late, *brother*," my father all but growls.

"Can we please fly? I so love flying." And not discussing how close they are. Thankfully, they aren't blood brothers, but they are best friends, which makes my relationship with Lore a tad odd.

After a final glower his king's way and a handful of muttered Crow words, my father gives me a sharp nod. His skin bursts into feathers, and his arms elongate into wings. Thank the gods Lore's realm was scaled the way it was, because its inhabitants are massive.

My father crouches, extending one wing so that I may climb aboard. Lore holds out his hand, and although it makes my father's eyes burn a little blacker, I allow the king to help me up. The second I'm settled and my arms are looped around Cathal's neck, he takes off.

We travel down hallway after hallway, skirting Crows both in feathers and in skin, through the greenhouse where I just have time to wave to Lore's mother before Cathal dips beneath the archway. Three beats of his powerful wings later, we reach the Market Tavern. And then we are sailing across hallways that rise several stories high. Balconies—or rather landing pads—are carved into the stone. Most doors are closed but some are opened, allowing me glimpses of the no-frills abodes beyond.

I take *everything* in. Every scent and sight and sound. Each time we pass beneath a landing hatch, I tilt my face to the sky and let the rising sun beat down on my upturned face. How glad I am that Lore is in a pleasant mood, because I so love sunshine.

When my father finally lands, the sky beyond the narrow windows shines the cerulean of Isolacuorin canals. But Isolacuorin canals remind me of Dante, so I push all thoughts of them and him away and concentrate instead on the marvel of rock and timber before me.

Although crafted from the same elements as the other two taverns, the North Tavern has an entirely different feel to it. Perhaps because it's a medley of small nooks and crannies instead of an open space, and the seating has been scooped from the rock instead of built from wood.

The tables too are made of stone. The only elements made of wood are the pine trees—*actual* trees—planted in giant stone pots, arranged haphazardly throughout the room. They stretch so high their serrated crowns skim the myriad of tiny convex mirrors that span the ceiling and glitter with both sunlight and torchlight.

After I hop off my father's back, I twirl on myself and gape in awe.

"Your mother wanted us to move here—well, in a nearby apartment." My father has shifted back into skin. Like me, he is gazing upward. "She'd found us the perfect"—his Adam's apple sharpens in his throat—"the perfect nest." His lids seal shut for a few long heartbeats.

"Is it no longer available?"

"I'm certain the owners will be up for a trade. After all, everyone prefers to live down south. In the dead of winter, the air doesn't turn quite as brisk as it does up here." He gestures to one of the half-moon nooks, and I sit.

The stone is cool beneath my thighs and the table smooth as marble beneath my forearms. A female Crow approaches with a smile that wavers at the sight of me. My lackluster reputation has clearly traveled far and wide. I refuse to let it affect my mood. She might know *of* me, but she does not know me.

My father asks what I want, and I tell him that I eat everything save for fish and meat. This seems to stun him. He returns his attention to the tavern maiden and shoots out a long list of dishes before refocusing on me.

Once she leaves, he links his hands in front of him on the table and studies his blunt nails and knuckles, which are bruised. I'm about to ask him what happened when he says, "Your mother doesn't eat animals either, like most Shabbins. It helps that the slaughter of animals is prohibited on Shabbe. Crows are exempt from that rule, for our bodies need animal protein."

"And Fae?"

"Fae have to abide by Shabbin law, the same way Shabbins were made to abide by Fae law when they could still venture out into the world."

"You've traveled there?"

"I have. Many times."

I'd love to ask him to fly me around the isle, but I'm afraid he may try to pitch me through the wards. I decide to ask Lore. Surely, he'll accept and won't try to toss me onto the pink isle.

"It's one of the most beautiful places on our earth."

"Where do people live? It seems like such a small island."

A smile touches my father's lips. "It's an illusion cast by the Cauldron. Once you penetrate the sandstone walls, the queendom unfurls, as wide and long as Luce and as lush as Tarespagia."

My jaw must've come unhinged, because my father blinks at me. "Were you not aware of this?"

"No."

"I suppose you've never met a Shabbin, and the few Fae

who've traveled there in recent years haven't journeyed back. I'm surprised that Lore hasn't told you about your mother's homeland, though."

"We weren't on the best of terms until...well, until yesterday." My cheeks warm.

My father sighs. "Your mother once jested that you'd be more than his curse breaker. I was not a fan of that joke."

I cannot stifle my smile, which is mostly due to the twin red slashes rising beneath my father's black makeup. "My mother sounds like an outspoken woman. I cannot wait to meet her."

The glow recedes from his cheeks and eyes, and he suddenly seems so lost that I reach out and clasp his bruised hands.

"Which will be soon, Dádhi."

He stares at my face, and although the sorrow doesn't instantly recede from his features, the corners of his mouth lift a fraction. He nods before steering the conversation off Daya and onto my upbringing. He wants to know all about Nonna and Mamma. All about my schooling and friendships.

So I tell him everything. I focus on the happy moments, because each time I mention a grievance, however trivial it may be, his mood takes a turn for the worse.

Our food comes and goes, and with it, the morning. And still I talk. I'm apparently full of stories.

"Just like your mother," he says with a smile. "She always had a story to—"

His mouth snaps shut, and his eyes glaze over. I think the memory must be too difficult to voice, but then he stands abruptly, and I realize Lore must've spoken to him.

My heart climbs into my throat just as fast as my father shot off the stone bench. "What is it?"

His deep-brown gaze grabs my wide violet one. "Your friends have arrived...and they haven't come alone."

58

My friends? Which ones? Is it Syb? Did they find Antoni?"

My father doesn't answer me, because he's already shifted into his Crow.

The second he extends his wing, I swing myself atop him. He takes off and flies so fast that I realize the pace he'd set on the way here was one of extreme leisure. When we reach the Market Tavern, he plummets and lands beside a stall that roasts headless animals on spits. The smell and sight turn my already spasming stomach.

I vault off his back and give the rotisserie stall a wide berth. Once the aroma of barbecued flesh stops punching up my nose, I stand still and wait for my father to shift, but instead, he soars and shoots up into the sky through the wide landing hatch that bathes the market in light.

I grind my jaw, stopping myself from calling him back, electing to stay patient. If my friends are here, they'll soon be carried inside. If only there was a window I could peer through, though.

I scan the market walls, my eyes adjusting to the darker parts until I find tiny squares of light.

Teeth clenched from the sheer pain of moving, I walk to one side, but all I see is jungle. *Ugh.*

Although awash with adrenaline, my legs are incapable of speed, so I hobble to the opposite side of the tavern. When I finally reach the window, I lean my forehead against the cold glass in order to peer as far down as possible.

"Álo, Fallon." Arin's voice makes me jump and knock my head into the window. "Dalich."

Daleh is a word I'm familiar with thanks to Aoife. "You've nothing to feel sorry about." I smile as I rub the tender spot.

Her eyes are soft on my face. "I glad you back."

"I'm glad I'm back too." Although I've only spent a few hours with this woman, I somehow feel like I know her. I wonder if it's a side effect of being mated to her son. Does that automatically create ties between the other family members? "Learning Lucin, I see."

"Phoebus teach me. He good teach."

Phoebus! I forgot to bring him breakfast. I wonder if he's awake. I glance around the Market Tavern, even though the odds of him having trekked all the way here are slim to none.

"I sorry about friends, Fallon."

My fingers freeze on my forehead, and I whirl back toward the window, eyes wide with alarm and dread. I can just glimpse the rump of two horses and the convoy of dark birds gliding through the azure. The crows are all monstrous, save for two with golden eyes.

Lore promised Bronwen to stay put, yet two of his crows are out in the open! I don't realize I'm trembling until I feel a comforting palm breeze across my forearm.

"Can you hear"—my lungs are so tight that I wheeze—"what they're saying?"

Arin doesn't grasp my question, so I point to the esplanade, then point to my ear.

Her lips form a soft *Oh*. "The Fae kill one friend."

My ribs squeeze around my heart. "Which friend?"

"The boy with dark hair."

"Antoni?"

"No. Red eyes."

"Riccio?"

Arin nods, her long, salt-and-pepper hair frolicking around her shoulders. "Tà. And girl, Giana—she… How you say it?"

"She arrested," a grave voice completes Arin's sentence.

Like a weathercock, I spin again, this time toward Aoife. "Arrested? By whom? For what?"

"By Dante. For crime against the Fae crown."

The blood drains from my face. "What?"

"Gabriele reached Sybille and Mattia before they caught and guided horses up mountain for safety."

Heart thudding in my jaw, in my cheeks, in my lids, I gape between Aoife and Arin.

Aoife's throat dips. "Immy was with Vance, the Racoccin rebel. They vanish in tunnels last night."

Last night, while I was in a state of bliss, my friends' world was toppling. "And Lore isn't able to get in touch with her?"

Aoife shakes her head, and although her face isn't a mess of wild heart palpitations like my own, her eyes gleam with anger. "No."

"Has he tried calling her?"

She nods.

"And?"

"She not come back."

"How can that be?" I ask.

Aoife closes her eyes. "Forever Crows lose power to communicate."

The market's noise vanishes as the whole world comes to a screeching standstill, every vendor frozen beside their stalls, every lit flame immobile, every conversation suspended in midair, never landing. My lips shape the word *No*.

"Lorcan wants to fly in valley and over forest, but your father and uncle have told him that if he do that, they toss him in Shabbe." I'm not sure how, but Aoife manages to raise a smile. It's brittle but there.

There and gone.

Arin has gone as white as the linens I'd launder by hand when I still believed myself a halfling with, for my only prospect, a small life in Tarelexo. How narrow my world was back then. How wide it's become, thanks to Lore.

Caws echo across the marketplace as black bird after black bird dives through the cupola and melts into skin and armor. Lore's eyes find mine through the darkness and don't let go as he pounds across the rapidly dimming cavern toward me. Whatever sun he'd let shine over Luce winks out of existence as woolen clouds flock over the blue like sheep.

Aoife steps aside so that he does not have to circle her to get to me. He steals my trembling fingers from my side and wraps his solid hand over them, then leans over to press his cheek to his mother's.

Words are spoken, volleyed back between mother and son. My eardrums quiver so frenziedly that I don't even try to concentrate on the conversation.

"Could Imogen be out of range?" I finally ask, my voice as tremulous as the rest of me.

"Perhaps. Or perhaps Dante locked her in an obsidian cage. Obsidian blots out our powers." His mouth sets into a grim line. "All of them." Lore speaks softly as though he senses that a stronger pitch will unmoor my heart. "Why don't you go see your friends, Little Bird?"

He nods to the heart of the tavern where Sybille and Mattia stand huddled together beside a blindfolded male with long blond hair and a soiled white shirt untucked from dark breeches. It takes me a moment to remember that Gabriele was the one to intercept them and bring them up here.

I glance at Lore, who kisses my knuckles before releasing my hand, then take a step in Sybille's direction but stop and turn back toward the sky king. "You're staying, right? You're not...not—"

"I'm not going anywhere."

I sink my teeth into my lower lip to keep it from wobbling, then take off like a minnow freed from a fisherman's net, sore muscles be damned. "Syb!" I yell her name.

She presses away from Mattia's side, picks up her skirts, and sprints toward me. We collide in a tear-filled hug and hold each other a long moment before either of us manages to utter a single word. Not that words are necessary with true friends; I already know all that must be racing through her head.

When we finally pull apart, her wet cheeks look like polished obsidian, and her eyes shine like silver medallions.

She sniffles. "Gia was arrested."

"I heard."

"And Antoni... We didn't find him. And...and...Imogen and Vance..."

"I heard." I squeeze her, calm, the Cauldron only knows how. "On what grounds were they arrested?"

"Tavo said...he said they stole classified information from Isolacuori, and he had an order to raid the house. Gia wouldn't let them in, so they blasted the door with a cannonball and...and Riccio was standing—" Her voice breaks. "He's dead. And they took Gia after they found...after they opened the cellar door."

"We'll get Giana out, Syb. She'll be fine. Dante will release her. Drugs may be illegal, but they're hardly a crime against the crown."

I'm not sure if Sybille hears me, because she says, "Catriona's the one who told Dargento about the dust. We should never have let her inside our home."

I sigh. Blaming a dead woman will lead us nowhere. "They were probably just biding their time, waiting to convict you on any offense."

Her nostrils flare. "I'm going to tell the whole fucking world that Dante ordered his brother's death. Just you wait and see."

Mattia steps over, hands stuffed in the pockets of his dusty slacks, the whites of his eyes as crimson as the top of Sybille's dress. We may have lost a friend, but he lost his cousin. I cannot even begin to imagine how his heart must ache.

The cool breeze that is my mate slicks across my neck and shoulders before funneling into his two-legged shape. "Cian went to negotiate Gia's release."

"If she's hurt, I will kill all of them. Tavo first. Dargento second. And then Dante. All of them!" Sybille threads her arms around Mattia's waist and leans into him.

His big body is so slumped I'm not certain which one is supporting the other. He presses his mouth to the crown of her head. "How about you leave the killing to"—he glances at Lore, then around at the other Crows who stand at a distance from us— "other people, Sybille?"

Lore spears his fingers through mine and squeezes my hand. "It will be our pleasure to rid Luce of these Fae, Mattia."

My breath snags in my throat as I realize what this means. War is no longer on our doorstep.

War has come.

59

war we will win. Lore's growl rolls through my marrow at the same time as the sky detonates.

Rain begins to plummet against the cupola, pelting the space that I assumed was open but apparently is not.

They're wards.

I glance up at Lore, struck dumb by his confession. I hadn't realized Crows could create wards.

"They were created by the Shabbins," he explains.

Sybille is staring so hard at our linked hands that her eyes look about ready to bug out.

"Why don't we all take a seat? Lunch is served." Lore nods to one of the communal tables set with a river of steaming dishes.

My father guides a still-blindfolded Gabriele and orders him to "Bloody sit his Fae ass down."

The Lucin commander obeys, feeling out carefully for his chair before sinking onto it. "I understand why you want me to wear a blindfold, Ríhbiadh, but I swear I will not bring your secrets home."

"Many men have sworn oaths to me, Moriati." Lore steers us to the table. "Few have upheld them, even when those bargains were stitched into their skin."

"How is that possible? Fae bargains—I mean *supernatural* bargains are unbreachable."

Lore pulls out the chair in front of Gabriele and tips his chin for me to sit. "Most preferred death to repaying their dues."

Gabriele inhales a sharp breath, probably imagining his life cut short by an iron beak.

"Where's Pheebs?" Sybille asks, about to take a seat beside me.

"Right here, scazza." Both Sybille and I whirl to find our friend standing there in dark trousers and a gossamer pink shirt that brings out the blond in his hair. "Since breakfast didn't come to me, I had to go to it."

I mouth a quick *Sorry*, just as Sybille smacks his pecs, muttering a watery, "Scazza, really?" before throwing her arms around his neck and towing his tall frame into hers.

Phoebus's eyebrows arch high when a wail bubbles out from her lips. "Did you expect me to be reduced to Fae jerky?"

A new sob lurches from her throat.

"Cauldron, you really did…" He strokes her back. "As you can tell, I'm alive and in tip-top—"

"Riccio is dead, Pheebs," she cries. "And Antoni is gone. And Gia was arrested."

Phoebus's good humor vanishes like footfalls in wet sand, and he blinks at me over Sybille's head before moving his attention toward Mattia, who white knuckles the back of a chair, vacant gaze fixed on a plate.

Once Sybille releases Phoebus, he places his hand on the blond sailor's shoulder and gives it a squeeze. "I'm sorry for your loss."

Mattia doesn't look at him as he nods, the bumpy movement exhorting new tears from his puffy eyes that noiselessly trip off his trembling chin. His quiet sorrow makes me knead the skin over my heart. The only muscle unharmed by last night's activities now aches like everywhere else.

Phoebus's gaze skates over the table that is dotted by Crows.

He smiles at Arin, who's taken residence farther down, since every seat in Lore's vicinity has been snagged by members of the Siorkahd. Well, besides the one I sit in.

As Lore takes the seat beside mine, my father drops into the one beside Gabriele. On the commander's other side sits Erwin, a male just as huge and frightening as my father. The Fae resembles a pamphlet stuck between two hefty tomes. He's better off blindfolded.

"So tell me, Moriati." Although Lore's voice is placid, the commander jumps. "Why is it you helped two outlaws escape? What were you hoping to gain?"

"Nothing."

Lore rubs the sharp edge of his jaw. "The truth."

"It is the truth. Don't you think I'd have bargained with them if I wanted something?" After a breath, Gabriele says, "Give me salt if you don't believe me."

"Salt no longer affects your king," Lore says as Phoebus drags a chair between mine and Sybille's.

The apple in Gabriele's throat rolls. "I'm not Dante."

"So you have not been ingesting the same poison he has?"

"What poison?"

Lore leans forward, his chair creaking like his leather armor. "You are his commander, are you not?"

"I don't see—"

"My commanders know all I do."

Gabriele's lips squeeze. "Dante and I've had some disagreements as of late. In case you've failed to hear, he's been thinking of reinstating Dargento."

"We've heard." Lore loses his solid edges, and his shadows coil around me as though to protect me from the vile man. "Where is that pointy-eared louse anyway?"

"With Dante."

"Where?"

"I wasn't told where. I was only told that Tavo and I needed to remain in Isolacuori to protect it during the king's absence."

"He must trust you and Tavo immensely, considering the influx of Nebban soldiers."

Gabriele's cheeks hollow as though he's bitten into something sour. "They were brought in to keep his betrothed safe."

I snort, which garners me quite a few stares.

My father tilts his head to the side. "What is it, ínon?"

"Roy does not care a lick for his daughter. He probably stationed them there to keep a foothold in Luce."

Gabriele startles. "Fallon?"

"Hi, Gabriele."

"You're alive?"

"You did *just* hear me speak."

"I forgot to mention"—Sybille leans past Phoebus to look at me—"Lucins think you perished. We knew you hadn't, thanks to Imogen." She scans the table until her gaze lands on Aoife, who sits beside Arin, stiff-backed, stiff-necked, stiff-jawed.

"Does Dante believe me dead?" I ask to steer the attention away from her missing sister.

"He's the one who made the announcement," Gabriele says. "He's warned everyone that the Crows will come to retaliate, and that was why Roy was lending us his troops."

"Why do you think my nephew went into hiding, Fallon?" Bronwen asks as she pads into the Market Tavern. "He may not have given the order to kill you, but your alleged death happened in his part of the realm."

My father stands and goes to her side. Although she may not ask for help or want it most of the time, she accepts his proffered arm. After she's seated in front of Mattia, Cathal returns to his own chair.

"Nephew?" The line of Gabriele's shoulders is as sharp as the tips of his ears that poke out from the blindfold. "Dante is related to your kind?"

"Through wedlock," Lore replies.

"Are you one of his mother's sisters?"

"I was Andrea's older sister, actually. *Half*-sister."

Gabriele sucks in a breath, then releases it along with the name, "Aurora? I thought—I thought she perished in her father's flames."

"Aurora perished in her father's flames. *I* walked out of her ashes."

"Does Dante know you live?"

"No, and I'd like to keep it that way. I may have been Costa's bastard daughter, but I was still his daughter. Cauldron forbid Dante believes me desirous of a throne that does not even belong to him."

"I will keep your secret."

"I know you will. I've foreseen your fate."

Gabriele goes as pale as Bronwen's eyes. "Excuse me?"

"Bronwen has flashes of the future." Lore does not add that her soothsaying was granted by the Shabbins.

"What have you foreseen?" Gabriele's voice is full of nerves.

"Luce falling to the rightful king." Bronwen's gaze drapes over Lore before shifting toward me.

Our eyes hold, and although Bronwen cannot speak into my mind, I hear the thoughts huddled behind the waxy skin of her forehead: Lore's future hinges on me, the magicless girl who helped an unworthy man seize a throne that wasn't his to take.

I sit up straighter. "Bronwen, can you see where Dante is hiding?"

If she could, Behach Éan—Lore's smoke coils around my clenched fingers, as slippery and cold as Minimus's scales—*she would not tell you, for she and I struck a little bargain this morning.*

Lore...

Have I put a wrench in your plans, my love?

I know it comes from a noble sentiment, but yes, my mate's protectiveness does throw an immense wrench in my plans. *What if that's the only way to get you on the throne?*

His shadows form back into a hand, one that pries my fist wide to slot his long fingers through.

I'd rather live another thousand years without a throne than a day without my mate.

"They can talk to each other, can't they?" I hear Sybille whisper to Phoebus, who must nod, because she hisses, "I knew it! I fucking knew it."

"What does the future hold for me, Bronwen?" Gabriele asks.

"Sometimes, ignorance is bliss."

"Tell me."

"Very well." She sighs. "You will perish before the next full moon."

The Fae in front of me turns deathly still along with every Crow at the table. "Have you ever been wrong?"

"Never."

When goose bumps bloom across my skin, Lore slackens his grip and begins to sketch circles on my palm.

"So I'm to leave this mountain in a body bag?" Gabriele's voice ropes my attention. Everyone's attention. "I suppose that does ensure that your secrets remain safe."

Bronwen slides her forearms onto the table as though to get a better line of sight on Gabriele past Aoife. "You will not die at our hands, Gabriele. You will die at the hands of your Fae general."

60

Gabriele has not uttered a single word since Bronwen proclaimed Tavo would end his life. I suppose I wouldn't be all that talkative either if she'd announced that Sybille or Phoebus were going to stab me in the back and send me into the overworld. Or the under one. My soul is, after all, not all that pure anymore. Sure, I've yet to kill Dargento, but I've contemplated it at length.

"What if Gabriele remains here, in the sky kingdom?" I suddenly ask.

Gabriele looks up—or rather cants his head in my direction. He's still blindfolded.

A few Crows hiss as though I've suggested arming the man with obsidian.

"You'd only delay his death," Bronwen says.

"Would he be welcome to stay?" I ask Lore.

Lore flicks his citrine gaze over the members of his Siorkahd. "I suppose a cell"—*a true one*—"could be put at his disposal." *I know you trust the male, but he was Dante's right hand. Until I've ascertained where his loyalties lie, I will keep him behind bars.*

Give him salt.

I will. Eventually. Once I'm certain no chemical can linger in his blood.

He said he didn't take the chemical.

And I should believe him why? Because he gifted you a one-eyed horse?

I drop the subject, because I understand his reticence, but then my mind zips to Arina.

"She's being fed," he murmurs softly. "Sybille rode up on her."

My relief that she wasn't left behind removes a thin layer of the Lucin grime my friends' arrival has splattered over my mood. I even start to smile until I remember Riccio didn't make it, Giana's in Fae custody, Antoni's been swallowed by these elusive tunnels I still know nothing about, and Imogen has vanished along with the human rebel leader.

The circles Lore draws on the inside of my hand become tighter. "Cathal, remove his blindfold, but his wrists stay bound."

Once the cloth is removed, Gabriele blinks and blinks, then stares and stares.

"Not what you expected, Moriati, is it?" Phoebus asks.

Gabriele's gray eyes land on Phoebus. As he shakes his head, his attention moves to me. I smile, but I'm not certain he catches it, because Lore's shadows coalesce in front of me.

I claw through them, but they linger, a veil between Gabriele and me. *What are you doing? He knows I'm alive and well.*

Then what need does he have to stare?

I taper my gaze on the dark billows. *He's probably surprised to see me sitting at your side.*

The same way your people were surprised when you took my hand.

His low *harrumph* makes me smile until he says, **Our** *people.* After shifting back into flesh, Lore hooks a serving bowl filled with a mix of barley and green vegetables and drags it over to us. "Let's eat!" He spoons some onto my plate, then onto his, then proceeds to heap many more things onto the dark ceramic before me. "Are you hungry, Moriati?"

"Not hungry enough to be spoon-fed."

"I could have your hands bound in front of you so you can use them."

Gabriele sighs. "That won't be necessary. The news of my death has rid me of…" His voice dies out as his gaze lands on Bronwen. *The woman forged by fire.*

"Pretty," Lore murmurs. "You should tell her this. She'll like the metaphor."

I doubt it. My aunt doesn't like me all that much.

Lore turns fully toward me. "Why do you say that?"

I raise an eyebrow. *She talks to me as though I'm a toddler.*

Give her time. She's been without her mate for five centuries. It takes a toll on the kindest of hearts.

"What would happen if the general died, Bronwen?" Phoebus asks. "Would that alter Gabriele's fate?"

She sets down her glass of water and swallows. "No." And then her gaze shifts to Gabriele, who seems to cower back in his chair. "You'll die heroically. I imagine that does not make your fate easier to accept, but know that your last breath won't be for naught."

Gabriele lowers his gaze to a wheel of cheese with a rind so purple it's tinted the creamy flesh a similar color. Has Bronwen's prophecy begun to color his opinion of Tavo and Dante, or had he already lost faith in their humanity when they rose to power and began to act like despots?

Lore reclines in his chair and crosses his long legs. "I understand your pain, Moriati. My general, Costa Regio, stabbed me in the back five centuries ago. Of course, he had help in the form of his Shabbin mistress. Nonetheless, his treachery left a terrible taste in my mouth."

If Gabriele finds the parallel unfair considering Lore still has breath in his lungs, he doesn't contest, merely glares at the sky cheese sitting in front of him as though it were his executioner's face.

"I've got an offer for you. One that would allow you to remain in the sky kingdom for as long as you'd like."

"What of the prophecy?"

"Although I'm not in the business of doling out false hope, we are still masters of our fate. At least that is my belief."

Bronwen's crumpled skin crumples some more. She obviously does not share Lore's mindset.

"So you'll allow me to remain in a cell until I decide I'm ready to head back into the Fae lands to die my hero's death?" Gabriele's voice has acquired a bitter edge, one I've never heard the even-tempered Fae use before.

"Those lands will not belong to the Fae for much longer. Once they're ours again, I will see to the dissolution of Dante's administration."

I imagine that *dissolution* is a euphemism for Lore's true intent, but I suppose his true intent may frighten a Fae.

"As for your accommodations, it'll be a cell at first, but once you've proven yourself a friend to my people"—Lore gestures to the Fae sitting beside me—"you'll walk freely amongst them."

Gabriele's pewter gaze finally lifts from the inanimate block of aged goat's milk. "What is it you're offering me, Lorcan?"

"My protection against the Lucin crown's secrets. All of them."

Gabriele closes his eyes.

"You should not interfere with prophecies, Mórrgaht." Bronwen's voice is low yet cracks over the table like a whip. "You will anger the Great Cauldron, who will lash out with a crueler fate."

"If I wanted your opinion on how to rule my kingdom, Bronwen, I would've asked for it." Lore's retort and tone snap Bronwen's mouth closed.

"Very well." She presses away from the table, and without anyone's help—perhaps because no one offers her support this time—she makes her way toward the giant archway of Murgadh'Thábhain.

I watch her leave until her form is gulped down by the shadows. I understand that she's been given a gift that she's been using for the good of Lore's people, but being the designated soothsayer shouldn't give one the right to disrespect one's king, especially in front of others.

I nibble on my lip as I recall the number of times I've disrespected Lore in front of his people. I whisper a quick but soul-felt apology through the bond.

Although he doesn't answer me with words, he steals my hand off my lap and cocoons it in his. "So, Gabriele? Will you work with us or against us?"

"With you, Lorcan Ríhbiadh of the sky."

61

Lore decides to move the conversation to a more private part of the kingdom—his rooms. Although he invites me to join him, I choose to spend time with Sybille and Phoebus. I'll learn all that Lore does later, once he is done squeezing Gabriele's mind like a lemon.

I wrinkle my nose at the visual.

"Oh come on, it's not *that* revolting," Phoebus says, and I think he must be addressing Sybille, since I haven't spoken in a handful of minutes, but when I find them both looking my way, I realize they're mistaking my grimace for a response to one of their many topics of conversation.

My mind is in such disarray from the emotional upheaval of the day that I've been having trouble keeping everything straight. It has not helped that I've projected myself into Lore's war chambers twice, startling myself more than him. After quick touches to my face and neck to calm my striking pulse and murmured promises of a tell-all later, I returned into my body, which is at present sandwiched between Sybille and Phoebus on my bed.

A bed that smells so strongly of Lore that my body, when not transporting itself into Lore's chambers, has begun to replay the evening.

"I'm sorry, but what is not that revolting?" I ask.

"A finger in the ass," Sybille says.

My cheeks heat so fast that I'm tempted to roll away from the two bodies hemming me in.

"I'm personally not a fan," she adds, "but Mattia is."

I wrinkle my nose. "I did not need to know that."

"Yes, you did, Piccolina."

"Why did I need to know Mattia's kink, Pheebs?"

He grins. "I meant the *fondling a man's ass* part."

I try to wriggle out from between them before I begin to sweat from how hard I blush, but the mattress is so soft that I merely get bogged down.

"Are we getting you hot and bothered?" Phoebus all but cackles.

"No," I reply, while my face steams. "This bed is huge. Must you crowd me?"

Phoebus turns onto his side, and so does Sybille. They both wrap one arm around my torso, extending their hands to reach each other's waist, until we are bound as tight as the Crow tome on my nightstand.

"And some men like more than a finger—"

"Phoebus," I hiss.

"Just trying to teach you ladies the way to a man's—"

"—ass?" Sybille interjects.

He shoots her a crooked grin. "I was going to say *heart*."

"Sure you were." Sybille lets out a rickety laugh that peters out too fast, replaced by a lung-racking sob.

Although discussing sex was her idea—a way not only to avoid dwelling on her sister and Riccio but also to learn all I was willing to share about my fledgling relationship with Lore—it has not uprooted her sorrow and anxiety, merely buried both under a thin layer of dirt.

"Gods, I missed us," she croaks.

"I missed us more," I say.

"I missed us most." Phoebus tosses me a look. "After all, I was the highland castaway." He's undoubtedly intending to appear vexed, but his eyes are so watery they don't retain his exasperation, only his love.

Although I can hardly move, I bend my arms and wrap my fingers around each of their forearms. "To never being apart again."

"Hear, hear," they say in unison.

Our embrace tightens, and although I know life will get in the way, because life always does, I pray to the Cauldron that our friendship will thrive for centuries to come.

When Sybille begins to cry silently, I release Phoebus's arm and twist onto my side to slip both my arms around her shaking body and pull her into me, and then Phoebus pulls us both into him. We must drift off, all tangled together, because the next thing I know, a disturbance in the air whisks my lids up.

Moonlight shapes the dark edges of my mate's leather armor and ignites his golden gaze as he stands over my bed, watching us with a soft smile.

I didn't mean to wake you, Little Bird.

My friends must sense his presence, because they both stir, and then Phoebus flops onto his back with a groan while Sybille scrubs at her swollen lids.

"Oh my gods." She rolls up into a sitting position. "What time is it?"

"Nearing ten in the evening," Lore answers.

"Ugh. I'm the worst girlfriend. I shouldn't have left Mattia alone all this time." She turns back toward me, then leans over and plants a kiss on my cheek. "Love you. Whatever the hour, wake me for breakfast, all right?" She blows Phoebus a kiss before hopping out of bed and heading to the door in her crumpled red dress. "Mórrgaht, any news from Cian?"

"Not yet, I'm afraid. The second I hear anything, I will tell you."

"No matter the time." Her voice rattles with distress.

"No matter the time, Sybille."

Sighing deeply, she murmurs, "Good night, Lore. And thank you for letting us stay."

Although Lore nods, his eyes don't stray to her; they stay on me.

Phoebus rakes back his hair. "Well, I'll be going." He rises from the bed, scooping up the book on my nightstand, then lingers there a second, his gaze skipping between Lore and me, moving the book from one hand to the other. "Off to the tavern I go." Yet he does not go. "You're staying, right, Mórrgaht?" Here I thought he was hoping to cop a look at Lore disrobing, but no…my wonderful friend is checking that I don't stay alone.

"I am. If Fallon will allow it."

I roll my eyes. As if I'd send him away. Even if he was staying only to grouse about Fae, I'd rather he do it here.

Grouse?

I smile. *Let me guess… Real kings don't grouse?*

His smile grows.

"All right then. Have fun, kids." Phoebus slaps a palm over his mouth. "I did not just say that. My sincerest apologies."

"You're forgiven." Lore's fingers have already started unbuckling his armor. "But only if you show yourself out this very minute."

Phoebus scrambles away so quickly that his outline blurs.

"Must you truly frighten my friends, Lore? Can't you settle for only terrifying your enemies?"

"I've a reputation to maintain, mo khrá."

I shake my head, but a smile slinks over my lips. A smile he matches with one of his own. As his clothes drop, so does my gaze and subsequently the arch of my lips, because one cannot grin at a work of art. One can only gape in awe.

Lore looks as though he was carved out of the starlit rock of his kingdom—his silver scars are strikes of a chisel, his blood veins of precious minerals, his hair wisps of night sky, and his eyes chips of gold. Even his scent seems to have been born from the mountain and the sky he commands.

He kneels on the foot of the bed, thick cock bobbing between his muscled thighs, straining against the air as he scales my clothed body. "Mórrígan, how I've missed you," he rasps as he runs the sharp tip of his nose from my navel to the hollow of my collarbone. He trails a line of kisses up the length of my throat, each gentle peck of his mouth sparking a little moan that vibrates the darkened air.

By the time he crests the point of my chin and reaches my parted lips, my lungs burn from the speed at which I'm breathing, and my rib cage aches from the velocity at which my heart pounds. When he touches his lips to mine, I dissolve into a puddle of want.

I lift my hands and run my nails around his naked waist, luxuriating at the feel of his skin pebbling. Once I reach the base of his taut spine, I cannot decide whether to head north or south. I want to touch him everywhere at once. I flatten my palms against his flesh, dividing and conquering. One hand skims up, the other down. His muscles flex beneath my fingertips, and he groans into my mouth, deepening the swishes of his tongue.

Supporting his body on one arm, he reaches down and unfastens my pants, then shoves his hand inside my underwear. When he uncovers the damp fabric, he looses another groan that sounds almost animalistic.

Without separating our mouths, he plunges one finger into my heat, then draws it out. *Sore?* he rasps into my mind.

No, I choke out.

He soaks another finger inside me, and a cry flees my lips, breaking our kiss. He must sense it's a cry of pleasure, because to my absolute delight, he repeats the thrusts several more times. Once his fingers are coated with me, he slicks them over that magical nub.

Open your eyes, mo khrá, so I can see how your heart beats for me.

Through my eyes? I'm somehow lucid enough to ask, even though my thoughts are as choppy as the waters of Monteluce.

Your pupils dilate when you desire me.

I desire him so much that my pupils must've flooded the whites of my eyes. My thought, or perhaps the circumference of those black dots, makes a liquid smile spill across Lore's mouth and into his eyes.

He slows his caresses, and I pout. *Lore, please...*

Chuckling, he kisses the hinge of my jaw, dips his fingers back inside me, then spreads the wetness to my hardened bud, rubbing and rolling until an orgasm ripples up my spine and wrenches a sharp gasp from my lungs. It's so intense that it feels as though I've left my body and traveled to the farthest reaches of the universe.

When he begins to caress me again, I almost still his wrist. My flesh is so raw that his fingers feel tipped in talons, but then he slows his ministrations, and the shallow ache turns into renewed need. My fingers sink into his skin at the same time as his sink into me, playing my sensitive flesh with such dexterity that in seconds, I am swept under again, into that place spun from sugar and sunshine where only Lore and I exist.

The male kisses the slope of my neck as he grips my pants and drags them down. I lift so that he doesn't feel the need to shred these. Once he's rolled them off me and, with them, my underwear, he takes his hardened length in his hand and rubs it against my wet folds.

I moan as his silken tip plows between my lips and flicks my orgasm switch. I go off. I'm uncertain which one of us is more startled that I've come again, but Lore blinks at me while I attempt to locate my heart, which feels as though it has dissolved, because it beats everywhere.

He slams his mouth against mine. *I need to be inside you, Behach Éan.*

I need you to be inside—

With a pump of his hips, he thrusts the whole thing in, every thick centimeter, and Holy Cauldron, there are many, many of those.

I just lie there, stunned. And full. Really, *really* full. "Were you this big yesterday?"

"I'm quite certain I stopped growing everywhere a few centuries ago."

"All right then." When he still hasn't moved, probably afraid it may crackle my insides, I ask, "Are you planning on playing dead?"

The male blinks at me, and then he laughs, that beautiful booming laughter of his that resonates in every corner of my bedroom and body. When he begins to roll his hips, his length glides in and out of me so smoothly that it feels as though he's coated in oil.

I'm coated in you.

The wet glide of our skin sets my cheeks ablaze.

Balancing himself on one arm, he slides one hand down my front, over my peaked nipples. When he reaches the hem of my shirt, he rolls it up to reveal my breasts, which he gazes at with great fondness. I can tell he hungers to suckle them, and it takes everything in him not to take them in his mouth. *Someday, Little Bird, I will feast on those pretty pink nipples.* He keeps rocking his hips steadily—neither fast nor slow but rather like a male not pressed for this to end.

His fingers trace the seam of my rib cage before traveling farther. When he reaches my engorged nub, he flicks it, which makes me tighten around him.

Focá. He flicks me again and again, and my core chokes his cock.

He snarls a series of undecipherable words, quickening the pace of both his thumb and hips. When my muscles clench and

I cry out his name, he groans. And then he glides out of me completely and moves down my body, replacing his hard length with his tongue.

Mórrígan, how I've craved kissing your sweet slit all fucking day. He spreads my thighs wide and laps at me, gorging himself on my taste.

My blood burns so hot that my veins feel incinerated and my lungs like useless mounds of ash. As he groans against me, savoring the mess between my thighs, my core clenches and fills his mouth anew. He licks until he's sopped up every last drop, then he rises onto his knees, seizes my hips, and flips me onto my stomach.

He grabs a pillow and props it beneath my stomach, then grips my hips and drags the head of his cock along the crease of my ass. He better not be contemplating sticking it in *there*. I don't care what my friends claim. I'm not ready to be gored, especially since Lore's cock is a forearm, not a dainty finger.

He chuckles, the sound deep and velvety. *I promise not to penetrate that hole tonight.*

Or any other night. I try to twist my neck to better see him. *Or day for that matter.*

I swear to only stretch your ass with your consent, mo khrá.

Unlike earlier, he feeds himself into my core slowly. My body begins to hum as he moves in languid thrusts, because this new angle feels…divine. His thumbs squeeze the base of my spine and knead, and Santo Caldrone, I see stars, and not from my window but on the backs of my lids.

Lore, I moan as the imaginary stars streak across my mind.

Come with me, Behach Éan. His hips set a punishing rhythm, striking me in that sensitive spot over and over until my stomach clenches like a fist and I shout out his name for his entire kingdom to hear.

Our kingdom, Lore growls, a thin sheen of sweat misting

his forehead. "*Ours*," he repeats, out loud this time, his timbre as rough as his pace.

I swallow. The beast making love to me may be my king, but I'm not yet his queen.

Today, Behach Éan. Today, we— Eyes shaded black, he pumps himself one final time and stills. Only the buried part of him moves, twitching as he pours himself into me in long, fiery bursts.

Is it strange that I even love the feel of him painting my walls with his seed?

We shall remedy this today, he rasps, thumbs still drawing arcs over the base of my languid spine.

My brain must've turned to mush, because I cannot for the life of me figure out what the two of us must remedy.

Every brick of muscle strains against his pearlescent skin as he leans over me to press a kiss to my shoulder blade. *Making you my queen.*

62

After Lorcan Ríhbiadh decided that today was to be my coronation, my heart seized and hasn't resumed beating. He still lies over me, his cock softening unlike his resolve to set a crown upon my brow.

He asks me where I'd prefer the ceremony to take place—either in the Market Tavern or in the orchard, since those are the largest rooms in the kingdom.

My tongue must've fused with my palate and my thoughts with my skull, because I cannot manage to answer him, neither out loud nor through the mind link.

Lore suddenly stops his manic planning, stops kneading my spine, stops peppering my shoulder with kisses. "Don't you want to be my queen, Behach Éan?"

I twist around, unsheathing him from my core, in order to roll onto my back. My silence has frayed the mask of assurance Lore forever wears. I lift my hand to his cheek and stroke the tattooed feather there. "I want nothing more, but I don't want it today. I want Nonna and my mother—*mothers*—to be in attendance. I'd also like for Gia to be present. I also want Dante to be gone so that Luce belongs only to us, Lore. And although this may seem silly to you—"

"Nothing you desire ever feels silly to me."

My throat knots with emotion. I have to swallow to finish spilling the reasons for my reticence out loud. "I want to have unlocked my magic. I want to deserve that throne, not because the Cauldron made me your mate but because I'll have earned my place at the top."

"You've already earned your place. You brought me back to life." The edges of his confidence firm, like the outline of his body, which had begun to unspool, and another part of him. "But I also understand why you care to wait, my love." He nudges my lips open with his mouth, then nudges my slit apart with his cock.

Since his seed has yet to dribble out of me, what with the pillow propped under my hips, he glides right in. My stomach tightens as he seats the full length of himself inside me, then clenches some more when he draws out, delivering the delicious friction he's slowly making me addicted to.

This time, his mouth doesn't leave mine as he makes love to me. He kisses me gently, from one corner of my lips to the other. He leaves no millimeter of skin untouched, neither on my face nor on the rest of my body. His fingertips bump over my ribs, tracing their curves, before venturing to whichever part of me he can reach.

His scent deepens as his skin heats, and little beads of charcoal-flecked salt roll into our fused mouths. I taste every beat of his heart as he kisses me with slow, precious sweeps of his tongue. I cannot decide if I favor this deliberate pace over his rougher one. Both drive my pulse wild. He traces the rounded shape of my breasts with the cool pad of his finger, his circles tightening like my breaths as he reaches the pinker flesh tipped with hardened pearls.

My lungs squeeze as a deep, hot pressure builds in both my core and chest. His name forms in my throat and climbs onto my tongue, but he brushes it away before I can utter it.

Although my climax is sharp, it unspools like a fugitive ball of yarn, rolling on and on until my limbs feel woolen. I am still coming when his hips and mouth finally still and he spills into me without making a sound.

I drift, drunk on him and his beautiful mouth and his steady breaths and his sensual hands and his outstanding cock. Gods, to think I may get to do this forever.

He pulls his mouth off mine so suddenly it feels as though he's removed a layer of my skin. "There is no *may*, Behach Éan."

I tangle my hand in his hair that's as wild as the eyes boring down on me and drag his head back toward mine so he doesn't glimpse the flicker of fear that sparks whenever I think of the future.

So many things could go wrong, thinks the Fallon who's been betrayed and crushed and shot at with a poisoned arrow.

I long for the optimistic version of myself, but she died the day Lore came back to life.

Hours later, as we lie in the dark, my head nestled in the crook of his shoulder, legs tangled with his, fingers twined over his scarred chest, I finally ask him whether Gabriele brought something new to the table.

"Dante has kept him in the dark. He wasn't even aware that tunnels existed beneath the kingdom."

"Do you think he kept him in the dark because he deemed him too weak and untrustworthy?"

Although my gaze remains fastened to our linked fingers, I can feel his drift across my forehead and linger. "Why else?"

"You once kept me in the dark to protect me."

"You wound me, Little Bird. Comparing me to that spineless, guileful male who cares about no one other than himself." He runs his fingers through my damp locks, which he insisted on washing while we soaked in my tub.

It was divine—both the bath and the feel of Lore's long fingers kneading my scalp. I could get used to how much he spoils me. "He and Gabriele were truly close once upon a time, Lore. He's still thick as thieves with Tavo it seems."

"And mark my words, he'd probably dispose of Tavo in the blink of an eye if the fire-Fae went against his will." He untangles our hands to scrub his palm down his face, which is bare of makeup. "When Mórrígan made me, when she gave me the responsibility of a kingdom, I not only brought my friends along, but I also kept them close because they had integrity and loyalty in spades and because they never hesitated to knock me down a peg when my ego required it. Especially your father." Tangible fondness colors his tone.

"How many of your Crows are stuck behind the wards?" I ask, tracing the silver scar beneath his bruise-colored nipple.

"Too many."

"More than half?"

"Far more than half. Before surrendering to Marco so he'd spare the humans in the cavern, I urged my people to flock to Shabbe. Only the stubborn remained." His skin is cold again, as clammy as his voice.

"The tunnels… Are you planning on storming them?"

"We tried." He swallows. "We cannot enter them."

I lift my head off his arm and twist to look at him. "Why not?"

"Obsidian doors. Antoni was trying to blast through them when he went missing."

The information floats inside my skull before settling like silt. "Do you believe he's dead?"

"I don't know." He squeezes the bridge of his nose and shuts his eyes for a long moment as though worried I may try to tiptoe into his mind to glimpse his true opinion on Antoni's state of existence.

"You told Sybille you had no news from Cian. Was that the truth?"

"No." He stares at the timbered beams over my bed, his fingers drifting off his face.

"You have news?"

"The negotiations continue."

"Can you be any more vague? What did you offer Tavo?"

"Gold."

"What does he want?"

Shadows puff off Lore's skin like grains of Selvatin sand during my furious gallop across the desert with Furia. "Nothing I am willing to give."

My fingers pause against one of his many scars, one that is perfectly round and slightly concave, probably leftover from an obsidian spike. "Tell me."

"We should sleep. In case your father decides to beat down your door again at fuck o'clock in the morning."

"For someone so intent on making me speak properly, you've a filthy mouth, Your Majesty."

"You love my mouth."

"I do love your mouth, Lore, but I'd love it even more if it offered an answer to my Gia question."

"Fallon." His sigh lifts his chest, which in turn lifts my hand.

"Did he ask for Gabriele? Is that it?"

Lore's lips flatten, and his fingers halt their slow slide through my dark locks. "He asked for a pint of your blood."

"I thought he believed me dead?"

"Giana, under the influence of salt, let it slip that you weren't."

Ah… "Does Dante know of my undeadness?"

"I'd imagine the news has found its way to wherever he hides."

I roll fully atop him. "Does my blood have a special scent or taste?"

"We're not giving Tavo—or any fucking Fae, for that matter—your blood."

"I repeat, you obtuse man, does my blood have a special scent or taste?" I remember his crow darting out his tongue to taste his bloodstained talon the first time we met.

"It contains iron, so it tastes metallic, unlike Fae blood."

"Like Crow blood then?"

"Somewhat, but saltier." His nostrils twitch. "I had to drink a filled goblet to activate Mórrígan's spell."

I wrinkle my nose at the idea of drinking blood. "Does Crow blood have any magical properties once outside the body?"

His eyebrows bend. "No."

"So let's give him a pint of *my*"—I add air quotes around the preposition—"blood. We'll just add some salt, then you'll taste test it, and voilà."

"You crafty female."

"How did the idea not cross your mind?"

"My mind was busy deciding how best to murder Tavo without using my beak or talons."

"Or hand, since you're not to leave your kingdom." I kiss the scar on his chest, the one on his right pec, and his nipple tightens when my lips meet skin. "Right?"

His molten eyes have slipped to mine, to the narrow space between his pebbled skin and my parted lips.

"Right?" I repeat, running my mouth along his sensitive skin before flicking his nipple with my tongue.

The gold in his eyes flares in time with his pulse.

"Lore?" My hot breath wafts against the bead of dark skin, sharpening it some more. "You will not leave these walls, right?"

He glares at my lips as though they're tricking him into striking oaths he doesn't care for. In a tremendously grumpy tone, he grunts, "Right."

"Good, because if you did, I'd never put my mouth on your body again."

His gaze narrows. "Is that right?"

431

"Yes. Like you said, I'm crafty." I shoot him a dark little smile. "Perhaps I should have you ink the terms with a quill, like you—"

He flips us around. "I've no need for a quill." He binds my wrists with his fist and holds them over my head, then proceeds to compose his promise on my chest with his tongue.

Moans and giggles alternately escape as he scrawls his invisible words. When he reaches my navel, he cranes his neck to peer at my flushed, wide-eyed expression. I'm no longer laughing.

"I've run out of space to sign my oath," he murmurs, his cool breath skimming the loops of damp he's left behind.

I stare and stare, mind full of lust that transforms into anticipation at the wicked rise of his mouth's corners.

"Oh…wait." He spreads my legs and lowers his head, his nose dragging through my curls. "I've found the perfect spot."

There, on the throbbing intersection between my thighs, he indolently tongues his full name.

63

I'm awoken by pangs of hunger, which is a first. Then again, considering my recent nocturnal exercise regimen, it's entirely unsurprising. As my stomach gurgles again, I stretch out and groan, then turn to ask Lore if he has time to have breakfast with me, only to discover a lone sheet of paper discarded on his side of the bed.

Mo khrá,

I'm off to conquer the world. As vowed, from the confines of my castle. although I'd much rather have done so from the juncture of your thighs.

Your mate.

I trace the words *your mate* with a fingertip, a smile cleaving my face in half. How incredible that I, Fallon Báeinach, possess a mate. A king, no less.

I reread each pretty word before reverently folding the note and hunting my sun-soaked bedroom for a place to store it. My nightstand has no drawers, and neither does the low table in front of the hearth. I consider placing it in my closet, but I assume someone enters it from time to time to replace the clothes I slide into the wash.

I wonder who it could be and make a note to ask Lore so I can not only thank the person but also accompany them to the magical laundry room. Now that I'm well again and settled, it's time I pick up some slack. Perhaps I can help tidy more rooms than just my own. Or perhaps, since I know my way around a kitchen and bar, I can give Connor and Reid a hand at the tavern.

Deciding the safest place for my note will be my underwear drawer, I hop out of bed. At least that's how I imagine myself moving. In reality, I unpick my carcass bone by bone from the sex-rumpled sheets and totter toward my closet, muscles throbbing.

After slipping the folded paper beneath underthings made of white lace and selecting a pair for the day ahead, I scan the row of clothing, settling on brown suede pants and a white cotton blouse that ties at the neck and wrists with silk ribbons. Instead of silk slippers, I choose sturdier footwear—tall boots polished to a high shine. Like everything else in the closet, they must never have been worn, because they sport not a single crease.

As I stand in front of the mirror propped against my closet wall, my heart performs merry little pirouettes. The clothes Sybille filled my closet with back at Antoni's had probably never been worn, but they'd clearly been bought off a rack. These were handstitched just for me. They've never graced anyone else's body, not even a mannequin's, not even a potential customer's.

Thinking of Antoni's home frays the edges of my delight, because I cannot think of *it* without thinking of *him*. I shut my eyes when I begin to picture him bleeding in some dank tunnel. Is he alive? Wouldn't the Fae have tried to ransom him if he were, though?

I blink back the heat that creeps up into my eyes. Antoni is strong and cunning. If anyone can survive the impossible, it's him. "Be alive," I whisper as I head toward my bathing chamber.

After unsnarling the mess atop my head with the boar bristle hairbrush beside my sink, I eye the block of black charcoal and hesitantly pick it up. Although I believe Lore may appreciate seeing my face painted, I worry it will attract unwanted attention and unkind whispers.

I can already hear his people murmuring that the girl who spreads her legs for their monarch doesn't merit warrior stripes. My face grows as hot as my chest. Gods, why must I care so deeply about other people's opinions of me?

I set down the block and wipe my palms on a towel, then set out toward Sybille and Mattia's bedroom.

"Syb?" I knuckle the wood gently so as not to disturb her boyfriend.

I stand and wait. And wait. Then try the handle, but there's no give.

"Syb?" I say it a little louder this time, and I hear footfalls.

The lock clicks twice before the door sweeps open, and for a second, my breath catches and I think Giana is standing before me, because the woman who greets me sports a halo of kinky curls. But then she steps into the beam of torchlight, and I expel my trapped hope, because this woman's skin is blacker and the shape of her face softer.

I smile as Sybille attempts to pry apart her squinty eyes.

"Is it morning?"

I nod.

"Is Gia—do you have any news?"

I don't want to raise my friend's hopes until the transaction is done and her sister is handed over, so I shake my head. "I expect we'll have some in no time, though. Still up for breakfast?"

She stares down at her bare, shapely legs as though to check whether she's wearing appropriate attire. "Would it be very odd if I went to breakfast wearing Mattia's shirt? I really don't want to don that red dress again."

"I've done it before. It got me looks."

"His shirt it is then. Let me just get some shoes and—" She's running her fingers through her hair or attempting to; they get stuck at the root. "Oh. My. Gods." She rolls her eyes as though to cop a look at her hair. "Fuck... I slept on wet hair. Fuck." She tugs on the strands to force them to straighten.

"Syb, I know you hate your curls, so you may not care about my opinion, but I'm still giving it to you. You look gorgeous."

She narrows her eyes as though she expects me to break out into a fit of giggles. Except I'm not, because I meant what I said. "I'm glad my curls appeal to you, but they do not appeal to me."

"Syb..."

"Is there anyone in your rooms? Like, a slumbering king?"

I smile. "No."

"Fantastic. Can I borrow a shower and a dress?"

"Of course." My stomach gurgles so loudly that it hitches the downturned corners of Sybille's mouth.

"Go to the tavern. I'll meet you there as soon as I can tame my Giana hair." The mention of her sister's name makes a swallow jostle her throat.

I grip her hand and give it a squeeze. "Lore will get her back. I swear he will."

She nods, then glances over her shoulder at the large shape burrowed beneath her covers.

I drop my voice. "Is he still asleep?"

"Yeah. I suspect he's going to try and sleep his heartache away."

Is that even possible?

"Better apathy than vengeance, right?" she murmurs.

I don't remind her of the different stages of grief, that anger will undoubtedly follow the dispiritedness. She doesn't need additional worries. Besides, deep down, I think she knows her boy-friend will someday thirst to avenge his cousin's death.

We part ways after she closes her door. While she heads south, I head north to the Sky Tavern where only one person is seated—Bronwen. I'll admit the hour is odd—long past breakfast but way too early for lunch.

I sidle up to the bar where Connor is arranging cloves of garlic and sprigs of rosemary in glass jars. He does it with such care that one can tell he enjoys the task.

"Morning, Connor."

He looks up, and lo and behold, he smiles. At me. I'm so surprised that I don't automatically return the sentiment. Yet it doesn't seem to irk him, since the corners of his full lips stay lifted. What have I done to deserve such a kind look?

I finally wrangle my mouth into an answering grin. "I'd like to order everything on your breakfast menu." I realize that I've never given him coin for all the food and drink I've ingested in the past and suddenly wonder how to pay. "Do I have a tab here?"

"No."

"Then...um..." I play with the ribbon I tied loosely around my neck. "How do I pay you?"

"No one pays in sky kingdom. We trade." His accent roughens his words but not his tone.

My decision firms. "If you'll have me, I'd like to help out here. I used to work in a tavern so I know..." His eyes have gone so round that I ask, "Did I say something wrong?"

He tugs on the black collar of his long-sleeved top, dragging it so low that a necklace pops out from behind the fabric. "Sorry, but Lorcan's mate not wait tables."

My head rears back. "Why the ever-loving Cauldron not?"

"Because you're...you're..."

At his third *you're*, I mutter, "The king's mate?"

"Yes."

I snare my lower lip with my teeth. Had I married Dante, I'd have had to quit my job at Bottom of the Jug and move to Isolacuori. Though Lore is not Dante, he probably wouldn't appreciate me serving food and drink to his people. I wish I had other skills I could put to use. I suppose that now's as good a time as any to pick up a new one.

Nonna taught me to tend plants. I could garden with Arin! That way, I could get to know her and—

"Fallon?" Bronwen's voice steers my thoughts off Lore's mother. "Come and have tea with me."

Although there was no question mark or please at the end of that request, the manners Nonna drilled into me kick in. "Coming, zia."

When I turn back around to ask Connor for a pitcher of coffee, the sun catches on the pendant strung to the leather cord, and the sight halts my breath. It's a rock. Not a precious one, yet the engraving is precious. To me anyway, because it's that curved V, the same one that graces Mamma's rock. Yes, I realize Vs aren't extremely original pieces of art, yet instead of straight, the diverging bars are curved in the same way as on my rock.

I jerk my gaze to Connor's. "What does your pendant symbolize?"

He frowns.

I gesture to his necklace.

"Ah. It symbol of us. Crows." He smiles fondly at the flat stone resting just beneath his collarbone. "My son make it."

"Did he make one for my mother?"

Connor blinks, then shakes his head. "No. Cathal would not be pleased that Reid gift love stone to his mate."

"A love stone?"

"That's what he call it. He make it for the people he love."

I gape at him.

"What?"

A shiver shoots up my spine. "When I said mother, I meant—I meant my Fae mother. Agrippina?"

"Fallon?" Bronwen's voice cuts through my frothing thoughts.

"I'll be right there." My voice is as thin as a tidemark, but since Bronwen is Fae, I've no doubt she hears me loud and clear. "Did Reid once give a love stone to Agrippina?"

Connor's lips thin. "Ask my son."

Except he's not here, and I *need* to know. "Please tell me."

Connor glances toward the window, and although he doesn't have a direct view of Shabbe, I sense that's the direction of his gaze. "Tà," he finally murmurs, unraveling one of the many mysteries of my existence.

No wonder Reid loathes me. I destroyed both the mind and body of the woman he loved.

64

Y our tea has gone cold." Bronwen pushes it toward where
I sit, spine stiff, mind devoured by guilt.

"Did you know about Agrippina and Reid, Bronwen?"

"I know everything."

Anger rips through my reverie. "Then why didn't you ever
tell me?"

"You never asked."

I blink at her, then blink at the milky tea in the earthen mug.
She's right. I never did ask. Foolish me.

When I don't seize the cup, she says, "Drink."

"I'd prefer coffee."

"Tea is better for your digestive system."

My eyebrows bend. "Perhaps, but I favor—"

"Fallon, don't offend me."

I grind my teeth together. This woman can be so infuriating.
I seize the cup and drink the whole thing down to please her. It
tastes foul, like a sweetened puddle of dirt with a dash of rot,
like—I fling my gaze off the empty mug and onto her white eyes.
"It's to keep my womb bare, isn't it?"

Without missing a beat, she says, "Yes."

My anger takes on a whole new dimension. "You could've

asked whether I wanted to poison my insides."

"Now isn't the time to bring a child into the world."

Although I agree with her, I'm still annoyed. That Nonna did it to save me from birthing a bastard child was one thing, but Lore is my mate. This should be *our* decision. *Not* Bronwen's.

"I've seen your future, Fallon. You will bear three babes. *Eventually*."

"Eventually being *after* I murder Dante?" I mutter.

The sun reflects in her milky eyes. "Yes."

"Do you hate me, Bronwen?"

"The only people I've ever hated were my father and Meriam. I'm indifferent to most everyone else and love few."

Oddly enough, after the wash of anger, it's pity that I feel. Pity that her father's flame penetrated her rib cage and charred her heart.

My stomach spasms. Gods, I'm not sure I'll be able to wait for Sybille to get here. I am ravenous. So much so that I feel somewhat queasy. And hot. Very hot. I untie the ribbon around my neck to allow more cool air to touch my skin.

Worry slams into me, because Nonna's drink hadn't made my veins feel ablaze. "What have you given me?"

"Lazarus made the infusion. You may be having an allergic reaction. It'll pass."

"Are you trying to poison me?"

"Don't be daft, Fallon. You're the reason my mate is home. You're the reason the Crows have risen. You're the key to breaking Lore's curse. Here. Hand me your cup."

Still not entirely reassured, I give it to her. "It's empty."

She sticks her fingers inside to scoop up the renegade droplets, then sticks them in her mouth and sucks. "See?"

"That you haven't dropped dead, yes. Then again, you had a sip, and I had an entire cup."

"Poison is poison. A droplet and one's dead. Once you eat, you'll feel better." She pushes a basket of bread my way. When I don't pinch a roll out, she sighs and reaches for my hand as though sensing exactly where it lies. "Fallon, I know I'm not the aunt of your dreams."

She can say that again.

"But I respect and love both Lore and Cathal like brothers. I would *never* harm you, because it would harm them."

Even though my stomach squirms and my body temperature still rises, I relent and select a dark, miniature loaf, which I wolf down. As promised, I start to feel better.

"Will you return your…um…*gift* after all this is done?"

Bronwen's mouth eases into a ghost of a smile. "Yes. I will shed both the cloak upon my eyes and skin to be reborn anew in the Cauldron. With wings this time."

My heart hiccups. "The Cauldron can really do that?"

"The Cauldron gave life to every being on this earth, Fallon."

A rush of floral fragrance hits my nose as Sybille, black spirals tamed into sleek waves that brush her shoulders, sinks onto the bench beside me. "Hello, Bronwen."

"Sybille." She nods as she presses herself to standing. "I'll see you later, Fallon."

To think that someday, she truly will *see* me.

Sybille trails Bronwen with her eyes. The woman moves with such grace that I wonder how I ever mistook her for a human.

"So what have I missed?"

So many things, Syb. So many things.

I tell her what Bronwen said about the Cauldron.

Sybille's irises glitter. "So I could ask it to make my ears pointy?"

"Maybe." I try to ask Lore through the bond, but he must be busy, because he doesn't answer me.

At some point, Phoebus arrives. Although he sits at our table, his gaze almost never wavers off the barkeep.

"How's that going?"

My friend snags his lip. "I'm trying to get him to come to the baths, but the man prefers showering in his room."

"Why don't you go shower in his room then?" Sybille asks with a smile that doesn't quite reach her eyes.

"I–I—" Phoebus's cheeks pinken.

Sybille leans over the table. "Do you not know where his rooms are?"

"I do." He nods to the kitchen.

My eyebrows scale my forehead. "He lives in the kitchen?"

"No. He lives farther north, on the third floor. Since I don't have wings, I cannot exactly pop in."

"I see how that can be a problem." I look between Connor, who's busy slicing cheese, and Phoebus, who's busy staring at the Crow as though he were cheese. "How about you just ask him if he'd be interested in showering in your room, Pheebs?"

My friend makes a choking sound. "I could never."

"Where is all this shyness coming from? You were never the shy one."

Phoebus stares down at his empty plate. "He dislikes Fae, Fal. Like most Crows. I may not feel like one of my kind, but my ears say differently."

Never in my life could I have imagined someone not wanting points on their ears.

How I've changed…

How we've all changed.

I reach out and cocoon Phoebus's fist between my palms. "Pheebs, you may be Fae, but underneath it all, you're a man, like him, with a heart, like his. He sees you. We all do. Now square those shoulders, and ask him out."

He peeks up at me from beneath his lowered blond lashes. "What if he says no?"

"What if he says yes?"

Although I try to reach out to Lore after I depart from the tavern and then again throughout the afternoon, he never once answers me. I don't expect a king to be at my beck and call, but his prolonged silence irks me.

As the sun dips beneath the horizon, painting the sky crimson and gold, I finally leave my bedchamber to seek him out. My trek to his rooms is interrupted by the shrill sound of my name and the churning of wings.

"Fallon!" Bronwen's eyes glow as bright as the moon beyond the magical cupola above her head. "You must come with me at once. One of Lore's crows was shot down."

65

My heart has not beat a single time since I climbed astride Aoife's body behind Bronwen.

One of Lore's crows got struck down by an obsidian arrow in the Racoccin woods. Bronwen saw it as it was happening. She swears there was no Shabbin blood on the whittled stone, so there are no chances that he was turned into a forever Crow, yet my lungs refuse to draw breath.

He promised he wouldn't put himself at risk.

He swore it to me.

He painted his vow on my body.

But he just *had* to go and save the day himself.

I pour my anger through the mind link. He must hear it. After all, he only needs one crow to hear me. To speak, he needs two. Since he hasn't answered me, I imagine he hasn't risked reassembling his other crows. I'd deem that smart if I didn't deem him venturing out of his castle's walls incredibly stupid.

As we fly nearer to the clearing at the foot of the mountain, I squint to make out the gleam of iron, but mist blankets the ground, making it impossible to see anything beyond.

"Here, Aoife," Bronwen shouts at our winged steed.

As soon as we land, I vault off her back, bypassing her extended wing.

"Where?" My voice is as sharp as a thorn and stabs the cloying silence. "Where is he?"

"Inside the cavern." Bronwen nods to a small depression inside the jutting bedrock of the mountain.

I begin to sprint, but Aoife catches up to me. "Slow, Fallon. And stay quiet."

Heart trembling as violently as my limbs, I creep toward the cavern. Just as I'm about to enter, a guttural gasp tears through the silence. I whirl around just as Aoife's body slams into the ground.

I yell her name and rush back toward her, but Bronwen flings out her palms and shoves me back. "Get inside the cavern, Fallon. Now!"

"But Aoife—" My heart feels as though it's crushing my throat, grinding each one of my ribs to dust.

"Lore will call her back, but in order for him to do so, you must save him. Go!"

I stare at the fletching that sticks out of Aoife's waist. "Let me pull it out—"

Bronwen mutters under her breath. "Get in that cavern now."

It strikes me that no other arrow has come whizzing our way. If we'd been under attack, wouldn't a regimen of Fae have charged us by now?

Something is amiss.

Lore! When he doesn't answer me, I shriek his name out loud.

"Quiet, girl!" Bronwen hisses.

But I scream my mate's name at the top of my lungs.

Bronwen slaps me. I lunge back, nursing the sting off my cheek.

"If you care about him, Fallon—if you care about the Crows— get inside that cavern *now*."

"We're not under attack, are we? *You* struck Aoife down?" I turn my head to the sky. "Lorcan Ríhbiadh!"

"He cannot hear you, Fallon."

"What did you do to him?" My fingers clench into fists as I stare around me for something to use as a weapon. If only I could reach Aoife and steal the arrow from her stone body.

I eye the feathered hilt, then throw myself on my powerless friend. Just as my fingertips graze the scrawny fletching, wind claps into my body and sends me hurtling into the cavern wall. My skull jounces against the rock, and my vision fractures.

Bronwen is an earth-Fae, not an air-Fae, which means…which means other Fae are here.

I lie on my stomach, stunned, for precious seconds, but then adrenaline drenches me, and jaw gritted, I drag myself onto all fours.

"I'll take it from here." The deep voice pins my heart to my ribs. "Hello, Fal."

I twist my head toward the cavern just as a male dressed in gold armor appears in its darkened mouth, bracketed by four pointy-eared soldiers. Although Bronwen is still present, Dante has eyes only for me.

I slam my gaze on Bronwen. "You tricked me." My lungs are in such a tight vise that every inhale burns as though the air were made of fire.

Hoofbeats vibrate the ground, amplifying the booming beats of my heart. I pray for the rider to be a friend but am greeted by a one-eyed, riderless horse—Arina.

I think the sweet mare has come to save me, but Dante bursts my fragile hope. "Dargento, help my aunt climb astride her steed."

My skin breaks out in gooseflesh at the sound of that name, but also…*my aunt*? Bronwen told him? Just yesterday, she was asking Gabriele to keep his silence.

"Immediately, Maezza."

I peer through the mist at the bladed face of the male who's wanted me dead for weeks now.

"I've no need for help." Bronwen seizes Arina's reins and climbs atop the filly with the grace of a seasoned equestrian. It's evident that she, like Nonna, must've once had a stable full of horses at her disposal.

My gaze drops to Aoife. Although she is stone, sound penetrates. When she awakens, she will tell Lore everything.

Lore… "Was Lore even struck, Bronwen, or was it all a ruse?"

Arina jerks her head at the sound of my voice, her eye growing large. As much as I want her to pad closer, to toss Bronwen off her back and choose me, I fear that Dante or one of his brutes will harm her if she does.

"I'm speaking to you, Bronwen!" Still, she doesn't answer me. "At least have the decency to tell me why you pitched me onto Dante's lap!"

"I will let my nephew explain. After all, you two will have plenty of time for chats in the coming days."

A pair of shiny black boots outfitted with gleaming spurs stops in front of me, blocking my view of the duplicitous seer. "Shall we get on with our evening?" Dante crouches, his cold blue eyes boring down on mine.

"Fuck you," I snarl. "I'm not going anywhere with you."

"That's no way to speak to your king."

"You're not my king! You're not my anything!"

Lore!!! I shout down our bond.

My heart jolts when the sky rumbles.

Did he finally hear my call? "Looor—"

Dante springs open his fingers, sending a reedy cord of water into my mouth. I gag on the icy trickle.

"Better not tarry, Dante. I suspect Lorcan has noticed her absence." As Arina paws at the mist, Bronwen nods to Aoife. "And take the Crow into the tunnels with you, or Lorcan will awaken her with his call, and she'll disclose your whereabouts."

I snort. The only reason Bronwen wants Aoife out of Lore's

range is because she fears her involvement will be revealed. "Lore and my father will shred you once they learn of your betrayal, Bronwen. And Cian... He'll despise you."

"Except none of them will ever find out. Unlike you, child, I've learned to guard my mind." She stares at me with her moon eyes before kicking Arina's flanks and taking off toward Lore's mountain.

I will the sky to fill with wingbeats.

I will this to have been a marvelous trick to draw Dante out of hiding.

I will Bronwen not to have left me here alone.

"Bron—" Water fills my mouth again, and I choke, because this time, it isn't a weak ooze but an unending gush. One that's coming from the raised palm of the blue-eyed soldier beside Dante.

"Are you quite done shouting, Fallon? Or does my guard need to feed you more water?"

I snap my lips closed and use the mind link. Since my words aren't reaching Lore, I picture him and will my soul to leap toward his. Yes, I'd be leaving my body unguarded, but it isn't as though I'm doing a swell job at protecting it as it is.

However hard I try, the valley doesn't fade, and Lore's face doesn't overtake Dante's. I blink away my frustration. Why is the bond not working? The answer hits me at the same time as vines tangle around Aoife's stone body. The tea Bronwen made me ingest wasn't for my womb, it was to hush the bond! That has to be it.

I've hated the sightseer many times in the past, but never more than at this moment.

As Aoife is dragged into the cavern, I stare at the arrow protruding from her waist. If I sprinted, I could reach her and pluck it out. At least she'd be saved.

One of the Fae must sense the direction of my thoughts, because the second I leap to my feet, vines tangle around my ankles and send me sprawling face-first into the ground.

Dargento crouches beside me, simpering. "Looks like you've gotten yourself in a bind, Crow-charmer."

My chest beats with such fury that I roll onto my back and shriek at the top of my lungs, hoping a passing Crow will hear my distress.

"Quiet her, Silvius," Dante hisses, just as rain begins to pelt the valley.

The former—current?—commander shoves his hand against my mouth. "You so much as make a peep, and I roast your face."

I roll my wild eyes, trying to glimpse Dante's expression. Is he on board with torching me? Does he want me dead? Why bring me into the tunnels if he wants to snuff out my life? So that Lore doesn't find my remains out in the open and massacre every Fae involved?

"Do *not* use your fire on her, Silvius." The Fae king's gaze is taped to the howling sky. "Get her inside. Now!"

When Dargento heaves me onto his shoulder, I clobber his back with my fists. If only I had talons…

"Can one of you bind her fucking wrists?" he growls.

"Right away, Commander," one of the green-eyed Fae calls out.

Of fucking course he's regained his position. The question is did he regain it before or after Gabriele took refuge in the sky kingdom?

As he walks me toward the mouth of the cavern, my fingertips graze the jeweled hilt of the sword strapped to the man's waist. I'd have called myself lucky, but I don't believe in chance.

I crane my head to see if anyone stares my way, but the few soldiers who accompanied Dante have penetrated the cavern. Only he still stands out in the open, lightning glazing his stern face and dripping off his golden breastplate. His gaze is turned toward the forest, and although rain lashes at my eyes, I don't miss his head bobbing with a nod.

Who is he nodding to?

I squint as shadows slink between the dark trunks. Oh my gods, a whole army stands there in wait, garbed in dark uniforms to blend into the night.

Merda. Merda. Merda.

My heart, which had begun to drop because of my potato-sack position, squeezes right into my throat. ***Lore!!*** I scream into the mind link right before Dargento strides into the cave, snuffing out my view of the world beyond.

Remembering Dargento's sword, I stretch my fingers and wrap them around the hilt, and then I arch my back, level the point at his spine, and swing my torso to drive steel into the monster.

66

Hot blood sprays my face.

Dargento freezes. I can only imagine his chin dropping to watch the point that protrudes from his navel. If only my blow had nicked his heart…

As a choked "Maezza" curls from his lips, my fingers tighten around the ruby hilt.

Is Dante near enough to hear Dargento's garbled voice over the smash of thunder?

"Wheel the obsidian door into place!" I hear the cruel monarch bark. "Now!"

I drive my shoulder into my lids to clear my sight of faerie blood, then blink up to find Dante filling the grotto's entrance, the jewels speared into his braids and ears gleaming like the toxic plants in Xema Rossi's fabled grove.

The ground gives a hard shudder that makes dust and small rocks plink off the ceiling. And then raucous grinding fills the blackened hull of the mountain as a panel of stone begins to descend like a giant maw over the opening in the rock.

The only opening.

"Move, Dargento!" Dante barks.

My insides turn to ice while my lungs fill with fire. I cannot even rejoice when Dargento's knees finally buckle and he lists to the side. I brace myself for impact, injecting my biceps with all the strength I possess, unwilling to lose my grip on the sword.

The momentum of his collapse tears the blade from his abdomen but not the pommel from my fingers. As we go down, my torso unfurls and smacks against something jagged.

Again, I see stars.

I blink them away, then kick at Dargento's heavy body with my bound feet until I've managed to squirm out from beneath him.

My temper burns so hot that I plot to kill every last Fae in this colossal coffin.

You will kill Dante. You will plot and plan his death.

Oh my gods... Is this why Bronwen brought me here? Because she foresaw me murdering the Fae king under this mountain on this dark night?

The thought does not quell my anger. Yes, there may be a reason to her madness, but she is still fucking *mad*. The second I get out of here, I will punch my aunt. In the heart.

"What the underworld?" Dante murmurs. "Dargento?"

I'm glad that his heightened pureblood senses have yet to kick in.

Quietly, quietly, I snip the vine off my ankles with the steel blade. Before using it on the one binding my wrists, I roll onto my knees and pat the ground until I find the lump that is Dargento's head. I skim my palms across his back until I locate his right shoulder blade. I'm glad for the darkness, for as much as I crave seeing the life bleed out of Dargento's eyes, I don't care for the sight of flesh tearing and blood gushing.

"Maezza?" someone calls out, probably one of the Fae who dragged in Aoife.

Dante must sense something is going on, because he doesn't answer. I strain to grasp sounds—breathing, heartbeats, anything that will pinpoint his location. But between my lackluster hearing, the tempestuous drum of my pulse, and the rolls of thunder jarring the mountain, I hear nothing.

Sensing I have mere seconds left, I position the steel tip beneath the bladed bone and the knobs of Dargento's spine, then, praying that I'm at the right spot, I rise to my feet and put all my weight and rage into the sword.

It plunges straight through him.

A wet rattle disturbs the deathly stillness. *Merda.* I must've pierced one of his lungs instead of his heart. I pull the blade out and slam it back down. This time, Dargento doesn't even squeak.

Arms snag my waist and hoist me up, tearing my boots off the floor.

Possessed, I fling my head back, and my skull smashes against my captor's face. Racked with adrenaline, I feel no pain, but my jailer must, because he growls and his grip slackens.

I jump away from him, then wheel around, sword extended. When it strikes armor, I know who grabbed me: Dante. I grunt as the force of my blow reverberates inside my arms. I suddenly wish the cavern would flood with light so he could see what his betrayal has done to me…who it's turned me into.

Although I stand my ground, sword held aloft, my arms shake so hard I worry Dante will spot the bob of the gleaming steel or hear my chaotic swallows. I keep my lips sealed to avoid producing a sound and begin to back up.

My foot crunches against something, and the pop echoes through the noiseless blackness.

As Lore would say, *focá.* A surge of anguish rushes up my spine when the ground shakes. I pray it's his thunder. I pray it's because he's violently angry with me for having left the castle. I pray it's not the hoofbeats of Dante's army.

The silence thickens until I think I may choke on it.

Suddenly, a flame erupts and chews away the cloak of night.

Cold fear slickens my skin, because the only amber-eyed Fae I spotted around Dante was Dargento. Did he—did he survive?

When I catch flames steaming off a torch and Dargento's supine body sprawled at Dante's feet, I begin to expel a sigh, but then my breathing shortens because...

Because the fire splashes two faces I haven't seen in weeks.

One I revile.

One I adore.

"Goccolina," Nonna chokes out as Justus's arm tightens around her long, slender neck.

67

Nonna?" The blood drains from my cheeks so fast that I feel lightheaded.

Lore said she was in Shabbe.

Giana said…

Did they lie to keep me from storming Luce to find her?

Tears gloss her green eyes and spill, coursing down her pallid cheeks.

"Drop your sword," Justus says calmly, "or Ceres dies."

This cannot be happening.

This must be a trick.

I swing my attention around the cavern, my gaze striking Dargento's limp body before lifting to Dante's stern face.

"I'd do as Justus asks, Fallon. My general is a ruthless man." He stands closest to me but not close enough for my sword to reach his head, the only part of him not covered in armor.

"General? You've replaced Tavo too?"

He doesn't bother answering me.

"You could've chosen peace, Dante." My voice is as strong and sharp as the sword I hold, even though everything inside me is melting like sunbaked snow.

"*Peace?* Come on, Fal. Peace was never an option. The demon you awakened would never have settled for *half* a kingdom."

"The only demon I awakened was you, Dante," I spit out just as the vine tightens around my wrists and motes of dirt spill from the cavern ceiling.

The soldiers who bound Aoife gawk from the low ceiling to the enormous slab of obsidian propped against the entrance.

Dante's blue eyes shine with horrible delight. "The heroic vulture must've finally joined the party. A little late." To his green-eyed soldiers, he says, "Take the Crow down into the tunnels!"

They jump to attention, then heft Aoife past where Justus stands and tip her black body into a wide pit. Stone bangs against stone as she clatters out of sight, the two soldiers clambering down after her.

Lore is here, I tell myself. *He's here.*

Even though a mountain stands between us, I want to weep in relief. How long will it take him to breach the stone walls if he transforms into smoke?

Does he need a crack to glide through, or can he penetrate—

Dante knows how to make forever Crows. The memory glides through my mind, popping my fragile hope. Oh gods, Lore cannot come inside.

"You have ten seconds to toss away my sword or your grandmother perishes, Fallon." Justus's ultimatum tears my attention off my pissed-off mate. "Ten."

I stare at Nonna's wet cheeks.

"Nine."

I swallow hard, but the lump in my throat is so jagged that my spit doesn't slip past it.

"Eight."

My grandmother's green eyes flare.

"Seven."

"Stop! Don't hurt her!"

"Six."

"Let her go, and I will throw down my sword."

"Sword first, Fallon. Five."

I stare at Nonna and release the sword. It clanks onto the ground and rolls, stopping when it hits…when it hits…

A skull.

One of hundreds.

There are bones *everywhere*. And amidst the bones are scattered thousands of black weapons—*obsidian*.

"Good girl."

I grit my teeth. "Release her, or I don't step forward."

He tosses Nonna aside the same way I discarded my sword.

Dante takes a step forward and scoops up the steel sword, then nods to the pit. "Now, Fal."

Dust streams from the rocky ceiling as the force of Lore's anger continues to sock the mountain.

"Move," he says, "or I slip this blade through her heart."

I leap forward. "Don't harm her!" I give the reddened point of Dante's sword a wide berth as I advance toward the frightful male who stands between me and my fallen grandmother. "Can I just— can I just have a minute with her?"

Justus's mouth curls. "Why…go ahead."

I frown, not expecting him to accept, much less smile. As I roll my grandmother onto her back, I catch a look passing between Dante and Justus. My forehead grooves harder, until I lower my gaze to Nonna's.

I bounce away, one of my feet rolling on a bone. As I go down, I gape at the blond Fae I was about to embrace.

The soldier smiles, dusting his pristine uniform.

"Blood casting is incredible, isn't it?" Dante seizes my bound wrists and hauls me to my feet before shoving the steel blade against my bobbing throat. "Meriam is a fount of knowledge."

I thought he was holding that woman prisoner, but he's working *with* her?

I stagger forward as the soldier who resembled Nonna only a moment ago straightens and takes the torch from Justus's hand, wiping drips of blood off his forehead.

Dante hands my grandfather back his sword, then winds his arm around my throat. "I don't want to hurt you, Fal, but I will if you fight me."

"Eat sprite shit, you prick." I jerk my face down in the hopes of sinking my teeth into his flesh, but he anticipates my move, because he tightens his grip, blocking my chin from dipping through the noose of muscle and bone.

"I said, *behave*."

I wheeze as he walks me to the pit and forces me down a whole bunch of steep steps. By the time we reach the belly of the earth, my vision has grayed and I'm panting as though I've raced across the Selvatin desert.

Fallon! Lore's voice explodes inside my mind—or is it inside my ears?

I try to tear myself out of Dante's hold, but the Fae king's limb is unyielding. *Lore?*

Justus and the guard who pretended to be Nonna sidestep us, the torch burning away the darkness before illuminating another slab of black.

Justus seizes my bound hands. As he raises his palm to the wall—door?—he stares at the soldier who pretended to be my grandmother. "Wash away the sigils as soon as we're through. The abounding obsidian will weaken them and prevent them from shifting into smoke. Strike down as many as you can, and don't forget to soak your blade in the witch's blood." He hands the soldier a glass vial speared onto a leather cord that the male swiftly loops around his neck.

Behach Éan? Lore hollers.

Tears cling to my fluttering lashes like sequins. *Lore, they're taking me down into the tunnels.* I pray my words ring loud and clear into his mind. *They're leaving only one soldier behind, but he has access to Shabbin blood and has been told how to use it. Get away from the mountain! Please! And don't come after me.*

Mo khrá, if you didn't want me to come after you, you shouldn't have run away.

I... The word *didn't* fades to air as Justus slams his palm against the black stone and carries us through it.

Through a wall!

A wall!

I gasp when he releases my fingers, my gaze hitting Aoife's immobilized body, which Dante's soldiers are carting down a narrow, torchlit passageway like draft horses.

"Gods, you look like them." Justus's blue eyes draw over every millimeter of my face as he wipes his palm along his long velvet jacket that is the color of night—a blue so dark it melts into the abounding obsidian. "How I ever believed you shared my blood is beyond me."

Same, you monster. Same.

Wait...

Did he just say... "Them?" I rasp.

"Your mother and grandmother." Dante's mouth is too near my ear for comfort.

"They're both here?" My voice patters against the tunnel walls, amplified by the stretch of black stone that covers *every* surface.

Justus's smile chills me to the core. "I see Aurora hasn't been very forthcoming."

My heart jounces at Bronwen's Fae-given name.

"I suppose that female stockpiles her secrets better than my mother hoards her jewels," Justus adds under his breath.

Is he saying that Bronwen knew where my mother was all this time?

Lore?

Silence.

Lore?

As Dante shoves me forward, I stare over my shoulder at the slab of obsidian we passed through. When Lore doesn't reply, I swallow. Has the tea's effect taken ahold of me again, or is it the stone that silences the bond?

Or did that soldier…

No.

My mate may thirst for vengeance, but he cares about his people and would never doom them to save me. Right?

Not to mention—but I will mention it for my sanity's sake—Bronwen foresaw him becoming a forever Crow *only* if I died. As long as my heart beats, his human one will too.

I steel my spine and hike up my chin. "So what's the plan, Fae?" I speak the word like one would say "ladies," with poised contempt.

Throwing me a venomous glower, Justus pounds ahead of us in the tunnel to shout orders at the soldiers.

"The plan is that I'm about to make your dream come true, Fal." Dante's unctuous voice slithers against my eardrum.

"You and Justus are going to drop dead at my feet?"

His grip tightens around my throat, and he yanks me backward until my spine is flush with his armor and the lump on my skull is throbbing in the crook of his neck. "You, Serpent-charmer, are about to become queen of Luce."

Since I doubt he's offering to let me go wild on his jugular with Justus's sword, my eyebrows dip. "And you brought me down into this obsidian maze for what reason? To throw me an impromptu gilding revel before my nuptials to Lore?"

His hold grows harsher, along with his timbre. "That animal is no king, only a peasant with feathers. I am the true king of Luce."

When he runs his nose along my cheek, I growl like a cornered wildcat. "Don't fucking touch me, Dante."

His lips curve against my earlobe. "A king has every right to touch his queen."

"I'm not your queen!"

"Not yet," he murmurs.

"Not ever," I hiss.

EPILOGUE

Lore

I'm no stranger to rage, but never has it blistered my heart like tonight.

Around me, the valley is littered with corpses, the earth saturated with Fae blood, the sky gashed by the dregs of my wrath. I've killed before, but never so many.

Every last Nebban soldier that sprang out of the Racoccin woods to attack us has fallen. Some on this battlefield, others in the forest as they beat a hasty retreat, pleas of mercy trembling upon their lips.

I showed no mercy. None of my people did.

After all, the Fae robbed me of my single most precious possession.

As my boots squelch against the blood-soaked mud, I imagine Fallon grumbling that she belongs to no one. Instead of ferrying a smile to my lips, it floods me with such vehemence that I take it out on the sky and land.

My Crows swerve and dip as I whip the mountain with my tempest. The enormous trunk they felled almost slips from their talons. Somehow, perhaps because they're used to my storms, they manage to fly through the wet gusts.

I watch as they reach the cavern, as they slam the wood into the obsidian wall blocking the entrance. The din matches the furious bangs of the scarlet muscle barely contained by my iron armor.

Cathal stands beside me, silent in his anger. I realize that I too haven't voiced many words. The last ones I propelled into my people's minds were the warning Fallon managed to slip me before our mind link went dark.

Again.

If only I'd sought her out earlier when she didn't answer my invitation to nap.

If only Erwin hadn't insisted on one more round of practice with our swords.

If only I hadn't listened to Cian's entreaty to preserve the staircase for his wingless mate.

If only I'd freed the horses Fallon's friends rode up on.

If only I'd heeded Bronwen's advice and headed to Shabbe to break the curse.

The obsidian barrier groans as it finally tips and smashes into the ground, cracking into chunks that glitter like a rug of glass shards.

Fallon! The foolish tendrils of hope that she'd hear me once we tore down the door unravel as her silence lingers. With her name poised on my cold lips, ready to flock from my lungs, I take a step forward.

Cathal flings out his arm to stop me. "We wait, Lore."

I shove his arm and stalk forward. I'm done waiting.

My friend streaks in front of me, more smoke than flesh, and plants his boots wide. "You take one more step, Lorcan Ríhbiadh, and I will carry you to Shabbe this very night."

I glare at him but stop advancing.

We don't possess many weapons—we've never had need for more than our talons and beaks—but thanks to Antoni and Vance, we've begun to amass a sizeable arsenal. Firearms that shoot iron bullets, hallucinogenic powder they've nicknamed "dust," and liquid salt that can be injected into veins or mouths, depending on the need.

I've had all three brought into the valley tonight.

Connor sets fire to a burlap sack filled with the hallucinogenic dust that his son snatches with his talons and hurls into the grotto. There's no explosion. After all, it's no cannonball. But there is smoke. At first, only a lavender trickle escapes, but that trickle swiftly thickens into a cloud of glittering purple.

If Fallon is in the cavern, this will not hurt her.

Behach Éan? I whisper into the void that stretches between us.

My lids slip closed when her beautiful voice doesn't irradiate the gathering darkness between my temples. But then a dull cough comes, and my lids snap open.

Take to the sky, I command my people.

Every one of them dissolves into feathers, becoming one with the starlit darkness.

I break into my five crows, all my eyes fixated on the mouth of the cavern and the faint smear of white staggering just beyond it. A Lucin soldier trips over the crumbled obsidian but rights himself against the cavern wall and blinks at the field.

The Fae's hands are bare of weapons. As he stumbles farther out, I fill his mind with the image of every soldier I tore through tonight. When I reveal how I plan on killing him, his pants grow sticky with piss.

I merge two of my crows in order to whisper into his mind that I will spare him if he brings me Fallon.

Although his eyes are unfocused by the drugs pumping into his system, he stammers, "I w-wiped the sigils off the d-door. C-can't get through without them."

How fortunate that you're in possession of Shabbin blood.

"Rossi d-drew them. Only he—"

The blood he entrusted you with. Where is it?

He stares at his palms, then flips them over and proceeds to blink at his knuckles, and then he touches his neck. "I must've—must've d-dropped it."

Should we kill him? Reid asks, impatience staining the boy's voice.

Not yet. To the soldier, I say, ***Who else is in the cavern?***

He shakes his head, making his blond hair flap around. "No one. Except...except..." The skin between his brows creases as though he has to give my question actual thought. "Commander Dargento."

The name stills the beat of my wings and coaxes one of my crows nearer to the grotto's opening.

As my eyes acclimate to the ambient darkness, he says, "He's d-dead, though. The Beast-charmer k-killed him."

Cathal drops in front of the man and morphs into skin. "My daughter killed Silvius Dargento?"

The Fae's eyes bulge at the sight of my general, who stands a full head taller than he does. A monstrous man—but not a monster.

I am the only monster present tonight.

"Y-yes." The air is rife with the stench of his soiled trousers. "Your"—he swallows—"your d-daughter k-k-killed him."

"How?"

Nostrils pulsating with terrified intakes of air, the Fae proceeds to give us a detailed account that swells my pride while also feeding my fury. "That is everything. Can I...please... Will you—"

I interrupt his embryonic plea. ***Fetch me Dargento's body.***

"And then I can go?"

One of my crows flies into the cavern, but my skin blisters and my eyes sting. There is too much obsidian. Around the crumbled door, black blades and spikes lie like refuse atop the grotto's floor amidst a jumble of ancient bones—relics from the Battle of Primanivi.

Fetch. His. Fucking. Body. My tone makes the soldier whirl.

He slips in the mud, adding brown smears to his white pants, and darts into the cave.

"What did you ask him for?" Cathal murmurs.

To bring us the body of Justus's pet asshole.

It takes the lone soldier several minutes to return, but he finally appears, corpse in tow.

The back of the commander's white jacket is crimson and torn in three places. Three places that my Fallon must've pierced with a blade. I try to picture her wielding a sword, but it only serves to deteriorate my mood. I detest that she found herself in a situation where she had to fight for her life.

"What are Regio's plans for my daughter?"

The soldier snaps his lids open and closed many times. "P-plans?"

Cathal's nostrils flare. "Why did he bring her into the fucking tunnels?"

"Oh." The man runs shaky fingers through his waist-long hair that I consider shearing off before carving into his neck, just to show the Fae how I feel about their inane status symbol. "I d-don't know."

Wrong answer. My body unspools until I am one with the lashing rain.

The man jerks out both palms as though two tender appendages could hold me back. I may have smiled had my mate… my curse breaker…my everything not been stolen from me and brought into a place I cannot reach.

"The k-king w-wants M-Meriam to-to-to—"

To?

Cathal's patience wears thin, and he cinches the man's throat. "Finish your fucking sentence, Fae."

A whimper burbles out of the soldier.

"What does that gutless turd want Meriam to do?" Cathal's howl blows back the man's pale tresses.

"I h-heard whispers of wed-wedlock."

My blood runs cold.

Cathal's head rears back. "Wedlock?"

"Between the B-Beast-charmer and our k-king."

Cathal turns his attention toward the oil spill I've become.

The sky roars and brightens.

I want this mountain disemboweled before sunrise! I command my people, who begin to pound the friable gray rock with their iron beaks and talons.

Mórrígan, how I will eviscerate Regio and all those he holds dear.

"C-can I leave?"

Cathal's talons must sprout, for the next thing I know, he's holding the man's head, and it's no longer attached to the rest of the body. "I will kill him."

Cian, who's landed beside his brother, says, "I believe you've already done so, brother."

"I meant—"

"I know who you meant." He raises his eyes to mine, and although his do not fill with prophecies like his mate's, I see Bronwen's words scroll across his dark irises: *Fallon will kill Dante.*

The sky calms, as though holding its breath. Is that why Fallon hushed our bond, stole through the hidden staircase, and took off on horseback toward the valley? To fulfill a fucking prophecy?

How did she even know how to mute our mating link? Did Lazarus brew her an elixir? If he aided her, may Mórrígan take pity on his soul.

"Daya." Cathal's skin has become so bleak beneath the drips of charcoal that I press out of my mind and land at his side.

"What about Daya?" Cian asks.

"I forgot to ask if she was in the tunnels. I forgot to ask—" He rubs at his iron breastplate. "I forgot to ask if she was alive."

Pity extracts a lie from my lips. "She is."

Where Cian's brows bend, Cathal's arch high.

"The Fae told me before you rid him of his ability to speak." Does deceiving my most loyal friend make me more of a monster?

Does it matter? The fact remains that I am a creature of nightmares. One whose heart lies deadened in a cage of bones and feathers.

"You mustn't have heard him over my storm." I claimed to understand Cathal's agony, but as I stand in a field of corpses, mind bare of Fallon's voice, skin bare of her touch, I realize that I understood nothing of it before tonight.

"We underestimated the princeling," Cian says, clipping the heavy silence. "Not only did he manage to dispose of the soldiers Roy left behind to 'aid' in the running of Luce, but he also managed to make us their executioners."

I roll my shoulders back, then stretch my neck. "It was only a matter of time before Nebba declared war."

I'm prepared for war. What I'm not prepared for is a life without my mate. If I must level this entire island to find her, then so be it.

Fight for us, Behach Éan. Your monster is coming.

Read on for an exclusive bonus retelling of chapter 44 from Lore.

44

Lore

Hands clasped behind my back, I pace the rug in front of my hearth as Lazarus incises my mate's body and my mother packs the newest gaping wound with herbs she grew in the orchard. Though they've helped resorb the bloating, Fallon is still unconscious, deathly pale, and agonizingly quiet. Not a single whimper has escaped her wan lips, not a single thought has breached her beautiful mind since I flew her out of the Fae lands.

I should never have let her out of my kingdom. She would've hated me for having kept her imprisoned in my stone walls, but I could've lived with that. What I cannot live without is her. If the poison…if…

I stop walking and scrape both my hands down my haggard face. "Where would that rat have hidden the crystals?" I bark at poor Lazarus who hasn't left Fallon's side since our return.

He rolls his lips as he prods my mate's milky flesh to locate another nascent boil. "Probably the tunnels, Mórrgaht."

Those fucking tunnels… *Naoise, Cian, are you on your way home?* I bark through the mind link that connects me to them, since I cannot, for the life of me, concentrate on the tether that binds me to both males and allows me to track them.

We're still in Glace, Lore. Cian's voice smacks with tension. *Why the fuck are you still in Glace?*

The negotiations are taking a little longer than expected.

For Mórrigan's sake, negotiate faster! I should've flown to Glace myself. *Give Vlad whatever he wants.*

The only thing he wants is something you aren't willing to give, Cian replies quietly.

I roll my neck because I know what Cian is alluding to: marrying Alyona. It has never been on the table and never will never be. Not even if…

I fist my fingers until I've crushed the thought to ash. "Can you heal Fallon without more crystals, Lazarus?"

A beat. Two. Three. I'm about to reiterate my question when he finally says, "I will try my best, Mórrgaht."

Though no one stakes me with a piece of obsidian, my heart deadens, because his best might not be enough. *Naoise, Cian, change of plans. Steal the fucking crystals.*

That'll start a war, Naoise all but wheezes.

A crazed smile seizes my lips. *And?*

We won't come home without the crystals. Cian sounds calm and resolved, unlike my other Siorkahd member. *Take care of your mate, Lore. Naoise and I will take care of Vlad.*

Mother selects a branch of dried herbs and rolls it between her palms to loosen the leaves. "Go eat something, Son."

I snort.

"That was not a suggestion, my love. Get out of this room. Go eat. Go fly. Go hunt."

Tonight was the last time I let Fallon out of my sight. Never again. Not until she's immortal. Perhaps not even then.

"Your energy is interfering with our healing."

"My…*energy?*" I mean my mother no disrespect, but does she realize what she's asking of me?

It strikes me that she does not. After all, she's never had a mate since my father passed on to the next world, before Queen Mara of Shabbe and the Cauldron transformed me and my people into winged shifters. Perhaps my father was her mate. Or perhaps he was merely the man she chose to love and have a child with. It is a mystery that will forever be left unsolved. But that mystery is neither here nor there. The only thing of import at the moment is Fallon's delicate life.

"Lorcan," she murmurs around a sigh.

"Do not ask me to leave for I cannot, Mother." I close my eyes, my skin loosening to smoke before tightening to flesh. "I cannot be away from her."

I pace my stone floors a moment longer and then I crouch in front of my hearth and poke at the embers. I add a log, two. When I turn back toward the bed, my mother has left to gather more herbs, but Lazarus is still there, still drawing his small knife through my mate's flesh, relieving it of the noxious fumes the poison generates when it breaches her vessels and seeps into her muscles.

"Is her fever breaking?" My voice rolls like thunder through the room.

"No." The Fae healer rinses the crimson stain of Fallon's blood in the little bowl he carried with him. The water is red but since he diluted a crystal inside, he's forbidden Mother from refreshing it. Once clean, he drags the blade to the flickering candle that is burning down to a stump on my nightstand.

He studies Fallon's flayed, bleeding back quietly while I rage like the sky over Luce and simmer like the sea biting the rocky cliffs outside my windows. I'm seized with the desire to decimate every last Fae roaming my kingdom. Maybe I should heed my mother's words and take a stroll through Luce's streets.

Just as my gaze cuts to the lightning-marbled sky, a shallow gasp sounds from my bed. One that is too high-pitched and feminine to have been produced by Lazarus. I soar across the room— half smoke, half man.

"Lore?" Fallon murmurs.

I draw my fingers through her hair. "I'm right here, Little Bird. Right here."

"Where is—" Fallon lets out a cry that shreds my fucking soul.

"Shh." I keep twisting my fingers through her hair, careful to keep my touch gentle even though rage sizzles inside my veins.

Is raising the dead one of your powers, Lore? Pain rucks the delicate skin around her eyes.

Why? Did you want me to revive the wildling so you could kill her again?

What? She grits her teeth. *I think I'm dying.*

Would I ever let that happen? If only I could suck the poison from her system. If only I could take away her pain and make it mine.

You may control many things, Lorcan Ríhbiadh, but you surely cannot control the rhythm of my heart.

I crouch beside her, my fingers tangling in her sweat- and blood-soaked hair. *I control all that belongs to me, Behach Éan.*

My heart belongs to you?

I swallow, dragging my index finger down the slope of her neck. When I feel her pulse nip my skin, I glide my finger back up to her jaw and trace a line to that pointed chin of hers which I fucking adore. *It's always belonged to me. I'm hoping that soon you'll understand this, so you stop wasting its precious beats on males who aren't me.*

She expels a soft breath into her pillow. *You are most delusional, Mórrgaht.*

Her breathing slows, and I think she is sinking back into unconsciousness when I hear her think: *I want so much to live and wander the world. And fly. Oh, how I long to fly, and not as a spirit.*

My finger freezes on the hinge of her jaw, but then I shake away her doubts…and mine. *I swear to you, Fallon Báeinach, that you will live, wander, and fly.*

Her throat moves over a small swallow. *Another one of your empty promises?*

For a moment, I am as silent and still as Lazarus who watches me, watches Fallon. But then Fallon whimpers, and I dissolve into smoke and roll over her fiery flesh to cool the fever enveloping her.

Stay with me, Fallon! Although her heart beats alongside mine, her mind wanders to a place I cannot reach. *Come back to me, mo khrá.*

ACKNOWLEDGMENTS

I expect that many of you want to hand me over to Dante and let him have his murderous way with me for the way I ended this book. I apologize for the cliffhanger. I would've preferred concluding this novel elsewhere, but I have so much planned for Fallon in these tunnels. Too much to fit into this sequel.

What an adventure my witches, Fae, and Crows have taken me on. Yes, *me*. I wrote an outline for this series last year, and let me tell you, nothing is going according to plan. My characters are making their own decisions and steering their own fate.

This is usually the case with my stories, so I'm not alarmed in any way. In truth, I'm excited to see where Fallon and the gang lead me.

Next up, the final chapter: *House of Striking Oaths*. Expect more magic, more romance, more banter, more surprises, more world building (I'm taking you to Shabbe in this one).

Off I go. Meet me there, dear reader?

Before leaving, I'd like to thank my extraordinary street team for all the early love and praise and typo catches (looking at you, Aimie, Kat, Julie, Traci, Jordan, Christina, and Steff).

Every time I publish a new story, I worry about disappointing my readers—especially those who've been with me since the beginning. Every time I manage to enchant you anew, it fills me with the greatest joy.

Maria, my first reader, thank you for keeping me and my characters real. *House of Pounding Hearts* owes much of its pounding (heart) to you.

Laetitia and Rachel, thank you for smoothing out all the rough edges of my manuscript and for being flexible about my chaotic deadlines. ♥

To my family, thank you for loving me unconditionally.

ABOUT THE AUTHOR

Olivia Wildenstein is a *USA Today* bestselling author of romantasy. When she's not swooning over her characters' steamy escapades or plotting their demise, you can find her sipping wine and crafting her next twisted, romantic masterpiece, all while trying to convince her children and leading man that she loves them more than her laptop.

Website: oliviawildenstein.com
Facebook: Olivia's Darling Readers
Instagram: @olives21
TikTok: @OWildWrites